WHEN GRAVITY FAILS

GEORGE ALEC EFFINGER

BANTAM BOOKS
NEW YORK · TORONTO · LONDON · SYDNEY · AUCKLAND

This edition contains the complete text of the original hardcover edition.
NOT ONE WORD HAS BEEN OMITTED.

WHEN GRAVITY FAILS

A Bantam Spectra Book / January 1988

PRINTING HISTORY

Hardcover edition published by
Arbor House Publishing Company December 1986

Grateful acknowledgment is made for permission to reprint extracts from the following:

The Simple Art of Murder *by Raymond Chandler. Copyright 1950 by Raymond Chandler. Copyright © renewed 1978 by Helga Greene. Reprinted by permission of Houghton Mifflin Company and Ed Victor Ltd, England.*

"Just Like Tom Thumb's Blues" by Bob Dylan. Copyright © 1965 by Warner Bros. Inc. All Rights Reserved. Used by permission.

Bantam Books are published by Bantam Books, a division of Bantam Double-day Dell Publishing Group, Inc. Its trademark, consisting of the words "Bantam Books" and the portrayal of a rooster, is Registered in U.S. Patent and Trademark Office and in other countries. Marca Registrada. Bantam Books, 666 Fifth Avenue, New York, New York 10103.

PRINTED IN THE UNITED STATES OF AMERICA

RAD   14 13 12 11 10 9 8 7 6

PRAISE FOR
GEORGE ALEC EFFINGER
AND
WHEN GRAVITY FAILS

"Buy, read and marvel . . . or else." —Harlan Ellison

"A brilliantly written, knife-edged futuristic detective story . . . destined to be the year's most intense and emotionally involving SF work." —*Houston Post*

"A terrific story—fast, cool, clever, beautifully written absolutely authoritative. A kind of cyberpunk Raymond Chandler book with dashes of Roger Zelazny, Ian Fleming and Scheherazade—but altogether original . . . I loved it." —Robert Silverberg

"Wry and black and savage . . . there's a knife behind every smile." —George R. R. Martin

"This book blindsided me . . . Ingenious, layered, sophisticated, and consistently bloodcurdling, *When Gravity Fails* kept me awake long after I had finished reading it." —Spider Robinson

"Muscular, convincing, yet continuously surprising." —Richard A. Lupoff

"One of the best cyberpunk novels I've read . . . Effinger's prose is terse, direct, vivid and often laced with an enchanting sense of humor . . ." —*The Providence Sunday Journal*

"Wry, inventive, nearly hallucinatory . . . a well-written, baroque riff on the time-honored themes of Raymond Chandler." —*Publishers Weekly*

BOOKS BY GEORGE ALEC EFFINGER

What Entropy Means to Me
Relatives
Mixed Feelings
Irrational Numbers
Those Gentle Voices
Dirty Tricks
Heroics
The Wolves of Memory
Idle Pleasures
The Nick of Time
The Bird of Time
When Gravity Fails
Shadow Money
A Fire in the Sun

. . . He must be the best man in his world and a good
enough man for any world. . . .
He is a lonely man and his pride is that you will
treat him as a proud man or be very sorry you ever saw
him. He talks as the man of his age talks—
that is, with rude wit, a lively sense of the
grotesque, a disgust for sham, and a contempt
for pettiness.
—RAYMOND CHANDLER
"The Simple Art of Murder"

When you're lost in the rain in Juarez and it's
  Eastertime too
And your gravity fails and negativity don't pull
  you through
Don't put on any airs when you're down on Rue
  Morgue Avenue
They got some hungry women there and they really
  make a mess out of you.
—BOB DYLAN
Just Like Tom Thumb's Blues

1

Chiriga's nightclub was right in the middle of the Budayeen, eight blocks from the eastern gate, eight blocks from the cemetery. It was handy to have the graveyard so close-at-hand. The Budayeen was a dangerous place and everyone knew it. That's why there was a wall around three sides. Travelers were warned away from the Budayeen, but they came anyway. They'd heard about it all their lives, and they'd be damned if they were going home without seeing it for themselves. Most of them came in the eastern gate and started up the Street curiously; they'd begin to get a little edgy after two or three blocks, and they'd find a place to sit and have a drink or eat a pill or two. After that, they'd hurry back the way they'd come and count themselves lucky to get back to the hotel. A few weren't so lucky, and stayed behind in the cemetery. Like I said, it was a very conveniently situated cemetery, and it saved a lot of time and trouble all around.

I stepped into Chiri's place, glad to get out of the hot, sticky night. At the table nearest the door were two women, middle-aged tourists, with shopping bags filled with souvenirs and presents for the folks back home. One had a camera and was taking hologram snapshots of the people in the nightclub. The regulars usually don't take kindly to that, but they were ignoring these tourists. A man couldn't have taken those pictures without paying for it. Everyone was ignoring the two women except a tall, very thin man wearing a dark European suit and tie. It was as outrageous a costume as I'd seen that night. I wondered what

1

his routine was, so I waited at the bar a moment, eaves-dropping.

"My name is Bond," said the guy. *"James* Bond." As if there could be any doubt.

The two women looked frightened. "Oh, my God," one of them whispered.

My turn. I walked up behind the moddy and grabbed one of his wrists. I slipped my thumb over his thumbnail and forced it down and into his palm. He cried out in pain. "Come along, Double-oh-seven, old man." I murmured in his ear, "let's peddle it somewhere else." I escorted him to the door and gave him a hefty shove out into the muggy, rain-scented darkness.

The two women looked at me as if I were the Messiah returning with their personal salvations sealed in separate envelopes. "Thank you," said the one with the camera. She was speaking French. "I don't know what else to say except thanks."

"It's nothing," I said. "I don't like to see these people with their plug-in personality modules bothering anybody but another moddy."

The second woman looked bewildered. "A moddy, young man?" Like they didn't have them wherever she came from.

"Yeah. He's wearing a James Bond module. Thinks he's James Bond. He'll be pulling that trick all night, until someone raps him down and pops the moddy out of his head. That's what he deserves. He may be wearing Allah-only-knows-what daddies, too." I saw the bewildered look again, so I went on. "Daddy is what we call an add-on. A daddy gives you temporary knowledge. Say you chip in a Swedish-language daddy; then you understand Swedish until you pop it out. Shopkeepers, lawyers, and other con men all use daddies."

The two women blinked at me, as if they were still deciding if all that could be true. "Plugging right into the brain?" said the second woman. "That's horrifying."

"Where are you from?" I asked.

They glanced at each other. "The People's Republic of Lorraine," said the first woman.

That confirmed it: they probably had never seen a moddy-driven fool before. "If you ladies wouldn't mind a piece of advice," I said, "I really think you're in the wrong neighborhood. You're definitely in the wrong bar."

"Thank you, sir," said the second woman. They fluttered and squawked, scooping up their packages and bags, leaving behind their unfinished drinks, and hurried out the door. I hope they got out of the Budayeen all right.

Chiri was working behind the bar alone that night. I liked her; we'd been friends a long time. She was a tall, formidable woman, her black skin tattooed in the geometric designs of raised scars worn by her distant ancestors. When she smiled—which she didn't do very often—her teeth flashed disturbingly white, disturbing because she'd had her canines filed to sharp points. Traditional among cannibals, you know. When a stranger came into the club, her eyes were shrewd and black, as empty of interest as two bullet holes in the wall. When she saw me, though, she shot me that wide welcoming grin. "*Jambo!*" she cried. I leaned across the narrow bar and gave her a quick kiss on her patterned cheek.

"What's going on, Chiri?" I said.

"*Njema,*" she said in Swahili, just being polite. She shook her head. "Nothing, nothing, same goddamn boring job."

I nodded. Not much changes on the Street; only the faces. In the club were twelve customers and six girls. I knew four of the girls, the other two were new. They might stay on the Street for years, like Chiri, or they might run. "Who's she?" I said, nodding at the new girl on stage.

"She wants to be called Pualani. You like that? Means 'Heavenly Flower,' she says. Don't know where she's from. She's a real girl."

I raised my eyebrows. "So you'll have someone to talk to now," I said.

Chiri gave me her most dubious expression. "Oh, yeah," she said. "You try talking to her for a while. You'll see."

"That bad?"

"You'll see. You won't be able to avoid it. So, did you come in here to waste my time, or are you buying anything?"

I looked at the digital clock blinking on the cash register

behind the bar. "I'm meeting somebody in about half an hour."

It was Chiri's turn to raise her eyebrows. "Oh, business? We're working again, are we?"

"Hell, Chiri, this is the second job this month."

"Then buy something."

I try to stay away from drugs when I know I'm going to meet a client, so I got my usual, a shot of gin and a shot of bingara over ice with a little Rose's lime juice. I stayed at the bar, even though the client was coming, because if I sat at a table the two new girls would try to hustle. Even if Chiri warned them off, they'd still try. There was time enough to take a table when this Mr. Bogatyrev showed up.

I sipped my drink and watched the girl onstage. She was pretty, but they were all pretty; it went with the job. Her body was perfect, small and lithe and so sweet that you almost ached to run your hand down that flawless skin, glistening now with sweat. You ached, but that was the point. That's why the girls were there, that's why you were there, that's why Chiri and her cash register were there. You bought the girls drinks and you stared at their perfect bodies and you pretended that they liked you. And they pretended that they liked you, too. When you stopped spending money, they got up and pretended that they liked someone else.

I couldn't remember what Chiri had said this girl's name was. She'd obviously had a lot of work done: her cheekbones had been emphasized with silicone, her nose straightened and made smaller, her square jaw shaved down to a cute rounded point, oversized breast implants, silicone to round out her ass . . . they all left telltale signs. None of the customers would notice, but I'd seen a lot of women on a lot of stages in the last ten years. They all look the same.

Chiri came back from serving customers farther down the bar. We looked at each other. "She spill any money for brainwork?" I asked.

"She's just amped for daddies, I think," said Chiri. "That's all."

"She's spent so much on that body, you'd think she'd go the whole way."

"She's younger than she looks, honey. You come back in six months, she'll have her moddy plug, too. Give her time, and she'll show you the personality you like best, hardcore slut or tragic soiled dove, or anything in-between."

Chiri was right. It was just a novelty to see someone working in that nightclub using her own brain. I wondered if this new girl would have the stamina to keep working, or if the job would send her back where she came from, content with her perfectly modified body and her partially modified mind. A moddy and daddy bar was a tough place to make money. You could have the most dazzling body in the world, but if the customers were wired too, and paying more attention to their own intracranial entertainment, you might as well be home yourself, chipping in.

A cool, imperturbably voice spoke in my ear. "You are Maríd Audran?"

I turned slowly and looked at the man. I supposed this was Bogatyrev. He was a small man, balding, wearing a hearing aid—this man had no modifications at all. No visible ones, anyway. That didn't mean that he wasn't loaded with a module and add-ons I couldn't see. I've run into a few people like that over the years. They're the dangerous ones. "Yes," I said. "Mr. Bogatyrev?"

"I am glad to make your acquaintance."

"Likewise," I said. "You're going to have to buy a drink or this barmaid will start heating up her big iron cooking pot." Chiri gave us that cannibal leer.

"I'm sorry," said Bogatyrev, "but I do not consume alcohol."

"It's all right," I said, turning to Chiri. "Give him one of these." I held up my drink.

"But—" objected Bogatyrev.

"It's all right," I said. "It's on me, I'll pay for it. It's only fair—I'm going to drink it, too."

Bogatyrev nodded: no expression. Inscrutable, you know? The Orientals are supposed to have a monopoly on that, but these guys from Reconstructed Russia aren't bad, either. They practice at it. Chiri made the drink and I paid

her. Then I steered the little man to a table in the back.
Bogatyrev never glanced left or right, never gave the
almost-naked women a moment of his attention. I've known
men like that, too.

Chiri liked to keep her club dark. The girls tended to
look better in the dark. Less voracious, less predatory.
The soft shadows tended to clothe them with mystery.
Anyway, that's what a tourist might think. Chiri was just
keeping the lights off whatever private transactions might
be occurring in the booths and at the tables. The bright
lights on the stage barely penetrated the gloom. You could
see the faces of the customers at the bar, staring, dreaming, or hallucinating. Everything else in the club was in
darkness and indistinct. I liked it that way.

I finished my first drink and slid the glass to the side. I
wrapped my hand around the second one. "What can I do
for you, Mr. Bogatyrev?"

"Why did you ask me to meet you here?"

I shrugged. "I don't have an office this month," I said.
"These people are my friends. I look out for them, they
look out for me. It's a community effort."

"You feel you need their protection?" He was sizing me
up, and I could tell that I hadn't won him over yet. Not all
the way. He was intensely polite about it the whole time.
They practice that, too.

"No, it isn't that."

"Do you not have a weapon?"

I smiled. "I don't carry a weapon, Mr. Bogatyrev. Not
usually. I've never been in a situation where I needed one.
Either the other guy has one, and I do what he says, or he
doesn't, and I make him do what *I* say."

"But surely if you had a weapon and showed it first, it
would avoid unnecessary risk."

"And save valuable time. But I have plenty of time, Mr.
Bogatyrev, and it's *my* hide I'm risking. We all have to get
our adrenaline flowing somehow. Besides, here in the
Budayeen we work on kind of an honor system. They
know I don't have a weapon, I know they don't. Anybody
who breaks the rules gets broken right back. We're like
one big, happy family." I didn't know how much of this
Bogatyrev was buying, and it wasn't really important. I

was just pushing a little, trying to get a sense of the man's temper.

His expression turned just a tiny bit sour. I could tell that he was thinking about forgetting the whole thing. There are lots of private strongarms listed in the commcodes. Big, strong types with lots of weapons to reassure people like Bogatyrev. Agents with shiny bright seizure guns under their jackets, with lush, comfortable suites in more attractive neighborhoods, with secretaries and computer terminals hooked into every data base in the known world and framed pictures of themselves shaking hands with people you feel you ought to recognize. That wasn't me. Sorry.

I saved Bogatyrev the trouble of asking. "You're wondering why Lieutenant Okking recommended me, instead of one of the corporations in the city."

Not a flicker out of Bogatyrev. "Yes," he said.

"Lieutenant Okking's part of the family," I said. "He tosses business my way, I toss business his way. Look, if you went to one of those chrome-plated agents, he'd do what you need done; but it would cost you five times more than my fee; it would take longer, I can guarantee you that; and the high-velocity guys have a tendency to thunder around with their expensive equipment and those attention-getting weapons. I do the job with less noise. Less likely that your interests, whatever they are, will end up decorated with laser burns themselves."

"I see. Now that you have brought up the subject of payment, may I ask your fee?"

"That depends on what you want done. There are certain kinds of work I don't do. Call it a quirk. If I don't want to take the job, though, I can refer you to someone good who will. Why don't you just start at the beginning?"

"I want you to find my son."

I waited, but Bogatyrev didn't seem to have anything further to say. "Okay," I said.

"You will want a picture of him." A statement.

"Of course. And all the information you can give me: how long he's been missing, when you last saw him, what was said, whether you think he ran away or was coerced. This is a big city, Mr. Bogatyrev, and it's very easy to dig in and hide if you want to. I have to know where to start looking."

"Your fee?"

"You want to haggle?" I was beginning to get annoyed. I've always had trouble with these New Russians. I was born in the year 1550—that would be 2172 in the calendar of the infidel. About thirty or forty years before my birth, Communism and Democracy died in their sleep from exhausted resources and rampant famine and poverty. The Soviet Union and the United States of America fractured into dozens of small monarchies and police states. All the other nations of the world soon followed suit. Moravia was an independent country now, and Tuscany, and the Commonwealth of the Western Reserve: all separate and terrified. I didn't know which Reconstructed Russian state Bogatyrev came from. It probably didn't make much difference.

He stared at me until I realized he wasn't going to say anything more until I quoted a price. "I get a thousand kiam a day and expenses," I said. "Pay me now for three days in advance. I'll give you an itemized bill after I find your son, *inshallah.*" If Allah wills, that is. I had named a figure ten times my usual fee. I expected him to haggle me down.

"That is entirely satisfactory." He opened a molded plastic briefcase and took out a small packet. "There are holotapes here, and a complete dossier on my son, all his interests, his vices, his aptitudes, his entire psychological profile, all that you will need."

I squinted at him across the table. It was odd that he should have that package for me. The Russian's tapes were natural enough; what struck me as fishy was the rest of it, the psych profile. Unless Bogatyrev was obsessively methodical—and paranoid to boot—I didn't see why he'd have that material prepared for me. Then I had a hunch. "How long has your son been missing?" I asked.

"Three years." I blinked; I wasn't supposed to wonder why he'd waited so long. He'd probably already been to the city jobbers and they hadn't been able to help him.

I took the package from him. "Three years makes a trail go kind of cool, Mr. Bogatyrev," I said.

"I would greatly appreciate it if you would give your full attention to the matter," he said. "I am aware of the difficulties, and I am willing to pay your fee until you succeed or decide that there is no hope of success."

I smiled. "There's always hope, Mr. Bogatyrev."

"Sometimes there is not. Let me give you one of your own Arab proverbs: Fortune is with you for an hour, and against you for ten." He took a thick roll of bills out of a pocket and sliced off three pieces. He put the money away again before the sharks in Chiri's club could sniff it, and held out the three bills to me. "Your three days in advance."

Someone screamed.

I took the money and turned to see what was happening. Two of Chiri's girls were throwing themselves down on the floor. I started to get out of my chair. I saw James Bond, an old pistol in his hand. I was willing to bet it was a genuine antique Beretta or Walther PPK. There was a single shot, as loud in the small nightclub as the detonation of an artillery shell. I ran up the narrow aisle between the booths and tables, but after a few steps I realized that I'd never get near him. James Bond had turned and forced his way out of the club. Behind him, the girls and the customers were shrieking and pushing and clawing their way to safety. I couldn't make my way through the panic. The goddamn moddy had taken his little fantasy to the ultimate tonight, firing a pistol in a crowded room. He'd probably replay that scene in his memory for years. He'd have to be satisfied with that, because if he ever showed his face around the Street again, he'd get jammed up so bad he'd have to be modified to hell and back just to pass as a human being again.

Slowly the club quieted down. There'd be a lot to talk about tonight. The girls would need plenty of drinks to soothe their nerves, and they'd need lots of comforting. They'd cry on the suckers' shoulders, and the suckers would buy them lots of drinks.

Chiri caught my eye. "Bwana Marîd," she said softly, "put that money in your pocket, and then get back to your table."

I realized that I was waving the three thousand kiam around like a handful of little flags. I stuffed the bills in a pocket of my jeans and went back to Bogatyrev. He hadn't moved an inch during all the excitement. It takes more than a fool with a loaded gun to upset these steely-nerved types. I sat down again. "I'm sorry about the interruption," I said.

I picked up my drink and looked at Bogatyrev. He didn't answer me. There was a dark stain spreading slowly across the front of his white silk Russian peasant blouse. I just stared at him for a long time, sipping my drink, knowing that the next few days were going to be a nightmare. At last I stood up and turned toward the bar, but Chiri was already there beside me, her phone in her hand. I took it from her without a word and murmured Lieutenant Okking's code into it.

2

The next morning, very early, the phone started to ring. I woke up, bleary and sick to my stomach. I listened to the ringing, waiting for it to stop. It wouldn't. I turned over and tried to ignore it; it just kept ringing and ringing. Ten, twenty, thirty—I swore softly and reached across Yasmin's sleeping body and dug for the phone in the heap of clothing. "Yeah?" I said when I found it at last. I didn't feel friendly at all.

"I had to get up even earlier than you, Audran," said Lieutenant Okking. "I'm already at my desk."

"We all sleep easier, knowing you're on the job," I said. I was still burned about what he'd done to me the night before. After the regular questioning, I'd had to hand over the package the Russian had given me before he died. I never even had a chance to peek inside.

"Remind me to laugh twice next time, I'm too busy now," Okking said. "Listen, I owe you a little something for being so cooperative."

I held the phone to my ear with one hand and reached for my pill case with the other. I fumbled it open and took out a couple of little blue triangles. They'd wake me up fast. I swallowed them dry and waited to hear the fragment of information Okking was dangling. "Well?" I said.

"Your friend Bogatyrev should have come to us instead. It didn't take us very long to match his tapes with our files. His missing son was killed accidentally almost three years ago. We never had an identification on the body."

There was a few seconds of silence while I thought about that. "So the poor bastard didn't have to meet me

11

last night, and he didn't have to end up with that red, ragged hole in his shirt."

"Funny how life works out, isn't it?"

"Yeah. Remind me to laugh twice next time," I said. "Tell me what you know about him."

"Who? Bogatyrev or his son?"

"I don't care, either or both. All I know is some little man wanted me to do a job. He wanted me to find his son for him. I wake up this morning, and both he and the kid are dead."

"He should have come to us," said Okking.

"They have a history, where he came from, of not going to the police. Voluntarily, that is."

Okking chewed that over, deciding whether he liked it or not. He let it ride. "So there goes your income," he said, pretending sympathy. "Bogatyrev was some kind of political middleman for King Vyacheslav of Byelorussia and the Ukraine. Bogatyrev's son was an embarrassment to the Byelorussian legation. All the petty Russias are working overtime to establish their credibility, and the Bogatyrev boy was getting into one scandal after another. His father should have left him at home, then they'd both still be alive."

"Maybe. How'd the boy die?"

Okking paused, probably calling up the file on his screen to be certain. "All it says is that he was killed in a traffic accident. Made an illegal turn, was broadsided by a truck, the other driver wasn't charged. The kid had no identification, the vehicle he was driving was stolen. His body was kept in the morgue for a year, but no one claimed it. After that . . ."

"After that it was sold for scrap."

"I suppose you feel involved in this case, Marîd, but you're not. Finding that James Bond maniac is a police matter."

"Yeah, I know." I made a face; my mouth tasted like boiled fur.

"I'll keep you posted," said Okking. "Maybe I'll have some work for you."

"If I run into that moddy first, I'll wrap him up and drop him by your office."

"Sure, kid." Then there was a sharp click as Okking banged his phone down.

We're all one big, happy family. "Yeah, you right," I muttered to myself. I laid my head down on the pillow, but I knew I wasn't going back to sleep. I just stared at the peeling paint on the ceiling, hoping that I'd get through another week without it falling on me.

"Who was that? Okking?" murmured Yasmin. She was still turned away from me, curled up with her hands between her knees.

"Uh huh. You go back to sleep." She already *was* back to sleep. I scratched my head for a little while, hoping the tri-phets would hit before I gave in and got sick. I rolled off the mattress and stood up, feeling a pounding in my temples that hadn't been there a moment ago. After the friendly shakedown by Okking last night, I'd gone up the Street, knocking back drinks in one club after another. Somewhere along the line I must have run into Yasmin, because here she was. The proof was indisputable.

I dragged myself to the bathroom and stood under the shower until I ran out of hot water. The drugs still hadn't come on. I toweled myself mostly dry, debating whether to take another blue triangle or just blow off the whole day and go back to bed. I looked at myself in the mirror. I looked awful, but I always look awful in the mirror. I keep myself going with the firm belief that my real face is much better looking. I brushed my teeth and that took care of the terrible taste in my mouth. I started to brush my hair, but it seemed like too much effort, so I went back out into the other room and pulled on a clean shirt and my jeans.

It took me ten minutes to hunt down my boots. They were under Yasmin's clothes, for some reason. Now I was dressed. If only the goddamn *pills* would kick in, I could face the world. Don't talk to me about eating. I'd done that the day before yesterday.

I left Yasmin a note telling her to lock the door on her way out. Yasmin was one of the few people I trusted alone in my apartment. We always had a good time together, and I think we really cared about each other in some unspoken, fragile way. We were both afraid to push it, to test it, but we both knew it was there. I think it's because

Yasmin hadn't been born a girl. Maybe spending half of your life one sex and half of your life the other does something to your perceptions. Of course, I knew lots of other sex-changes I couldn't get along with at all. Well, you just can't get away with generalizations. Not even to be kind.

Yasmin was fully modified, inside and out, body and mind. She had one of those perfect bodies, one of the ones you order out of a catalog. You sit down with the guy in the clinic and he shows you the book. You say, "How about these tits?" and he tells you how much, and you say, "This waist?" and he gives you an estimate for breaking your pelvic bones and resetting them, and you have your Adam's apple shaved down and you pick out your facial features and your ass and your legs. Sometimes you could even go for new eye color. They can help you with your hair, and the beard is a matter of drugs and one magical clinical procedure. You end up with a customized self, just like restoring an old gasoline automobile.

I looked across the room at Yasmin. Her long, straight, black hair—that's what I thought was her best asset, and she was born with it. It was hers all the way. There wasn't much else about her that was original equipment—even when she was chipping in, her personality—but it all looked and functioned real nice. There was always something about a change, though, something that gave her away. The hands and feet, for instance; the clinics didn't want to touch them, there were too many bones. Female changes always had big feet, men's feet. And for some reason, they always had this slight nasal voice. I could always pick that up, even if nothing else told the T.

I thought I was an expert on reading people. What did I know? That's why I stuck myself out on a limb and handed down an ax to whoever felt like taking a whack.

Outside in the hall, the tri-phets finally flowered. It was like the whole world suddenly took a deep breath, expanding like a balloon. I caught my balance by grabbing at the railing, and then started downstairs. I didn't exactly know what I was going to do, but it was about time to start hustling up some money. The rent was coming due, and I didn't want to have to go to The Man to borrow it. I shoved my hands in my pockets and felt bills. Of course. The Russian had given me three big ones the night before. I took the money out and counted it; there was about twenty-eight hundred kiam left. Yasmin and I must have had some wild party on the other two hundred. I wished I remembered it.

When I hit the sidewalk, I was almost blinded by the sun. I don't function very well in the daytime. I shaded my eyes with a hand and looked up and down the street. No one else was about; the Budayeen hides from the light. I headed toward the Street with the vague idea of running a few errands. I could afford to run them now, I had money. I grinned; the drugs were pumping me up, and the twenty-eight hundred kiam lifted me the rest of the way. I had my rent made, all my expenses paid for the next three months or so. Time to lay in supplies: replenish the stock in the pill case, treat myself to a few luxury caps and tabs, pay off a couple of debts, buy a little food. The rest would go in the bank. I have a tendency to fritter away money if it sits around too long in my pocket. Better to salt it away, turn it into electronic credit. I don't allow myself to carry a credit charge-card—that way I can't bankrupt myself some night when I'm too loaded to know what I'm doing. I spend cash, or I don't spend at all. You can't fritter bytes, not without a card.

I turned toward the eastern gate when I got to the Street. The nearer I came to the wall the more people I saw—my neighbors going out into the city like me, tourists coming into the Budayeen during the slack time. The outsiders were just fooling themselves. They could get into just as much trouble in broad daylight.

There was a little barricade set up at the corner of Fourth Street, where the city was doing some street repair. I leaned against the posts to overhear the conversations of a couple of hustlers out for the early trade—or, if they hadn't yet made enough money to go home, it might still be last night for them. I'd listened to this stuff a million times before, but James Bond had got me pondering moddies, and so these negotiations took on a slightly new meaning today.

"Hello," said this short, thin mark. He was wearing

European clothing, and he spoke Arabic like someone who had studied the language for three months in a school where no one, neither teacher nor pupils, had ever come within five thousand miles of a date palm.

The bint was taller than he by about a foot and a half, but give some of that to the black spike-heeled boots. She probably wasn't a real woman, but a change or a pre-op deb; but the guy didn't know or care. She was impressive. Hustlers in the Budayeen *have* to be impressive, just to be noticed. We don't have a lot of plain, mousy housewives living on the Street. She was dressed in a kind of short-skirted black frilly thing with no back or sleeves, lots of visibility down the front, cinched around the waist with a solid silver chain with a Roman Catholic rosary dangling from it. She wore dramatic purple and pink paints and a beautiful mass of auburn hair, artfully arranged to frame her face in defiance of all known laws of natural science. "Lookin' to go out?" she asked. When she spoke, I read her for someone who still had a masculine set of chromosomes in every one of her refurbished body's cells, whatever was beneath that skirt.

"Maybe," said the trick. He was playing it cagey.

"Lookin' for anybody special?"

The man licked his lips nervously. "I was hoping to find Ashla."

"Uh uh, baby, sorry. Lips, hips, or fingertips, I don't do no Ashla." She looked away for a second and spat. "You go by that girl, I think she got Ashla." She pointed to a deb I knew. The trick nodded his thanks and crossed the street. I accidentally caught the first whore's eyes. "Fuck, man," she said, laughing a little. Then she was watching the Street again, looking for lunch money. A couple of minutes later another man came up to her and had the same conversation. "Lookin' for anybody special?"

This guy, a little taller than the first and a lot heavier, said "Brigitte?" He sounded apologetic.

She dug in her black vinyl purse and brought out a plastic rack of moddies. A moddy is a lot bigger than a daddy, which usually just chips right into a socket on the side of the moddy you're using, or onto the cory plug in your skull if you're not wired for moddies or if you just feel like being yourself. The girl held a pink plastic moddy in one hand and put the rack back in her purse. "Here she go, your main woman. Brigitte, she be real popular, she get a lot of airplay. She cost you more."

"I know," said the trick. "How much?"

"You tell me," she said, thinking he might be a cop setting her up. That kind of thing still happened whenever the religious authorities ran out of infidels to persecute. "How much you got to spend?"

"Fifty?"

"For *Brigitte,* man?"

"A hundred?"

"An' fifteen for the room. You come with me, sugar." They walked off along Fourth Street. Ain't love grand.

I knew who Ashla was and who Brigitte was, but I wondered who all the other moddies in that rack might be. It wasn't worth a hundred kiam a throw to find out, though. Plus fifteen for the room. So this Titian-haired hustler goes off with her sweetheart and chips Brigitte in, and she *becomes* Brigitte, and she's everything he remembers her being; and it would always be the same, whoever used a Brigitte moddy, woman, deb, or sex-change.

I went through the eastern gate and I was halfway to the bank when I stopped suddenly in front of a jewelry store. Something was gnawing at the edge of my mind. There was some idea trying to burst its way into my consciousness. It was an uncomfortable, ticklish feeling; there didn't seem to be any way to help it, either. Maybe it was only the tri-phets I'd taken; I can get pretty carried away with meaningless thoughts when I'm humming like that. But no, it was more than just drug inspiration. There was something about Bogatyrev's murder or the conversation I'd had on the phone with Okking. There was something wrong.

I thought over as much of that business as I could remember. Nothing stood out in my memory as unusual; Okking's bit had been a brush-off, I realized, but it was just the standard cop brush-off: "Look, this is a matter for the police, we don't need you sticking your nose into it, you had a job last night but it blew up in your face, so thank you very much." I've heard the same line from

Okking before, a hundred times. So why did it feel so wonky today?

I shook my head. If there was something to it, I'd figure it out. I filed it away in my backbrain; it would stew there and either boil away into nothing or simmer down into a cold, hard fact that I could use. Until then, I didn't want to bother about it. I wanted to enjoy the warmth and strength and confidence I was getting from the drugs. I'd pay for that when I crashed, so I wanted to get my money's worth.

Maybe ten minutes later, just as I was getting to the bank's sidewalk teller terminals, my phone rang again. I plucked it off my belt. "Yeah?" I said.

"Marîd? This is Nikki." Nikki was a crazy change, worked as a whore for one of Friedlander Bey's jackals. About a year ago I had been pretty friendly with her, but she was just too much trouble. When you were with her, you had to keep track of the pills and the drinks she was taking; one too many and Nikki got belligerent and completely incoherent. Every time we went out, it ended up in a brawl. Before her modifications, Nikki had been a tall, muscular male, I guess—stronger than I am. Even after the sex change, she was still impossible to handle in a fight. Trying to drag her off the people she imagined had insulted her was an ordeal. Getting her calmed down and safely home was exhausting. Finally I decided that I liked her when she was straight, but the rest of it just wasn't worth it. I saw her now and then, said hello and gossiped, but I didn't want to wade into any more of her drunken, screaming, senseless conflicts.

"Say, Nikki, where you at?"

"Marîd, baby, can I see you today? I really need you to do me a favor."

Here we go, I thought. "Sure, I guess. What's up?"

There was a short pause while she thought about how she was going to phrase this. "I don't want to work for Abdoulaye anymore." That was the name of Friedlander Bey's bottleholder. Abdoulaye had about a dozen girls and boys on wires all around the Budayeen.

"Easy enough," I said. I've done this kind of work a lot, picking up a few extra kiam now and then. I've got a good relationship with Friedlander Bey—within the walls we all called him Papa; he practically owned the Budayeen, and had the rest of the city in his pocket, as well. I always kept my word, which was a valuable recommendation to someone like Bey. Papa was an old-timer. The rumor was that he might be as much as two hundred years old, and now and then I could believe it. He had an archaic sense of what was honor and what was business and what was loyalty. He dispensed favors and punishments like an ancient idea of God. He owned many of the clubs, whorehouses, and cookshops in the Budayeen, but he didn't discourage competition. It was all right with him if some independent wanted to work the same side of the street. Papa operated on the understanding that he wouldn't bother you if you didn't bother him; however, Papa offered all kinds of attractive inducements. An awful lot of free agents ended up working for him after all, because they couldn't get those particular benefits for themselves. He didn't just *have* connections; Papa *was* connections.

The motto of the Budayeen was "Business is business." Anything that hurt the free agents eventually hurt Friedlander Bey. There was enough to go around for everybody; it might have been different if Papa had been the greedy type. He once told me that he used to be that way, but after a hundred and fifty or sixty years, you stop wanting. That was about the saddest thing anyone ever said to me.

I heard Nikki take a deep breath. "Thanks, Maríd. You know where I'm staying?"

I didn't pay that much attention to her comings and goings anymore. "No, where?"

"I'm staying by Tamiko for a little while."

Great, I thought, just great. Tamiko was one of the Black Widow Sisters. "On Thirteenth Street?"

"Yeah."

"I know. How about if I come by, say, two o'clock?"

Nikki hesitated. "Can you make it one? I've got something else I need to do."

It was an imposition, but I was feeling generous; it must have been the blue triangles. For old times' sake I said, "All right, I'll be there about one, *inshallah*."

"You're sweet, Marîd. I'll see you then. Salaam." She cut the connection.

I hung the phone on my belt. It didn't feel, at that moment, like I was getting into something over my head. It never does, before you take the leap.

3

It was twelve forty-five when I found the apartment building on Thirteenth Street. It was an old two-story house, broken up into separate flats. I glanced up at Tamiko's balcony overlooking the street. There was a waist-high iron railing on three sides, and in the corners were lacy iron columns twined with ivy, reaching up toward the overhanging roof. From an open window I could hear her damn koto music. Electronic koto music, from a synthesizer. The shrieking, high-pitched singing that accompanied it gave me chills. It might have been a synthetic voice, it might have been Tami. Did I tell you that Nikki was a little crazy? Well, next to Tami, Nikki was just a cuddly little white bunny. Tamiko'd had one of her salivary glands replaced with a plastic sac full of some high-velocity toxin. A plastic duct led the poison down through an artificial tooth. The toxin was harmless if swallowed, but loose in the bloodstream, it was horribly, painfully lethal. Tamiko could uncap that tooth anytime she needed to—or wanted to. That's why they called her and her friends the Black Widow Sisters.

I punched the button by Tami's name, but no one responded. I rapped on the small pane of Plexiglas set into the door. Finally I stepped into the street and shouted. I saw Nikki's head pop out of the window. "I'll be right down," she called. She couldn't hear anything over that koto music. I've never met anybody else who could even *stand* koto music. Tamiko was just bughouse nuts.

The door opened a little, and Nikki looked out at me. "Listen," she said worriedly, "Tami's in kind of a bad mood. She's a little loaded, too. Just don't do or say anything to set her off."

I asked myself if I really wanted to go through with this, after all. I didn't really need Nikki's hundred kiam that much. Still, I'd promised her, so I nodded and followed her up the stairs to the apartment.

Tami was sprawled on a heap of brightly patterned pillows, with her head propped against one of the speakers of her holo system. If that music had sounded loud down in the street, I was now learning what "loud" meant. The music must have been throbbing in Tami's skull like the world's worst migraine, but she didn't seem to mind. It must have been throbbing in time to whatever drug she had in her. Her eyes were half-closed and she was slowly nodding. Her face was painted white, as stark white as a geisha's, but her lips and eyelids were flat black. She looked like the avenging specter of a murdered Kabuki character.

"Nikki," I said. She didn't hear me. I had to walk right up next to her and shout into her ear. "Why don't we get out of here, where we can talk?" Tamiko was burning some kind of incense, and the air was thick with its overwhelming sweet scent. I really wanted some fresh air.

Nikki shook her head and pointed to Tami. "She won't let me go."

"Why not?"

"She thinks she's protecting me."

"From what?"

Nikki shrugged. "Ask *her*."

As I watched, Tami canted over alarmingly and toppled in slow motion, until her white-daubed cheek was pressed against the bare, dark-varnished wood of the floor. "It's a good thing you can take care of yourself, Nikki."

She laughed weakly. "Yeah, I guess so. Look, Marîd, thanks for coming over."

"No problem," I said. I sat in an armchair and looked at her. Nikki was an exotic in a city of exotics: her long, pale blond hair fell to the small of her back. Her skin was the color of young ivory, almost as white as the paint on Tami's face. Her eyes were unnaturally blue, however, and glittered with a flickering hint of madness. The delicacy of her facial features contrasted disconcertingly with the bulk and strength of her frame. It was a common enough error; people chose surgical modifications that they admired in others, not realizing that the changes might look out of place in the context of their own bodies. I glanced at Tami's inert form. She wore the emblem of the Black Widow Sisters: immense, incredible breast implants. Tami's bust probably measured fifty-five or sixty inches. It was funny to see the stunned expression on a tourist's face when he accidentally bumped into one of the Sisters. It was funny unless you thought a little about what was likely to happen.

"I just don't want to work for Abdoulaye anymore," said Nikki, watching her fingers twist a lock of her champagne-colored hair.

"I can understand that. I'll call and arrange a meeting with Hassan. You know Hassan the Shiite? Papa's mouthpiece? That's who we have to deal with."

Nikki shook her head. Her bright gaze flicked about the room. She was worried. "Will it be dangerous or anything?" she asked.

I smiled. "Not a chance," I said. "There'll be a table set up, and I'll sit on one side with you, and Abdoulaye will sit on the other. Hassan sits between us. I present your side of the story, Abdoulaye gives his, and Hassan thinks about it. Then he makes his judgment. Usually you have to make some kind of payment to Abdoulaye. Hassan will name the figure. You'll have to grease Hassan a little afterward, and we ought to bring some kind of gift for Papa. That helps."

Nikki didn't look reassured. She stood up and tucked her black T-shirt into her tight black jeans. "You don't know Abdoulaye," she said.

"You bet your ass I do," I said. I probably knew him better than she did. I got up and crossed the room to Tami's Telefunken holo. With a stiff forefinger I silenced the koto music. Peace flooded in; the world thanked me. Tamiko moaned in her sleep.

"What if he doesn't keep his part of the agreement? What if he comes after me and forces me to go back to work for him? He likes to beat up girls, Marîd. He likes that a lot."

"I know all about him. But he has the same respect for Friedlander Bey's influence that everyone else does. He won't dare cross Hassan's decision. And you better not, either. If you skip out without paying, Papa will send his thugs after you. You'll be back to work for sure, then. After you heal."

Nikki shuddered. "Has anybody ever skipped out on you?" she asked.

I frowned. It had happened just one time: I remembered the situation all too well. It had been the last time I'd ever been in love. "Yeah," I said.

"What did Papa and Hassan do?"

It was a lousy memory, and I didn't like calling it up. "Well, because I represented her, I was responsible for the payment. I had to come up with thirty-two hundred kiam. I was stone broke, but believe me, I got the money. I had to do a lot of crazy, dangerous things to get it, but I owed it to Papa because of what this girl did. Papa likes to be paid quickly. Papa doesn't have a lot of patience at times like that."

"I know," said Nikki. "What happened to the girl?"

It took me a few seconds to get the words out. "They found out where she'd split to. It wasn't difficult for them to trace her. They brought her back with her legs fractured in three places each, and her face was ruined. They put her to work in one of their filthiest whorehouses. She could earn only one or two hundred kiam a week in a place like that, and they let her keep maybe ten or fifteen. She's still saving up to get her face fixed."

Nikki couldn't say anything for a long time. I let her think about what I told her. Thinking about it would be good for her.

"Can you call to make the appointment now?" she asked at last.

"Sure," I said. "Is next Monday soon enough?"

Her eyes widened. "Can't we do it tonight? I need to get it finished tonight."

"What's your hurry, Nikki? Going somewhere?"

She gave me a sharp look. Her mouth opened and closed. "No," she said, her voice shaky.

"You can't just set up appointments with Hassan whenever you want."

"Try, Marîd. Can't you just call him and try?"

I made a little gesture of surrender. "I'll call. I'll ask. But Hassan will make the appointment at his convenience."

Nikki nodded. "Sure," she said.

I unclipped my phone and unfolded it. I didn't have to ask Info for Hassan's commcode. The phone rang once and was answered by one of Hassan's stooges. I told him who I was and what I wanted, and I was told to wait; they always tell you to wait, and you *wait*. I sat there, watching Nikki twisting her hair, watching Tamiko breathing slowly, listening to her snoring softly on the floor. Tamiko was wearing a light cotton kimono, dyed matte black. She never wore any kind of jewelry or ornament. With the kimono, her ornately arranged black hair, her surgically altered eyelids, and the painted face, she looked like an assassin-geisha, which is what she was, I guess. Tamiko looked very convincing, with the epicanthic folds and all, for someone who hadn't been born an Oriental.

A quarter of an hour later, with Nikki fidgeting nervously around the apartment, the stooge spoke into my ear. We had an appointment for that evening, just after sunset prayers. I didn't bother to thank Hassan's flunky; I have a certain amount of pride, after all. I clipped the phone back on my belt. "I'll come by and get you about seven-thirty," I said to Nikki.

I got that nervous eye-flick again. "Can't I meet you there?" she asked.

I let my shoulders sag. "Why not? You know where?"

"Hassan's shop?"

"You go straight back through the curtain. There's a storeroom behind there. Go through the storeroom, through the back door into the alley. You'll see an iron door in the opposite wall. It'll be locked, but they'll be expecting you. You won't have to knock. Get there on *time*, Nikki."

"I will. And thanks, Marîd."

"The hell with thanks. I want my hundred kiam now."

She looked startled. Maybe I'd sounded a little too tough; too bad. "Can't I give it to you after—"

"*Now*, Nikki."

She took some money out of her hip pocket and counted off a hundred. "Here." There was a new coldness between us.

"Give me another twenty for Papa's little gift. And you're responsible for Hassan's *baksheesh*, too. I'll see you tonight." And then I got out of that place before the rampant craziness began to seep into *my* skull.

I went home. I hadn't slept enough, I had a splitting headache, and the edge of the tri-phet glow had disappeared somewhere in the summer afternoon. Yasmin was still asleep, and I climbed onto the mattress next to her. The drugs wouldn't let me nap, but I really wanted to have a little piece and quiet with my eyes shut. I should have known better; as soon as I relaxed, the tri-phets began thrumming in my head louder than ever. Behind my closed eyelids, the red darkness began to flash like a strobe light. I felt dizzy; then I imagined patterns of blue and dark green, swirling like microscopic creatures in a drop of water. I opened my eyes again to get rid of the strobing. I felt involuntary twitches in my calf muscles, in my hand, in my cheek. I was strung tighter than I thought: no rest for the wicked.

I stood up again and crumpled the note I'd left for Yasmin. "I thought you wanted to go out today," she said sleepily.

I turned around. "I did go out. Hours ago."

"What time is it?"

"About three o'clock."

"*Yaa salaam!* I'm supposed to be at work at three today!"

I sighed. Yasmin was famous all over the Budayeen for being late for just about everything. Frenchy Benoit, the owner of the club where Yasmin worked, fined her fifty kiam if she came in even a minute late. That didn't get Yasmin to move her pretty little ass; she took her sweet old time, paid Frenchy the fifty nearly every day, and made it back in drinks and tips the first hour. I've never seen anyone who could separate a sucker from his money so fast. Yasmin worked hard, she wasn't lazy. She just loved to sleep. She would have made a great lizard, basking on a hot rock in the sun.

It took her five minutes to leap out of bed and get dressed. I got an abstract kiss that landed off-center, and she was going out the door, digging in her purse for the module she'd use at work. She called something over her shoulder in her barbaric Levantine accent.

Then I was alone. I was pleased with the turn my fortunes had taken. I hadn't been this flush in many months. As I was wondering if there was something I wanted, something I could blow my sudden wealth on, the image of Bogatyrev's bloodstained blouse superimposed itself over the spare, shabby furnishings of my apartment. Was I feeling guilty? Me? The man who walked through the world untouched by its corruption and its crude temptations. I was the man without desire, the man without fear. I was a catalyst, a human agent of change. Catalysts caused change, but in the end they remained unchanged themselves. I helped those who needed help and had no other friends. I participated in the action, but was never stung. I observed, but kept my own secrets. That's how I always thought of myself. That's how I set myself up to get hurt.

In the Budayeen—hell, in the whole world, probably—there are only two kinds of people: hustlers and marks. You're one or the other. You can't act nice and smile and tell everybody that you're just going to sit on the sidelines. Hustler or mark or sometimes a little of each. When you stepped through the eastern gate, before you'd taken ten steps up the Street, you were permanently cast as one or the other. Hustler or mark. There was no third choice, but I was going to have to learn that the hard way. As usual.

I wasn't hungry, but I forced myself to scramble some eggs. I ought to pay more attention to my diet, I know that, but it's just too much trouble. Sometimes the only vitamins I get are in the lime slices in my gimlets. It was going to be a long, hard night, and I was going to need all my resources. The three blue triangles would be wearing off before my meeting with Hassan and Abdoulaye; in fact, it figured that I'd show up at my absolute worst:

depressed, exhausted, in no shape at all to represent Nikki. The answer was stunningly obvious: *more* blue triangles. They'd boost me back up. I'd be operating at superhuman speed, with computer precision and a prescient knowledge of the rightness of things. Synchronicity, man. Tapped into the Moment, the Now, the convergence of time and space and life and the holy fuckin' tide in the affairs of men. At least, it would seem that way to me; and across the table from Abdoulaye, putting up a good front was every bit as good as the real thing. I would be mentally alert and morally straight, and that son of a bitch Abdoulaye would *know* I hadn't shown up just to get my ass kicked. These were the persuasive arguments I gave as I crossed my crummy room and hunted for my pill case.

Two more tri-phets? Three, to be on the safe side? Or would that wind me too tight? I didn't want to go spanging off the wall like a snapping guitar string. I swallowed two, pocketed the third just in case.

Man, tomorrow was going to be one godawful scurvy day. Better Living Through Chemistry didn't mind lending me the extra energy up front, in the form of pretty pastel pills; but, to use one of Chiriga's favorite phrases, paybacks are a bitch. If I managed to survive the stupifying crash that was coming due, it would be an occasion for general rejoicing all around the throne of Allah.

The pace picked up again in about half an hour. I showered, washed my hair, trimmed my beard, shaved the little places on my cheeks and neck where I don't want the beard, brushed my teeth, washed out the sink and the tub, walked naked through my apartment searching for other things to clean or rearrange or straighten up—and then I caught myself. "Hold on, kid," I muttered. It was good that I took the two extra bangers so early; I'd settle down before it was time to leave.

Time passed slowly. I thought of calling Nikki to remind her to get going, but that was pointless. I thought of calling Yasmin or Chiri, but they were at work now, anyway. I sat back against the wall and shivered, almost in tears: Jesus, I really *didn't* have any friends. I wished I had a holo system like Tamiko's; it would have killed some time. I've seen some holoporn that made the real thing seem fetid and diseased.

At seven-thirty I dressed: an old, faded blue shirt, my jeans, and my boots. I couldn't have looked pretty for Hassan if I'd wanted to. As I was leaving my building, I heard the crackle of static, and the amplified voice of the muezzin cried *"laa 'illaha 'illallaahu"*—it is a beautiful sound, that call to prayer, alliterative and moving even to a blaspheming dog of an unbeliever like myself. I hurried through the empty streets; hustlers stopped their hustling for prayer, marks overcame their cullibility for prayer. My footsteps echoed on the ancient cobblestones like accusations. By the time I reached Hassan's shop, everything had returned to normal. Until the final, evening call to prayer, the hustlers and the marks could return to their rock 'n' roll of commerce and mutual exploitation.

Minding Hassan's shop at that hour was a young, slender American boy everyone called Abdul-Hassan. Abdul means "the slave of," and is usually rounded out with one of the ninety-nine names of God. In this case, the irony was that the American boy was Hassan's, in every respect you could think of except, perhaps, genetically. The word around the Street was that Abdul-Hassan had not been born a boy, in exactly the same way that Yasmin had not been born a girl; but no one I knew had the time or the inclination to launch a full-scale investigation.

Abdul-Hassan asked me something in English. It was a mystery to the casual bargain hunter just what Hassan's shop dealt in. That was because it was virtually empty; Hassan's shop dealt in everything, and so there was no vital reason to display anything. I couldn't understand English, so I just jerked my thumb toward the stained, block-printed curtain. The boy nodded and went back to his daydreaming.

I passed through the curtain, the storeroom, and the alley. Just as I came to the iron door, it swung outward almost silently. "Open sesame," I whispered. Then I stepped into a dimly lighted room and looked around. The drugs made me forget to be afraid. They made me forget to be cautious, too; but my instincts are my livelihood, and my instincts are firing away morning and evening, drugs or no drugs. Hassan reclined on a small mountain of cushions, puffing on a narjîlah. I smelled the tang of hashish; the burbling of Hassan's water pipe was the only sound in the room. Nikki sat stiffly on the edge of a rug, evidently terrified, with a cup of tea in front of her crossed legs. Abdoulaye rested on a few cushions, whispering into Hassan's ear. Hassan's expression was as empty as a handful of wind. This was his tea party; I stood and waited for him to speak.

"*Ahlan wa sahlan!*" he said, smiling briefly. It was a formal greeting, meaning something like "you have come to your people and level ground." It was intended to set the tone for the rest of this parlay. I gave the proper response, and was invited to be seated. I sat beside Nikki; I noticed that she was wearing a single add-on in the midst of her pale blond hair. It must have been an Arabic-language daddy, because I knew she couldn't understand a word of it without one. I accepted a small cup of coffee, heavily spiced with cardamom. I raised the cup to Hassan and said, "May your table last forever."

Hassan wafted a hand in the air and said, "May Allah lengthen your life." Then I was given another cup of coffee. I nudged Nikki, who had not drunk her tea. You just can't expect business to start immediately, not until you'd drunk at least three cups of coffee. If you declined sooner, you risked insulting your host. All the while the coffee- and tea-drinking was going on, Hassan and I asked after the health of the other's family and friends, and called on Allah to bless this one and that one and protect all of us and the whole Muslim world from the depredations of the infidel.

I murmured under my breath to Nikki to keep downing the odd-tasting tea. Her presence here was distasteful to Hassan for two reasons: she was a prostitute, and she wasn't a real woman. The Muslims have never made up their minds about that. They treated their women as second-class citizens, but they weren't exactly sure what to do with men who became women. The Qur'ân evidently makes no provisions for such things. The fact that I myself wasn't exactly a devotee of the Book in which there is no doubt didn't help matters. So Hassan and I kept drinking and

nodding and smiling and praising Allah and trading pleas-
antries tit for tat, like a tennis match. The most frequent
expression in the Muslim world is *inshallah*, if God wills. It
removes all guilt: blame it on Allah. If the oasis dries up
and blows away, it was Allah's will. If you get caught
sleeping with your brother's wife, it was Allah's will. Getting your hand or your cock or your head chopped off in
reprisal is Allah's will, too. Nothing much gets done in the
Budayeen without discussing how Allah is going to feel
about it.

The better part of an hour passed this way, and I could
tell that both Nikki and Abdoulaye were getting antsy. I
was doing fine. Hassan was smiling broader every minute;
he was inhaling hashish in heroic quantities.

At last, Abdoulaye couldn't stand it any longer. He
wanted the conversation to get around to money. Specifi-
cally, how much Nikki was going to have to pay him for her
freedom.

Hassan wasn't pleased by this impatience. He raised his
hands and looked wearily heavenward, reciting an Arab
proverb that meant "Greed lessens what is gathered." It
was a ludicrous statement, coming from Hassan. He looked
at Abdoulaye. "You have been this young woman's protector?" he asked. There are many ways of expressing "young
woman" in this ancient language, each with its own subtle
undertone and shade of meaning. Hassan's careful choice
was *il-mahroosa*, your daughter. The literal meaning of
il-mahroosa is "the guarded one," and seemed to fit the
situation nicely. That's how Hassan got to be Papa's ace
strongarm, by threading his way unerringly between the
demands of culture and the necessities of the moment.

"Yes, O Wise One," replied Abdoulaye. "For more than
two years."

"And she displeases you?"

Abdoulaye's forehead wrinkled up. "No, O Wise One."

"And she has not harmed you in any way?"

"No."

Hassan turned to me; Nikki was beneath his notice.
"The guarded one wishes to live in peace? She plots no
malice against Abdoulaye Abu-Zayd?"

"I swear this is true," I said.

Hassan's eyes narrowed. "Your oaths mean nothing here, unbeliever. We must leave aside the honor of men, and make a contract of words and silver."

"Those who hear your words, live," I said.

Hassan nodded, pleased by my manners, if by nothing else about me or Nikki. "In the name of Allah, the Beneficent, the Merciful," declared Hassan, his hands raised, palms upward, "I render now my judgment. Let all who are present hear and obey. The guarded one shall return all jewelry and ornaments given to her by Abdoulaye. She shall return all gifts of value. She shall return all costly clothing, keeping for herself only that clothing seemly for daily attire. On his part, Abdoulaye Abu-Zayd must promise to let the guarded one pass about her business unhindered. If some dispute arises in this, I shall decide." He glared from one to the other, making it clear that there would be no dispute. Abdoulaye nodded, Nikki looked unhappy. "Further, the guarded one shall pay unto Abdoulaye Abu-Zayd the sum of three thousand kiam before noon prayer tomorrow. This is my word, Allah is Most Great."

Abdoulaye grinned. "May you be healthy and happy!" he cried.

Hassan sighed. *"Inshallah,"* he murmured, fitting the mouthpiece of the narjîlah between his teeth again.

I was forced by convention to thank Hassan, too, although he'd stung Nikki pretty badly. "I am obliged to you," I said, standing and dragging Nikki to her feet. Hassan waved a hand, as if shooing a buzzing fly out of his presence. As we passed through the iron door, Nikki turned and spat.

She shouted the worst insults her add-on could supply: *"Himmar oo ibn-himmar! Ibn wushka! Yil'an 'abook!"* I grabbed her more firmly and we ran. Behind us came the laughter of Abdoulaye and Hassan. They'd hustled their share for the evening and were feeling generous, letting Nikki escape unpunished for her obscenities.

When we got back to the Street, I slowed down, out of breath. "I need a drink," I said, leading her into the Silver Palm.

"Bastards," Nikki growled.

"Don't you have the three thousand?"

"I've got it. I just don't want to give it to them, that's all. I had other plans for it."

I shrugged. "If you want to get out from under Abdoulaye bad enough . . ."

"Yeah, I know." She still didn't look happy about it.

"Everything will be all right," I told her, steering her through the dark, cool bar.

Nikki's eyes opened wide, she threw up her hands. "Everything will be all right," she said, laughing. *"Inshallah."* Her mockery of Hassan sounded hollow. She tore off the Arabic daddy. That's about the last I remember of that night.

4

Y ou know what a hangover is. You know about the pounding headache, the vague and persistent sick stomach, the feeling that you'd just rather lose consciousness entirely until the hangover went away. But do you know what a massive hypnotic-drug hangover is like? You feel as if you're in somebody else's dream; you don't feel real. You tell yourself, "I'm not actually going through all this now; this happened to me years and years ago, and I'm just remembering it." Every few seconds you realize that you *are* going through it, that you *are* here and now, and the dissonance starts a cycle of anxiety and an even greater feeling of unreality. Sometimes you're not sure where your arms and legs are. You feel like someone carved you out of a block of wood during the night, and if you behave, someday you'll be a real boy. "Thought" and "motion" are foreign concepts; they are attributes of *living* people. Add all *that* on top of a booze hangover, and throw in the abysmal depression, bone-breaking fatigue, more nausea, more anxiety, tremors, and cramps that I owed from all the tri-phets I'd taken the day before. That's how I felt when they woke me up at dawn. Death warmed over—ha! I hadn't been warmed over at all.

Dawn, yet. The loud banging on my door started just as the muezzin was crying, "Come to prayer, come to prayer. Prayer is better than sleep. Allah is Most Great!" I might have laughed at the "prayer is better than sleep" part, if I'd been able. I rolled over and faced the cracked green wall. I regretted that simple action immediately; it had felt

34

like a slow-motion film with every other frame missing. The universe had begun to stutter around me.

The banging on the door wouldn't go away. After a few moments, I realized that there were several fists trying to slam their way in. "Yeah, wait a minute," I called. I crawled slowly out of bed, trying not to jar any part of my body that might still be alive. I made it to the floor and rose up very slowly. I stood there and wobbled a little, waiting to feel real. When I didn't, I decided to go to the door anyway. I was halfway there when I realized I was naked. I stopped. All this decision-making was getting on my nerves. Should I go back to the bed and throw on some clothes? Angry shouts joined the pounding fists. The hell with the clothes, I thought.

I opened the door and saw the most frightening sight since some hero or other had to face Medusa and the other two Gorgons. The three monsters that confronted me were the Black Widow Sisters, Tamiko, Devi, and Selima. They all had their preposterous breasts crammed into thin black pullovers; they were wearing tight black leather skirts and black spike-heeled shoes: their working outfits. My sluggish mind wondered why they were dressed for work so early. Dawn. I don't ever see dawn, unless I'm coming at it from the other side, going to bed after the sun rises. I supposed the sisters hadn't been to—

Devi, the refugee from Calcutta, shoved me backward into my room. The other two followed, slamming the door. Selima—Arabic for "peace"—turned, drew her right arm up and, snarling, jabbed the hard point of her elbow up into my gut just below my breastbone. All the air was forced out of my lungs, and I collapsed to my knees, gasping. Someone's foot kicked my jaw viciously, and I went over backward. Then one of them picked me up and the other two worked me over, slowly and carefully, not missing a single tender and unprotected spot. I had been dazed to begin with; after a few deft and punishing blows, I lost all track of what was happening. I hung limply in someone's grasp, almost grateful that this wasn't really happening to me, that it was some terrible nightmare that I was merely remembering, safely in the future.

I don't know how long they beat me. When I came to, it

was eleven o'clock. I just lay on the floor and breathed; some ribs must have been cracked, because even breathing caused agony. I tried to order my thoughts—at least the drug hangover had abated a little. My pill case. Got to find my pill case. Why can't I ever find my damn pill case? I crawled very slowly to the bed. The Black Widow Sisters had been thorough and efficient; I learned that with every movement. I was badly bruised almost everywhere, but they hadn't shed a drop of blood. It occurred to me that if they'd wanted to kill me, one playful nip would have done the job. This was all supposed to mean something. I'd have to ask them about it the next time I saw them.

I hauled myself onto the bed and across the mattress to my clothes. My pill case was in my jeans, where it usually was. I opened it, knowing I had some escape-velocity painkillers in there. I saw that my entire stash of beauties— butaqualide HCl—was gone. They were illegal as hell all over and just as plentiful. I'd had at least eight. I must have taken a handful to get me to sleep over the screaming tri-phets; Nikki must have taken the rest. I didn't care about them now. I wanted *opiates,* any and all opiates, *fast.* I had seven tabs of Sonneine. When I got them down, it would be like the sun breaking through the gloomy clouds. I would bask in a buzzy, warm respite, an illusion of well-being rushing to every hurt and damaged part of my body. The notion of crawling to the bathroom for a glass of water was too ridiculous to consider. I summoned both spit and courage, and downed the chalky sunnies, one by one. They'd take twenty minutes or so to hit, but the anticipation was enough to ease the throbbing torment just a little.

Before the sunnies ignited, there was a knock on my door. I made a little, involuntary cry of alarm. I didn't move. The knock, polite but firm, came again. *"Yaa shabb,"* called a voice. It was Hassan. I closed my eyes and wished I believed in something enough to pray to it.

"A minute," I said. I couldn't shout. "Let me get dressed." Hassan had used a more-or-less friendly form of address, but that didn't mean a damn thing. I made it to the door as quickly as I could, wearing only my jeans. I opened the door and saw that Abdoulaye was with Hassan. Bad news.

I invited them in. *"Bismillah,"* I said, asking them to enter in God's name. It was a formality only, and Hassan ignored it.

"Abdoulaye Abu-Zayd is owed three thousand kiam," he said simply, spreading his hands.

"Nikki owes it. Go bother *her.* I'm in no mood for any of your greasy nattering."

It was probably the wrong thing to say. Hassan's face clouded like the western sky in a simoom. "The guarded one has fled," he said flatly. "You are her representative. You are responsible for the fee."

Nikki? I couldn't believe that Nikki'd do this to me. "It isn't noon yet," I said. It was a lame maneuver, but it was all I could think of.

Hassan nodded. "We will make ourselves comfortable." They sat on my mattress and stared at me with fierce eyes and voracious expressions I didn't like at all.

What was I going to do? I thought of calling Nikki, but that was pointless; Hassan and Abdoulaye had certainly already visited the building on Thirteenth Street. Then I realized that Nikki's disappearance and the working-over I'd gotten from the Sisters were very likely related in some way. Nikki was their pet. It made some sort of sense, but not to me, not yet. All right, I thought, it looked as if I was going to have to come across with Abdoulaye's money, and wring it out of Nikki when I caught up with her. "Listen, Hassan," I said, wetting my swollen split lips, "I can give you maybe twenty-five hundred. That's all I have in the bank right now. I'll pay the other five hundred tomorrow. That's the best I can do."

Hassan and Abdoulaye exchanged glances. "You will pay me the twenty-five hundred today," said Abdoulaye, "and another *thousand* tomorrow." Another exchange of glances. "I correct myself: another *fifteen hundred* tomorrow." I got it. Five hundred to repay Abdoulaye, five hundred juice to him, and five hundred juice to Hassan.

I nodded sullenly. I had no choice at all. Suddenly, all my pain and anger were focused on Nikki. I couldn't wait to run into her. I didn't care if it was in front of the Shimaal Mosque, I was going to put her through every copper fiq's worth of hell she'd caused me, with the Black Widow Sisters and these two fat bastards.

"You seem to be in some discomfort," said Hassan pleasantly. "We will accompany you to your bank machine. We will use my car."

I looked at him a long time, wishing there was some way I could excise that condescending smile from his face. Finally I just said, "I am quite unable to express my thanks."

Hassan gave me his negligent wave of the hand. "No thanks are needed when one performs a duty. Allah is Most Great."

"Praise be to Allah," said Abdoulaye.

"Yeah, you right," I said. We left my apartment, Hassan pressed close against my left shoulder, Abdoulaye close against my right.

Abdoulaye sat in the front, beside Hassan's driver. I sat in the back with Hassan, my eyes closed, my head pressed back against the genuine leather upholstery. I'd never in my life before been in such a car, and at that moment I couldn't care less. The pain was grinding and growing. I felt droplets of sweat run slowly down my forehead. I must have groaned. "When we have concluded our transaction," Hassan murmured, "we must see to your health."

I rode the rest of the way to the bank wordlessly, without a thought. Halfway there the sunnies came on, and suddenly I was able to breathe comfortably and shift my weight a little. The rush kept coming until I thought I was going to faint, and then it settled into a wonderful, lambent aura of promise. I barely heard Hassan when we arrived at the teller machine. I used my card, checked my balance, and withdrew twenty-five hundred and fifty kiam. That left me with a grand total of six kiam in my account. I handed the twenty-five big ones to Abdoulaye.

"Fifteen hundred more, tomorrow," he said.

"Inshallah," I said mockingly.

Abdoulaye raised a hand to strike me, but Hassan caught it and restrained him. Hassan muttered a few words to Abdoulaye, but I couldn't make them out. I shoved the remaining fifty in my pocket, and realized that I had no other money with me. I should have had *some*—the money

I'd had the day before plus Nikki's hundred, less whatever I'd spent last night. Maybe Nikki had clipped it, or one of the Black Widow Sisters. It didn't make any difference. Hassan and Abdoulaye were having some sort of whispered consultation. Finally Abdoulaye touched his forehead, his lips, and his chest, and walked away. Hassan grasped my elbow and led me back into his luxurious, glossy black automobile. I tried to speak; it took a moment. "Where?" I asked. My voice sounded strange, hoarse, as if I hadn't used it in decades.

"I will take you to the hospital," said Hassan. "If you will forgive me, I must leave you there. I have pressing obligations. Business is business."

"Action is action," I said.

Hassan smiled. I don't think he bore me any personal animosity. *"Salaamtak,"* he said. He was wishing me peace.

"Allah yisallimak," I replied. I climbed out of the car at the charity hospital, and went to the emergency clinic. I had to show my identification and wait until they called up my records from their computer memory. I took a seat on a gray steel folding chair with a printed copy of my records on my lap, and waited for my name to be called. I waited eleven hours; the sunnies faded after ninety minutes. The rest of the time was a delirious hell. I sat in a huge room filled with sick and wounded people, all poor, all suffering. The wail of pain and the shrieks of babies never ended. The air reeked of tobacco smoke, the stink of bodies, of blood and vomit and urine. A harried doctor saw me at last, muttered to himself as he examined me, asked me no questions at all, taped my ribs, wrote out a prescription, and ordered me away.

It was too late to get the scrip filled at a pharmacy, but I knew I could score some expensive drugs on the Street. It was now about two in the morning; the action would be strong. I had to limp all the way back to the Budayeen, but my rage at Nikki fueled me. I had a score to settle with Tami and her friends, too.

When I got to Chiriga's club, it was half-empty and oddly quiet. The girls and debs sat listlessly; the customers stared into their beers. The music was blaring as loud as usual, of course, and Chiri's own voice cut through that noise with her shrill Swahili accent. But laughter was missing, the undercurrent of double-edged conversations. There was no action. The bar smelled of stale sweat, spilled beer, whiskey, and hashish.

"Marîd," said Chiri when she saw me. She looked tired. It had evidently been a long, slow night with little money in it for anybody.

"Let me buy you a drink," I said. "You look like you could use one."

She managed a tired smile. "When have I ever said no to that?"

"Never that I can recall," I said.

"Never will, either." She turned and poured herself a drink out of a special bottle she kept under the bar.

"What's that?" I asked.

"Tende. An East African speciality."

I hesitated. "Let me have one of those."

Chiri's expression became very mock-serious. "Tende no good for white bwana. Knock white bwana on his mgongo."

"It's been a long, rotten day for me, too, Chiri," I said. I handed her a ten-kiam note.

She looked sympathetic. She poured me some tende, and raised her glass in a toast. "*Kwa siha yako,*" she said in Swahili.

I picked up my drink. "*Sahtayn,*" I said in Arabic. I tasted the tende. My eyebrows went up. It tasted fiery and unpleasant; still I knew that if I worked at it, I could develop a taste for it. I drained the glass.

Chiri shook her head. "This nigger girl scared for white bwana. Wait for white bwana to throw up all over her nice, clean bar."

"Another one, Chiri. Keep 'em coming."

"Your day's been that bad? Honey, step over here by the light."

I went around the edge of the bar where she could see me better. My face must have looked ghastly. She reached up gently to touch the bruises on my forehead, around my eyes, my purple, swollen lips and nostrils. "I just want to get drunk fast, Chiri," I said, "and I'm broke, too."

"You couped three thousand off that Russian, didn't

you tell me about that? Or did I hear that from somebody else? Yasmin, maybe. After the Russian ate that bullet, you know, both of my new girls quit, and so did Jamila." She poured me some more tende.

"Jamila is no great loss." She was a deb, a pre-op transsexual who never intended to get the operation. I started on my second drink. It seemed to be on the house.

"Easy for you to say. Let's see *you* lure tourists in here without naked boobies shaking on stage. You want to tell me what happened to you?"

I shook the glass of liquor back and forth, gently. "Another time."

"You looking for anybody in particular?"

"Nikki."

Chiri gave a little laugh. "That explains some of it, but Nikki couldn't bust you up that bad."

"The Sisters."

"*All three?*"

I grimaced. "Individually and in concert."

Chiri glanced upward. "Why? What did you do to them?"

I snorted. "I haven't figured that out yet."

Chiri cocked her head and looked at me sideways for a moment. "You know," she said softly, "I did see Nikki today. She came by my place about ten this morning. She said to tell you 'thank you.' She didn't say why, but I suppose you know. Then she went off looking for Yasmin."

I felt my anger starting to bubble up again. "Did she say where she was going?"

"No."

I relaxed again. If anyone in the Budayeen knew where Nikki was, it would be Tamiko. I didn't like the thought of facing that crazy bitch again, but I was sure as hell going to. "You know where I can seize some stuff?"

"What you need, baby?"

"Oh, say, half a dozen sunnies, half a dozen tri-phets, half a dozen beauties."

"And you say you're broke, too?" She reached down under the bar again and found her bag. She rummaged through it and came up with a black plastic cylinder. "Take this into the men's room and pocket what you need. You can owe me. We'll work something out—maybe I'll take you home with me tonight."

That was an exciting though daunting thought. I haven't been intimidated by many women, changes, debs, or boys in my time; I mean, I'm no superhuman sex machine, but I get along. Chiri, though, was a scary proposition. Those evil, patterned scars and filed teeth ... "I'll be right back," I said, palming the black cylinder.

"I just got Honey Pílar's new module," Chiri called after me. "I'm dying to try it out. You ever want to jam Honey Pílar?"

It was a very tempting suggestion, but I had other business for the next hour or so. After that ... with Honey Pílar's personality module plugged in, Chiri would *become* Honey Pílar. She'd jam the way Honey had jammed when the module was recorded. You close your eyes and you're in bed with the most desirable woman in the world, and the only man she wants is you, begging for *you* ...

I took some tabs and caps from Chiri's caddy and came back out into the club. Chiri looked down along the bar casually as I put the black cylinder in her hand. "Nobody's making no money tonight," she said dully. "Another drink?"

"Got to run. Action is action," I said.

"Business is business," said Chiri. "Such as it is. It *would* be if these cheap motherfuckers would spend a little money. Remember what I said about my new moddy, Marîd."

"Listen, Chiri, if I get finished and you're still here, we'll break it in together. *Inshallah.*"

She gave me that grin of hers that I liked so much. "*Kwa heri,* Marîd," she said.

"*As-salaam alaykum,*" I said. Then I hurried out into the warm, drizzling night, taking a deep breath of the sweet scent of some flowering tree.

The tende had lifted my spirits, and I had swallowed a tri-phet and a sunny. I'd be doing all right when I booted my way into Tamiko's phony geisha rat's nest. I practically ran the whole way up the Street to Thirteenth, except I discovered I couldn't. I used to be able to run a lot farther than that. I decided it wasn't age that had slowed me down, it was the abuse my body had taken that morning. Yeah, that was it. Sure.

Two-thirty, three in the morning, and koto music is coming out of Tami's window. I pounded on her door until my hand started to hurt.

She couldn't hear me; it was either the loud music or her drugged state. I tried to force the door and found that it was unlocked. I went slowly and quietly up the stairs. Almost everyone around me in the Budayeen is modified somehow, with personality modules and add-ons wired down deep into their brains, giving them skills and talents and inputs of information; or even, as with the Honey Pílar moddy, entirely new personalities. I alone walked among them unaltered, relying on nerve and stealth and savvy. I outhustled the hustlers, pitting my native wits against their computer-boosted awareness.

Right now, my native wits were yelling at me that something was wrong. Tami wouldn't have left her door open. Unless she did it for Nikki, who'd left her key behind. . . .

At the top of the stairs I saw her, in much the same position I'd seen her in the day before. Tamiko's face was painted the same stark white with the same gruesome black highlights. She was naked, though, and her unnatural, surgically enhanced body was pale against the hardwood floor. Her skin had a wan, sick pallor to it, except for the dark burn marks and the bruises around her wrists and throat. There was a wide slash from her right carotid artery to the left, and a great pool of blood had formed, into which her white makeup had run off a little. This Black Widow would never sting anyone again.

I sat near her on the cushions and looked at her, trying to understand it. Maybe Tami had just picked up the wrong trick, and he'd pulled his weapon before she could uncap hers. The burn marks and the bruises spelled torture, long, slow, painful torture. Tami had been paid back many times over for what she'd done to me. *Qadaa oo qadar*—a judgment of God and fate.

I was about to call Lieutenant Okking's office when my phone rang on my belt. I was so lost in thought, staring at Tami's corpse, that the ringing startled me. Sitting in a room with a staring dead woman is scary enough. I answered the phone. "Yeah?" I said.

"Marîd? You've got to—" And then I heard the line go

dead. I wasn't even sure whose voice it had been, but I thought I recognized it. It sounded like Nikki's.

I sat there a little longer, wondering if Nikki had been trying to ask me for something or warn me. I felt cold, unable to move. The drugs took effect, but this time I barely noticed. I took a couple of deep breaths and spoke Okking's commcode into the phone. No Honey Pílar tonight.

5

I learned an interesting fact.

It didn't make up for the particularly foul day I'd had, but it was a fact I could file in my highly regarded cerebrum: police lieutenants are rarely enthusiastic about homicides reported less than half an hour before they're supposed to go off duty. "Your second cadaver in less than a week," Okking observed, when he showed up at the Thirteenth Street apartment. "We're not going to start paying you commissions on these, if that's what you're after. On the whole, we try to discourage this sort of thing, if we can."

I looked at Okking's tired, florid face and guessed that in the middle of the night, this passed for wry cop humor. I don't know where Okking was from—one or another dilapidated, bankrupt European country I guess, or one of the North American federations—but he had a genuine gift for getting along with the innumerable squabbling factions residing under his jurisdiction. His Arabic was the worst I'd ever heard—he and I usually held our acerbic conversations in French—yet he was able to handle the several Muslim sects, the devoutly religious and the nonpracticing, Arab and non-Arab, the rich and poor, honest and slightly bent, all with the same elegant touch of humanity and impartiality. Believe me, I hate cops. A lot of people in the Budayeen fear cops or distrust cops or just plain don't like them. I *hate* cops. My mother had been forced into prostitution when I was very young, to keep us both fed and sheltered. I remember with painful clarity the games the cops had played with her then. That had been in Algeria a long time ago, but cops were cops to me. Except for Lieutenant Okking.

The medical examiner's usually stoic expression showed a little distaste when he saw Tamiko. She had been dead about four hours, he said. He could get a general description of the murderer from the handprints on her neck and other clues. The killer had plump, stubby fingers, and mine are long and tapered. I had an alibi, too: I had the receipt from the hospital stamped with the time of my treatment, and the written prescription. "Okay, friend," said Okking, still jovial in his sour way, "I guess it's safe to let you back out on the streets."

"What do you think?" I asked, indicating Tami's body.

Okking shrugged. "It looks like we've got some kind of maniac. You know these whores end up like this every so often. It's part of their overhead, like face paint and tetracycline. The other whores write it off and try not to think about it. They'd *better* think about it, though, because whoever did this is likely to do it again; that's been my experience. We might end up with two or three or five or ten dead people before we catch up with him. You go tell your friends what you saw. You tell it to them so they listen. Get the word around. Spread it among the six or eight sexes we've got in these walls not to accept dates with men about five and a half feet tall, heavyset, with short, fat fingers and a yen for the ultimate sadism while he's getting laid." Oh, yeah: the M.E. found that the killer had taken a trip around the world while he'd been beating Tami, branding her naked skin, and strangling her. Traces of semen had been found in all three orifices.

I did my best to get the word out. Everyone agreed with my own secret opinion: whoever had killed Tami had better watch his *own* ass. Anybody who jammed with the Black Widow Sisters usually got *himself* jammed up, and trashed. Devi and Selima would be picking up every guy they could find who fit the general description, just in the hope he was the right one. I had the feeling they wouldn't slip the toxin to him at the first chance, either. I'd learned how much they enjoyed what *they* thought of as foreplay.

The next day was Yasmin's day off, and about two in the afternoon I gave her a call. She hadn't been home all night; it was none of my business where she'd been. I was amused and startled to find out that I was, however, just the least bit jealous. We made a date for dinner at five at our favorite café. You can sit at a table on the terrace and watch the traffic on the Street. Only two blocks from the gate, the Street isn't so tawdry. The restaurant was a good place to relax. I didn't tell Yasmin about any of the previous day's trouble over the phone. She would have kept me talking all afternoon, and she needed the three hours to make the dinner date on time.

As it was, I had two drinks while I waited for her at the table. She arrived about quarter to six. Three quarters of an hour late is about average for Yasmin; in fact, I hadn't really expected her until after six o'clock. I wanted to get a couple of drinks ahead. I'd had only about four hours of sleep, and I struggled with terrible nightmares the whole time. I wanted to get some liquor into me, and a good meal, and have Yasmin hold my hand while I told her of my ordeal.

"Marhaba!" she called gaily as she wove her way between the iron tables and chairs.

I signaled to Ahmad, our waiter, and he took Yasmin's drink order and left menus. I looked at her as she studied her menu. She was wearing a light cotton European-style summer dress, yellow with white butterflies. Her black hair was brushed down sleek and lustrous. She wore a silver crescent on a silver chain around her darkly tanned neck. She looked lovely. I hated to bother her now with my news. I decided to put it off as long as I could.

"So," she said, looking up at me and grinning, "how was your day?"

"Tamiko's dead," I said. I felt like a fool. There must have been a way to begin the story with less of an awful thud.

She sort of goggled at me. She murmured an Arabic superstitious phrase to ward off evil.

I took a deep breath and let it out. Then I started with dawn, yesterday morning, and my enthusiastic wake-up call from the Sisters. I went through the whole day, ending with my dismissal by Okking and my weary and lonely walk home.

I saw a tear slide slowly down one of her carefully blushed cheeks. She wasn't able to speak for several seconds. I didn't know she'd be so upset; I berated myself for my clumsiness.

"I wish I'd been with you last night," she said at last. She didn't realize how hard she was squeezing my hand. "I had a date, Marîd, some guy from the club. He's been coming in to see me for weeks, and finally last night he offered me two hundred kiam to go out with him. He's a nice guy, I suppose, but—"

I raised a hand. I didn't need to hear this. I didn't care how she paid her rent. I would have liked to have had her with me last night, too. I would have liked to have held her between the nightmares. "It's all over now, I guess," I said. "Let me blow the rest of my fifty kiam on this dinner, and then let's go for a long walk."

"Do you really think it's all over?"

I chewed my lip. "Except for Nikki. I wish I knew what that phone call meant. I just can't understand her running out on me like that, sticking me for Abdoulaye's three thousand. I mean, in the Budayeen, you can never be sure how loyal your friends are; but I'd gotten Nikki out of one or two scrapes before. I thought that might have counted for something with her."

Yasmin's eyes opened wider, then she laughed. I couldn't see what she thought was so humorous. My face still looked swollen and bruised, and by ribs still hurt like the devil. The day before had been anything but clownish. "I saw Nikki yesterday morning," said Yasmin.

"You did?" Then I remembered that Chiriga had seen Nikki about ten o'clock, and that Nikki had left Chiri's to find Yasmin. I hadn't connected that visit to Chiri with Nikki's later skip-out.

"Nikki looked very nervous," said Yasmin, "and she told me she'd quit her job and had to move out of Tami's apartment. She wouldn't tell me why. She said she'd tried to call you again and again, but there wasn't any answer." Of course not; when Nikki was trying to call me, I was lying unconscious on my floor. "She gave me this envelope and told me to be sure you got it."

"Why didn't she just leave it with Chiri?" That would have saved a lot of mental and physical anguish.

"Don't you remember? Nikki worked in Chiri's club, oh, a year ago, maybe longer. Chiri caught Nikki shortchanging customers and stealing from the other girls' tip jars."

I nodded; now I recalled that Nikki and Chiri left each other pretty much alone. "So Nikki went to Chiri just to get your address?"

"I asked her a lot of questions, but she wouldn't answer a thing. She just kept saying, 'Make sure Marîd gets this,' over and over."

I hoped it was a letter, an apology maybe, with an address where I could reach her. I wanted my money back. I took the envelope from Yasmin and tore it open. Inside was my three thousand kiam, and a note written in French. Nikki wrote:

My dearest Marîd:

I so much wanted to give you the money in person. I called many times, but you did not answer. I am leaving this with Yasmin, but if you never get it, how will you know? You will hate me forever, then. When we meet again, I will not understand. My feelings are so confused.

I am going to live with an old friend of my family. He is a wealthy businessman from Germany, who always brought me presents whenever he visited. That was when I was a shy, introverted little boy. Now that I am, well, what I am, the German businessman has discovered that he is even more inclined to give me presents. I was always fond of him, Marîd, although I can't love him. But being with him will be so much more pleasant than staying with Tamiko.

The gentleman's name is Herr Lutz Seipolt. He lives in a magnificent house on the far side of the city, and you must ask the driver to take you to (I have to copy this down for you) Bayt il-Simsaar il-Almaani Seipolt. That ought to get you to the villa.

Give my love to Yasmin and to everyone. I will visit the Budayeen when I can, but I think I will enjoy playing the mistress of such an estate for a while. I am sure you, of all people, Marîd, will understand: Business is business, mush hayk? (And I'll bet you thought I never learned a single word of Arabic!)

With much love,
Nikki

When I finished reading the letter, I sighed and handed it to Yasmin. I'd forgotten that she couldn't read a word of French, and so I translated it for her.

"I hope she'll be happy," she said when I folded the letter up.

"Being kept by some old German bratwurst? Nikki? You know Nikki. She needs the action as much as I do, as much as you do. She'll be back. Right now, I guess, it's sugar-daddy time on the Princess Nikki Show."

Yasmin smiled. "She'll be back, I agree; but in her own time. And she'll make that old bratwurst pay for every minute of it." We both laughed, and then the waiter brought Yasmin's drink, and we ordered dinner.

As we finished the meal, we lingered over a last glass of champagne. "What a day yesterday was," I said bemusedly, "and now everything is back to normal. I have my money, except I'll be out a thousand kiam in interest. When we leave here, I want to find Abdoulaye and pay him."

"Sure," said Yasmin, "but even then, everything won't be back to normal. Tami's still dead."

I frowned. "That's Okking's problem. If he wants my expert advice, he knows where to find me."

"Are you really going to talk to Devi and Selima about why they beat you?"

"You bet your pretty plastic tits. And the Sisters better have a damn good reason."

"It must have something to do with Nikki."

I agreed, although I couldn't imagine what. "Oh," I said, "and let's stop by Chiriga's. I owe her for the stuff she let me have last night."

Yasmin gazed at me over the rim of her champagne glass. "It sounds like we might not get home until late," she said softly.

"And when we do get home, we'll be lucky to find the bed."

Yasmin made a sweeping, mildly drunken gesture. "Fuck the bed," she said.

"No," I said, "I have more worthy goals."

Yasmin giggled a little shyly, as if our relationship were beginning all over again from the very first night together. "Which moddy do you want me to use tonight?" she asked.

I let out my breath, taken by her loveliness and her quiet, unaffected charm. It *was* as if I were seeing her again for the first time. "I don't want you to use any moddy," I said quietly. "I want to make love with *you*."

"Oh, Marîd," she said. She squeezed my hand, and we stayed like that, staring into each other's eyes, inhaling the perfume of the sweet olive, hearing the songs of thrushes and nightingales. The moment lasted almost forever . . . and then . . . I remembered that Abdoulaye was waiting. I had better not forget Abdoulaye; there is an Arabic saying that a clever man's mistake is equal to the mistakes of a thousand fools.

Before we left the café, however, Yasmin wanted to consult the book. I told her that the Qur'ân didn't contain much solace for me. "Not the Book," she said, "the wise mention of God. The *book*." She took out a little device about the size of a pack of cigarettes. It was her electronic *I Ching*. "Here," she said, giving it to me, "switch it on and press H."

I didn't have a lot of faith in the *I Ching*, either; but Yasmin had this fascination with fate and the unseen world and the Moment and all of that. I did as she told me, and when I pressed the square white spot marked H, the little computer played a reedy, tinkling tune, and a woman's tinny voice spoke up. "Hexagram Eighteen. Ku. Work on that which has been spoiled. Changes in the fifth and sixth lines."

"Now hit J, for Judgment," said Yasmin.

I did, and the calculator peeped out its goddamn little song again and said, "Judgment:

Putting effort into what has been ruined
Brings great success.
It profits one to cross the great water.
Heed three days before beginning.
Heed three days before completing.

"What has been ruined can be made good again through effort. Do not fear danger—crossing the great water. Success depends on forethought; be cautious before beginning. A return of ruin must be avoided; be cautious before completing.

"The superior man arouses the people and renews their spirit."

I looked at Yasmin. "I hope you're getting something out of all of this," I said, "because it doesn't mean a camel's glass eye to me."

"Oh, sure," said Yasmin in a hushed voice. "Now, go on. Press L for the Lines."

I did as I was told. The spooky machine continued: "A six in the fifth place means:

Repairing what the father has ruined.
One's actions are praiseworthy.

"A nine at the top means:

He does not serve kings and princes,
Sets himself higher goals."

"Who's it talking about, Yasmin?" I asked.

"You, darling, who else?"

"Now what do I do?"

"You find out what the changing lines turn the hexagram into. Another hexagram. Push CH for Change."

"Hexagram Forty-seven. K'un. Oppression."

I pressed J.

"Judgment:

Oppression. Success. Perseverance.
The great man causes good fortune.
There is no blame.

When one has something to say,
It is not believed.

"A great man remains confident through adversity, and this confidence leads to later success. It is a strength greater than fate. It must be accepted that for a time he is not granted power, and his counsel is ignored. In times of adversity, it is important to maintain confidence and speak but little.

"If one is weak in adversity, he remains beneath a bare tree and falls more deeply into sorrow. This is an inner delusion that must be overcome at all costs."

That was it: the oracle had spoken. "Can we go now?" I asked plaintively.

Yasmin was looking dreamily into some other Chinese dimension. "You're destined for great things, Marîd," she murmured.

"Right," I said, "but the important thing is, can that talking box guess my weight? What good is it?" I didn't even have the motherless good sense to know when I'd been told off by a book.

"You've got to find something to believe in," she said seriously.

"Look, Yasmin, I keep trying. Really, I do. Was that some kind of prediction? Was it reading my future?"

Her brow furrowed. "It's not really a prediction, Marîd. It's kind of an echo of the Moment we're all part of. Because of who you are and what you think and feel, and what you've done and plan to do, you could have drawn no other hexagram than Number Eighteen, with the changes in just those two lines. If you did it again, right this very second, you'd get a different reading, a different hexagram, because the first one changed the Moment and the pattern is different. See?"

"Synchronicity, right?" I said.

She looked puzzled. "Something like that."

I sent Ahmad off with the check and a stack of kiam notes. It was a warm, lush, dry evening, and it would be a beautiful night. I stood up and stretched. "Let's go find Abdoulaye," I said. "Business is business, damn it."

"And afterward?" She smiled.

"Action is action." I took her hand, and we started up the Street toward Hassan's shop.

The good-looking American boy was still sitting on his stool, still gazing off toward nowhere. I wondered if he was actually having thoughts, or if he was some kind of electronically animated figure that only came to life when someone approached or he caught the crackle of a few kiam. He looked at us and smiled, and asked some question in English again. Maybe a lot of the customers who came into Hassan's place spoke English, but I doubted it. It wasn't a place for tourists; it wasn't that kind of souvenir shop. The boy must have been all but helpless, unable to speak Arabic and without a language daddy. He must have been helpless; that is, dependent. On Hassan. For so *many* things.

I know a little simple English; if it's spoken slowly enough, I can understand a few words. I can say, "Where is the toilet?" and "Big Mac and fries" and "Fuck you," but that's about the extent of my vocabulary. I stared at the boy; he stared back. He smiled slowly. I think he liked me.

"Where is the Abdoulaye?" I asked in English. The kid blinked and rattled off some indecipherable reply. I shook my head, letting him know that I hadn't understood a word. His shoulders slumped. He tried another language; Spanish, I think. I shook my head again.

"Where is the Sahîb Hassan?" I asked.

The boy grinned and rattled off another string of harsh-sounding words, but he pointed at the curtain. Great: we were communicating.

"*Shukran,*" I said, leading Yasmin to the back of the shop.

"You're welcome," said the boy. That stumped me. He knew that I'd said "thanks" in Arabic, but he didn't how how to say "you're welcome." Dumb kid. Lieutenant Okking would find him in an alleyway some night. Or *I* would, with my kind of luck.

Hassan was in the storeroom, checking some crates against an invoice. The crates were addressed to him in Arabic script, but other words were stenciled in some European language. The crates could have contained anything from static pistols to shrunken heads. Hassan didn't care what he bought and sold, as long as he turned a profit. He was the Platonic ideal of the crafty merchant.

He heard us come through the curtain, and greeted me like a long-lost son. He embraced me and asked, "You are feeling better today?"

"Praise be to Allah," I replied.

His eyes flicked from me to Yasmin and back. I think he may have recognized her from the Street, but I don't think he knew her personally. I saw no need to introduce her. It was a breach of etiquette, but tolerated in certain situations. I made the determination that this was one of those times. Hassan extended a hand. "Come, join me in some coffee!"

"May your table last forever, Hassan, but we've just dined; and I am in a hurry to find Abdoulaye. I owe him a debt, you recall."

"Yes, yes, quite so." Hassan's brow creased. "Marîd, my darling, clever one, I haven't seen Abdoulaye for hours. I think he's entertaining himself elsewhere." Hassan's tone implied Abdoulaye's entertainment was any of several possible vices.

"Yet I have the money now, and I wish to end my obligation."

Hassan pretended to mull this problem over for a moment. "You know, of course, that a portion of that money is indirectly to be paid to me."

"Yes, O Wise One."

"Then leave the whole sum with me, and I will give Abdoulaye his portion when next I see him."

"An excellent suggestion, my uncle, but I would like to have Abdoulaye's written receipt. Your integrity is beyond reproach, but Abdoulaye and I do not share the same bond of love as you and I."

That didn't sit well with Hassan, but he could make no objection. "I think you will find Abdoulaye behind the iron door." Then he rudely turned his back on us and continued his labor. Without turning to face us, he spoke again. "Your companion must remain here."

I looked at Yasmin, and she shrugged. I went through the storeroom quickly, across the alley, and knocked on the iron door. I waited a few seconds while someone

identified me from somewhere. Then the door opened.
There was a tall, cadaverous, bearded old man named
Karîm. "What do you wish here?" he asked me gruffly.

"Peace, O Shaykh, I have come to pay my debt to
Abdoulaye Abu-Zayd."

The door closed. A moment later, Abdoulaye opened it.
"Let me have it. I need it now." Over his shoulder, I could
see several men engaged in some high-spirited gambling.

"I have the whole sum, Abdoulaye," I said, "but you're
going to write me out a receipt. I don't want you claiming
that I never paid you."

He looked angry. "You dare imagine I'd do such a thing?"

I glared back at him. "The receipt. Then you get your
money."

He called me a couple of foul names, then ducked back
into the room. He scrawled out the receipt and showed it
to me. "Give me the fifteen hundred kiam," he said,
growling.

"Give me the receipt first,"

"Give me the accursed money, you pimp!"

For a second I thought about hitting him hard with the
edge of my hand across the flat of his nose, breaking his
face for him. It was a delicious image. "Christ, Abdoulaye!
Get Karîm back here. Karîm!" I called. When the gray-
bearded old man returned, I said to him, "I'm going to
give you some money, Karîm, and Abdoulaye is going to
give you that piece of paper in his hand. You give him the
money, and give me the paper."

Karîm hesitated, as if the transaction were too compli-
cated for him to follow. Then he nodded. The trade was
made in silence. I turned and went back across the alley.
"Son of a whore!" cried Abdoulaye. I smiled. That is one
hell of an insult in the Muslim world; but, as it happened
to be true, it's never offended me very much. Still, because
of Yasmin and our plans for the evening, I had let
Abdoulaye abuse me beyond my usual limit. I promised
myself that soon there would be a settling of that account,
as well. In the Budayeen, it is not well to be thought of as
one who meekly submits to insolence and intimidation.

As I passed through the storeroom and went to Yasmin,
I said, "You can collect your cut from Abdoulaye, Hassan.

You'd better do it fast: I think he's losing big." Hassan nodded but said nothing.

"I'm glad that's taken care of," said Yasmin.

"Not any more than I am." I folded the receipt and pushed it down into a hip pocket.

We went to Chiri's, and I waited until she'd finished serving three young men in Calabrian naval uniforms. "Chiri," I said, "we can't stay long, but I wanted to give you this." I counted out seventy-five kiam and put the money on the bar. Chiri didn't make a move toward it.

"Yasmin, you look beautiful, honey. Marîd, what's this for? The stuff last night?" I nodded. "I know you make a thing about keeping your word and paying your debts and all that honorable choo. I wouldn't charge you Street prices, though. Take some of this back."

I grinned at her. "Chiri, you risk causing offense to a Muslim."

She laughed. "Muslim, my black ass. Then you two have a drink on me. There's a lot of action tonight, a lot of loose money. The girls are in a good mood, and so am I."

"We're celebrating, Chiri," said Yasmin. They exchanged some kind of secret signal—maybe that kind of occult, gender-specific transfer of knowledge goes along with the sex-change operation. Anyway, Chiri understood. We took the free drinks she'd offered, and got up to go.

"You two have a good night," she said. The seventy-five kiam had long since disappeared. I don't remember seeing it happen, though.

"*Kwa heri*," I said as we left.

"*Kwa herini ya kuonana*," she said. Then, "All right, which one of you lazy, fat-assed whores is supposed to be up on stage dancing? Kandy? Well, get your fuckin' clothes off and get to work!" Chiri sounded happy. All was well with the world.

"We could pass by Jo-Mama's," said Yasmin. "I haven't seen her in weeks." Jo-Mama was a huge woman, nearly six feet tall, somewhere between three and four hundred pounds, with hair that changed according to some esoteric cycle: blonde, redhead, brunette, midnight black; then a dull brown would start to grow out, and when it was long enough, it was transformed by some sorcery into blonde hair again. She was a tough, strong woman, and no one caused trouble in *her* bar, which catered to Greek merchant seamen. Jo-Mama had no scruples against pulling her needle gun or her Solingen perforator and creating general peace in gory heaps all around her. I'm sure Jo-Mama could easily have handled *two* Chirigas at the same time, and simultaneously still have the unruffled calm to mix a Bloody Mary from scratch for a customer. Jo-Mama either liked you a lot or she hated your guts. You *really* wanted her to like you. We stopped in; she greeted both of us in her usual loud, fast-talking, distracted way. "Marîd! Yasmin!" She said something to us in Greek, forgetting that neither of us understood that language; I can say even less in Greek than I can in English. All that I know I've picked up from hanging out in Jo-Mama's: I can order ouzo and retsina; I can say *kalimera* (hello); and I can call somebody *maláka,* which seems to be their favorite insult (as far as I can make out, it means "jerk-off").

I gave Jo-Mama the best hug I could manage. She's so plentiful that Yasmin and I together probably couldn't circumscribe her. She included us in a story she was telling to another customer. " . . . so Fuad comes running back to me and says, 'That black bitch clipped me!' Now, you and I both know that nothing gives Fuad a thrill like being clipped by some black whore." Jo-Mama looked questioningly at me, so I nodded. Fuad was this incredibly skinny guy who had this fascination with black hookers, the sleazier and the more dangerous, the better. Nobody liked Fuad, but they used him to run and fetch; and he was so desperate to be liked that he'd run and fetch all night, unless he ran into the girl he happened to be in love with that week. "So I asked him how he managed to get clipped this time, because I was figuring he knew all the angles by now, I mean, God, even Fuad isn't as stupid as Fuad, if you know what I mean. He says, 'She's a waitress over by Big Al's Old Chicago. I bought a drink, and when she brought my change back, she'd wet the tray with a sponge and held the tray up above where I could see it, see? I had to reach up and slide my change off the tray, and the bottom bill stuck on the wet part.' So I grabbed him by the ears and shook his head back and forth. 'Fuad, Fuad,' I said, 'that's the oldest scam in the book. You must have seen that one worked a million times. I remember when Zainab pulled that one on you last year.' And the stupid skeleton nods his head, and his big lump of an Adam's apple is going up and down and up and down, and he says to me, he says, 'Yeah, but all those other times they was one-kiam bills. Nobody ever done it with a ten before!' As if that made it all different!" Jo-Mama started to laugh, the way a volcano starts to rumble before it goes blam, and when she really got into the laugh, the bar shook, and the glasses and bottles on it rattled, and we could feel the vibrations clear across the bar on our stools. Jo-Mama laughing could cause more damage than a smaller person throwing chairs around. "So what you want, Marîd? Ouzo, and retsina for the young lady? Or just a beer? Make up your mind, I don't have all night, I got a crowd of Greeks just in from Skorpios, their ship's carrying boxes full of high explosives for the revolution in Holland and they got a long way to sail with it and they're all nervous as a goldfish at a cat convention and they're drinking me dry. What the hell do you want to drink, goddamn it! Getting an answer out of you is like prying a tip out of a Chink."

She paused just long enough for me to cram a few words in. I got myself my gin and bingara with Rose's, and Yasmin had a Jack Daniels with a Coke back. Then Jo-Mama started in on another story, and I watched her like a hawk, because sometimes she starts the stories so you'll get all caught up in them and forget you've got change coming. I never forget. "Let me have the change all in singles, Mama," I said, interrupting her story and reminding her, in case my change had slipped her mind. She gave me an amused look and made the change, and I kicked her a whole kiam for a tip. She stuffed it into her bra. There was plenty of room in there for all the money I'd ever see in my lifetime. We finished our drinks after two or three more stories, kissed her good-bye, and wandered further up the Street. We stopped in Frenchy's and a few other places, and we were satisfactorily loaded by the time we got home.

We didn't say a word to each other; we didn't even pause to turn on a light or go to the bathroom. We had our clothes off and were lying close together on the mattress. I ran my fingernails up the back of Yasmin's thighs; she loves that. She was scratching my back and chest; that's what I like. I used the tips of my thumb and fingers to touch her skin very lightly, just barely tickling her, from her armpit up her arm to her hand, and then I tickled her palm and her fingers. I ran my fingertips back down her arm, down her side, and across her sexy little ass. Then I began touching the sensitive creases of her groin the same way. I heard her start to make soft sounds, and she didn't realize her own hands had fallen beside her; then she began touching her breasts. I reached over and grabbed her wrists, pinning her arms to the bed. She opened her eyes in surprise. I grunted softly and kicked her right leg aside, a little roughly, then I spread her left leg with mine. She gave a little shudder and moan. She tried to reach down to touch me, but I wouldn't let go of her wrists. I held her immobile, and I felt a strong, almost cruel sense of control, yet it was expressed in the most caring and tender way. It sounds like a contradiction; if you don't feel the same thing sometimes, I can't explain it to you. Yasmin was giving herself to me wordlessly, completely; at the same time I was taking her, and she *wanted* me to take her. She liked me to get a little wild now and then; the moderate force I permitted myself to use only aroused her more. Then I entered her, and we let out our breath together in a sigh of pleasure. We began to move slowly, and her legs lifted; she put her heels on my hips, digging in and holding on, as close to me as she could get, while I was driving into her as close to *her* as possible. We jammed like that, slowly, drawing out every gentle touch, every surprise shock of roughness, for a long while. Yasmin and I still clung to each other, our hearts thumping and our breath ragged and quick. We clung until our bodies quieted, and still we held each other, both satisfied, both exhilarated by this restatement of our mutual need and our mutual trust and, above all else, our mutual love. I suppose at some time we separated, and I suppose at some time we fell asleep; but in the late morning when I awoke, our legs were still entwined, and Yasmin's head was on my shoulder.

Everything had been fixed, everything had indeed returned to normal. I had Yasmin to love, I had money in my pocket to last a few months, and whenever I wanted it, there was action. I smiled softly and slowly drifted back into untroubled dreams.

6

It was one of those rare times of shared happiness, of perfect contentment. We had a feeling of expectation, that what was already wonderful would only get better and better as time went on. These moments are one of the rarest, most fragile things in the world. You have to seize the day; you have to recall all the rotten, dirty things you endured to earn this peace. You have to remember to enjoy each minute, each hour, because although you may feel like it's going to last forever, the world plans otherwise. You want to be grateful for every precious second, but you simply can't do it. It's not in human nature to live life to the fullest. Haven't you ever noticed that equal amounts of pain and joy are not, in fact, equal in duration? Pain drags on until you wonder if life will ever be bearable again; pleasure, though, once it's reached its peak, fades faster than a trodden gardenia, and your memory searches in vain for the sweet scent.

Yasmin and I made love again when we woke at last, this time on our sides, with her back to me. We held each other close when we finished, but only for a few moments, because Yasmin wanted to live life to the fullest again. I reminded her that this, too, was just not in human nature—at least as far as I was concerned. I wanted a little longer to savor the gardenia, which was still pretty fresh in my mind. Yasmin really wanted another gardenia. I told her to wait another minute or two.

"Sure," she said, "tomorrow, with the apricots." That's the Levantine equivalent of "when pigs fly."

I would have loved to jam her right then until she cried

for mercy, but my flesh was still weak. "This is the part they call the afterglow," I said. "Sensitive, voluptuous people like me value it as much as the jamming itself."

"Fuck that, man," she said, "you're just getting old." I knew she wasn't being serious, that she was just riding me—or trying to. Actually, I was beginning to feel my weak flesh beginning to stir already, and was almost ready to proclaim my remaining youth, when there was a knock at the door.

"Uh oh, there goes your surprise," I said. For a recluse, I was sure entertaining a lot of visitors lately.

"I wonder who it is. You don't owe anyone any money."

I grabbed my jeans and crammed myself into them. "Then it's got to be somebody trying to borrow," I said, heading for the peephole in the door.

"From you? You wouldn't give a copper fîq to a beggar who knew the Secret of the Universe."

As I got to the door, I looked back at Yasmin. "The universe doesn't have secrets," I said cynically, "only lies and swindles." My indulgent mood vanished in a split second when I looked through the peephole. "Son of a bitch," I said under my breath. I went back to the bed. "Yasmin," I said softly, "give me your bag."

"Why? Who is it?" She found her purse and passed it to me.

I knew she always carried a low-grade seizure gun for protection. I don't carry a weapon like that; alone and unarmed I walked among the cutthroats of the Budayeen, because I was special, exempt, proud, and stupid. I had these delusions, you see, and I lived a kind of romantic fallacy. I was no more eccentric than your average raving loon. I took the gun and went back to the door. Yasmin watched me, silently and anxiously.

I opened the door. It was Selima. I held the seizure gun pointed between her eyes. "How nice to see you," I said. "Come on in. There's something I've been wanting to ask you."

"You won't need the gun, Marîd," said Selima. She brushed by me, seemed unhappy to see Yasmin, and looked in vain for somewhere to sit. She was extremely uncomfortable, I noticed, and very upset about something.

"So," I said cruelly, "you just want to get in a few last whacks before somebody lays you out like Tami?"

Selima glowered, reached back, and slapped me hard across the face. I'd earned it.

"Sit on the bed, Selima. Yasmin will move over. As for the gun, it would have come in handy when you and your friends dropped by and started my morning with such a bang. Or don't you remember about that?"

"Marîd," she said, licking her glossy red lips, "I'm sorry about that. It was a mistake."

"Oh, well, that makes it all better, then." I watched Yasmin cover herself with the sheet and crawl as far away from Selima as she could, with her knees drawn up and her back in the corner. Selima had the immense breasts that was the trademark of the Black Widow Sisters, but otherwise she was almost unmodified. She was naturally prettier than most sex-changes. Tamiko had turned herself into a caricature of the modest and demure geisha; Devi accentuated her East Indian heritage, complete with a caste mark on her forehead to which she was not entitled, and when she was not working, she wore a brightly-colored silk sari, embroidered in gold. Selima, on the contrary, wore the veil and the hooded cloak, a subtle fragrance, and the demeanor of a middle-class Muslim woman of the city. I think, but I'm not sure, that she was religious; I can't imagine how she squared her thievery and frequent violence with the teachings of the Prophet, may prayers and peace be upon him. I'm not the only self-deluded fool in the Budayeen.

"Please, Marîd, let me explain." I'd never seen Selima—or either of her Sisters, for that matter—in such a state of near-panic. "You know that Nikki left Tami's." I nodded. "I don't think she wanted to go. I think someone forced her."

"That isn't the message *I* got. She wrote me a letter about some German guy and what a wonderful life she was going to have, and that she had a real fish on the line here and she was going to play him for everything he had."

"We all got the same letter, Marîd. Didn't you notice anything suspicious about it, though? Maybe you don't know Nikki's handwriting as well as I do. Maybe you didn't pay attention to her choice of words. There were clues in the note that made us think she was trying to get something across between the lines. I think someone was standing over her, making her write the letters so no one would think twice when she disappeared. Nikki was right-handed, and the letters were written with her left hand. The script was awful, nothing like her usual writing. She wrote our notes in French, although she knows perfectly well that none of us understands that language. She spoke English, and both Devi and Tami could have read that; that's the language she used with them. She never mentioned an old German friend of her family; there may well have been such a man when she was younger, but the way she called herself 'a shy, introverted little boy,' well, that just underlined the bad feeling we had about the whole letter. Nikki told lots of stories about her life before she had her change. She was vague about most of the details—where she was really from, things like that—but she always laughed about what a terror she—he—had been. She wanted to be just like us, and so she went into these biographical accounts of her hell-raising. She was anything but shy and introverted. Marîd, that letter smelled from beginning to end."

I let my hand with the gun drop. Everything Selima had said made sense, now that I thought about it. "That's why you're so shaken up," I said thoughtfully. "You think Nikki's in some kind of trouble."

"I think Nikki's in trouble," said Selima, "but that's not why I'm so rabbity. Marîd, Devi's dead. She's been murdered, too."

I closed my eyes and groaned. Yasmin gave a loud gasp; she uttered another superstitious formula—"far from you"—to protect us from the evil that had just been mentioned. I felt weariness, as if I'd overdosed on shocking news and just couldn't work up the proper reaction. "Don't tell me," I said, "let me guess: just like Tami. Burn marks, bruises around her wrists, jammed coming and going, strangled, and her throat cut. And you think someone's out to get all three of you, and you're next."

I was astonished by her reply. "No, you're wrong. I

found her lying in her bed, almost like she was peacefully asleep. She'd been shot, Marîd, with an old-fashioned gun, the kind that used metal bullets. There was a bullet hole exactly centered on her caste mark. No signs of a fight or anything. Nothing disturbed in her apartment. Just Devi, part of her face blown away, a lot of blood splattered on the bedclothes and the walls. I threw up. I've never seen anything like it. Those old weapons were so bloody and, well, brutal." This from a woman who'd slashed enough faces in her time. "I'll bet no one's been shot with a bullet in fifty years." Selima evidently didn't know about my Russian, whatever his name had been; dead bodies didn't cause much scandal and gossip in the Budayeen; they weren't all that rare. Corpses were more of an inconvenience than anything else. Getting large quantities of bloodstains out of nice silk or cashmere is a tedious job.

"Have you called Okking yet?" I asked.

Selima nodded. "It wasn't his shift. Sergeant Hajjar came and asked all the questions. I wish it'd been Okking instead."

I knew what she meant. Hajjar was the kind of cop I think of when I think of "cop." He walked around as if he had a cork up his ass, looking for petty rowdies to blast into grand mal seizures. He had a particular hard-on for Arabs who were inattentive to their spiritual duties: people like me and almost everyone else in the Budayeen.

I put the gun back in Yasmin's bag. My mood had changed entirely; now suddenly, and for the first time, I felt sympathy for Selima. Yasmin put her hand on Selima's shoulder in a comforting gesture. "I'll make some coffee," I said. I looked at the last Black Widow Sister. "Or would you rather have tea?"

She was grateful for our kindness, and our company, too, I think. "Tea, thank you," she said. She had begun to calm down.

I put the kettle on to boil. "So just tell me one thing: why *did* the three of you work out your kinks on my body the other day?"

"Allah have mercy on me," said Selima. She took a folded scrap of paper from her bag and brought it to me. "This is Nikki's usual handwriting, but it's obvious she was in a terrible hurry." The words were written in English, scrawled quickly on the back of an envelope.

"What does it say?" I asked.

Selima glanced at me and quickly looked back down at the paper. "It says, 'Help. Hurry. Marîd.' That's why we did what we did. We misunderstood. We thought you were responsible for whatever trouble she was in. Now I know that you had done her the service of negotiating her release from that pig Abdoulaye, and that she owed you money. She wanted us to let you know that she needed help, but didn't have time to write anything more. She was probably lucky just to scribble this down."

I thought about the beating they'd given me; the hours of unconsciousness; the pain I'd suffered and still suffered; the long, nightmarish wait at the hospital; the anger I'd felt toward Nikki; the thousand kiam it had cost me. I added all that up and tried to cancel it. I couldn't. I still felt an unaccustomed rage inside me, but now it seemed I had no one to vent it on. I looked at Selima. "Just forget it," I said.

Selima wasn't moved. I thought she'd meet me halfway at least, but then I remembered who I was dealing with. "It isn't all right, you know," she reminded me. "I'm still worried about Nikki."

"The letter she wrote *might* be true, after all," I said, pouring tea into three cups. "Those clues you mentioned, they might all have some innocent explanation." I didn't believe a word of it, even as I said it. It was only to make Selima feel better.

She took her cup of tea and held it. "I don't know what to do now," she said.

"It may be some crazy trick is after all three of you," Yasmin suggested. "Maybe you ought to hide out for a while."

"I thought of that," Selima said. Yasmin's theory didn't sound likely to me: Tamiko and Devi had been killed in such completely different ways. Of course, that didn't rule out the possibility of a creative murderer. Despite all the old cop truisms about a criminal's modus operandi, there wasn't a reason in the world why a killer couldn't use two offbeat techniques. I kept quiet about this, too.

"You could stay in my apartment," said Yasmin. "I could stay here with Marîd." Both Selima and I were startled by Yasmin's offer.

"That's good of you to offer," said Selima. "I'll think about it, sugar, but there are a couple of other things I want to try. I'll let you know."

"You'll be all right if you just keep your eyes open," I said. "Don't do any business for a few days, don't mix with strangers." Selima nodded. She handed me her tea, which she hadn't even tasted.

"I have to go," she said. "I hope everything is straight now between us."

"You have more important things to worry about, Selima," I said. "We've never been very close before. In a morbid way, maybe we'll end up better friends because of this."

"The price has been high," she said. That was all too true. Selima started to say something else, then stopped. She turned and went to the door, let herself out, and closed the door quietly behind her.

I stood by the stove with three cups of tea. "You want one of these?" I asked.

"No," said Yasmin.

"Neither do I." I dumped the tea into the sink.

"There's either one mighty twisted bastard out there killing people," mused Yasmin, "or what's worse, two different motherfuckers working the same side of the street. I'm almost afraid to go to work."

I sat down beside her and stroked her perfumed hair. "You'll be all right at work. Just listen to what I told Selima: don't pick up any trick you don't already know. Stay here with me instead of going home alone."

She gave me a little smile. "I couldn't bring a trick here to your apartment," she said.

"You're damn straight about *that*," I said. "Forget about turning tricks at all until this business is over and they've caught the guy. I've got enough money to support both of us for a little while."

She put her arms around my waist and laid her head on my shoulder. "You're all right," she said.

"You're okay, too, when you're not snoring like a go-devil," I said. In reprisal, she raked my back hard with her long, claret-colored fingernails. Then we stretched out on the bed and played around again for half an hour.

I got Yasmin out of bed about two-thirty, made her something to eat while she showered and dressed, and urged her to get to work without getting fined for being late: fifty kiam is fifty kiam, I always reminded her. Her answer to that was, "So why worry? One fifty-kiam bill looks just like all the others. If I don't bring home one, I'll bring home another." I couldn't quite get her to see that if she just hustled her bustle a little more, she could bring them *both* home.

She asked me what I was going to do that afternoon. She was a little jealous because I'd earned my money for the next few weeks; I could sit around in some coffeehouse all day, bragging and gossiping with the boyfriends of the other dancers and working girls. I told her that I had some errands to run, and that I'd be busy, too. "I'm going to see what the story is with Nikki," I said.

"You didn't believe Selima?" Yasmin asked.

"I've known Selima a long time. I know she likes to go overboard in these situations. I'd be willing to bet that Nikki is safe and happy with this Seipolt guy. Selima just had to invent some story to make her life sound exotic and risky."

Yasmin gave me a dubious look. "Selima doesn't *have* to make up stories. Her life *is* exotic and risky. I mean, how can you exaggerate a bullet hole through the forehead? Dead is *dead*, Marîd."

She had a point there, but I didn't feel like awarding it to her out loud. "Go to work," I said, kissing her and fondling her and booting her out of the apartment. Then I was all alone. "Alone" was much quieter now than ever before; I think I almost preferred having a lot of noise and people and provocation around. That's a bad sign for a recluse. It's even worse for a solitary agent, for a tough character who lives for action and menace, the kind of bold, competent guy I liked to think I was. When the silence starts to give you the nervous jimjams, that's when you find out you're *not* a hero, after all. Oh, sure, I knew a lot of truly dangerous people, and I'd done a lot of dangerous things. I was on the inside, one of the sharks rather than one of the minnows; and I had the respect of the other sharks as well. The trouble was that having Yasmin around all the time was getting to be enjoyable, but that didn't fit the lone wolf's profile.

I said all of this to myself while I shaved my throat, looking in the bathroom mirror. I was trying to persuade myself of something, but it took me a while to do it. When I did, I wasn't happy about my conclusion: I hadn't accomplished very much during the last several days; but three times now, people had dropped dead near me, people I knew, people I didn't know. If this trend went on, it could endanger Yasmin.

Hell, it could endanger *me*.

I had said that I thought Selima was getting excited over nothing. That was a lie. While Selima was telling me her story, I was recalling the brief, frantic phone call I'd gotten: "Marîd? You've got to—" I hadn't been sure before that it had been from Nikki; but I was certain now, and I was feeling guilty because I hadn't acted on it. If Nikki had been hurt in any way, I was going to have to live with that guilt for the rest of my life.

I put on a white cotton *gallebeya;* covered my head with the familiar Arab headdress, the white *keffiya,* and held it in place with a rope *akal.* I put some sandals on my feet. Now I looked like every other poor, scruffy Arab in the city, one of the *fellahîn,* or peasants. I doubt if I'd dressed like this more than ten times in all the years I'd lived in the Budayeen. I've always affected European clothing, in my youth in Algeria and later when I'd wandered eastward. I did not now look like an Algerian; I wanted to be taken for a local *fellah.* Maybe only my reddish beard whispered a discordant note, but the German would not know that. As I left my apartment and walked along the Street toward the gate, I didn't hear my name called once or catch a glance of recognition. As I walked among my friends, they did not know me, so unusual was it for me to dress this way. I felt invisible, and with invisibility goes a certain power. My uncertainty of a few minutes before evaporated, replaced by my old confidence. I was dangerous again.

Just beyond the eastern gate was the broad Boulevard il-Jameel, lined with palm trees on both sides. A spacious neutral ground separated the north- and southbound traffic, and was planted with several varieties of flowering shrub. There was something blooming every month of the year, filling the air along the boulevard with sweet scents, distracting the eyes of those who passed by with their blossoms' startling colors: luscious pinks, flaming carmine, rich pansy purple, saffron yellow, pristine white, blue as varied as the restless sea, and still more. In the trees and lodged high above the street on rooftops sang a multitude of warblers, larks, and ringdoves. The combined beauties moved one to thank Allah for these lavish gifts. I paused on the neutral ground for a moment; I had emerged from the Budayeen dressed as what I truly was—an Arab of few kiam, no great learning, and severely limited prospects. I had not anticipated the feeling of excitement this aroused in me. I felt a new kinship with the other scurrying *fellahîn* around me, a kinship that extended—for the moment—to the religious part of daily life that I had neglected for so long. I promised myself that I would tend to those duties very soon, as soon as I had the opportunity; I had to find Nikki first.

Two blocks north of the Budayeen's eastern gate in the direction of the Shimaal Mosque, I found Bill. I knew he'd be near the walled quarter, sitting behind the steering wheel of his taxi, watching the people passing by on the sidewalk with patience, love, curiosity, and cold fear. Bill was almost my size, but more muscular. His arms were covered with blue-green tattoos, so old that they had blurred and become indistinct; I wasn't even certain what they had once represented. He hadn't cut his sandy-colored hair or beard in years, many years; he looked like a Hebrew patriarch. His skin, where it was exposed to the sun as he drove around the city, was burned a bright red, like forbidden crayfish in a pot. In his red face, his pale blue eyes stared with an insane intensity that always made me look quickly away. Bill was crazy, with a craziness he'd chosen for himself as carefully as Yasmin had chosen her high, sexy cheekbones.

I met Bill when I first came to the city. He had already learned to live among the outcasts, wretches, and bullies of the Budayeen years before; he helped me fit myself easily into that questionable society. Bill had been born in the United States of America—that's how old he was—in the part that is now called Sovereign Deseret. When the North American union broke into several jealous, balkanized nations, Bill turned his back on his birthplace forever. I don't know how he earned a living until he learned the way of life here; Bill doesn't remember, either. Somehow he acquired enough cash to pay for a single surgical modification in his body. Rather than wiring his brain, as many of the lost souls of the Budayeen choose to do, Bill selected a more subtle, more frightening bodmod: He had one of his lungs removed and replaced with a large, artificial gland that dripped a perpetual, measured quantity of some fourth-generation psychedelic drug into his bloodstream. Bill wasn't sure which drug he'd asked for, but judging from his abstracted speech and the quality of his hallucinations, I'd guess it was either l.-ribopropylmethionine—RPM—or acetylated neocorticine.

You can't buy RPM or acetylated neocorticine on the street. There isn't much of a market for either drug. They both have the same long-term effect: After repeated doses of these drugs, a person's nervous system begins to degenerate. They compete for the binding sites in the human brain that are normally used by acetylcholine, a neurotransmitter. These new psychedelics attack and occupy the binding sites like a victorious army swooping down upon a conquered city; they cannot be removed, either by the body's own processes or by any form of medical therapy. The hallucinatory experiences are unparalleled in pharmacological history, but the price in terms of damage is exorbitant. The user, more literally than ever before, burns out his brain, synapse by synapse. The resulting condition is symptomatically indistinguishable from advanced Parkinson's and Alzheimer's diseases. Continued use, when the drugs begin interfering with the autonomic nervous system, probably proves fatal.

Bill hadn't reached that state yet. He was living a day-long, nightlong dreamlife. I remembered what it had been like sometimes, when I had dropped a less-dangerous psychedelic and had been struck by the crippling fear that "I would never come down," a common illusion that you use to torture yourself. You feel as if this time, this particular drug experience, unlike all the pleasant experiences in the past, *this time* you've gone and broken something in your head. Trembling, terrified, promising that you'll never take another pill again, you huddle up against the onslaught of your own darkest dreams. At last, however, you do recover; the drug wears off, and sooner or later you forget just how bad the horror was. You do it again. Maybe this time you'll be luckier, maybe not.

There were no maybes with Bill. Bill was *never* coming down, ever. When those moments of utter, absolute dread began, he had no way to lessen the anxiety. He couldn't tell himself that if he just held out long enough, in the morning he'd be back to normal. Bill would never be back to normal. That's the way he wanted it. As for the cell-by-cell death of his nervous system, Bill only shrugged. "They all gonna die someday, right?"

"Yes," I replied, clinging nervously to the rear seat of his taxi as he plunged through narrow, twisting alleys.

"And if they go all at once, everybody *else* has a party at your funeral. You don't get *nothin'*. You get *buried*. This way, I get to say good-bye to my brain cells. They all done a lot for me. Good-bye, good-bye, farewell, it's been good to know ya. Give each goddamn little fucker its own little send-off. If you die like a regular person, bam! you're dead, violent stopping of every goddamn part of you, sugar in the gas tank, water in the carburetor, come to a grinding halt, you get one second, maybe two seconds, to scream to God that you're on your way. Awful way to come to an end. Live a violent life, live a violent death. Me, I'm sneaking across the bar one neuron at a time. If I have to go into that good night, I'm goin' *gentle;* the hell with whoever said not to. That sucker's *dead,* man, so what did he know? Not even the courage of his convictions. Maybe after I'm dead the *afrit* won't know I'm there if I keep my mouth shut. Maybe they'll leave me alone. I don't want to be fucked with after I'm dead, man. How can you protect yourself after you're dead? Think about *that*, man. I'd like to get my hands on the guy who invented demons, man. And they call *me* crazy."

I didn't want to discuss it any further.

Bill drove me out to Seipolt's. I always had Bill drive me when I went into the city for any reason. His insanity distracted me from the pervasive normalness all around, the lack of chaos imposed on everything. Riding with Bill was like carrying a little pocket of the Budayeen around with me for security. Like taking a tank of oxygen with you when you went into the deep, dark depths.

Seipolt's place was far from the center of the city, on the southeast edge. It was within sight of the realm of the everlasting sand, where the dunes waited for us to relax just a little, and then they'd cover us all like ashes, like dust. The sand would smooth out all conflicts, all works, all hopes. It would swoop down, a victorious army upon a conquered city, and we would all lie in the deep, dark depths beneath the sand forever. The good night would come—but not just yet. No, not here, not yet.

Seipolt saw that order was maintained and the desert held back; date palms arched around the villa, and gardens bloomed because water was forced to flow in this inhospitable place. Bougainvillea flowered and the breeze was perfumed with enticing aromas. Iron gates were kept in repair, painted and oiled; long, curving drives were kept clean and raked; walls were whitewashed. It was a magnificent residence, a rich man's home. It was a refuge against the creeping sand, against the creeping night that waits so patiently.

I sat in the back of Bill's taxi. His engine idled roughly, and he muttered and laughed to himself. I felt small and foolish—Seipolt's mansion awed me, despite myself. What was I going to say to Seipolt? The man had power—why, I couldn't hold back even a handful of sand, not if I tried with all my might and prayed to Allah at the same time.

I told Bill to wait, and I watched him until I saw that somewhere down in his careening mind he understood. I got out of the taxi and walked through the iron gate, up the white-pebbled drive toward the front entrance to the villa. I knew that Nikki was crazy; I knew that Bill was crazy; I was now learning that *I* wasn't entirely well, either.

As I listened to my feet crunching the small stones, I wondered why we all just didn't go back where we'd come from. That was the real treasure, the greatest gift: to be where you truly belonged. If I was lucky, someday I would find that place. *Inshallah.* If Allah willed.

The front door was a massive thing made of some kind of blond wood, with great iron hinges and an iron grille. The door was swinging open as I raised my hand to grasp the brass knocker. A tall, lean, blond European stared down at me. He had blue eyes (unlike Bill's, this man's eyes were the kind you always hear described as "piercing" and, by the Prophet's beard, I felt pierced); a thin, straight nose with flaring nostrils; a square chin; and a tight-lipped mouth that seemed set in a permanent expression of mild revulsion. He spoke to me in German.

I shook my head. " *'Anaa la 'afham,"* I said, grinning like the stupid Arab peasant he took me for.

The man with the blond hair looked impatient. He tried English. I shook my head again, grinning and apologizing and filling his ears with Arabic. It was obvious that he couldn't make any sense out of my language, and he wasn't going to try any harder to find another that I might understand. He was just on the point of slamming the heavy door in my face, when he saw Bill's taxi. That made him think. I looked like an Arab; to this man, all Arabs were pretty much the same, and one of their shared qualities was poverty. Yet I had hired a taxi to drive out to the residence of a rich and influential man. He was having trouble making sense of that, so now he wasn't so ready to dismiss me out of hand. He pointed at me and muttered something; I supposed it was "Wait here." I grinned, touched my heart and my forehead, and praised Allah three or four times.

A minute later, Blondie returned with an old man, an Arab in the employ of the household. The two men spoke together briefly. The old *fellah* turned to me and smiled. "Peace be upon you!" he said.

"And upon you," I said. "O neighbor, is this man the honored and excellent one, Lutz Seipolt Pasha?"

The old man laughed a little. "You are mistaken, my nephew," he said. "He is but the doorman, a menial even as I am." I really doubted that they were all *that* equal. Evidently the blond man was part of Seipolt's retinue, brought from Germany.

"On my honor, I am a fool!" I said. "I have come to ask an important question of His Excellency." Arabic terms of address frequently make such use of elaborate flattery. Seipolt was a businessman of some sort; I had already called him Pasha (an obsolete title used in the city for ingratiation) and His Excellency (as if he were some sort of ambassador). The old, leather-skinned Arab understood what I was doing well enough. He turned to the German and translated the conversation.

The German seemed even less pleased. He replied with a single, curt sentence. The Arab spoke to me. "Reinhardt the doorman wishes to hear this question."

I grinned into Reinhardt's hard eyes. "I'm only looking for my sister, Nikki."

The Arab shrugged and relayed the information. I saw Reinhardt blink and make the beginning of some gesture, then catch himself. He said something to the old *fellah*. "There is no one by that name here," the Arab told me. "There are no women at all in this household."

"I am certain that my sister is here," I said. "It is a matter of my family's honor." I sounded threatening; the Arab's eyes opened wide.

Reinhardt hesitated. He was undecided whether to slam the door in my face, after all, or kick this problem upstairs. I figured him for a coward; I was right. He didn't want to take the responsibility for the decision, so he agreed to convey me somewhere inside the cool, lavishly furnished house. I was glad to get out of the hot sun. The old Arab disappeared, returning to his duties. Reinhardt did not deign to look at me or address a word in my direction; he merely walked deeper into the house, and I followed. We came to another heavy door, this one of a fine-grained dark hardwood. Reinhardt rapped; a gruff voice called out, and Reinhardt answered. There was a short pause, then the gruff voice gave an order. Reinhardt turned the doorknob, pushed the door open just a little, and walked away. I entered the room, putting the dumb-Arab look back on my face. I pressed my hands together in supplication and dipped my head a few times for good measure. "You are His Excellency?" I asked in Arabic.

I was looking at a heavy, coarse-featured, bald man in his sixties, with a moddy and two or three daddies plugged into his sweat-shiny skull. He sat behind a heavily-littered desk, holding a telephone in one hand and a large, blued-steel needle gun in the other. He smiled at me. "Please do me the honor of coming closer," he said in unaccented Arabic; it was probably a language daddy speaking for him.

I bowed again. I was trying to think, but my mind was like a blank parchment. Needle guns do that to me sometimes. "O Excellent One," I said, "I beg your pardon for intruding."

"To hell with all that 'Excellent One' bull. Tell me why you're here. You know who I am. You know I don't have a lot of time to waste."

I pulled Nikki's letter from my shoulder bag and gave it to him. I guessed he'd figure it out quickly enough.

He read it through and then put down the telephone—but not the needle gun. "You're Marîd, then?" he said. He'd stopped smiling.

"I have that privilege," I said.

"Don't get smart with me," said Seipolt. "Sit down in that chair." He waved me aside with the pistol. "I've heard one or two things about you."

"From Nikki?"

Seipolt shook his head. "Here and there in the city. You know how Arabs like to gossip."

I smiled. "I didn't realize I had such a reputation."

"It's nothing to get excited about, kid. Now, what makes you think this Nikki, whoever she is, is here? This letter?"

"Your house seemed like a good place to start looking. If she's not here, why is your name so prominent in her plans?"

Seipolt looked genuinely bewildered. "I don't have any idea, and that's the truth. I've never heard of your Nikki, and I don't have the least interest in her. As my staff will attest, I haven't had an interest in *any* woman in many years."

"Nikki's not just any woman," I said. "She's a simulated woman built on a customized boy's chassis. Maybe that's what's been stirring your interest during those years."

Seipolt's expression grew impatient. "Let me be blunt, Audran. I no longer have the apparatus to get sexually interested in anyone or anything. I no longer have the desire to have that condition repaired. I have found that I prefer business. *Versteh'*?"

I nodded. "I don't suppose you'd allow me to search your lovely home," I said. "I needn't disturb you while you work: don't mind me, I'll be quiet as a jerboa."

"No," he said, "Arabs steal things." His smile grew slowly until it was an evil thing.

I don't taunt easily, so I just shook that one off. "May I have the letter back?" I asked. Seipolt shrugged; I went to his desk and picked up Nikki's note, tucked it back in my shoulder bag. "Import-export?" I asked.

Seipolt was surprised. "Yes," he said. He looked down at a stack of bills of lading.

"Anything in particular, or the usual odds and ends?"

"What the hell difference does it make to you *what* I—" I waited for him to reach the middle of his outraged reply, then swiftly hit the inside of his right forearm with my left hand, swinging the muzzle of the needle gun away, and slapped him across his plump, white face with my right hand. Then I tightened my grip on his left wrist. We struggled silently for a moment. He was sitting, and I was standing over him, balanced, with momentum and surprise on my side. I twisted his wrist outward, abusing the small bones in his forearm. He grunted and dropped the needle gun to the desk, and with my right hand I swept it all the way across the room with one motion. He made no attempt to retrieve it. "I have other weapons," he said softly. "I have alarms to summon Reinhardt and the others."

"I do not doubt that," I said, not relaxing my hold on his wrist. I felt my little sadistic streak beginning to enjoy this. "Tell me about Nikki," I said.

"She's never been here, I don't know a damn thing about her," said Seipolt. He was starting to suffer. "You can hold the gun on me, we can fight and wrestle around the room, you can battle my men, you can search the house. Goddamn it, I don't know *who* your Nikki is! If you don't believe me now, there isn't a damn thing in the world I can say that will change your mind. Now, let's see how smart you really are."

"At least four people received that same letter," I said, thinking out loud. "Two of them are dead now. Maybe the police could find some clue here, even if I couldn't."

"Let go of my wrist." His voice was icy and commanding. I let go of his wrist; there didn't seem to be much point in holding it any longer, anyway. "Go ahead and call the police. Let them search. Let *them* persuade you. Then after they leave, I will make you sorry you ever stepped onto my property. If you don't get out of my office right now, you uncivilized idiot, you may never get another chance. *Versteh'?*"

"Uncivilized idiot" was a popular insult in the Budayeen that doesn't translate well. I was doubtful that it had been included in Seipolt's daddy vocabulary; I was amused that he had picked up the idiom in his years among us.

I cast a quick glance at his needle gun, lying on the carpet about a dozen feet from me. I would have liked to take it with me, but that would be bad manners. I wasn't going to fetch it for Seipolt, though; let him have Reinhardt pick it up. "Thanks for everything," I said, with a friendly look on my face. Then I changed my expression to the very respectful, dumb Arab. "I am obliged to you, O Excellent One. May your day be happy, may you awaken tomorrow in health!" Seipolt only stared at me hatefully. I backed away from him—not because of any wariness, but only to exaggerate the Arabic courtesy I was mocking him with. I passed through the office door and closed it softly. Then I stared up into Reinhardt's face again. I grinned and bowed; he showed me out. I paused on my way to the front door to admire some shelves filled with various kinds of rare artworks: pre-Columbian, Tiffany glass, Lalique crystal, Russian religious icons, ancient Egyptian and Greek statuary fragments. Among the hodgepodge of periods and styles was a ring, obscure and inconspicuous, a simple band of silver and lapis lazuli. I had seen that ring before, around one of Nikki's fingers while she played endlessly, twisting the locks of her hair. Reinhardt was studying me too closely; I wanted to grab the ring, but it was impossible.

At the door, I turned and began to give Reinhardt some Arabic formula of gratitude, but I didn't have the chance: this time, with great relish, the blond Aryan bastard flung the door shut, almost breaking my nose. I went back along the pebble drive, lost in thought. I got into Bill's cab. "Home," I said.

"Huh," Bill grunted. "Play hurt, play with pain. Easy for *him* to say, the son of a bitch. And there's the best defensive line in history waiting for me to twitch my little pink ass, waiting to tear my head off and hand it to me, right? 'Sacrifice.' So I hoped they'd call some dinky pass play and let me rest; but no, not today. The quarterback was an *afrit,* he only looked like a human being. I had him spotted, all right. When he handed it off, the ball was always hot as coals. I should have guessed something was up, even back then. Fire demons. A little bit of burning brimstone and smoke, see, and the referee can't see them grabbing at your facemask. *Afrits* cheat. *Afrits* want you to know what it's going to be like for you after you're dead, when they can do anything they want to you. They like to play with your mind like that. *Afrits.* Kept calling off-tackle plunges all afternoon. Hot as hell."

"Let's go home, Bill," I said more loudly.

He turned to look at me. "Easy for *you* to say," he muttered. Then he started his old taxi and backed out of Seipolt's drive.

I called Lieutenant Okking's commcode during the ride back to the Budayeen. I told him about Seipolt and Nikki's note. He didn't seem to be very interested. "Seipolt's nobody," said Okking. "He's a rich nobody from reunited Neudeutschland."

"Nikki was scared, Okking," I told him.

"She probably lied to you and the others in those letters. She lied about where she was going, for some reason. Then it didn't work out the way she'd planned, and tried to get in touch with you. Whoever she'd gone with didn't let her finish." I could almost hear him shrug. "She didn't do a smart thing, Marîd. She's probably been hurt because of it, but it wasn't Seipolt."

"Seipolt may be nobody," I said bitterly, "but he lies very well under pressure. Have you figured out anything about Devi's murder? Some connection with Tamiko's killing?"

"There probably isn't any connection, buddy, as much as you and your criminal colleagues want there to be. The Black Widow Sisters are the kind of people who get themselves murdered, that's all. They ask for it, so they get it. Just coincidence that the two of them were postmarked so close together."

"What kind of clues did you find at Devi's?"

There was a brief silence. "What the *hell*, Audran, all of a sudden I have a new partner? Who the fuckin' hell do you think you *are*? Where do you get off questioning *me*? As if you didn't know I couldn't talk police business with you like that, even if I wanted to, which is not in the most minute sense true. Go away, Marîd. You're bad luck." Then he snapped the connection.

I put my phone in my bag and closed my eyes. It was a long, dusty, hot ride back to the Budayeen. It would have been quiet, except for Bill's constant monologue; and it would have been comfortable, except for Bill's dying taxi. I thought about Seipolt and Reinhardt; Nikki and the sisters; Devi's killer, whoever he was; Tamiko's mad torturer, whoever *he* was. None of it made any sense to me at all.

Okking had just been telling me that very thing: It didn't make sense because there *was* no sense. You can't find a point in a pointless killing. I had just become aware of the random violence in which I had lived for years, part of it, ignoring it, believing myself immune to it. My mind was trying to take the unrelated events of the last several days and make them fit a pattern, like making warriors and mythical beasts out of scattered stars in the night sky. . Senseless, pointless; yet the human mind seeks explanations. It demands order, and only something like RPM or Sonneine can quiet that clamoring or, at least, distract the mind with something else.

Sounded like a great idea to me. I took out my pill case and swallowed four sunnies. I didn't bother offering anything to Bill; he'd paid in advance, and anyway he had a private screening.

I had Bill let me out at the eastern gate of the Budayeen. The fare was thirty kiam; I gave him forty. He stared at the money for a long time until I took it back and pushed it into the pocket of his shirt. He looked up at me as if he'd never met me before. "Easy for *you* to say," he murmured.

I needed to learn a few things, so I went directly to a modshop on Fourth Street. The modshop was run by a twitchy old woman who'd had one of the first brain jobs. I think the surgeons must have missed what they'd been aiming for just slightly, or else Laila had always made you feel like getting out of her presence as quickly as possible. She couldn't talk to you without whining. She crooked her head and stared up at you as if she were some kind of garden mollusc and you were about to step on her. You sometimes considered stepping on her, but she was too quick. She had long, straggly gray hair; bushy gray eyebrows; yellow eyes; bloodless lips and depopulated jaws; black skin, scaled and scabrous; and the same crooked, clawed fingers that a witch ought to have. She had one moddy or another plugged in all day, but her own personality—and it wasn't a likable personality at all—bled through as if the moddy weren't exciting the right cells, or enough of them, or strongly enough. You'd get Janis Joplin with static-like flashes of Laila, you'd get the Marquise Josephine Rose Kennedy with Laila's nasal whine, but it was her shop and her merchandise, and if you didn't want to put up with her, you went elsewhere.

I went to Laila because even though I wasn't wired, she let me "borrow" any moddy or daddy she had in stock, by plugging it into herself. If I needed to do a little research,

I went to Laila and hoped that she didn't distort what I had to learn in any lethal way.

This afternoon she was being herself, with only a bookkeeping add-on and an inventory-management add-on plugged in. It was that time of the year again; how the months fly when you take a lot of drugs.

"Laila," I said. She was so much like the old hag in *Snow White* that you couldn't think of more to say to her. Laila was one person with whom you didn't make small talk, whatever you wanted from her.

She looked up, her lips mumbling stock numbers, quantities, markups, and markdowns. She nodded.

"What do you know about James Bond?" I asked.

She put her microrecorder down and tapped it off. She stared at me for a few seconds, her eyes getting very round, then very narrow. "Marîd," she said. She managed to whine my name.

"What do you know about James Bond?"

"Videos, books, twentieth-century power fantasies. Spies, that kind of action. He was irresistible to women. You want to be irresistible?" She whined at me suggestively.

"I'm working on that on my own, thanks. I just want to know if anybody's bought a James Bond moddy from you lately."

"No, I'm sure of it. Haven't even had one in stock for a long time. James Bond is kind of ancient history, Marîd. People are looking for new jams. Cloak-and-dagger is too quaint for words." When she stopped talking, numbers formed on her lips as her daddies went on speaking to her brain.

I knew about James Bond because I'd read the books—actual, physical books made out of paper. At least, I'd read *some* of them, four or five. Bond was a Eur-Am myth like Tarzan or Johnny Carson. I wish Laila had had a Bond moddy; it might have helped me understand what Devi's killer was thinking. I shook my head; something was tickling my mind again. . . .

I turned my back on Laila and left her shop. I glanced at a holographic advertisement playing on the sidewalk outside her display window. It was Honey Pílar. She looked about eight feet tall and absolutely naked. When you're

Honey Pílar, naked is the only way to go. She was running her lascivious hands over her superluminally sexy body. She shook her pale hair out of her green eyes and stared at me. She slid the pink tip of her tongue across her unnaturally full, luscious lips. I stood watching the holoporn, mesmerized. That was what it was for, and it was working just fine. At the edge of my consciousness, I was aware that several other men and women had stopped in their tracks and were staring, too. Then Honey spoke. Her voice, enhanced electronically to send chills of desire through my already lust-ridden body, reminded me of adolescent longings I hadn't thought of in years. My mouth was dry; my heart was pounding.

The hologram was selling Honey's new moddy, the one Chiri already owned. If I bought one for Yasmin. . . .

"My moddy lies over the ocean," said Honey in a breathy, soft voice, while her hands slid slowly down the copious upper slopes of her perfect breasts. . . .

"My moddy lies over the sea." Her hands tweaked her nipples hard, then found their way to the delicious undersides of those breasts and continued southward. . . .

"Now someone is jamming my moddy," she confided, as her fiery fingernails lightly touched her flat belly, still searching, still seeking. . . .

"Now he knows what it's like to jam *me!*" Her eyes were half-closed with ecstasy. Her voice became a drawn-out moan, pleading for the continuation of that pleasure. She was begging *me* as her hands at last slipped out of sight between her suntanned thighs.

As the hologram faded, another woman's voice overdubbed the details of manufacturer and cost. "Haven't you tried modular marital aids? Are you still using holoporn? Look, if using a rubber is like kissing your sister, then holoporn is like kissing a *picture* of your sister! Why stare at a holo of Honey Pílar, when with her new moddy you can jam the livin' daylights out of her again and again, whenever you want! Come on! Give your girlfriend or boyfriend the new Honey Pílar moddy today! Modular marital aids are sold as novelty items only."

The voice faded away and let me have my mind back. The other spectators, similarly released, went on about their business a little unsteadily. I turned toward the Street, thinking first about Honey Pílar, then about the moddy I would give Yasmin as an anniversary present (as soon as possible, for the anniversary of *anything*. Hell, I didn't care), and at last the tantalizing thing that had been bothering me. I'd thought of it first after I spoke with Okking about the shooting in Chiriga's nightclub, and again today.

Someone who just wanted to have a little Fun With Murder wouldn't have used a James Bond moddy. No, a Bond moddy is too specialized and too sterile. James Bond didn't get pleasure from killing people. If some psychotic wanted to use a personality module to help him murder more satisfyingly, he might have chosen any of a dozen rogues. There were underground moddies, too, that weren't on sale in the respectable modshops: for a big enough pile of kiam, you could probably get your hands on a Jack the Ripper moddy. There were moddies of fictional characters, or real people, recorded right from their brains or reconstructed by clever programmers. I felt ill as I thought about the perverse people who wanted the illicit moddies, and the black-market industry that catered to them with Charles Manson modules or Nosferatu modules or Heinrich Himmler modules.

I was sure that whoever had used the Bond module had done so for a different purpose, knowing in advance that it wouldn't give him much pleasure. It wasn't pleasure the false James Bond had been after. His goal had not been excitement, but execution.

Devi's death—and, of course, the Russian's—had not been the work of a mad slasher among the dregs of society. Both murders had been, in fact, assassinations. Political assassinations.

Okking would not listen to any of this without proof. I had none. I wasn't even certain in my own mind what this all meant. What connection could there be between Bogatyrev, a minor functionary in the legation of a weak and indigent Eastern European kingdom, and Devi, one of the Black Widow Sisters? Their worlds didn't intersect at all.

I needed more information, but I didn't know where it was going to come from. I found myself walking determinedly somewhere. Where was I going? I asked myself. Devi's apartment, of course. Okking's men would still be combing the premises for clues. There'd be barriers up, and a cordon with signs warning CRIME SCENE. There'd be—

Nothing. No barriers, no cordon, no police. A light was on in the window. I went up to the green shutters that were used to cover the doorway. They were thrown open, so that Devi's front room was clearly visible from the sidewalk. A middle-aged Arab was down on his hands and knees, painting a wall. We greeted each other, and he wanted to know if I wanted to rent the place; it would be fixed up in another two days. That's all the memorial Devi got. That's all the effort Okking would put into finding her killer. Devi, like Tami, didn't deserve much of the authorities' time. They hadn't been good citizens; they hadn't earned the right to justice.

I looked up and down the block. All the buildings on Devi's side of the street were the same: low, whitewashed, flat-roofed houses with green-shuttered doors and windows. There would have been no place for "James Bond" to hide, to waylay Devi. He could only have concealed himself inside her apartment in some way, waiting for her to come home after work; or else he'd waited someplace nearby. I crossed the old, cobbled street. On the opposite side, some of the houses had low stoops with iron handrails. Directly across from Devi's house, I sat on the topmost step and looked around. On the ground below me, to the right of the stairs, were a few cigarette butts. Someone had sat on this stoop, smoking; maybe it was the person who lived in the house, maybe not. I squatted down and looked at the butts. There were three gold bands on each, around the filters.

In the James Bond books, he smoked cigarettes made up specially for him of some particular mixture of tobaccos, and his blend was marked with the three gold bands. The assassin took his job seriously; he used a small-caliber pistol, probably a Walther PPK, like Bond's. Bond kept his cigarettes in a gunmetal cigarette case that held fifty; I wondered if the assassin had one of those, too.

I put the cigarette butts in my shoulder bag. Okking

wanted proof, I had proof. That didn't mean Okking would agree. I looked up into the sky; it was getting late, and there would be no moon tonight. The slender sliver of the new moon would appear tomorrow night, bringing with it the beginning of the holy month of Ramadân.

The already-frantic Budayeen would get more hysterical after nightfall tomorrow. Things would be deathly quiet during the day, though. Deathly quiet. I laughed softly as I walked in the direction of Frenchy Benoit's bar. I'd seen enough of death, but the notion of peace and quiet sounded very inviting.

What a fool I was.

7

Bismillah ar-Rahman ar-Raheem. In the name of Allah, the Compassionate, the Merciful.

In the month of Ramadân, in which was revealed the Qur'ân, a guidance for mankind, and clear proofs of the guidance, and the Criterion of right and wrong. And whosoever of you is present, let him fast the month, and whosoever of you is sick or on a journey, let him fast the same number of days. Allah desireth for you ease; He desireth not hardship for you; and He desireth that ye should complete the period, and that ye should magnify Allah for having guided you, and that it may be that ye be thankful.

That was the one hundred eighty-fifth verse of the sûah Al-Baqarah, The Cow, the second sûrah in the noble Qur'ân. The Messenger of God, may the blessing of Allah be on him and peace, gave directions for the observance of the holy month of Ramadân, the ninth lunar month of the Muslim calendar. This observance is considered one of the five Pillars of Islam. During the month, Muslims are prohibited from eating, drinking, and smoking from dawn until sunset. The police and the religious leaders see that even those like myself, who are negligent at best about spiritual duties, comply. Nightclubs and bars are closed during the day, and the cafés and restaurants. It is forbidden to take so much as a sip of water until after dusk. When night falls, when it is proper to serve food, the Muslims of the city enjoy themselves. Even those who shun the Budayeen the rest of the year may come and relax in a café.

Night would replace day completely in the Muslim world during the month, were it not for the five-times-daily call to prayer. These must be heeded as usual, so the respectful Muslim rises at dawn and prays, but does not break his fast. His employer may let him go home for a few hours in the afternoon to nap, to catch up on the sleep he loses by staying awake into the early hours of the morning, taking his meals and enjoying what he cannot enjoy during the day.

In many ways, Islam is a beautiful and elegant faith; but it is the nature of religions to put a higher premium on your proper attention to ritual than on your convenience. Ramadân can be very inconvenient to the sinners and scoundrels of the Budayeen.

Yet at the same time, it made some things simpler. I merely shifted my schedule several hours later on the clock, and I wasn't put out at all. The nightclubs made the same alteration in their hours. It might have been worse if I had other things to attend to during the day; say, for instance, facing Mecca and praying every now and then.

The first Wednesday of Ramadân, after I'd settled myself into the changed daily scheme, I sat in a small coffee-house called the Café Solace, on Twelfth Street. It was almost midnight, and I was playing cards with three other young men, drinking small cups of thick coffee without sugar, and eating small bites of *baqlaawah*. This was just what Yasmin had been envious of. She was over at Frenchy's, shaking her fine little behind and charming strangers into buying her champagne cocktails; I was eating sweet pastries and gambling. I didn't see anything wrong with taking it easy when I could, even if Yasmin still had to put in a long, exhausting ten hours. It seemed to be the natural order of things.

The three others at my table were a mixed collection. Mahmoud was a sex-change, shorter than me but broader through the shoulders and hips. He had been a girl until five or six years ago; he'd even worked for Jo-Mama for a while, and now he lived with a real girl who hustled in the same bar. It was an interesting coincidence.

Jacques was a Moroccan Christian, strictly heterosexual, who felt and acted as if he had special privileges because he was three-quarters European, therefore beating me out by a full grandparent. Nobody listened to Jacques very much, and whenever celebrations and parties were planned, Jacques learned about them just a little too late. Jacques was included in card games, however, because somebody has to be there to lose, and it might as well be a miffy Christian.

Saied the Half-Hajj was tall and well-built, rich, and strictly homosexual; he wouldn't be seen in the company of a woman, real, renovated, or reconverted. He was called the Half-Hajj because he was so scatterbrained that he could never start one project without getting distracted in the middle by two or three others. Hajj is the title one gets after completing the holy pilgrimage to Mecca, which is one of the other Pillars of Islam. Saied had actually begun the journey several years ago, made about five hundred miles, and then turned back because he'd had a magnificent money-making idea that he forgot before he reached home again. Saied was somewhat older than I was, with a carefully trimmed mustache that he was very proud of. I don't know why; I've never thought of a mustache as an achievement, unless you'd started out life like Mahmoud. Female, that is. All three of my companions had had their brains wired. Saied was wearing a moddy and two daddies. The moddy was just a general personality module; not a particular person but a particular type—he was being strong, silent, rough trade today, and neither of the add-ons could have been giving him card-playing help. He and Jacques were making me and Mahmoud richer.

These three ill-assorted louts were my best male friends. We wasted a lot of afternoons (or, during Ramadân, late evenings) together. I had two prime sources of information in the Budayeen: these three, and the girls in the clubs. The information I got from one person often contradicted the version I heard from another, so I'd long ago gotten into the habit of trying to hear as many different stories as I could and averaging them all out. The truth was in there somewhere, I knew it; the problem was coaxing it into the open.

I had won most of the money on the table, and Mahmoud the rest. Jacques was about to throw in his cards and quit the game. I wanted something more to eat, and the Half-Hajj agreed. The four of us were just about to leave the Solace and find somewhere else to have lunch, when Fuad ran up to us. This was the scrawny, spindle-legged son of a camel who was called (among other things) Fuad il-Manhous, or Fuad the Chronically Unlucky. I knew right off that I wasn't going to get anything to eat for a while. The look on il-Manhous's face told me that a little adventure was about to begin.

"Praise Allah that I found you all here," he said, snapping quick glances at each of us.

"Go with Allah, my brother," said Jacques tartly. "I think I see Him heading that way, toward the north wall."

Fuad ignored him. "I need some help," he said. He sounded more frantic than usual. He has little adventures fairly often, but this time he seemed really upset.

"What's wrong, Fuad?" I asked.

He looked at me gratefully, like a child. "Some black bitch clipped me for thirty kiam." He spat on the ground.

I looked at the Half-Hajj, who only looked heavenward for strength. I looked at Mahmoud, who was grinning. Jacques looked exasperated.

"Them bitches get you pretty regularly, don't they, Fuad?" asked Mahmoud.

"You just think so," he replied defensively.

"What happened this time?" asked Jacques. "Where? Anybody we know?"

"New girl," he said.

"It's always a new girl," I said.

"She works over at the Red Light," said the Cursed One.

"I thought you were banned out of there," said Mahmoud.

"I was," Fuad tried to explain, "and I still can't spend any money in there, Fatima won't let me, but I'm working for her as a porter, so I'm in there all the time. I don't live by Hassan's shop anymore, he used to let me sleep in his storeroom, but Fatima lets me sleep under the bar."

"She won't give you a drink in her place," said Jacques, "but she lets you carry out her garbage."

"Uh huh. And sweep up and clean off the mirrors."

Mahmoud nodded wisely. "I've always said that Fatima has a soft heart," he said. "You've all heard me."

"So what *happened*?" I asked. I hate having to listen to Fuad circumambulate the point for half an hour every time.

"I was in the Red Light, see," he said, "and Fatima had just told me to bring in another couple bottles of Johnny Walker and I'd gone back and told Nassir and he gave me the bottles and I brought them up to Fatima and she put them under the bar. Then I asked her, I said, 'What do you want me to do now?' and she said, 'Why don't you go drink lye?' and I said, 'I'm going to go sit down for a while,' and she said, 'All right,' so I sat down by the bar and watched for a while, and this girl came over and sat down next to me—"

"A black girl," said Saied the Half-Hajj.

"Uh huh—"

The Half-Hajj gave me a look and said, "I have a special sensitivity in these matters." I laughed.

Fuad went on. "Uh huh, so this black girl was real pretty, never saw her before, she said she just started working for Fatima that night, and I told her it was a pretty rowdy bar and that sometimes you have to watch yourself because of the crowd they get in there, and she said she was real grateful because I gave her the advice and she said people in the city were real cold and didn't care about anybody but themselves, and it was nice to meet a nice guy like me. She gave me a little kiss on my cheek, and she let me put my arm around her, and then she started—"

"To feel you up," said Jacques.

Fuad blushed furiously. "She wanted to know if she could have a drink, and I said I only had enough money to live on for the next two weeks, and she asked me how much I had, and I said I wasn't sure. She said she bet I probably had enough to get her *one* drink and I said, 'Look, if I've got more than thirty, I will, but if I've got less than thirty, I can't,' and she said that sounded fair, so

I took out my money and guess what? I had exactly thirty, and we hadn't said what we were going to do if I had exactly thirty, so she said it was okay, I didn't have to buy her a drink. I thought that was real nice of her. And she kept kissing on me and hugging me and touching me, and I thought she really liked me a lot. And then, guess what?"

"She took your money," said Mahmoud. "She wanted you to count it just to see where you kept it."

"I didn't know she done it until later, when I wanted to get something to eat. It was all gone, like she reached into my pocket and took it."

"You've been clipped before," I said. "You *knew* she was going to do it. I think you *like* being clipped. I think you get off on it."

"That's not true," said Fuad stubbornly. "I really thought she liked me a lot, and I liked her, and I thought maybe I could ask her out or something later, after she got off work. Then I saw my money was gone, and I knew she done it. I can put two and two together, I'm no dummy."

We all nodded without saying anything.

"I told Fatima, but she wouldn't do anything, so I went back to Joie—that's what she calls herself, but she told me it wasn't her real name—and she got real mad, saying she never stole nothing in her life. I said I knew she done it, and she got madder and madder, and then she pulled a razor out of her purse, and Fatima told her to put it away, I wasn't worth it, but Joie was still real mad and come at me with the razor, and I got out of there and looked all over the place for you guys."

Jacques closed his eyes wearily and rubbed them. "You want us to go get your thirty kiam back. Why the hell *should* we, Fuad? You're an imbecile. You want us to walk up to some screaming crazy flatbacker who's waving a razor around, just because you can't hang onto your own roll."

"Don't argue with him, Jacques," said Mahmoud, "it's like talking to a brick wall." The actual Arabic phrase is, "You talk in the east, he answers in the west," which is a very perceptive description of what was happening with Fuad il-Manhous.

The Half-Hajj, though, was wearing this moddy that

made him into a Man of Action, so he just twirled his mustache and gave Fuad a small, rugged smile. "Come on," he said, "you show me this Joie."

"Thanks," said the skinny Fuad, fawning all over Saied, "thanks a whole lot. I mean, I don't have another goddamn fîq, she has all the money I had saved for the next—"

"Just shut up about it," said Jacques. We got up and followed Saied and Fuad to the Red Light. I shook my head; I didn't want to be involved in this at all, but I had to go along. I hate eating by myself, so I told myself to be patient; we'd all go by the Café de la Fée Blanche afterward and have lunch. All of us except the Cursed One, I mean. In the meantime, I swallowed two tri-phets, just for luck.

The Red Light Lounge was a rough place, and you went into in knowing it was a rough place, so if you got rolled or clipped in there, it was hard to find someone to give you a little sympathy. The police figured you were a fool to be there in the first place, so they would just laugh in your face if you made a complaint to them. Both Fatima and Nassir are interested only in how much profit they make on each bottle of liquor they sell and how many champagne cocktails their girls push; they couldn't be bothered keeping track of what the girls were doing on their own. It was free enterprise in its purest, most unhindered form.

I was reluctant to set foot in the Red Light because I didn't get along with either Fatima or Nassir, so I was last in our little group to sit down. We took a table away from the bar. They kept it as dark in there as Chiri kept her place. There was a heavy, sour smell of spilled beer. A hatchet-faced redhaired girl was dancing onstage. She had a nice little body unless your gaze strayed up past her neck. What she did on stage was designed to keep your attention away from her defects and focused intently on what she had to sell. Fanya, her name was, I remembered. They called her "Floor-show Fanya," because her notion of dance was mostly horizontal, rather than in the customary upright position.

It was still early in the night, so we ordered beers, but

virile old Saied the Half-Hajj, still listening to his manly moddy, got himself a double shot of Wild Turkey to go with his beer. No one asked the undernourished Fuad if he wanted anything. "That's her over there," he said in a loud whisper, pointing to a short, plain girl who was working on a European in a business suit.

"She's no girl," said Mahmoud. "Fuad, she's a deb."

"Don't you think I can tell the difference between a boy and a girl?" responded Fuad hotly. No one wanted to voice an opinion about that; as far as I was concerned, it was too dark for me to read her yet. I'd know later, when I saw her better.

Saied didn't even wait for his drink. He stood up and sort of strolled over to Joie. You know, "nothing can touch me because, deep inside, I'm Attila the Hun, and all you other faggots better watch your asses." He engaged Joie in conversation; I couldn't hear a word, and I didn't want to. Fuad followed the Half-Hajj like a pet lamb, piping up in his shrill voice now and then, agreeing vigorously with Saied or denying vigorously the new whore.

"I don't know nothing about this chump's thirty kiam," she said.

"She's got it, look in her purse," screeched the Unlucky One.

"I got more than that, you son of a bitch," cried Joie. "How you gonna prove some of it is yours?"

Tempers were igniting fast. The Half-Hajj had the sense to turn and send Fuad back to our table, but Joie followed the scrawny *fellah,* pushing him and calling him all kinds of foul names. I thought Fuad was almost on the verge of tears. Saied tried to pull Joie away, and she turned on him. "When my people gets here, he's gonna climb into your ass," she shouted.

The Half-Hajj gave her one of his little, heroic smiles. "We'll see about that when he gets here," he said calmly. "In the meantime, we're giving my friend here his money back, and I don't want to hear about you shaving him or any of my other friends again, or you'll have so many cuts on your face you'll have to turn tricks with a bag over your head."

It was at just this moment, with Saied holding Joie's

wrists together, with Fuad standing on her other side, blithering loudly into her ear, that Joie's pimp came into the bar. "Here we go," I murmured.

Joie called to him and quickly told him what was happening. "These cocksuckers are trying to take my money!" she cried.

The pimp, a big, one-eyed Arab named Tewfik who everybody called Courvoisier Sonny, didn't need to hear a word from anyone. He slapped Fuad aside without so much as a glance. He put one hand around Saied's right wrist and made him release Joie's hands. Then he shoved the Half-Hajj's shoulder and sent him backward, staggering. "Messing with my girl like that can get you cut, my brother," he said in a deceptively soft voice.

Saied strolled back to our table. "She *is* a deb," he said. "Just a man in a dress." He and Sonny were standing right above me, and I wished they'd take their negotiations outside. The disturbance hadn't seemed to draw the attention of either Fatima or Nassir. Meanwhile, Fanya had ended her turn on stage, and a tall, lanky black sex-change, American, began to dance.

"Your ugly, thieving, syphilitic whore took thirty kiam of my friend's money," said Saied in the same soft voice as Sonny.

"You gonna let him call me names, Sonny?" demanded Joie. "In front of all these other bitches?"

"Praise Allah," said Mahmoud sadly, "it has turned into an affair of honor. It was a lot simpler when it was just larceny."

"I won't let nobody call you nothing, girl," said Sonny. He had put a little growl into his soft voice. He turned to Saied. "I'm telling you now to shut the fuck up."

"Make me," said Saied, smiling.

Mahmoud, Jacques, and I grabbed our beers and got halfway out of our seats; we were too late. Sonny had a knife in the rope belt around his *gallebeya;* he reached for it. Saied got his knife out quicker. I heard Joie cry a warning to Sonny. I saw Sonny's eyes get narrow as he backed away a step. Saied swung his left fist hard at Sonny's jaw, and Sonny ducked away. Saied took a step forward, blocked Sonny's right arm, bent a little, and drove his knife into Sonny's side.

I heard Sonny make a little sound, a quiet, gurgling, surprised groan. Saied had slashed Sonny's chest and cut some big vessels. Blood spurted in all directions, more blood than you would think possible for one person to carry around. Sonny stumbled one step to his left, then two steps forward, and fell onto the table. He grunted, jerked and thrashed a few times, and slipped off the table to the floor. We were all staring at him. Joie hadn't made another sound. Saied hadn't moved; he was still in the same position he'd been in when his knife had cut open Sonny's heart. He slowly rose up straight, his knife-hand falling to his side. He was breathing heavily, loudly. He turned around and grabbed his beer; his eyes were glassy and expressionless. He was soaked with blood. His hair, his face, his clothing, his hands and arms, all were covered with Sonny's blood. There was blood all over the table. There was blood all over us. I was almost drenched in blood. It had taken me a moment, but now I realized how much blood I had on me, and I was horrified. I stood up, trying to pull my blood-soaked shirt away from my body. Joie began to scream, again and again; someone finally slapped her a few times, and she shut up. At last Fatima called Nassir out of the back room, and he called the police. The rest of us just sat down at another table. The music stopped, the girls went into their dressing room, the customers slipped out of the bar before the police could arrive. Mahmoud went to Fatima and got a pitcher of beer for us.

Sergeant Hajjar took his time coming around to see the aftermath. When he arrived at last, I was surprised to see that he'd come alone. "What's that?" he asked, indicating Sonny's corpse with the toe of a boot.

"Dead pimp," said Jacques.

"They all look the same, dead," said Hajjar. He noticed the blood splashed all over everything. "Big guy, huh?"

"Sonny," said Mahmoud.

"Oh, *that* motherfucker."

"He died for thirty lousy kiam," said Saied, shaking his head unbelievingly.

Hajjar looked around the bar thoughtfully, then looked straight at me. "Audran," he said, stifling a yawn, "come with me." He turned to walk back out of the bar.

"Me?" I cried. "I didn't have anything to do with it!"

"With what?" asked Hajjar, puzzled.

"With that knifing."

"The hell with the knifing. You got to come with me." He led me to his patrol car. He didn't care at all about this murder. If some rich-bitch tourist gets done in, the police break their buns lifting fingerprints and measuring angles and interrogating everybody twenty or thirty times. But let someone nip this gorilla one-eyed stable-boss or Tami or Devi, and the cops act as bored as an ox on a hill. Hajjar wasn't going to question anybody or take pictures or anything. It wasn't worth his time. To the officials, Sonny had only gotten what he had coming; in Chiriga's philosophy, "Paybacks are a motherfucker." The police didn't mind if the whole Budayeen decimated itself, one worthless degenerate at a time.

Hajjar locked me into the back seat, then slid behind the steering wheel. "Are you arresting me?" I asked.

"Shut up, Audran."

"Are you arresting me, you son of a bitch?"

"No."

That brought me up short. "Then what the hell are you holding me for? I told you I didn't have a goddamn thing to do with that killing in the bar."

Hajjar glanced back over his shoulder. "Will you forget about that pimp already? This doesn't have anything to do with that."

"Where are you taking me?"

Hajjar looked around again and gave me a sadistic grin. "Papa wants to talk to you."

I felt cold. "Papa?" I'd seen Friedlander Bey here and there, I knew all about him, but I'd never actually been summoned into his presence before.

"And from what I hear, Audran, he's spitting mad. You'd be better off if I *did* bring you in for murder."

"Mad? At me? What for?"

Hajjar just shrugged. "I don't know. I was just told to fetch you. Let Papa do his own talking."

Just at this moment of growing fear and menace, the tri-phets decided to kick in and race my heart even harder. It had started out to be such a nice evening, too. I'd won some money, I was looking forward to a pleasant meal, and Yasmin was going to spend the night again. Instead I was in the back of a police cruiser, my shirt and jeans still damp with Sonny's blood, my face and arms beginning to itch as the blood dried on them, heading toward some foreboding meeting with Friedlander Bey, who owned everybody and everything. I was sure it was some sort of accounting, but I couldn't imagine for what. I've always been extremely careful not to tread on Papa's toes. Hajjar wouldn't tell me any more; he only grinned wolfishly and said that he wouldn't want to be in my boots. I didn't want to be in my boots, either, but that's where I'd found myself too often lately. "It is the will of Allah," I murmured anxiously. Nearer My God to Thee.

8

Friedlander Bey lived in a large, white, towered mansion that might almost have qualified as a palace. It was a large estate in the middle of the city only two blocks from the Christian Quarter. I don't think anyone else had such a great expanse of property walled off. Papa's house made Seipolt's look like a Badawi tent. But Sergeant Hajjar didn't drive me to Papa's house: we were going in the wrong direction. I mentioned this to Hajjar, the bastard.

"Let *me* do the driving," he said in a surly voice. He called me "il-Maghrîb." Maghrîb may mean sunset, but it also refers to the vast, vague part of North Africa to the west, where the uncivilized idiots come from—Algerians, Moroccans, semihuman creatures like that. Lots of my friends will call me il-Maghrîb, or Maghrebi, and then it's only a nickname or an epithet; when Hajjar used it, it was definitely an insult.

"The house is back the other way about two and a half miles," I said.

"Don't you think I know that? Jesus Christ, would I love to have you handcuffed to a pole for fifteen minutes."

"Where on Allah's good, green earth are you taking me?"

Hajjar wouldn't answer any more questions, so I just gave up and watched the city go by. Riding with Hajjar was a lot like riding with Bill: you didn't learn very much and you weren't sure where you were going or how you were going to get there.

The cop pulled into an asphalt driveway behind a cinder-block motel on the eastern outskirts of the city. The cinder blocks were painted a pale green, and there was a small handlettered sign that said simply MOTEL NO VACANCY. I thought a motel with a permanent No Vacancy sign was a trifle unusual. Hajjar got out of the cop car and opened the back door. I slid out and stretched a little; the tri-phets had me humming in a high-velocity way. The combination of the drugs and my nervousness added up to a headache, a very sick stomach, and fidgeting that flirted with total emotional collapse.

I followed Hajjar to room nineteen of the motel. He rapped on the door in some kind of signal. The door was opened by a hulking Arab who looked like a block of sandstone that walked. I didn't expect him to be able to talk or think; when he did, I was astonished. He nodded to Hajjar, who didn't acknowledge it; the sergeant went back toward his car. The Stone looked at me for a moment, probably wondering where I'd come from; then he realized that I must have come with Hajjar, and that I was the one he was waiting to let into the damn motel room. "In," he said. His voice sounded like sandstone that spoke.

I shuddered as I passed by him. There were two more men in the room, another Stone That Speaks on the far side, and Friedlander Bey, sitting at a folding table set up between the king-sized bed and the bureau. All the furnishings were European, but a little worn and shabby.

Papa stood when he saw me come in. He was about five feet two inches tall, but almost two hundred pounds. He wore a plain, white cotton shirt, gray trousers, and slippers. He wore no jewelry. He had a few wisps of graying hair brushed straight back on his head, and soft brown eyes. Friedlander Bey didn't look like the most powerful man in the city. He raised his right hand in front of his face, almost touching his forehead. "Peace," he said.

I touched my heart and my lips. "And on you be peace."

He did not look happy to see me. The formalities would protect me for a short while and give me time to think. What I needed to plan was a way to bowl over the two Stones and get out of that motel room. It was going to be a challenge.

Papa seated himself at the table again. "May your day be

prosperous," he said. He indicated the chair across from him.

"May your day be prosperous and blessed," I said. As soon as I could, I was going to ask for a glass of water, and take as many Paxium as I had with me. I sat down.

His brown eyes caught mine and held them. "How is your health?" he asked. His voice was unfriendly.

"Praise Allah," I said. I felt the fear growing.

"We have not seen you in some time," said Friedlander Bey. "You have made us lonely."

"May Allah never let you feel lonely."

The second Stone served coffee. Papa took a cup and sipped from it to show me it wasn't poisoned. Then he handed it to me. "Be pleased," he said. There was little hospitality in his voice.

I took the cup. "May coffee be found forever in your house."

We drank some coffee together. Papa sat back and regarded me for a moment. "You have honored us," he said at last.

"May Allah preserve you." We had come to the end of the short form of the amenities. Things would begin to happen now. The first thing that happened was that I took out my pill case, dug up every tranquilizer I could find, and swallowed them with some more coffee. I took fourteen Paxium; some people would find that a large quantity. It wasn't, for me. I know lots of people in the Budayeen who can drink me under the table—Yasmin, for one—but I bow to no one in my capacity for pills and caps. Fourteen 10-milligram Paxium, if I was lucky, would only unscrew the tension a little; they wouldn't even begin to make me really tranquil. Right then, I'd need something with a little more velocity to it for that. Fourteen Paxium was barely Mach 1.

Friedlander Bey held out his coffee cup to his servant, who refilled it. Papa sipped a little of it, watching me over the rim of the small cup. He set it down precisely and said, "You understand that I have a great number of people in my employ."

"Indeed yes, O Shaykh," I said.

"A great number of people who depend on me, not

only for their livelihoods, but for much more. I am a source of security in their difficult world. They know that they may depend on me for wages and certain favors, as long as they perform their work for me in a satisfactory way."

"Yes, O Shaykh." The blood drying on my face and arms irritated me.

He nodded. "So when I learn that one of my friends has, indeed, been welcomed by Allah into Paradise, I am distressed. I am concerned for the well-being of all who represent me in the city, from my trusted lieutenants down to the poorest and most insignificant beggar who aids me however he can."

"You are the people's shield against calamity, O Shaykh."

He waved a hand, tired of my interruptions. "Death is *one* thing, my nephew. Death comes to all, there is no one who can run from it. The jar cannot remain whole forever. We must learn to accept our eventual demise; and more, we must look forward to our eternal delight and refreshment in Paradise. Yet death before death is due is unnatural. That is *another* thing completely; it is an affront to Allah, and must be set right. One cannot recall the dead to life, but one can avenge a murder. Do you understand me?"

"Yes, O Shaykh." It hadn't taken Friedlander Bey long to hear about Courvoisier Sonny's premature end. Nassir probably called Papa even before he called the police.

"Then, let me put this question to you: How does one revenge a murder?"

There was a long, glacial silence. There was only one answer, but I took a while to frame my reply in my mind. "O Shaykh" I said at last, "a death must be met with another death. That is the only revenge. It is written in the Straight Path, 'Retaliation is prescribed for you in the matter of the murdered'; and also, 'One who attacketh you, attack him in like manner as he attacked you.' But it also says elsewhere, 'The life for the life, and the eye for the eye, and the nose for the nose, and the ear for the ear, and the tooth for the tooth, and for wounds retaliation. But whoso forgoeth it in the way of charity, it shall be expiation for him.' I am innocent of this murder, O Shaykh, and to seek revenge wrongfully is a crime worse than the killing itself."

"Allah is Most Great," murmured Papa. He looked at me in surprise. "I had heard that you were an infidel, my nephew, and it caused me pain. Yet you have a certain knowledge of the noble Qur'ân." He stood up from the table and rubbed his forehead with his right hand. Then he crossed to the large bed and laid down on the bedspread. I turned to face him, but a huge brown hand clamped itself on my shoulder and forced me to turn around again. I could only stare across the table, at Friedlander Bey's empty chair. I could not see him, but I could hear him when he spoke. "I have been told that of all people in the Budayeen, you had most reason to want to murder this man."

I thought back over the recent months; I couldn't even remember the last time I'd even said hello to Sonny. I stayed out of the Red Light; I had nothing to do with the kind of debs, changes, and girls Sonny ran on the street; our circles of friends didn't seem to intersect at all, except for Fuad il-Manhous—and Fuad was no friend of mine and, I'm sure, no friend of Sonny's, either. Yet the Arab's concept of revenge is as fully developed and patient as the Sicilian's. Maybe Papa was thinking of some incident that had happened months, even years, ago, something I had forgotten completely, that could be construed as a motive to kill Sonny. "I had no reason at all," I said shakily.

"I do not enjoy evasions, my nephew. It happens very often that I must ask someone these difficult questions, and he always begins by making evasive answers. This continues until one of my servants persuades him to stop. The next stage is a series of answers that do not sound so evasive, but are clearly lies. Once again, my guest must be persuaded not to waste valuable time this way." His voice was tired and low. I tried to turn to face him again, and once more the huge hand grasped my shoulder, more painfully this time. Papa went on. "After a while, one is at last brought to the point where truth and cooperation seem far the most reasonable course, yet it often makes me sad to see what state my guest is in when he makes this discovery. My advice, then, is to pass through evasion and lies quickly—better still, not at all—and proceed directly to truth. We will all benefit."

The stone hand did not leave my shoulder. I felt as if my bones were slowly being crushed into white powder inside my skin. I made no sound.

"You owed this man a sum of money," said Friedlander Bey. "You owe him no longer, because he is dead. I will collect that sum, my nephew, and I will do that which the Book allows."

"I didn't owe him any money!" I cried. "Not one goddamn fîq!"

A second stone hand began to crush my other shoulder. "The dog's tail is still bent, O Lord," murmured the Stone That Speaks.

"I do not lie," I said, gasping a little. "If I tell you that I owed Sonny nothing, it is the truth. I am known everywhere in the city as one who does not lie."

"It is true that I have never had cause to doubt you before, my nephew."

"Perhaps he has found reasons to take up the practice, O Lord," murmured the Stone That Speaks.

"Sonny?" said Friedlander Bey, returning to the table. "No one cares about Sonny. He is no friend of mine, or of anyone; to that I can attest. If he is dead, too, then it but makes the air over the Budayeen more pleasant to breathe. No, my nephew, I have asked you to join me here to talk about the murder of my friend, Abdoulaye Abu-Zayd."

"Abdoulaye," I said. The pain was immense; I was beginning to see little flecks of red before my eyes. My voice was hoarse and barely audible. "I did not even know that Abdoulaye was dead."

Papa rubbed his forehead again. "There have been several deaths recently among my friends. More deaths than is natural."

"Yes," I said.

"You must prove to me that you did not kill Abdoulaye. No one else has such a reason to wish him ill fortune."

"And what reason do you think I have?"

"The obligation I mentioned. Abdoulaye was not well-loved, that is true; and he may well have been disliked, even hated. Yet everyone knew that he had my protection, and that a harmful thing done to him was a harmful thing done to me. His murderer will die, just as he died."

I tried to raise my hand, but I could not. "How did he die?" I asked.

Papa looked at me through lowered eyelids. "You must tell *me* how he died."

"I—" The stone hands left my shoulders; that only made the pain there get worse. Then I felt the fingers wrap themselves around my throat.

"Answer quickly," said Papa gently, "or very soon you will not be able to answer at all, ever again."

"Shot," I croaked. "Once. Small lead bullet."

Papa made a slight, flicking gesture with one hand; the stone fingers released my throat. "No, he was not shot. Yet two other people have been killed with just such an antique weapon in the last fortnight. It is interesting to me that you know of that matter. One of them was under my protection." He paused, a thoughtful look on his face. His coarse, trembling hands played with his empty coffee cup.

The pain receded quickly, although my shoulders would be sore for days. "If he was not shot," I said, "how *was* Abdoulaye murdered?"

His eyes jerked back to my face. "I am not yet certain that you are not his killer," he said.

"You have said that I have the only motive, that I had an obligation to him. That obligation was paid several days ago. I owed him nothing."

Papa's eyes opened wider. "You have some proof?"

I rose out of my chair just a bit, to get the receipt that was still in my hip pocket. The stone hands returned to my shoulders instantly, but Papa waved them away again. "Hassan was there," I said. "He'll tell you." I dug into my pocket and took out the paper, opened it, and passed it across the table. Friedlander Bey glanced at it, then studied it more closely. He looked beyond me, over my shoulder, and made a small motion with his head. I turned around, and the Stone had gone back to his post by the door.

"O Shaykh, if I may ask," I said, "who is it that told you of this debt? Who suggested to you that I was Abdoulaye's murderer? It must be someone who did not know that I paid the debt in full."

The old man nodded slowly, opened his mouth as if to tell me, then thought better of it. "Ask no more questions," he said.

I took a deep breath and let it out. I wasn't out of this room safely yet; I had to remember that. I couldn't feel anything from the Paxium. Those tranquilizers had been a goddamn waste of money.

Friedlander Bey looked down at his hands, which were toying again with his coffee cup. He signaled to the second Stone, who filled the cup with coffee. The servant looked at me, and I nodded; he gave me another cupful. "Where were you," asked Papa, "about ten o'clock tonight?"

"I was in the Café Solace, playing cards."

"Ah. What time did you begin playing cards?"

"About half past eight."

"And you were in that café until midnight?"

I thought back a few hours. "It was about half past twelve when we all left the Solace and went over to the Red Light. Sonny was stabbed somewhere between one o'clock and one-thirty, I'd say."

"Old Ibrihim at the Solace would not dispute your story?"

"No, he would not."

Papa turned and nodded to the Stone That Speaks behind him. The Stone used the room's telephone. A short time later, he came to the table and murmured in Papa's ear. Papa sighed. "I'm very glad for you, my nephew, that you can account for those hours. Abdoulaye died between ten and eleven o'clock. I accept that you did not kill my friend."

"Praise Allah the protector," I said softly.

"So I will tell you how Abdoulaye died. His body was found by my subordinate, Hassan the Shiite. Abdoulaye Abu-Zayd was murdered in a most foul manner, my nephew. I hesitate to describe it, lest some evil spirit seize the notion and prepare the same fate for me."

I recited Yasmin's superstitious formula, and that pleased the old man. "May Allah preserve you, my nephew," he said. "Abdoulaye lay in the alley behind Hassan's shop, his throat slashed and blood smeared over him. There was little blood in the alley, however, so he was murdered in some other place and removed to the spot where Hassan found him. There were the horrible signs that he had been burned many times, on his chest, on his arms, on his legs, on his face, even upon his organs of procreation. When the police examined the body, Hassan learned that the filthy dog who murdered Abdoulaye had first used my friend's body as a woman's, in the mouth and in the forbidden place of the sodomite. Hassan was quite distraught, and had to be sedated." Papa looked deeply agitated himself as he told me this, as if he had never seen or heard anything so profoundly unnerving. I knew that he had become accustomed to death, that he had caused people to die and that other people had died because of their association with him. Abdoulaye's case, though, affected him passionately. It wasn't really the killing; it was the absolute and appalling disregard for even the most elementary code of conscience. Friedlander Bey's hands were shaking even worse than before.

"It is the same way that Tamiko was killed," I said.

Papa looked at me, unable to speak for a moment. "How did you come to be in possession of that information?" he asked.

I could sense that he was playing again with the notion that I might be responsible for these killings. I seemed to have facts and details that otherwise shouldn't have been known to me. "I discovered Tami's body," I said. "I reported it to Lieutenant Okking."

Papa nodded and looked down again. "I cannot tell you how filled with hatred I am," he said. "It makes me grieve. I have tried to control such feelings, to live graciously as a prosperous man, if that is the will of Allah, and to give thanks for my wealth and do Allah honor by harboring neither anger nor jealousy. Yet my hand is always forced, someone always tries to probe for my weakness. I must respond harshly or lose all I have worked to attain. I wish only peace, and my reward is resentment. I will be avenged on this most abominable of butchers, my nephew! This mad executioner who defiles the holy work of Allah will die! By the sacred beard of the Prophet, I will have my vengeance!"

I waited a moment until he had calmed himself a little. "O Shaykh," I said, "there have been two people murdered by leaden bullets, and two who have been tortured and bled in this same way. I believe there may be more deaths to come. I have been seeking a friend who has disappeared. She was living with Tamiko, and she sent me a frightened message. I fear for her life."

Papa frowned at me. "I have no time for your troubles," he muttered. He was still preoccupied with the outrage of Abdoulaye's death. In some ways, from the old man's point of view, it was even more frightening than what the same killer had done to Tamiko. "I was prepared to believe that you were responsible, my nephew; if you had not proven your innocence, you would have died a lingering and terrible death in this room. I thank Allah that such an injustice did not occur. You seemed to be the most likely person upon whom to direct my wrath, but now I must find another. It is only a matter of time until I discover his identity." His lips pressed together into a cruel, bloodless smile. "You say you were playing cards at the Café Solace. Then the others with you will have the same alibi. Who were these men?"

I named my friends, glad to provide an explanation of their whereabouts; they would not have to face such an inquisition as this.

"Would you like some more coffee?" asked Friedlander Bey wearily.

"May Allah guide us, I have had enough," I said.

"May your times be prosperous," said Papa. He gave a heavy sigh. "Go in peace."

"By your leave," I said, rising.

"May you arise in the morning in health."

I thought of Abdoulaye. "*Inshallah*," I said. I turned, and the Stone That Speaks had already opened the door. I felt a great relief flood through me as I left the room. Outside, beneath a clear black sky pricked with bright stars, was Sergeant Hajjar, leaning against his patrol car. I was surprised; I thought he'd gone back to the city long ago.

"I see you made it out all right," he said to me. "Go around the other side."

"Sit in front?" I asked.

"Yeah." We got into the car; I'd never sat in the front of a police car before. If my friends could only see me now. . . . "You want a smoke?" Hajjar asked, taking out a pack of French cigarettes.

"No, I don't do that," I said.

He started the car and whipped it around in a tight circle, then headed back to the center of town, lights flashing and siren screaming. "You want to buy some sunnies?" he asked. "I know you do *that*."

I would have loved to get some more sunnies, but buying them from a cop seemed odd. The drug traffic was tolerated in the Budayeen, the way the rest of our harmless foibles were tolerated. Some cops don't enforce every law; there were undoubtedly plenty of officers one could safely buy drugs from. I just didn't trust Hajjar, not as far as I could kick him uphill in the dark.

"Why are you being so nice to me all of a sudden?" I asked.

He turned to me and grinned. "I didn't expect you to get out of that motel room alive," he said. "When you walked through that door, you had Papa Bey's Okay mark stamped on your forehead. What's okay with Papa is okay with me. Get it?"

I got it. I had thought that Hajjar worked for Lieutenant Okking and the police force, but Hajjar worked for Friedlander Bey, all the way.

"Can you take me to Frenchy's?" I said.

"Frenchy's? Your girlfriend works there, right?"

"You keep up on things."

He turned and grinned at me again. "Six kiam apiece, the sunnies."

"Six?" I said. "That's ridiculous. I can get them for two and a half."

"Are you crazy? There's nowhere in the city you can get them less than four, and you can't get them."

"All right," I said, "I'll give you three kiam each."

Hajjar rolled his eyes upward. "Don't bother," he said in a disgusted voice. "Allah will grant me a sufficient living without you."

"What is your lowest price? I mean your lowest."

"Offer whatever you think is fair."

"Three kiam," I said again.

"Because it's between you and me," said Hajjar seriously, "I'll go as low as five and a half."

"Three and a half. If you won't take my money, I can find somebody who will."

"Allah will sustain me. I hope your dealing goes well."

"What the hell, Hajjar? Okay, four."

"What, you think I'm making you a present of these?"

"They're no present at these prices. Four and a half. Does that satisfy you?"

"All right, I'll take my consolation from God. No gain to me, but give me the money and that ends it." And that is the way Arabs in the city bargain, in a souk over a beaten-brass vase, or in the front seat of a cop car.

I gave him a hundred kiam, and he gave me twenty-three sunnies. He reminded me three times on the way to Frenchy's that he had thrown in one free, as a gift. When we got to the Budayeen, he didn't slow down. He squealed through the gate and shot up the Street, predicting amiably that everyone would get out of his way; almost everyone did. When we got to Frenchy's, I started to get out of the car. "Hey," he said in a hurt tone of voice, "aren't you going to buy me a drink?"

Standing in the street, I slammed the door closed and leaned down to look in through the window. "I just can't do that, as much as I would like to. If my friends saw me drinking with a cop, well, think what that would do to my reputation. Business is business, Hajjar."

He grinned. "And action is action. I know, I hear that all the time. See you around." And he whipped the patrol car around again and bellowed off down the Street.

I was already sitting down at Frenchy's bar when I remembered all the blood on my clothes and my body. It was too late; Yasmin had already spotted me. I groaned. I needed something to set me up for the scene that was fast approaching. Fortunately, I had all these sunnies. . . .

9

I was wakened once again by the ringing of my telephone. It was simpler to find it this time; I no longer owned the jeans it had been clipped to the previous night, or the shirt I'd been wearing. Yasmin had decide that it would be much easier to dispose of them entirely than to try to wash the stains out. Besides, she said, she didn't want to think about Sonny's blood every time she ran her fingernails up my thigh. I had other shirts; the jeans were another matter. Finding a new pair was the first order of business for that Thursday.

Or so I had planned. The phone call changed that. "Yeah?" I said.

"Hello! Welcome! How are you?"

"Praise Allah," I said, "who *is* this?"

"I ask your pardon, O clever one, I thought you would recognize my voice. This is Hassan."

I squeezed my eyes shut and opened them. "Hello, Hassan," I said. "I heard about Abdoulaye last night from Friedlander Bey. The consolation is that you are well."

"May Allah bless you, my dear. Indeed, I am calling you to relay an invitation from Friedlander Bey. He desires that you come to his house and take breakfast with him. He will send a car and driver."

This was not my favorite way to begin a day. "I thought I persuaded him last night that I was innocent."

Hassan laughed. "You have nothing to worry yourself about. This is purely a friendly invitation. Friedlander Bey would like to make amends for the anxiety he may have caused you. Also, there are one or two things he would like to ask of you. There may be a large amount of money in it for you, Marîd, my son."

I had no interest in taking Papa's money, but I could not turn down his invitation; that was just not done in Papa's city. "When will the car be here?" I asked.

"Very soon. Refresh yourself, and then listen closely to whatever suggestions Friedlander Bey makes. You will profit from them if you are wise."

"Thank you, Hassan," I said.

"No thanks are needed," he said, hanging up.

I laid back on the pillow and thought. I had promised myself years ago that I would never take Papa's money; even if it represented legitimate pay for a service rendered, accepting it put you in that broad category of his "friends and representatives." I was an independent operator, but if I wanted to maintain that status, I'd have to walk carefully this afternoon.

Yasmin was still asleep, of course, and I did not disturb her—Frenchy's did not open until after sundown. I went to the bathroom and washed my face and brushed my teeth. I would have to go to Papa's dressed in the local costume. I shrugged; Papa would probably interpret that as a compliment. That reminded me that I ought to take some small gift with me; this was an entirely different sort of interview than last night's. I finished my brief toilet and dressed, leaving off the *keffiya* and wearing instead the knitted skullcap of my birthplace. I packed my shoulder bag with money, my telephone, and my keys, looked around the apartment with a vague feeling of foreboding, and went outside. I should have left a note telling Yasmin where I was going, but it occurred to me that if I never came home, the note wouldn't do me any good.

There was a warm, late afternoon sun-shower falling. I went to a shop nearby and bought a basket of mixed fruits, then walked back to my apartment building. I enjoyed the fresh, clean smell of the rain on the sidewalk. I saw a long black limousine waiting for me, its engine thrumming. A uniformed driver stood in the doorway of my building, out of the light rain. He saluted me as I got nearer, and he opened the expensive car's rear door. I got in, addressed a silent prayer to Allah, and heard the door slam. A moment later the car was in motion, heading toward Friedlander Bey's great house.

There was a uniformed guard at the gate in the high, ivy-covered wall, who passed the limousine through. The pebble-paved driveway curved gracefully through carefully tended landscaping. There was a profusion of bright tropical flowers blooming all around and, behind them, tall date palms and banana plants. The effect was more natural and more cheering than the artificial arrangements around Lutz Seipolt's place. We drove slowly, the tires of the car making loud popping sounds on the gravel. Inside the wall, everything was quiet and still, as if Papa had succeeded in keeping out the city's noise and clamor as well as unwanted visitors. The house itself was only two stories high, but it rambled over quite an expensive plot of midtown real estate. There were several towers—no doubt with guards in them, too—and Friedlander Bey's home had its own minaret. I wondered if Papa kept his own, private muezzin to call him to his devotions.

The driver pulled to a stop before the wide marble stairs of the front entrance. Not only did he open the car's rear door for me, but he also accompanied me up the stairs. It was he who rapped on the estate's polished mahogany door. A butler or some other servant opened the door, and the driver said, "The master's guest." Then the driver went back to the car, the butler bowed me in, and I was standing in Friedlander Bey's house. The beautiful door closed softly behind me, and the cool, dry air caressed my perspiring face. The house was faintly perfumed with incense.

"This way, please," said the butler. "The master is at his prayers just now. You may wait in this antechamber."

I thanked the butler, who sincerely wished that Allah do all sorts of wonderful things for me. Then he disappeared, leaving me alone in the small room. I walked about casually, admiring the lovely objects Papa had acquired during his long, dramatic life. At last, a communicating door opened, and one of the Stones signaled to me. I saw Papa inside, folding his prayer rug and putting it away in a cabinet. There was a mihrab in his office, the semicircular recess you find in every mosque indicating the direction of Mecca.

Friedlander Bey turned to face me, and his plump, gray face brightened with a genuine smile of welcome. He came toward me and greeted me; we proceeded through all the formalities. I offered him my gift, and he was delighted. "The fruits look succulent and tempting," he said, putting the basket on a low table. "I will enjoy them after the sun sets, my nephew; it was kind of you to think of me. Now, will you make yourself comfortable? We must talk, and when it is proper, I beg that you will join me at breakfast." He indicated an antique lacquered divan that looked like it was worth a small fortune. He relaxed on its mate, facing me across several feet of exquisite pale blue and gold rug. I waiting for him to begin the conversation.

He stroked his cheek and looked at me, as if he hadn't done enough of that last night. "I can see by your coloring that you are a Maghrîb," he said. "Are you Tunisian?"

"No, O Shaykh, I was born in Algeria."

"One of your parents was surely of Berber heritage."

That rankled me a little. There are long-standing, historical reasons for the irritation, but they're ancient and tedious and of no relevance now. I avoided the whole Berber-Arab question by saying, "I am a Muslim, O Shaykh, and my father was French."

"There is a saying," said Friedlander Bey, "that if you ask a mule of his lineage, he will say only that one of his parents was a horse." I took that as a mild reproof; the reference to mules and asses is more meaningful if you consider, as all Arabs do, the donkey, like the dog, to be among the most unclean of animals. Papa must have seen that he had only irked me more, because he laughed softly and waved a hand. "Forgive me, my nephew. I was only thinking that your speech is accented heavily with the dialect of the Maghrîb. Of course, here in the city our Arabic is a mixture of Maghrîb, Egyptian, Levantine, and Persian. I doubt if anyone speaks a pure Arabic, if such a thing exists at all anywhere but in the Straight Path. I meant no offense. And I must extend a further apology, for my treatment of you last night. I hope you can understand my reasons."

I nodded grimly, but I did not reply.

Friedlander Bey went on. "It is necessary that we return to the unpleasant subject we discussed briefly at the motel. These murders must stop. There is no acceptable alternative. Of the four victims thus far, three have been connected to me. I cannot see these killings as anything other than a personal attack, direct or indirect."

"Three of the four?" I asked. "Certainly Abdoulaye Abu-Zayd was one of your people. But the Russian? And the two Black Widow Sisters? No pimp would dare try to coerce the Sisters. Tamiko and Devi were famous for their fierce independence."

Papa made a small gesture of distaste. "I did not interfere with the Black Widow Sisters in regard to their prostitution," he said. "My concerns are on a higher plane than that, although many of my associates find profit in purveying all manner of vice. The Sisters were allowed to keep every kiam they earned, and they were welcome to it. No, they performed other services for me, services of a discreet, dangerous, and necessary nature."

I was astonished. "Tami and Devi were . . . your assassins?" I asked.

"Yes," said Friedlander Bey. "And Selima will continue to take on such assignments when no other solution is possible. Tamiko and Devi were paid well, they had my complete trust and confidence, and they always gave excellent results. Their deaths have caused me no little anguish. It is not a simple matter to replace such artists, particularly ones with whom I enjoyed such a satisfactory working partnership."

I thought this over for a little while; it wasn't hard to accept, although the information had come as quite a surprise. It even answered a few questions I'd entertained from time to time concerning the open daring of the Black Widow Sisters. They worked as secret agents of Friedlander Bey, and they were protected; or they were *supposed* to be protected. Yet two had died. "It would be simpler to understand this situation, O Shaykh," I said, musing out loud, "if both Tami and Devi had been murdered in the same way. Yet Devi was shot with the old pistol, and Tami was tortured and slashed."

"Those were my thoughts, my nephew," said Papa. "Please continue. Perhaps you will shed light on this mystery."

I shrugged. "Well, even that fact could be dismissed, if other victims hadn't been found slain in these same ways."

"I will find both killers," said the old man calmly. It was a flat statement of fact, neither an emotional vow nor a boast.

"It occurred to me, O Shaykh," I said, "that the murderer who uses the pistol is killing for some political reason. I saw him shoot the Russian, who was a minor functionary in the legation of the Byelorussian-Ukrainian Kingdom. He was wearing a James Bond personality module. The weapon is the same type of pistol the fictional character used. I think a common murderer, killing out of spite or sudden anger or in the course of a robbery, would chip in some other module, or none at all. The James Bond module might provide a certain insight and skill in the business of quick, clean assassination. That would be of value only to a dispassionate killer whose acts were part of some larger scheme."

Friedlander Bey frowned. "I am not convinced, my nephew. There isn't the slightest connection between your Russian diplomat and my Devi. The assassination idea occurred to you only because the Russian worked in some political capacity. Devi had no idea of world affairs at all. She was of no help or hindrance to any party or movement. The James Bond theme merits further inspection, but the motives you suggest are without substance."

"Do you have any ideas about either killer, O Shaykh?" I asked.

"Not yet," he said, "but I have only just begun to collect information. That is why I wanted to discuss this situation with you. You should not think that my involvement is solely a matter of revenge. It is that, of course, but it is a great deal larger than that. To put it simply, I must protect my investments. I must demonstrate to my associates and my friends that I will not permit such a threat to their safety to continue. Otherwise I will begin to lose the support of the people who make up the foundation and framework of my power. Taken individually, these four murders are repellent but not unheard-of occurrences:

murders take place every day in the city. Together, however, these four killings are an immediate challenge to my existence. Do you understand me, my nephew?"

He was making himself very clear. "Yes, O Shaykh," I said. I waited to hear the suggestions Hassan said would be made.

There was a long pause while Friedlander Bey regarded me pensively. "You are very different from most of my friends in the Budayeen," he said at last. "Almost everyone has had some modification made on his body."

"If they can afford it," I said, "I think they should have whatever mod they want. As for me, O Shaykh, my body has always been fine just the way it is. The only surgery I've ever had has been for therapeutic reasons. I am pleased with the form I was given by Allah."

Papa nodded. "And your mind?" he asked.

"It runs a little slow sometimes," I said, "but, on the whole, it's served me well. I've never felt a desire to have my brain wired, if that's what you mean."

"Yet you take prodigious quantities of drugs. You did so in my presence last night." I had nothing to say to that. "You are a proud man, my nephew. I've read a report about you that mentions this pride. You find excitement in contests of wit and will and physical prowess with people who have the advantage of modular personalities and other software add-ons. It is a dangerous diversion, but you seem to have emerged unscathed."

A few painful memories flashed through my mind. "I've been scathed, O Shaykh, more than a few times."

He laughed. "Even that has not prompted you to modify yourself. Your pride takes the form of presenting yourself—as the Christians say in some context—as being *in* the world but not *of* it."

"Untempted by its treasures and untouched by its evils, that's me." My ironic tone was not lost on Papa.

"I would like you to help me, Marîd Audran," he said. There it was, take it or leave it.

The way he put it, I was left in an extremely uncomfortable position: I could say, "Sure, I'll help you," and then I'd have compromised myself in precisely the way I swore I never would; or I could say, "No, I won't help you," and

I'd have offended the most influential person in my world. I took a couple of long, slow breaths while I sorted out my answer. "O Shaykh," I said at last, "your difficulties are the difficulties of everyone in the Budayeen; indeed, in the city. Certainly, anyone who cares about his own safety and happiness will help you. I will help you all that I can, but against the men who have murdered your friends, I doubt that I can be of much use."

Papa stroked his cheek and smiled. "I understand that you have no wish to become one of my 'associates.' Be that as it may. You have my guarantee, my nephew, that if you agree to aid me in this matter, it will not mark you as one of 'Papa's men.' Your pleasure is in your freedom and independence, and I would not take that from one who does me a great favor."

I wondered if he was implying that he might take away the freedom from one who refused to perform the favor. It would be child's play for Papa to steal my liberty; he could accomplish that by simply planting me forever, deep beneath the tender grass in the cemetery where the Street comes to its end.

Baraka: an Arabic word that is very difficult to translate. It can mean magic or charisma or the special favor of God. Places can have it; shrines are visited and touched in the hope that some of the *baraka* will rub off. People can have *baraka;* the derwishes, in particular, believe that certain fortunate people are specially blessed by Allah, and are therefore worthy of singular respect in the community. Friedlander Bey had more *baraka* than all the stone shrines in the Maghríb. I can't say if it was *baraka* that made him what he was, or if he attained the *baraka* as he attained his position and influence. Whatever the explanation, it was very difficult to listen to him and deny him what he asked. "How can I help you?" I said. I felt hollow inside, as if I had made a great surrender.

"I want you to be the instrument of my vengeance, my nephew," he said.

I was shocked. No one knew better than I how inadequate I was to the task he was giving me. I had tried to tell him that already, but he'd only brushed aside my objections as if they were just some form of false modesty. My mouth and throat were dry. "I have said that I will help you, but you ask too much of me. You have more capable people in your employ."

"I have stronger men," said Papa. "The two servants you met last night are stronger than you, but they lack intelligence. Hassan the Shiite has a certain shrewdness, but he is not otherwise a dangerous man. I have considered each of my friends, O my beloved nephew, and I have made this decision: none but you offers the essential combination of qualities I seek. Most important, I trust you. I cannot say the same of many of my associates; it is a sad thing to admit. I trust you because you do not care to rise in my esteem. You do not try to ingratiate yourself with me for your own ends. You are not a truckling leech, of which I have more than my share. For the important work we must do, I must have someone about whom I have no doubts; that is one of the reasons our meeting last night was so difficult for you. It was an examination of your inner worth. I knew when we parted that you were the man I sought."

"You do me honor, O Shaykh, but I am afraid I do not share your confidence."

He raised his right hand, and it trembled visibly. "I have not finished my speech, my nephew. There are further reasons why you must do as I ask, reasons that benefit you, not me. You tried to speak of your friend Nikki last night, and I would not permit it. I ask your forgiveness again. You were quite correct in your concern for her safety. I am certain that her disappearance was the work of one or the other of these murderers; perhaps she herself has already been slain, Allah grant that it not be true. I cannot say. Yet if there is any hope of finding her alive, it is in you. With my resources, together we will find the killers. Together we will deal with them, as the Wise Mention of God directs. We will prevent Nikki's death if we can, and who can say how many other lives we may save? Are these not worthy goals? Can you still hesitate?"

It was all very flattering, I suppose; but I wished like hell that Papa had picked somebody else. Saied would have done a good job, especially with his ass-kicking moddy chipped in. There was nothing I could do now, though, except agree. "I will do my best for you, O Shaykh," I said reluctantly, "but I do not abandon my doubts."

"That is well," said Friedlander Bey. "Your doubts will keep you alive longer."

I really wished he hadn't added that last word; he sounded as if I couldn't survive, no matter what I did, but my doubts would keep me around to watch myself suffer. "It will be as Allah wills," I said.

"May the blessing of Allah be on you. Now we must discuss your payment."

That surprised me, too. "I had no thought of payment," I said.

Papa acted as if he did not hear. "One must eat," he said simply. "You shall be paid a hundred kiam a day until this affair is concluded." Concluded is right: until either we put an end to the two murdering sons of bitches, or one of them put an end to me.

"I did not ask for such a wage," I said. A hundred a day; well, Papa had said one must eat. I wondered what he thought I was accustomed to eating.

Again he ignored me. He gestured to the Stone That Speaks, who approached and handed Friedlander Bey an envelope. "Here is seven hundred kiam," Papa said to me, "your pay for the first week." He gave the envelope back to the Stone, who brought it to me.

If I took the envelope, it was a symbol of my complete acceptance of Friedlander Bey's authority. There would be no turning back, no quitting, no ending but the ending. I looked at the white envelope in the sandstone-colored hand. My own hand rose a little, sank a little, rose again and took the money. "Thank you," I said.

Friedlander Bey looked pleased. "I hope it brings you pleasure," he said. It had damn well better; I was certainly going to earn every fuckin' fîq of it.

"O Shaykh, what are your instructions?" I asked.

"First, my nephew, you must go to Lieutenant Okking and put yourself at his disposal. I will inform him that we will cooperate completely with the police department in this matter. There are circumstances that my associates can manage with greater efficiency than the police; I'm sure the lieutenant will acknowledge that. I think that a temporary alliance of my organization with his will best serve the needs of the community. He will give you all the information he has on the killings, a probable description of the one who cut the throats of Abdoulaye Abu-Zayd and Tamiko, and whatever else he has so far withheld. In return, you will assure him that we will keep the police informed of such facts as we uncover."

"Lieutenant Okking is a good man," I said, "but he cooperates only when he feels like it, or when it's clearly to his advantage."

Papa gave me a brief smile. "He will cooperate with you now, I will make sure of that. He will soon learn that it is, indeed, in his own best interest." The old man would be as good as his word; if anyone could persuade Okking to help me, it was Friedlander Bey.

"And then, O Shaykh?"

He cocked his head and smiled again. For some reason I felt cold, as if a bitter wind had found its way into Papa's fortress. "Do you foresee a time, my nephew," he asked, "or can you imagine a circumstance, in which you would seek the modifications you have so far rejected?"

The icy wind blew more fiercely. "No, O Shaykh," I said, "I can't foresee such a time or imagine such a situation; that doesn't mean that it may not happen. Perhaps sometime in the future I'll have need to choose some modification."

He nodded. "Tomorrow is Friday, and I observe the Sabbath. You will need time to think and plan. Monday is soon enough."

"Soon enough? Soon enough for what?"

"To meet with my private surgeons," he said simply.

"No," I whispered.

Suddenly, Friedlander Bey ceased being the kindly uncle. He became, instantly, the commander of men's allegiance, whose orders cannot be questioned. "You have accepted my coin, my nephew," he said sternly. "You will do as I say. You cannot hope to succeed against our enemies unless your mind is improved. We know that at least one of the two has an electronically augmented brain. You must have the same, but to an even greater degree. My surgeons can give you advantages over the murderers."

The two sandstone hands appeared on my shoulders, holding me firmly in place. Now, truly, there was no way out. "What sort of advantages?" I asked apprehensively. I began to feel the cold sweat of utter fear. I had avoided having my brain wired more out of profound dread than principle. The idea produced terror in me, amounting to an irrational, paralyzing phobia.

"The surgeons will explain it all to you," said Papa.

"O Shaykh," I said, my voice breaking, "I do not wish this."

"Events have moved beyond your wishing," he replied. "You will change your mind on Monday."

No, I thought, it won't be me; it will be Friedlander Bey and his surgeons who will change my mind.

10

"Lieutenant Okking's out of his office at the moment," said a uniformed officer. "Can I help you with something?"

"Will the lieutenant be back soon?" I asked. The clock above the officer's desk said almost ten o'clock. I wondered how late Okking was going to work tonight; I had no desire to talk to Sergeant Hajjar, whatever his connection to Papa. I still didn't trust him.

"The lieutenant said he'd be right back, he's just gone downstairs for something."

That made me feel better. "Is it all right if I wait in his office? We're old friends."

The cop looked at me dubiously. "Can I see some identification?" he asked. I gave him my Algerian passport; it's expired, but it's the only thing I own with my photograph on it. He punched my name into his computer, and a moment later my whole history began spilling across his screen. He must have decided that I was an upright citizen, because he gave me back my passport, stared up into my face for a moment, and said, "You and Lieutenant Okking go back a ways together."

"It's a long story, all right," I said.

"He won't be another ten minutes. You can take a seat in there."

I thanked the cop and went into Okking's office. It was true, I *had* spent a lot of time here. The lieutenant and I had formed a curious alliance, considering that we worked opposite sides of the legal fence. I sat in the chair beside Okking's desk and waited. Ten minutes passed, and I began to get restless. I started looking at the papers piled in hefty stacks, trying to read them upside-down and sideways. His *Out* box was half-filled with envelopes, but there was even more work crammed into the *In* box. Okking earned whatever meager wages he got from the department. There was a large manila envelope on its way to a small-arms dealer in the Federated New England States of America; a handwritten envelope to some doctor in the city; a neatly addressed envelope to a firm called Universal Exports with an address near the waterfront—I wondered if it was one of the companies Hassan dealt with, or maybe it was one of Seipolt's; and a heavily stuffed packet being sent to an office-supplies manufacturer in the Protectorate of Brabant.

I had glanced at just about everything in Okking's office when, an hour later, the man himself appeared. "Hope I haven't kept you waiting," he said distractedly. "What the hell do you want?"

"Nice to see you, too, Lieutenant. I've just come from a meeting with Friedländer Bey."

That caught his attention. "Oh, so now you're running errands for sand-niggers with delusions of grandeur. I forget: is that a step up or a step down for you, Audran? I suppose the old snake charmer gave you a message?"

I nodded. "It's about these murders."

Okking seated himself behind his desk and gazed at me innocently. "What murders?" he asked.

"The two with the old pistol, the two throat-slashings. Sure, *you* remember. Or have you been too busy rounding up jaywalkers again?"

He shot me an ugly look and ran a finger along a heavy jaw that badly needed shaving. "I remember," he said bluntly. "Why does Bey think this concerns him?"

"Three of the four victims did odd jobs for him, back in the days when they had a little more spring in their step. He just wants to make sure that none of his other employees get the same treatment. Papa has a lot of civic consciousness that way. I don't think you appreciate that about him."

Okking snorted. "Yeah, you right," he said. "I always thought those two sex-changes worked for him. They looked like they were trying to smuggle cantaloupes under their sweaters."

"Papa thinks these murders are aimed at him."

Okking shrugged. "If they are, those killers are lousy marksmen. They haven't so much as nicked Papa yet."

"He doesn't see it that way. The women who work for him are his eyes, the men are his fingers. He said that himself, in his own warm and wonderful way."

"What was Abdoulaye, then, his asshole?"

I knew that Okking and I could go on like that all night. I briefly explained the unusual proposition Friedlander Bey had asked me to deliver. As I expected, Lieutenant Okking had as little faith as I. "You know, Audran," he said dryly, "official law-enforcement groups worry a lot about their public image. We get enough beating-up in the news media as it is, without having to go out on the front steps and kiss ass with somebody like Friedlander Bey because nobody thinks we can do a damn thing about these murders without him."

I patted the air to make it all better between us. "No, no," I said, "it isn't that at all. You're misunderstanding me, you're misunderstanding Papa's motives. No one's saying you couldn't nail these murderers without help. These guys aren't any more clever or dangerous than the scruffy, beetle-headed crumbs you pull in here every day. Friedlander Bey only suggests that because his own interests are directly involved, teamwork might save everybody time and effort, as well as lives. Wouldn't it be worth it, Lieutenant, if we keep just one of your uniformed cops from stopping a bullet?"

"Or one of Bey's whores from annexing a butcher knife? Yeah, listen, I already got a call from Papa, probably while you were on your way over here. We went through this whole song-and-dance already, and I agreed to a certain point. *A certain point*, Audran. I don't like you or him trying to make police policy, telling me how to run my investigation, interfering in any way. Understand?"

I nodded. I knew both Lieutenant Okking and Friedlander Bey, and it didn't make any difference what Okking *said* he didn't want; Papa'd get his way anyhow.

"Just so we understand each other on this," said the

lieutenant. "The whole thing is unnatural, like rats and mice going to church to pray for the recovery of a cat. When it's over, when we have those two killers, don't expect any more honeymoon. Then it will be seizure guns and batons and the same old harassment on both sides."

I shrugged. "Business is business," I said.

"I'm real tired of hearing that line," he said. "Now get out of my sight."

I got out and took the elevator down to the ground floor. It was a nice, cool evening, a swelling moon slipping in and out of gleaming metal clouds. I walked back to the Budayeen, thinking. In three days I was going to have my brain wired. I'd avoided that fact since I left Friedlander Bey's; now I had all the time in the world to think about it. I felt no excitement, no anticipation, only dread. I felt that, somehow, Marîd Audran would cease to be and someone new would awaken from that surgery, and that I'd never be able to put my finger on the difference; it would bother me forever, like a popcorn hull wedged permanently between my teeth. Everyone else would notice the change, but I wouldn't because I was on the inside.

I went straight to Frenchy's. When I got there, Yasmin was working on a young, thin guy wearing white baggy pants with drawstrings around the ankles and a gray salt-and-pepper sport coat about fifty years old. He probably bought his whole wardrobe in the back of some antique shop for one and a half kiam; it smelled musty, like your great-grandmother's quilt that has been left in the attic too long.

The girl on stage was a sex-change named Blanca; Frenchy had a policy about not hiring debs. Girls were all right with him, and debs who'd had their full changes, but the ones stuck indecisively in the middle made him feel that they might get stuck sometime in the middle of some other important transaction, and he just didn't want to be held responsible. You knew when you went into Frenchy's that there wasn't going to be anybody in there with a cock bigger than yours unless it was Frenchy himself or one of the other customers, and if you found out that awful truth you had nobody to blame but yourself.

Blanca danced in a peculiar, half-conscious way that was common among dancers all up and down the Street. They moved vaguely in time to the music, bored and tired and waiting to get out from under the hot lights. They stared at themselves incessantly in the smeared mirrors behind them, or they turned and stared at their reflections across the room behind the customers. Their eyes were fixed forever in some empty space about a foot and a half above the customers' heads. Blanca's expression was a faint attempt to look pleasant—"attractive" and "alluring" weren't in her professional vocabulary—but she looked as if she'd just had a lot of nerve-deadening drug pumped into her lower jaw and she hadn't decided if she liked it yet. While Blanca was on stage she was selling herself—she was promoting herself as a product entirely separate from her own self-image, herself as she would be when she came down from the stage. Her movements—mostly weary, half-hearted imitations of sexual motions—were supposed to titillate her watchers, but unless the customers had had a lot to drink or were otherwise fixated on this particular girl, the dancing itself would have little effect. I'd watched Blanca dance dozens, maybe hundreds, of times; it was always the same music, she always made the same gyrations, the same steps, the same bumps, the same grinds at the same instants of each song.

Blanca finished her last number and there was a scattering of applause, mostly from the mark who had been buying her drinks and thought he was in love with her. It takes a little longer for you to establish an acquaintance in a place like Frenchy's—or any of the other bars along the Street. That seems like a paradox, because the girls rushed up to grab any single man who strayed into the place. The conversation was so limited, though: "Hi, what's your name?"

"Juan-Javier."

"Oh, that's nice. Where you from?"

"Nuevo Tejas."

"Oh, that's interesting. How long have you been in the city?"

"A couple of days."

"Want to buy me a drink?"

That's all there is, there ain't no more. Even a top-notch international secret agent couldn't relay more information in that small amount of time. Beneath it all was a constant undercurrent of depression, as if the girls were locked into this job, although the illusion of absolute freedom hovered almost visibly in the air. "Any time you want to quit, honey, you just walk out that door." The way out the door, though, led to one of only two places: another bar just like Frenchy's, or the next step down the ladder toward the deadly bottom of the Life: "Hi, handsome, looking for some company?" You know what I mean. And the income gets lower and lower as the girl gets older, and pretty soon you get people like Maribel turning tricks for the price of a shot glass of white wine.

After Blanca, a real girl called Indihar came on stage; it might even have been her real name. She moved the same as Blanca, hips and shoulders swaying, feet almost motionless. As she danced, Indihar mouthed the words to the songs silently, completely unaware that she was doing it. I asked a few girls about that; they all mouthed the lyrics, but none of them realized they did it. They all got self-conscious when I mentioned the fact, but the next time they got up to dance, they sang to themselves just as they always had. Made the time go quicker, I guess, gave them something to do besides look at the customers. Back and forth the girls swayed, their lips moving, their hands making empty gestures, their hips swirling where habit told them to swirl their hips. It might have been sexy to some of the men who'd never seen such things before, it might have been worth what Frenchy charged for his drinks. I could drink for free because Yasmin worked there and because I kept Frenchy amused; if I'd had to pay, I would have found something more interesting to do with my time. Anything would have been more interesting; sitting alone in the dark in a soundless room would have been more interesting.

I waited through Indihar's set, and then Yasmin came out of the dressing room. She gave me a wide smile that made me feel special. There was some applause from two or three men scattered along the bar: she was mixing well tonight, making money. Indihar threw on a gauzy top and started hitting up the customers for tips. I kicked in a kiam and she gave me a little kiss. Indihar's a good kid. She plays by the rules and doesn't hassle anybody. Blanca could go to hell, as far as I was concerned, but Indihar and I could be good friends.

Frenchy caught my eye and motioned me down to the end of the bar. He was a big man, about the size of two average Marseilles enforcers, with a big, black, bushy beard that made mine look like the fuzz in a cat's ear. He glowered at me with his black eyes. "Where ya at, cap?" he asked.

"Nothing happening tonight, Frenchy," I said.

"Your girl's doing all right for herself."

"That's good," I said, "because I lost my last fiq through a hole in my pocket."

Frenchy squinted and looked at my *gallebeya*. "You don't have any pockets in that outfit, *mon noraf*."

"That was days ago, Frenchy," I said solemnly. "We've been living on love since." Yasmin had some orbital-velocity moddy chipped in, and her dancing was something to watch. People all up and down the bar forgot their drinks and the other girls' hands in their laps, and stared at Yasmin.

Frenchy laughed; he knew that I was never as flat-out broke as I always claimed to be. "Business is bad," he said, spitting into a small plastic cup. With Frenchy, business is always bad. Nobody ever talks prosperity on the Street; it's bad luck.

"Listen," I said, "there's some important thing I have to talk over with Yasmin when she's finished this set."

Frenchy shook his head. "She's working on that mark down there wearing the fez. Wait until she milks him dry, then you can talk to her all you want. If you wait until the mark leaves, I'll get someone else to take her next turn on stage."

"Allah be praised," I said. "Can I buy you a drink?"

He smiled at me. "Buy two," he said. "Pretend one's for me, one's for you. Drink them both. I can't stomach the stuff anymore." He patted his belly and made a sour face, then got up and walked down the bar, greeting his customers and whispering in the ears of his girls. I bought two drinks from Dalia, Frenchy's short, round-faced, informative barmaid; I'd known Dalia for years. Dalia, Frenchy, and Chiriga were very likely fixtures on the Street when the Street was just a goatpath from one end of the Budayeen to the other. Before the rest of the city decided to wall us in, probably, and put in the cemetery.

When Yasmin finished dancing, the applause was loud and long. Her tip jar filled quickly, and then she was hurrying back to her enamored mark before some other bitch stole him away. Yasmin gave me a quick, affectionate pinch on the ass as she passed behind me.

I watched her laughing and talking and hugging that cross-eyed bastard son of a yellow dog for half an hour; then his money ran out, and both he and Yasmin looked sad. Their affair had come to a premature end. They waved fond, almost passionate farewells and promised they'd never forget this golden evening. Every time I see one of those goddamn wogs climbing all over Yasmin—or any of the other girls, for that matter—I remember watching nameless men grabbing at my mother. That was a hell of a long time ago, but for certain things my memory works just too well. I watched Yasmin and I told myself it was just her job; but I couldn't help the sick, acid feeling that climbed out of my gut and made me want to start breaking things.

She scooted down beside me, drenched with perspiration, and gasped, "I thought that son of a slut would never leave!"

"It's your charming presence," I said sourly. "It's your scintillating conversation. It's Frenchy's needled beer."

"Yeah," said Yasmin, puzzled by my annoyance, "you right."

"I have to talk to you about something."

Yasmin looked at me and took a few deep breaths. She mopped her face with a clean bar towel. I suppose I sounded unusually grave. Anyway, I went through the events of the evening for her: my second meeting with Friedlander Bey; our—that is, *his*—conclusions; and how I had failed to impress Lieutenant Okking. When I finished, there was stunned silence from all around.

"You're going to do it?" asked Frenchy. I hadn't noticed

him returning. I wasn't aware that he'd been eavesdropping, but it was his place and nobody knew his eaves better.

"You're going to get *wired*?" asked Yasmin breathlessly. She found the whole idea vastly exciting. *Arousing*, if you get my meaning.

"You're crazy if you do," said Dalia. Dalia was as close to being a true conservative as you could find on the Street. "Look what it does to people."

"What *does* it do to people?" shouted Yasmin, outraged, tapping her own moddy.

"Oops, sorry," said Dalia, and she went to mop up some imaginary spilled beer at the far, far end of the bar.

"Think of all the things we could do together," said Yasmin dreamily.

"Maybe it's not good enough for you the way it is," I said, a little hurt.

Her expression fell. "Hey, Marîd, it's not that. It's just—"

"This is *your* problem," said Frenchy, "it's none of my business. I'm going in the back and count tonight's money. Won't take me very long." He disappeared through a ratty gold-colored cloth that served as a flimsy barrier to the dressing room and his office.

"It's permanent," I said. "Once it's done, it's done. There's no backing out."

"Have you ever heard me say that I wanted to have my wires yanked?" asked Yasmin.

"No," I admitted. It was just the *irrevocableness* of it that prickled my skin.

"I haven't regretted it for an instant, and neither has anybody else I know who's had it done."

I wet my lips. "You don't understand," I said. I couldn't finish my argument; I couldn't put into words what she didn't understand.

"You're just afraid," she said.

"Yeah," I said. That was a good starting point.

"The Half-Hajj has *his* brain wired, and he's not even a quarter of the man you are."

"And all it got him was Sonny's blood all over everything. I don't need moddies to make me act crazy, I can do that on my own."

Suddenly she got a faraway, inspired look in her eyes. I knew something fascinating had occurred to her, and I knew it most likely meant bad news for me. "Oh, Allah and the Virgin Mary in a motel room," she said softly. That had been a favorite blasphemy of her father's, I think. "This is working out just like the hexagram said."

"The hexagram." I had put that *I Ching* business out of my mind almost before Yasmin had finished explaining it to me.

"Remember what it said?" she asked. "About not being afraid to cross the great water?"

"Yeah. What great water?"

"The great water is some major change in your life. Getting your brain wired, for instance."

"Uh huh. And it said to meet the great man. I did that. Twice."

"It said to wait three days before beginning, and three days before completing."

I counted up quickly: tomorrow, Saturday, Sunday. Monday, when I was going to have this thing done, would be after three days. "Oh, hell," I muttered.

"And it said that nobody would believe you, and it said that you had to keep up your confidence during adversity, and it said that you didn't serve kings and princes but higher principles. That's my Marîd." And she kissed me; I felt ill. There was absolutely no way I could get out of the surgery now, unless I started running and began a new life in some new country, shoving goats and sheep around and eating a few figs every couple of days to stay alive like the other *fellahîn.*

"I'm a hero, Yasmin," I said, "and we heroes sometimes have secret business to attend to. Got to go." I kissed her three or four times, squeezed her right silicone tit for luck, and stood up. On the way out of Frenchy's I patted Indihar's ass, and she turned and grinned at me. I waved good-night to Dalia. Blanca I pretended didn't even exist.

I walked down the Street to the Silver Palm, just to see what people were doing and what was going on. Mahmoud and Jacques were sitting at a table, having coffee and sopping up *hummus* with pita bread. The Half-Hajj was absent, probably out kicking gigantic heterosexual stonecutters around for the hell of it. I sat down with my friends. "May your and so forth, and so forth," said Mahmoud. He was never one to worry about formalities.

"Yours too," I said.

"Getting yourself wired, I hear," said Jacques. "A crucial decision. A major undertaking. I'm sure you've considered both sides of the matter?"

I was a little astonished. "News travels fast, doesn't it?"

Mahmoud raised his eyebrows. "That's what news is for," he said, around a mouthful of bread and *hummus*.

"Permit me to buy you some coffee," said Jacques.

"Praise Allah," I said, "but I feel like something stronger."

"Just as well," said Jacques to Mahmoud. "Marîd has more money than the two of us together. He's on Papa's payroll now."

I didn't like the sound of that rumor at all. I went to the bar and ordered my gin, bingara, and Rose's. Behind the bar, Heidi grimaced, but she didn't say anything. She was pretty—hell, she was one of the most beautiful real women I'd ever met. She always fitted into her well-chosen clothing the way some of the debs and changes wished they could, with their store-bought bodies. Heidi had wonderful blue eyes and soft, pale bangs. I don't know why, but bangs on young women always make me jittery. I think it's the hebephile in me; if I examine myself closely enough, I find hints of every objectionable quality known to man. I'd always wanted to get to know Heidi *really* well, but I guess I wasn't her type. Maybe her type was available on a moddy, and after I got my brain wired . . .

While I was waiting for her to mix my drink, another voice spoke up about twenty feet away, beyond a group of Korean men and women who would soon learn, no doubt, that they were in the wrong part of town. "Vodka martini, dry. Pre-war Wolfschmidt's if you've got it, shaken and not stirred. With a twist of lemon peel."

Well, now, I said to myself. I waited until Heidi came back with my drink. I paid her and swirled the liquor and ice in tight, counterclockwise circles. Heidi brought my change; I tipped her a kiam, and she started some polite conversation. I interrupted her rather rudely; I was more interested in the vodka martini.

I picked up my glass and stepped back from the bar, just enough to get a good look at James Bond. He was just as I remembered him from the brief encounter in Chiri's place, and from Ian Fleming's novels: black hair parted on one side, a heavy lock of it falling in an unruly comma over the right eye, the scar running down the right cheek. He had straight, black brows and a long, straight nose. His upper lip was short and his mouth, though relaxed, somehow gave the impression of cruelty. He looked ruthless. He had paid a great deal of money to a team of surgeons to make him look ruthless. He glanced at me and smiled; I wondered if he recalled our previous meeting. His gray-blue eyes crinkled a bit at their edges as he observed me; I had the distinct feeling that I was, in fact, being observed. He was wearing a plain cotton shirt and tropical worsted trousers, no doubt of British manufacture, with black leather sandals suitable to the climate. He paid for his martini and came toward me, one hand extended. "Nice to see you again, old man," he said.

I shook hands with him. "I don't believe I've been granted the honor of making the gentleman's acquaintance," I said in Arabic.

Bond answered me in flawless French. "Another bar, another circumstance. It was of no great consequence. Everything turned out satisfactorily in the end." It had been satisfactory for him, at least. At the moment, the dead Russian had no opinion at all.

"May Allah forgive me, my friends are waiting," I said.

Bond smiled his famous half-smile. He gave me back an Arabic saying—in perfect local Arabic. "What has died has passed," he said, shrugging, meaning either that bygones were bygones, or that it would be good policy for me to begin forgetting all the recently dead; I wasn't sure which interpretation Bond intended. I nodded, disconcerted more by his facility with my language. Then I remembered that he was wearing a James Bond moddy, probably with an Arabic-language daddy chipped in. I took my drink to the table where Mahmoud and Jacques were sitting, and chose a chair from which I could keep an eye on the bar and its single entrance. By the time I'd seated myself, Bond had downed his martini and was going out into the cobbled

Street. I felt a chilly wave of indecision: what was I supposed to do? Could I hope to bring him down now, before I had my brain wired? I was unarmed. What possible good could come of attacking Bond prematurely? Yet surely Friedlander Bey would consider this an opportunity lost, one that might well mean the death of someone else, someone dear to me. . . .

I decided to follow. I left my drink untasted on the table and gave my friends no explanation. I got out of my chair and went to the open doorway of the Silver Palm, just in time to see Bond turn left into a side street. I crept along carefully behind. Evidently I wasn't careful enough, because when I stopped at the corner and peered cautiously around, James Bond was gone. There were no other streets parallel to the Street for him to have turned onto; he must have entered one of the low, whitewashed, flat-roofed dwellings on the block. That was *some* information, at least. I turned around again to walk back to the Silver Palm, when a flare of pain detonated behind my left ear. I crumpled to my knees, and a strong, tanned hand grabbed the light material of my *gallebeya* and dragged me back to my feet. I muttered some curses and raised my fist. The edge of his hand chopped at the point of my shoulder, and my arm dropped, numb and useless.

James Bond laughed softly. "Every time you see a well-setup European in one of your grimy, quaint rumshops, you think you can come along behind and relieve him of his pocketbook. Well, my friend, sometimes you choose to rob the wrong European." He slapped me across the face, not very hard, threw me away from himself against the rough face of the wall behind me, and stared at me as if I owed him an explanation or apology. I decided he was right.

"A hundred thousand pardons, *effendi*," I murmured. Somewhere in my mind arose the thought that this James Bond was handling himself a good sight better than he had when he let me escort him out of Chiri's a couple of weeks ago. Tonight, his goddamn black comma of hair wasn't even out of place. He wasn't even breathing hard. There was some logical explanation for all that, too; I'd let

Papa or Jacques or the *I Ching* figure it out: my head was throbbing too hard and my ears were chiming.

"And you needn't bother with that *'effendi'* bunk," he said grimly. "That's a Turkish flattery, and I still have more than one grudge against the Turks. You're no Turk, anyway, by the looks of you." His slightly cruel mouth gave me a slightly vicious sneer and he walked by me as if I were no threat at all to his safety or his wallet. That, in point of fact, was the plain truth. I had just had my second run-in with the man who called himself James Bond. At the moment, we each had a score of one, out of a possible two; I was in no hurry at all to play the rubber match. He seemed to have learned a lot since our last meeting, or for some reason of his own he had allowed me to chuck him so easily out of Chiri's. I knew I was badly outclassed here.

As I walked slowly and painfully back to the Silver Palm, I came to an important decision: I was going to tell Papa that I wouldn't help him. It wasn't merely a matter of being afraid to have my brain wired; hell, even with it goosed from here to the Prophet's Birthday, I was no competition for these killers. I couldn't even follow James Bond down one goddamn block in my own neighborhood without getting my ass kicked around. I didn't have a single doubt that Bond could have dealt more harshly with me, if he'd chosen to. He thought I was just a robber, a common Arab thief, and he merely treated me the way he treated all common Arab thieves. It must have been a daily occurrence for him.

No, there was nothing that could persuade me otherwise. I didn't need the three days to think about it—Papa and his wonderful scheme could just go to hell.

I went back to the Silver Palm and threw down my drink in two great gulps. Over the protestations of Mahmoud and Jacques, I said that I had to be going. I kissed Heidi on the cheek and whispered a licentious suggestion in her ear, the same suggestion I always whispered; and she replied with the same amused rejection. I walked thoughtfully back to Frenchy's to explain to Yasmin that I was not going to be a hero, that I was not going to serve higher principles than kings and princes and all the rest of that foolishness. Yasmin would be disappointed in me, and I probably wouldn't get into her pants for a week; but that was better than getting my throat slashed and having my ashes strewn over the sewage treatment plant.

I would have a lot of explaining to do to everybody. I would have a lot of apologizing to do, too. Everyone from Selima to Chiri to Sergeant Hajjar to Friedlander Bey himself would be after my balls, but I had made my decision. I was my own man, and I wouldn't be pressured into accepting a terrifying fate, however morally right and public-spirited they all made it sound. The drink at the Silver Palm, the two at Frenchy's, a couple of tri-phets, four sunnies, and eight Paxium all agreed with me. Before I found my way back to Frenchy's, the night was warm and safe and wholly on my side, and everybody who was urging me to wire my brain was stuffed down deep in a dark pit into which I planned never again to peek. They could all jam each other silly, for all I cared. I had my own life to lead.

11

Friday was a day of rest and recuperation. My body had been bruised and beaten by a lot of people lately, some of whom had been friends and acquaintances, some of whom I was just chafing to catch in a dark alley real soon. One of the best things about the Budayeen is the prevalence of dark alleys. They were planned purposefully, I think. Somewhere in somebody's sacred scripture it says, "And there shall be caused to be built dark alleys wherein the mockers and the unrighteous shall in their turn have their heads laid open and in like wise their fat lips busted; and even this shall be pleasing in the sight of Heaven." I couldn't quote you exactly where that verse comes from. I might have dreamt it up early Friday morning.

The Black Widow Sisters had had first crack at me; various lackeys of Lutz Seipolt, Friedlander Bey, and Lieutenant Okking had caused me grief, as had their smugly smiling masters; and just last night I'd been briefly chastized by this James Bond lunatic. My pill case was now completely empty: nothing but pastel-colored dust on the bottom that I could lick from my fingertips, hoping for a milligram of help. The opiates were the first to go; my supply of Sonneine, bought from Chiriga and then Sergeant Hajjar, had been downed in rapid succession as each of my body's movements brought new twinges and spasms of pain. When the sunnies were gone I tried Paxium, the little lavender pills that some people believe is the ultimate gift of the organic chemical universe, the Answer to All of Life's Little Worries, but which I'm coming to the conclusion aren't worth their weight in jackal snot. I ate them anyway and washed them down with about six ounces of Jack Daniels that Yasmin brought home from work with her. Okay, that left the full-throttle blue triangles. I didn't really know what they'd do for pain, but I was certainly willing to use myself as a research volunteer. Science Marches On. I dropped three tri-phets, and the effect was fascinating from a pharmacological standpoint: in about half an hour, I began taking a tremendous interest in my heartbeat. I measured my pulse rate at something like four hundred and twenty-two per minute, but I kept getting distracted by phantom lizards crawling around just at the edges of my peripheral vision. I'm almost certain that my heart wasn't really pumping that hard.

Drugs are your friends, treat them with respect. You wouldn't throw your friends in the garbage. You wouldn't flush your friends down the toilet. If that's the way you treat your friends or your drugs, you don't deserve to have either. Give them to me. Drugs are wonderful things. I won't listen to anybody trying to get me to give them up. I'd rather give up food and drink—in fact, on occasion, I have.

The effect of all the pills was to make my mind wander. Actually, any sign of life on its part was heartening. Life was taking on a kind of bleak, pungent, really penetrating, and awfully *huge* quality that I didn't enjoy at all.

On top of that, I remembered that I'd collected a couple of caps of RPM from Saied the Half-Hajj. This is the same junk that Bill the taxi driver has coursing through his bloodstream all the time, *all* the time, at the cost of his immortal soul. I've got to remember not to ride with Bill anymore. Jesus, that stuff is just really scary, and the worst part was that I actually *paid* cash money for the privilege of feeling so lousy. Sometimes I'm disgusted by the things I do, and I make resolutions to clean myself out. I promised, when that RPM wore off, if it ever did . . .

Friday was the Sabbath, a day of rest except for everybody in the Budayeen who went right back to work as soon as the sun went down. We observed the holy month of Ramadân, but the city's cops and the mosque's bullies let up on us a little on Fridays. They were happy to get whatever cooperation they could. Yasmin went to work and I stayed in bed, reading a Simenon I think I had read when I was about fifteen and again when I was about twenty and again a couple of other times. It's hard to tell with Simenon. He wrote the same book a dozen times, but he had so many different books that he wrote a dozen times each that you have to read all of them and then sort them out in some kind of rational order according to a logical, thematic basis that's always been far beyond me. I just start at the back (if it's printed in Arabic) or the front (if it's printed in French) or the middle (if I'm in a hurry or too full of my friends, the drugs).

Simenon. Why was I talking about Simenon? It was going to lead to a vital and illuminating point. Simenon suggests Ian Fleming: they're both writers; they're both clawed out thrillers in their individual fashions; they're both dead; and neither one of them knew the first thing about making a good martini—Fleming's "shaken and not stirred," my holy whoring mother's ineffable left tit; and Ian Fleming leads neatly and directly to James Bond. The man with the Bond moddy never again left another 007 trace in the city, not so much as the stub of a Morlands Special with the gold rings around the filter or a chomped-on slice of lemon peel or a Beretta bullet hole. Yeah, it was the Beretta he'd used on Bogatyrev and Devi. The Beretta was Bond's choice of pistols in the early Fleming novels, until some hotshot reader pointed out that it was a "lady's gun" with no stopping power; so Fleming had Bond switch to the Walther PPK, a smallish but reliable automatic. If our James Bond had used the Walther, it would have left a messier indentation in Devi's face; the Beretta made a rather tidier little hole, like the pop-top slot in a can of beer. That slapping-around I got from him was the last anyone saw or heard of James Bond in the city. He had a low tolerance for boredom, I guess.

That's another first-rate reason for getting to know your medicines and correctives. Boredom can be tedious, but not when you're counting your pulse at over four hundred a minute. By the life of my beard and the sacred shifting balls of the Apostle of God, may the blessings of Allah be on him and peace, I really just wanted to go to sleep! Every time I closed my eyes, though, a black-and-white strobe effect started flashing, and purple and green things swam by, gigantic things. I cried, but they wouldn't leave me alone. I couldn't see how Bill could drive his taxi through them all.

So that was Friday, in brief summary. Yasmin came home with the Jack Daniels, I killed the rest of my drug supply, passed out sometime near noon, and awoke to find Yasmin gone. It was now Saturday. I had two more days to enjoy my brain.

Early Saturday evening, I noticed my money seemed to have vaporized. I should have had a few hundred kiam left; I'd spent a little, of course, and I'd probably blown even more that I couldn't account for. Yet I had the feeling that I ought to have more than the ninety kiam I found in my shoulder bag. Ninety kiam wasn't going to get me much of anything; a new pair of jeans was going to cost me forty or more.

I began to suspect that Yasmin had been dipping into my finances. I hate that about women, even the ones whose genetic threads in their cells still said they were male. Jo-Mama says, "Just 'cause the cat had her kittens in the oven don't make them biscuits." Take a pretty boy, nip off his *couilles* and buy him a silicone balcony that could comfortably seat an underfed family of three, and before you know it, she's digging around in your wallet. They eat up all your pills and caps, spend your money, bitch about the goddamn sheet and the blanket, stare rapturously all afternoon at themselves in the bathroom mirror, make innocent little remarks about the devastating young plushes passing by in the other direction, want to be held for an hour after you've exhausted yourself jamming them into the floorboards, and then they climb up your back because you look out the window with a slightly irked expression on your face. What could you possibly be annoyed about, with a virtually perfect goddess hanging around the apartment, decorating your floor with her dirty underwear? You might take something to elevate your mood, but the precious bitch already consumed all that, remember?

Only another day and a half of Marîd Audran's brain as Allah the Protector in His wisdom had designed it. Yasmin was not speaking to me: she thought I was a coward and a

selfish son of a clapped-up ass for not going along with
Papa's plan. One minute, it was all set—on Monday morning, I was going to meet with Friedlander Bey's surgeons
and have my thoughts electrified. The next minute, I was
a rotten bastard who didn't care what happened to his
friends. She couldn't remember if I was going to get my
brain wired or not; she couldn't think back far enough to
recall the last argument (*I* could: I was *not* going to get my
brain wired, and that was the end of it). I didn't get out of
bed all day Friday or Saturday. I watched shadows get
longer and shorter and longer. I heard the muezzin call
the faithful to prayer; and then, what seemed to me like a
few minutes later, he called again. I stopped paying attention to Yasmin and her moods sometime on Saturday
evening, before she started to get ready for work.

She slammed her way back and forth across my room,
calling me all kinds of innovative foul names, some of
which I'd actually never heard before, despite my years of
wandering. It just made me love the little slut even more.
I didn't get out of bed until Yasmin left for Frenchy's. My
body alternated between rattling chills and flashes of fever
so bad I had to cool off in the shower. Then I'd lie back in
bed and shiver and sweat. I soaked the sheets and the
mattress cover, and clung with white-knuckled fingers to
the blanket. The phantom lizards were on my face and
arms now, but crawling around less frequently. I felt safe
enough to go to the bathroom again, something I'd been
thinking about for a long while. I wasn't hungry, but I was
getting pretty thirsty. I drank a couple of glasses of water,
then slid shakily back into bed. I wished Yasmin would
come home.

Despite the waning effects of the drug overdose and my
growing fear, I had made up my mind about Monday
morning. Saturday night passed with more cold sweats
and remittent fever, and I stared wakefully at the ceiling,
even after Yasmin came back and went drunkenly to sleep.
Sunday, just before sunset, while she was getting herself
ready to go to work again, I got out of bed and stood
naked behind her. She was putting on her eye makeup,
screwing her face into crazy expressions and glossing her
eyelids with loveliness from some rich-bitch department

store beyond the Budayeen. She wouldn't use inexpensive paint from the bazaars like everyone else, as if anyone in Frenchy's could get a good look at her in that dimness. The same makeup was on the racks in the souks, but Yasmin paid top prices for it across town. She wanted to look heartbreaking on stage, when not a juiced-up fool in the place would be looking at her *eyes*. She was going for a layered effect of blue and green below her narrow, sketched-in eyebrows. Then she worked on a tasteful sprinkle of gold glittery sparkles. The sparkles were the hard part. She put them on one by one. "Get to bed early," she said.

"Why?" I asked innocently.

"Because you have a busy day tomorrow," she said.

I shrugged.

"Your brain," she said, "remember?"

"My brain, I remember," I said. "It's not going anywhere unusual. I don't have anything particularly taxing lined up for it."

"You're getting the worthless thing wired!" She turned on me like a nesting falcon on a hawk.

"Not the last time I thought it over," I said.

She grabbed up her small blue overnight case. "Well, you son-of-a-bitching mother-ugly *kaffir*," she cried, "fuck you *and* the horse you rode in on!" She made more noise leaving my apartment than I thought was possible, and that was before she even slammed the door. After she slammed the door it got very quiet, and I was able to think. I couldn't think of anything to think about, though. I walked around the room a few times, put one or two things away, kicked some of my clothes from the right to the left and back again, and laid down on the bed. I'd been in the bed so long that it wasn't diverting to be there again now, but there wasn't that much else to do. I watched the darkness in the room stretch and reach out toward me. That wasn't so exciting anymore, either.

The pain had gone, the overdose-induced hysteria had gone, my money had gone, Yasmin had gone. This was peace and contentment. I hated every goddamn second of it.

In this silent center of motionless and mindlessness, free

of all the frenzy that had surrounded me for many days, I surprised myself with a piece of genuine intuition. It began by congratulating myself for figuring that the man with the James Bond moddy had a Beretta rather than a Walther. Then the Bond thought linked up to something else, and they hooked together with one or two more ideas, and it all illuminated an inexplicable detail that had been simmering in my memory for a couple of days, at least. I recalled my last visit to Lieutenant Okking. I remembered the way he didn't seem to be at all interested in my theories or Friedlander Bey's proposition. That wasn't so unusual; Okking resisted interference from anyone. He disliked positive interference, in the form of authentic assistance, just as much. It wasn't Okking himself to whom my thoughts kept returning; it was something in his office.

One of the envelopes had been addressed to Universal Export. I recalled wondering idly if Seipolt ran that firm, or if Hassan the Shiite ever received any curious crates from them. The company's name was so commonplace that there were probably a thousand "Universal Exports" all around the world. Maybe Okking was just sending off a mail order for some rattan patio furniture to put next to his backyard barbecue.

Of course, the very ordinariness of "Universal Export" was the reason that M., the head of James Bond's special 00 section, used it as a false cover and code name in Ian Fleming's books. The forgettable name would never have stuck in my memory without that connection to the Bond stories. Maybe "Universal Export" was a disguised reference to the man who'd worn the James Bond moddy. I wished that I had memorized the address on that envelope.

I sat up, startled. If the Bond explanation had any truth to it, why was that envelope in Lieutenant Okking's *Out* box? I told myself that I was getting as jumpy as a grasshopper on a griddle. I was probably looking for honey where there were no bees. Still, I felt my stomach turn sick again. I felt myself being drawn unwillingly into a morass of tortuous and deadly paths.

It was time for action. I had spent Friday, Saturday, and most of Sunday paralyzed between my worn and grimy sheets. It was the moment to get moving, to leave the apartment, to rid myself of this clinging morbidity and fear. I had ninety kiam; I could buy myself some buta-qualides and get some decent sleep.

I threw on my *gallebeya*, which was getting a little on the soiled side, my sandals, and my *libdeh*, the close-fitting cap. I grabbed my shoulder bag on the way out the door, and hurried downstairs. Suddenly I really wanted to score some beauties; I mean, I *really* wanted them. I'd just gotten over three horrible days of sweating too much of everything out of my system, and already I was rushing out to buy more. I made a mental note to slow down my drug intake; crumpled the mental note; and tossed it into my mental wastebasket.

Beauties, it seemed, were scarce. Chiriga didn't have any, but she gave me a free drink of tende while she told me about how much trouble she was having with a new girl working for her, and that she was still saving her Honey Pílar moddy for me. I remembered the holoporn ad outside old Laila's shop. "Chiri," I said, "I'm just getting over the flu or something; but I promise, we'll go have dinner some night next week. Then, *inshallah*, we'll burn your moddy out."

She didn't even smile. She looked at me as if she were watching a wounded fish flopping in the water. "Marîd, honey," she said sadly, "now really, listen to me: you got to cut out all these pills. You're wrecking yourself."

She was right, but you don't ever want to hear that kind of advice from anybody else. I nodded, gulped the rest of the tende, and left her club without saying good-bye.

I caught up with Jacques, Mahmoud, and Saied at Big Al's Old Chicago. They said they were all tapped out, financially and medicinally. I said, "Fine, see you around."

"Marîd," said Jacques, "maybe it's none of my—"

"It's not," I said. I passed by the Silver Palm: no action there, either. I passed by Hassan's shop, but he wasn't in the back and his American chicken just gazed at me with sultry eyes. I ducked into the Red Light—that's how desperate I was beginning to feel—and Fatima told me that one of the white girls' boyfriends had a whole suitcase full of different stuff, but that he wouldn't be in until maybe five in the morning. I said that if nothing else turned up by then, I'd come back. No free drink from Fatima.

Finally, at Jo-Mama's Hellenic hideaway, I ran into a little luck. I bought six beauties from Jo-Mama's second barmaid, Rocky, another hefty woman with short, brushy black hair. Rocky stung me a little on the price, but at that point I didn't care. She offered me a beer on the house to wash them down, but I told her I was just going to go home and take them and climb back into bed.

"Yeah, you right," said Jo-Mama, "you got to get to sleep early. You got to get up in the morning, dawlin', and have your skull drilled."

I shut my eyes briefly and sighed. "Where did you hear about that?" I asked her.

Jo-Mama pasted a slightly offended, wholly innocent look on her face. *"Everybody's* been knowin' it, Marîd. Ain't that the truth, Rocky? It's what everybody's been having trouble believing. I mean, *you* getting your brain wired. F'sure, the next thing we be hearing, Hassan'll be giving away free rugs or rifles or handjobs to the first twenty callers."

"I'll take that beer," I said, very tired. Rocky drew one; for a moment nobody knew if this was the free beer or if I'd turned that one down and this was another one that I had to pay for.

"It's on me," said Jo-Mama.

"Thanks, Mama," I said. "I'm not getting my brain wired." I took a big gulp of the beer. "I don't care *who* told *who,* I don't care who *they* heard it from. This is me, Marîd, talking: I am *not* getting my brain wired. *Comprendez?"*

Jo-Mama shrugged like she didn't believe me; after all, what was *my* word against the word of the Street? "I got to tell you what happened in here last night," she said, about to launch into one of her endless but entertaining stories. I half-wanted to hear it because I had to keep up with the news, but I was rescued.

"There you are!" shouted Yasmin, banging into the bar and whacking a vicious swipe at me with her purse. I ducked my head, but she cracked me in the side.

"What the hell—" I started to say.

"Take it outside," said Jo-Mama automatically. She looked as astonished as I felt.

Yasmin wasn't in the mood to listen to either of us. She grabbed me around the wrist—her hand was as strong as mine, and my wrist was *grabbed*. "You come with me, you cocksucker," she said.

"Yasmin, shut the fuck up and leave me alone," I said. Jo-Mama got off her stool; that ought to have been a warning, but Yasmin paid her no attention. She still had my wrist, and her fingers closed even tighter. She yanked on my arm.

"You're going to come with me," she said in an ominous voice, "because I got something pretty to show you, you goddamn yellow-bellied pussy."

I was really angry; I'd never been this angry with Yasmin before, and I still didn't know what she was talking about. "Slap her face for her," said Rocky from behind the bar. That always works in the holoshows for excitable heroines and panicking junior officers; I didn't think, though, that it would quiet Yasmin down. She'd probably just beat the living hell out of me, and then we'd go do whatever she wanted in the first place. I raised the arm she was still clutching, turned it outward a little, broke her grasp, and grabbed *her* wrist. Then I twisted her arm and forced it up behind her back in a tight hammerlock. She cried out in pain. I pushed her arm further, and she yelped again.

"That's for calling me those names," I said, growling softly, close to her ear. "You can do that at home if you want, but not in front of my friends."

"You want me to hurt you bad?" she said angrily.

"You can try."

"Later," she said. "I still got something to show you."

I let go of her arm, and she rubbed it for a moment. Then she snatched up her purse and kicked open Jo-Mama's door. I raised my eyebrows at Rocky; Jo-Mama was giving me an amused little smile, because all of this would eventually make a better story than the one she never got to tell me. Jo-Mama, at least, was going to come out ahead.

I followed Yasmin outside. She turned to me; before she could say a word, I put my right hand tightly around her throat and flung her up against an ancient brick wall. I didn't care how much I hurt her. "You're *never* going to do that again," I said in a dangerously calm voice. "You understand me?" And just for the pure sadistic pleasure of it, I knocked her head roughly against the bricks.

"*Fuck you,* asshole!"

"Anytime you think you're man enough, you mutilated, gelded son of a bitch," I said. And then Yasmin started to cry. I felt myself collapse inside. I felt I had done the worst thing I could ever do, and there was no way I could make up for it. I might crawl on my knees all the way to Mecca to pray for forgiveness, and Allah would forgive me, but Yasmin wouldn't. I would have given anything I had, anything I could steal, if the last few minutes hadn't happened; but they had, and they would be difficult for either of us to forget.

"Marîd," she whispered between sobs. I held her. Right then, there wasn't a damn thing in the world to say. We clasped each other that way, close together, Yasmin weeping, me wanting to but unable, for five or ten or fifteen minutes. A few people passed by on the sidewalk and pretended they didn't see us. Jo-Mama stuck her head out of the door and ducked back inside. A moment later, Rocky looked out as if she were just casually counting the crowd that didn't exist on this dark street. I wasn't thinking anything, I wasn't feeling anything. I just clung to Yasmin, and she clung to me.

"I love you," I murmured at last. When you find the appropriate time, it's always the best and only thing to say.

She took my hand and we started walking slowly toward the back of the Budayeen. I thought we were just wandering, but after a few minutes I realized that Yasmin was leading me somewhere. The grim certainty grew in me that I didn't want to see what she was going to show me.

A body had been stuffed into a large plastic trash bag, but someone had disturbed the pile of bags; Nikki's bag had split open, and she lay sprawled on the damp, filthy bricks of a tight blind alley. "I thought it was your fault she was dead," said Yasmin with a little whimper. "Because you didn't do very much to try and find her." I held Yasmin's hand and we just stood there for a while, staring down at Nikki's corpse, not saying anything more for a while. I *knew* that I'd see Nikki like this sometime, finally. I think I knew it from the beginning, when Tamiko had been murdered and Nikki made that short, frantic phone call.

I let go of Yasmin's hand and knelt down beside Nikki. There was a lot of blood all over her, in the dark green trash bag, on the moss-covered bricks of the pavement. "Yasmin, baby," I said, looking up into her bleak face, "you don't want to see this anymore. Why don't you call Okking, then go home? I'll be there in a little while."

Yasmin made a vague, meaningless gesture. "I'll call Okking," she said in a toneless voice, "but I got to go back to work."

"Frenchy can go fuck himself tonight," I said. "I want you to go home. Listen, honey, I *need* to have you there."

"All right" she said, smiling a little through the tears. Our relationship hadn't been destroyed, after all. With a little care it would be just as good as new, maybe even better. It was a relief to feel hopeful again.

"How did you know she was here?" I asked, frowning.

"Blanca found her," said Yasmin. "Her back door's down there, and she passes by here on her way to work." She pointed further up the alley, where a peeling, gray-painted door was set into the blank brick wall.

I nodded and watched Yasmin walk slowly toward the Street. Then I turned back to Nikki's ruined body. It had been the throat-slasher, and I could see the bruises on Nikki's wrists and neck, the burn marks, and a lot of small cuts and wounds. The killer had invested more time and expertise in finishing Nikki than he had with Tami or Abdoulaye. I was sure the medical examiner would find the traces of rape, too.

Nikki's clothing and purse had been thrown into the trash bag with her. I looked through her clothes, but I didn't find anything. I reached for the purse, but I had to lift Nikki's head. She had been clubbed cruelly and savagely until her skull and hair and blood and brains were all crushed together into a repellent mass. Her throat had been cut so brutally that her head was almost severed. I had never seen such profane, desecrating, perverse savagery in my life. I cleared the strewn refuse from a space and rested Nikki's corpse gently on the broken bricks. Then I walked away a few steps, knelt, and vomited. I heaved and retched until my stomach muscles began to ache. When the sickness passed, I made myself go back to look through her purse. I found two curious and noteworthy objects: a brass reproduction that I'd seen in Seipolt's house of an ancient Egyptian scarab; and a crude, almost homemade-looking moddy. I put both in my shoulder bag, chose the trash bag with the least stench surrounding it, and made myself as comfortable as I could. I addressed a prayer to Allah on behalf of Nikki's soul. Then I waited.

"Well," I said quietly, looking around at the squalid, mucky place where Nikki had been abandoned, "I guess I get up in the morning and get my brain wired." *Maktoob,* all right: It was written.

12

Muslims are often, by nature, very superstitious. Our co-travelers through Allah's bewildering creation include all sorts of *djinn, afrit,* monsters, and good and bad angels. Then there are legions of sorcerous people armed with dangerous powers, the evil eye being the most frequently encountered. All of this makes the Muslim culture no more irrational than any other; every group of people has its own set of unfriendly, unseen things waiting to pounce on the unwary human being. Commonly there are far more enemies in the spirit world than there are protectors, although there are supposed to be uncountable armies of angels and the like. Maybe they've all been on R&R since the deparadisation of Shaitan, I don't know.

Anyway, one of the superstitious practices clung to by some Muslims, particularly the nomadic tribes and the uncivilized *fellahîn* of the Maghrîb—i.e., my mother's people—is to name a newborn with an affliction or a dreadful quality to ward off the envy of whatever spirit or witch might be paying too much attention. I'm told that this is done all over the world by people who have never even heard of the prophet, may peace be on his name. I am called Marîd, which means "illness," and I was given it in the hope that I would not, in fact, suffer much illness in my lifetime. The charm seems to have had a certain positive effect. I had a burst appendix removed a few years ago, but that's a common, routine operation, and it is the only serious medical problem I've ever had. I guess that may be due to the improved treatments available in this age of wonders, but who can say? Praise Allah, and all that.

So I haven't had much experience with hospitals. When the voices woke me, it took me quite some time to figure out where I was, and then another while to recall why the hell I was there in the first place. I opened my eyes; I couldn't see anything but a dim blur. I blinked again and again, but it was like someone had tried to paste my eyelids closed with sand and honey. I tried to raise my hand to rub my eyes, but my arm was too weak; it wouldn't travel the negligible distance from my chest to my face. I blinked some more and squinted. Finally I could make out two male nurses standing near the foot of my bed. One was young, with a black beard and a clear voice. He held a chart and was briefing the other man. "Mr. Audran shouldn't give you too much trouble," he said.

The second man was a good deal older, with gray hair and a hoarse voice. He nodded. "Meds?" he asked.

The younger man frowned. "It's unusual. He can have almost anything he wants, with approval from his doctors. The way I understand it, he'll get that approval just by asking. As much and as often as he wants."

The gray-haired man let out an indignant breath. "What did he do, win a contest? An all-expense-paid drug holiday in the hospital of his choice?"

"Lower your voice, Ali. He isn't moving, but he may be able to hear you. I don't know who he is, but the hospital has been treating him like a foreign dignitary or something. What's being spent to ablate every little twinge of his discomfort could relieve the pain of a dozen suffering poor people on the charity wards."

Naturally, that made me feel like a filthy pig. I mean, *I* have feelings, too. I didn't ask for this kind of treatment—I didn't remember asking for it, at least—and I planned to put an end to it as soon as I could. Well, if not an *end* to it, that is, maybe ease it off a little. I didn't want to be handled like a feudal shaykh.

The younger man went on, consulting his chart. "Mr. Audran was admitted for some elective intracranial work. Elaborate circuit implants, very experimental, I understand. That's why he's been on bed rest this long. There may be some unforeseen side effects." That made me a little uneasy: *what* side effects? Nobody had ever mentioned them to me before.

"I'll take a look at his chart this evening," said the gray-haired man.

"He sleeps most of the time, he shouldn't bother you too much. Merciful Allah, between the etorphin bubble and the injections, he should sleep for the next ten or fifteen years." Of course, he was underestimating my wonderfully efficient liver and enzyme system. Everyone always thinks I'm exaggerating about that.

They began to leave the room. The older man opened the door and stepped out. I tried to speak; nothing came out, as if I hadn't used my voice for months. I tried again. There was a whispered croaking sound. I swallowed a little saliva and murmured, "Nurse."

The man with the black beard put my chart on the console beside my bed and turned to me, his expression blank. "Be right with you, Mr. Audran," he said in a cool voice. Then he went out and shut the door behind him.

The room was clean and plain and almost bare of decoration, but it was also comfortable. It was much more comfortable than the charity wards, where I had been treated after my appendix burst. That had been an unpleasant time; the only bright spots were the saving of my life, all thanks be to Allah, and my introduction to Sonneine, once again may Allah be praised. The charity wards were not wholly philanthropic—I mean, the *fellahîn* who could not afford private doctors were, indeed, given free medical attention; but the hospital's principle motive was to provide a wide range of unusual problems for the interns, residents, and student nurses to practice upon. Everyone who examined you, everyone who performed some sort of test, everyone who did some minor surgery at your bedside, had only a modest familiarity with his job. These people were earnest and sincere, but inexperienced: they could make the simple taking of blood an ordeal, and a more painful procedure a hellish torture. It was not so in this private room. I had comfort and ease and freedom from pain. I had peace and rest and competent care.

Friedlander Bey was giving this to me, but I would repay him. He would see to that.

I suppose that I dozed off for a little while, because when the door opened again I awoke with a start. I expected to see the nurse, but it was a young man in a green surgical outfit. He had dark, sunburnt skin and bright brown eyes, with one of the largest black mustaches I've ever seen. I imagined him trying to contain the thing within a surgical mask, and that made me smile. My doctor was a Turk. I had a little trouble understanding his Arabic. He had trouble understanding me, too.

"How are we today?" he said without looking at me. He glanced through the nurse's notes and then turned to the data terminal beside my bed. He touched a few keys, and displays changed on the terminal's screen. He made no sounds at all, neither the doctor's concerned clucking nor the encouraged humming. He stared at the scrolling parade of numbers and twirled the ends of his mustache. At last he faced me and said, "How are you feeling?"

"Fine," I said noncommittally. When I deal with doctors I always figure that they're after certain specific information; but they won't ever come out and ask you just what they need to know because they're afraid you'll distort the truth and give them what you think they *want* to hear, so they go about it in this circular way as if you're not still trying to guess what they want to know and distorting the truth anyway.

"Any pain?"

"A little," I said. It was a lie: I was drifted to the hairline—my former hairline, that is. You never tell a doctor that you're not suffering, because that might encourage him to lower your dosage of anodynes.

"Sleeping?"

"Yes."

"Had anything to eat?"

I thought for a moment. I was ravenously hungry, although the IV was dripping a glucose solution directly into the back of my hand. "No," I said.

"We might start you on some clear liquids in the morning. Been out of bed?"

"No."

"Good. Stay there for another couple of days. Dizzy? Numbness in your hands or feet? Nausea? Unusual sensations, bright lights, hearing voices, phantom limbs, anything like that?"

Phantom limbs? "No." I wouldn't tell him that if it *was* true.

"You're doing just fine, Mr. Audran. Coming along right on schedule."

"Allah be thanked. How long have I been here."

The doctor gave me a glance, then looked at my chart again. "A little over two weeks," he said.

"When did I have the surgery?"

"Fifteen days ago. You were in the hospital for two days of preparation before that."

"Uh huh." There was less than a week of Ramadân remaining. I wondered what had happened in the city during my absence. I certainly hoped a few of my friends and associates were left alive. If anyone had been hurt—killed, that is—it would be Papa who would have to bear the responsibility. That was just about as effective as blaming it on God, and as practical, too. You couldn't get a lawyer to sue either of them.

"Tell me, Mr. Audran, what is the last thing you remember?"

That was a tough one. I thought for a few moments; it was like diving into a dark, stormy cloudbank: there was nothing there but a grim feeling of foreboding down below. I had vague impressions of stern voices and the memory of hands rolling me over on the bed, and bolts of blazing pain. I remembered someone saying "Don't pull on that," but I didn't know who had said it or what it meant. I searched further and realized that I couldn't remember going into surgery or even leaving my apartment and coming to the hospital. The very last thing I could see clearly was . . .

Nikki. "My friend," I said, my mouth suddenly dry and my throat tight.

"The one who was murdered," said the doctor.

"Yes."

"That happened almost three weeks ago. You don't remember anything since?"

"No. Nothing."

"Then you don't recall meeting me before today? Our conversations?"

The dark cloudwall was rushing up to blot me out, and I figured now was a good time for it, too. I hated these gaps in my consciousness. They're a nuisance, even the little twelve-hour holes; a three-week slice missing from my mental pie was more trouble than I wanted to deal with. I just didn't have the energy to work up a decent panic. "I'm sorry," I said, "I just don't remember."

The doctor nodded. "My name is Dr. Yeniknani. I assisted your surgeon, Dr. Lisân. In the last several days you've gradually recovered some self-awareness. If, however, you've lost the content of our talks, it is very important that we discuss that information again."

I just wanted to go back to sleep. I rubbed my eyes with a weary hand. "And if you do explain it all to me again, I'll probably forget it and you'll just have to do it all over tomorrow or the next day."

Dr. Yeniknani shrugged. "That is possibly so, but you have nothing else to occupy your time, and I am paid well enough that I am more than willing to do what must be done." He gave me a broad smile to let me know he was joking—these fierce types have to do that or you'd never guess; the doctor looked like he ought to be shouldering a rifle in some mountain ambush rather than wielding clipboards and tongue depressors, but that's just my shallow mind making stereotypes. It keeps me amused. The doctor showed me his huge, crooked, yellow teeth again and said, "Besides, I have an overwhelming love for mankind. It is the will of Allah that I should begin to end all human suffering by having this same uninteresting interview with you each day until you at last remember it. It is for us to do these things; it is for Allah to understand them." He shrugged again. He was very expressive, for a Turk.

I blessed the name of God and waited for Dr. Yeniknani to launch into his bedside manner.

"Have you looked at yourself?" he asked.

"No, not yet." I'm never in a hurry to see my body after it's been offended in any serious way. I do not find wounds particularly fascinating, especially when they are my own.

When I had my appendix taken out, I couldn't look at myself below the navel for a month. Now, with my brain newly wired and my head shaved, I didn't want to look in a mirror; that would make me think about what had been done, and why, and where all this might lead. If I were careful and clever, I might stay in that hospital bed, pleasantly sedated, for months or even years. It didn't sound like so terrible a fate. Being a numb vegetable was preferable to being a numb corpse. I wondered how long I could malinger here before I was rudely dumped back on the Street. I was in no hurry, that's for sure.

Dr. Yeniknani nodded absently. "Your . . . *patron*," he said, choosing the word judiciously, "your patron specified that you were to be given the most comprehensive intracranial reticulation possible. That is why Dr. Lisân performed the surgery himself: Dr. Lisân is the finest neurosurgeon in the city, one of the most respected in the world. Quite a lot of what he has given you he invented or refined himself, and in your case Dr. Lisân has tried one or two new procedures that might be called . . . experimental."

That didn't soothe me, I didn't care how great a surgeon Dr. Lisân might be. I am of the "better safe than sorry" school. I could be just as happy with a brain lacking one or two "experimental" talents, but one that didn't run the risk of turning to tahini if I concentrated too long. But what the hell. I grinned a crooked, devil-may-care grin and realized that poking hot wires into unknown corners of my brain to see what happened was not much worse than gunning around the city in the back of Bill's taxi. Maybe I did have some kind of death wish, after all. Or some kind of plain stupidity.

The doctor raised the lid of the tray-table beside my bed; there was a mirror under there, and he rolled the table so that I could see my reflection. I looked awful. I looked like I'd died and started off toward hell and then got lost, and now I was stuck nowhere at all, definitely not alive but not decently deceased, either. My beard was neatly trimmed, and I had shaved every day or someone had done it for me; but my skin was pale, an unhealthy color like smudged newsprint, and there were deep shadows under my eyes. I stared into the mirror for a long moment before I even noticed that my head was indeed bald, just a fine growth of fuzz covering my scalp like lichen clinging to a senseless stone. The implanted plug was invisible, hidden beneath protective layers of gelstrip bandages. I raised a tentative hand as if to touch the crown of my head, but I couldn't bring myself to do it. I felt a strange, unpleasant tingling shoot up through my bowels, and I shuddered. My hand fell away and I looked at the doctor.

"When we take the gelstrips off," he said, "you'll notice that you have two plugs, one anterior and the second plug posterior."

"Two?" I'd never heard of anyone with two plugs before.

"Yes. Dr. Lisân has given you twice the augmentation of a conventional corymbic implantation."

That much capacity hooked into my brain was like putting a rocket engine on an oxcart; it would never fly. I closed my eyes feeling more than a little frightened. I started murmuring Al-Fâtihah, the first sûrah of the noble Qur'ân, a comforting prayer that always comes to me at times like this. It is the Islamic equivalent of the Christian Lord's Prayer. Then I opened my eyes and stared at my reflection. I was still afraid, but at least I had made my uncertainty known in heaven, and from here on I'd just accept everything as the will of Allah. "Does that mean I can chip in two different moddies at the same time, and be two people at once?"

Dr. Yeniknani frowned. "No, Mr. Audran, the second plug will accept only software add-ons, not a full personality module. You wouldn't want to try two modules at once. You might end up with a pair of charred cerebral hemispheres and a backbrain that would be completely useless except as a paperweight. We have given you the augmentation as—" (he almost committed an indiscretion and mentioned a name) "your patron directed. A therapist will instruct you in the proper use of your corymbic implants. How you choose to employ them after you leave the hospital is, of course, your own affair. Just remember that you're dealing directly with your central nervous system now. It isn't a matter of taking a few pills and staggering around for a while until you recover your sobriety. If you do something ill-advised with your implants, it may well have permanent effects. Permanent, frightening effects."

Okay, he had me sold. I did what Papa and everybody else wanted: my brain was wired. Good old Dr. Yeniknani had put the fear into me, though, and I told myself right there in the hospital bed that I'd never promised that I'd *use* the damn thing. I'd get out of the hospital as soon as I could, go home, forget about the implants, and go about my business as usual. It would be a cold day in Jiddah before *I* chipped in. Let the plugs sit there for decoration. When it came to Marîd Audran's subskullular amplification, pal, the batteries had definitely not been included, and I intended to leave it that way. Zinging my little gray cells with chemicals now and then didn't incapacitate them permanently, but I wasn't going to sizzle them in any electric frying pan. Only so far can I be pushed, and then my inborn perversity asserts itself.

"So," said Dr. Yeniknani more encouragingly, "with that mandatory warning out of the way, I suppose you're looking forward to hearing about what your improved mind and body are capable of doing for you."

"You bet," I said, without enthusiasm.

"What do you know about the activities of the brain and the nervous system?"

I laughed. "About as much as any hustler from the Budayeen who can barely read and write his name. I know that the brain is in the head, I've heard that it's a bad idea to let some thug spill it on the sidewalk. Beyond that, I don't know much." I did, truthfully, know some more, but I always hold something in reserve. It's a good policy to be a little quicker, a little stronger, and a little smarter than everybody thinks you are.

"Well, then, the posterior corymbic implant is completely conventional. It will enable you to chip in a personality module. You know that the medical profession is not unanimous in its sanction of these modules. Some of our colleagues feel that the potential for abuse far outweighs the benefits. Those benefits, actually, were very limited at first; the modules were produced on a limited basis as therapeutic aids for patients with certain severe neurological disturbances. However, the modules have been taken over by the popular media and are used for purposes grossly different from those their inventors originally intended." He shrugged again. "It's too late to do anything about that now, and those few who are outraged and would prohibit the modules' use can barely get an audience for their views. So you will have access to the entire range of personality modules for sale to the public, modules that are extremely serviceable and can save a good deal of drudgery as well as those that many people might find offensive." I thought immediately of Honey Pílar. "You can walk into any shop and become Salâh ad-Dîn, a genuine hero, the great sultan who drove out the Crusaders; or become the mythical Sultan Shahryar, and entertain yourself with the beautiful storyteller and the entire *Thousand Nights and a Night.* Your posterior implant can also accommodate up to six software add-ons."

"That's just the same kind of implant all my friends have," I said. "What about the experimental advantages you mentioned? How dangerous will they be to chip in?"

The doctor smiled briefly. "That's difficult to say, Mr. Audran; they are, after all, experimental. They've been tested on many animal subjects and just a few human volunteers. The results have been satisfactory, but not unanimously. A lot will depend on you, if Allah pleases. Let me explain by first describing the sort of controls we're talking about. Personality modules alter your consciousness, and make you believe temporarily that you are someone else. The add-ons feed directly into your short-term memory, and give you an instant knowledge of any subject; that vanishes when you remove the chip. The add-ons you can use with the anterior implant affect several other, more specialized diencephalic structures." He took a black felt-tip pen and sketched a rough map of the brain. "First, we have inserted an extremely thin silver, plastic-sheathed wire into your thalamus. The wire is less than a thousandth of an inch in diameter, too delicate to be manipulated by hand. This wire will connect your reticular system to a unique add-on we will provide you; it will enable you to damp out the neural network that catalogs sensory detail. If, for instance, it is vital for you to concentrate, you may choose to block out disturbing visual, audible, tactile, and other signals."

I raised my eyebrows. "I can see how that may come in handy," I said.

Dr. Yeniknani smiled. "It is only a tenth part of what we have given you—there are other wires, to other areas. Near the thalamus, in the center of your brain, is the hypothalamus. This organ is small, but it has many varied and vital functions. You will be able to control, augment, or override most of them. For example, you may decide to ignore hunger, if you wish; using the proper add-on, you will feel no hunger at all, however long you fast. You will have the same control over thirst and the sensation of pain. You may consciously regulate your body temperature, blood pressure, and the state of sexual arousal. Perhaps most usefully, you will be able to suppress fatigue."

I just sat and looked at him, wide-eyed, as if he had unwrapped for me a fabulous treasure or a real wishing-lamp. But Dr. Yeniknani was no enslaved *djinn*. What he offered was not magic, but as far as I was concerned it might as well have been: I didn't even know if I entirely believed him, except that I tended to believe fierce Turks in positions of authority. I humor them, at least, so I let him continue.

"You will find it simpler to learn new skills and information. Of course, you will have electronic add-ons to feed these things into your short-term memory; but if you want to transfer them permanently to your long-term memory, your hippocampus and other associated areas have been circuited for this. If you need to, you may alter your circadian and lunar clocks. You'll be able to fall asleep when you wish, and awaken automatically according to the chips you're using. The circuit to your pituitary will give you indirect control over your other endocrines, such as your thyroid and adrenal glands. Your therapist will go into more detail about just how you can take advantage of these functions. As you see, you may devote total attention to your tasks, without needing to interrupt them quite so often for the normal bodily necessities. Now, of course, one can't go indefinitely without sleep or taking in water or emptying one's bladder; but if you choose, you may dismiss the insistent and increasingly unpleasant warning signs."

"My patron doesn't want me distracted," I said dryly.

Dr. Yeniknani sighed. "No, he doesn't. Not by anything."

"Is there anything more?"

He chewed his lip for a moment. "Yes, but your therapist will cover all of it, and we'll give you the usual brochures and booklets. I may say that you'll be able to control your limbic system, which influences your emotions. That is one of Dr. Lisân's new developments."

"I'll be able to choose my feelings? Like I was choosing what clothes to wear?"

"To some extent. Also, in wiring these areas of the brain, we were often able to affect more than one function at one location. For instance, as a positive bonus, your system will be able to burn alcohol more efficiently, quicker than the standard ounce an hour. If you choose." He gave me a brief, knowing look, because of course a good Muslim does not drink alcohol; he must have been aware that I wasn't the most devout person in the city. Yet the subject was still a delicate one between two relative strangers.

"My patron will be pleased by that, too, I'm sure. Fine. I can't wait. I'll be a force for good among the unrighteous and corrupt."

"Inshallah," said the doctor. "As God wills."

"Praise Allah," I said, humbled by his honest faith.

"There is still one thing more, and then I wish to give you a personal word, a little of my own philosophy. The first thing is that as you must know, the brain—the hypothalamus, actually—has a pleasure center that can be electrically stimulated."

I took a deep breath. "Yes, I've heard about that. The effect is supposed to be absolutely overwhelming."

"Animals and people who have leads into that area and are permitted to stimulate the pleasure center often forget everything else—food, water, every other need and drive. They may continue exciting the pleasure center to the point of death." His eyes narrowed. *"Your* pleasure center has not been wired. Your patron felt it would have been too great a temptation for you, and you have more to accomplish than spending the rest of your life in some dream heaven."

I didn't know if I felt glad about that news or not. I didn't want to waste away as the result of some never-ending mental orgasm; but if the choice was between that or going up against two savage, mad assassins, I think, in a moment of weakness, I might pick exquisite pleasure that didn't fade or pall. It might take a little getting used to, but I'm sure I would get the hang of it.

"Near the pleasure center," said Dr. Yeniknani, "there is an area that causes rage and ferociously aggressive behavior. It is also a punishment center. When it is stimulated, subjects experience torment as great as the ecstasy of the pleasure center. This area *was* wired. Your sponsor felt that this might prove useful in your undertaking for him, and it gives him a measure of influence over you." He said this in a clearly disapproving tone of voice. I wasn't crazy about the news, either. "If you choose to use it to your advantage, you can become a raging, unstoppable creature of destruction." He stopped, evidently not liking how Friedlander Bey had exploited the neurosurgical art.

"My . . . patron gave this all a lot of thought, didn't he?" I said sardonically.

"Yes, I suppose he did. And so should you." Then the doctor did an unusual thing: he reached over and put his hand on my arm; it was a sudden change in the formal atmosphere of our talk. "Mr. Audran," he said solemnly, looking directly into my eyes, "I have a rather good idea of why you had this surgery."

"Uh huh," I said, curious, waiting to hear what he had to say.

"In the name of the Prophet, may peace be on his name and blessings, you need not fear death."

That rocked me. "Well," I said, "I don't think about it very much, I guess. Anyway, the implants aren't that dangerous, are they? I admit that I was afraid they'd roast my wits if something went wrong, but I didn't think they could kill me."

"No, you don't understand. When you leave the hospital, when you are in that situation for which you underwent this augmentation, you need not be afraid. The great English shâ'ir, Wilyam al-Shaykh Sebîr, in his splendid play, *King Henry the Fourth, Part II*, says, 'We owe God a death ... and, let it go which way it will, he that dies this year, is quit for the next.' So you see, death comes to us all. Death is inescapable. Death is desirable as our passage to paradise, may Allah be praised. So do what you must, Mr. Audran, and do not be hindered by an undue fear of death in your search for justice."

Wonderful: my doctor was some kind of Sufi mystic or something. I just stared at him, unable to think of a damn thing to say. He squeezed my arm and stood up. "With your permission," he said.

I gestured vaguely. "May your day be prosperous," I said.

"Peace be on you."

"And on you be peace," I replied. Then Dr. Yeniknani left my room. Jo-Mama would get a big kick out of this story. I couldn't wait to hear the way *she'd* tell it.

Just after the doctor went out, the young male nurse returned with an injection. "Oh," I said, starting to tell him that earlier I hadn't meant that I wanted a shot; I had only wanted to ask him a few questions.

"Roll over," said the man briskly. "Which side?"

I jiggled a little in bed, feeling the soreness in each hip, deciding that both were pretty painful. "Can you give it to me someplace else? My arm?"

"Can't give it to you in your arm. I can give it to you in your leg, though." He pulled back the sheet, swabbed the front of my thigh about halfway down toward the knee, and jabbed me. He gave the leg another quick swipe with the gauze, capped the syringe, and turned away without a word. I wasn't one of his favorite patients, I could see that.

I wanted to say something to him, to let him know that I wasn't the self-indulgent, vice-ridden, swinish person he thought I was. Before I could speak a word, though, before he'd even reached the door to my room, my head began to swirl and I was sinking down into the familiar warm embrace of numbness. My last thought, before I lost consciousness, was that I had never had so much fun in my life.

13

I did not expect to have many visitors while I was in the hospital. I'd told everyone that I appreciated their concern but that it was no big deal, and that I'd rather be left in peace until I felt better. The response I usually got, carefully considered and tacifully phrased, was that nobody was planning to visit me, anyway. I said, "Good." The real reason I didn't want people coming to look at me was that I could imagine the aftereffects of major brain surgery. The visitors sit on the foot of your bed, you know, and tell you how great you look, and how quickly you'll feel all better, and how everybody misses you, and—if you can't fall asleep fast enough—all about *their* old operations. I didn't need any of that. I wanted to be left alone to enjoy the final, straggling, time-released molecules of etorphin planted in a bubble in my brain. Sure, I was prepared to play a stoic and courageous sufferer for a few minutes every day, but I didn't have to. My friends were as good as their word: I didn't have a single, goddamn visitor, not until the last day, just before I was discharged. All that time, no one came to see me, no one even called or sent a card or a crummy plant. Believe me, I've got all that written down in my book of memories.

I saw Dr. Yeniknani every day, and he made sure to point out at least once each visit that there were worse things to fear than death. He kept dwelling on it; he was the most morbid doctor I've ever known. His attempt to calm my fearful spirit had absolutely the wrong effect. He should have stuck with his professional resources: pills. They—I mean the kind I got in the hospital, made by real pharmaceutical houses and all—are very dependable and can make me forget about death and suffering and anything else just like *that*.

So as the next few days passed, I realized that I had a clear idea of how vital my well-being was to the tranquility of the Budayeen: I could have died and been buried inside a brand-new mosque in Mecca or some Egyptian pyramid thrown together in my honor, and nobody would even know about it. Some friends! The question arises: Why did I even entertain the notion of sticking my own neck out for their well-being? I asked myself that over and over, and the answer was always: Because who else did I have? *Triste, non?* The longer I observe the way people really act, the happier I am that I never pay attention to them.

The end of Ramadân came, and the festival that marks the close of the holy month. I was sorry I was still in the hospital, because the festival, Îd el-Fitr, is one of my favorite times of the year. I always celebrate the end of the fast with towers of *ataïf*, pancakes dipped in syrup and sprinkled with orange-blossom water, layered with heavy cream, and covered with chopped almonds. Instead, this year I took some farewell shots of Sonneine, while some religious authority in the city was declaring that he'd sighted the new crescent moon, the new month had begun, and life could now return to normal.

I went to sleep. I woke up early the next morning, when the blood nurse came around for his daily libation. Everyone else's life may have gone back to normal, but mine was permanently doglegged in a direction I could not yet imagine. My loins were girded, and now I was needed on the field of battle. Unfurl the banners, O my sons, we will come down like a wolf on the fold. I come not to send peace, but a sword.

Breakfast came and went. We had our little bath. I called for a shot of Sonneine; I always liked to take one after all the heavy work of the morning was finished, while I had a couple of hours before lunch. A drifty little nap, then a tray of food: good stuffed grape leaves; *hamûd;* skewered *kofta* on rice, perfumed with onions, coriander, and allspice. Prayer is better than sleep, and food is better than drugs . . . sometimes. After lunch, another shot and a second nap. I was awakened by Ali, the older, disapproving nurse. He shook my shoulder. "Mr. Audran," he murmured.

Oh no, I thought, they want more blood. I tried to force myself back to sleep.

"You have a visitor, Mr. Audran."

"A visitor?" Surely there had been some mistake. After all, I was dead, laid to rest on some mountaintop. All I had to do now was wait for the grave robbers. Could it be that they were here already? I didn't even feel stiff, yet. They wouldn't even let me get cold in the tomb, the bastards. Ramses II was shown more respect, I'll bet. Haroun al-Raschîd. Prince Saalih ibn Abdul-Wahîd ibn Saud. Everybody but me. I struggled up to a sitting position.

"O clever one, you are looking well." Hassan's fat face was resting in its shabby business smile, the unctuous look that even the stupidest tourist could spot as too deceitful by half.

"It is as God pleases," I said groggily.

"Yes, praise Allah. Very soon you will be wholly recovered, *inshallah*."

I didn't bother to respond. I was just glad he wasn't sitting on the foot of my bed.

"You must know, my nephew, that the entire Budayeen is desolate without your presence to light our weary lives."

"So I understand," I said. "From the flood of cards and letters. From the crowds of friends that mob the hospital corridors day and night, anxious to see me or just hear word of my condition. From all your many little thoughtfulnesses that have made my stay here bearable. I cannot thank you enough."

"No thanks are necessary—"

"—for a duty. I know, Hassan. Anything else?"

He looked a little uncomfortable. It might have crossed his mind that *just possibly* I was mocking him, but usually he was impervious to that sort of thing. He smiled again. "I am happy that you will be among us again tonight."

I was startled. "I will?"

He turned over one fat palm. "Is it not so? You are to be discharged this afternoon. Friedlander Bey sent me with a message: You must visit him as soon as you feel well. Tomorrow will be soon enough. He does not wish for you to hurry your recuperation."

"I didn't even know that I was being released, and I'm supposed to see Friedlander Bey tomorrow; but he doesn't want to hurry me. I suppose your car is waiting to take me home."

Now Hassan looked unhappy. He didn't like my suggestion at all. "Oh darling, I wish it were so, but it cannot be. You must make other arrangements. I have business elsewhere."

"Go in safety," I said quietly. I laid my head back on the pillow and tried to find my dream again. It was long gone.

"*Allah yisallimak,*" murmured Hassan, and he was gone, too.

All the peace of the last few days disappeared, and it happened with disturbing suddenness. I was left with a pervasive feeling of self-loathing. I remembered one time a few years ago, when I had pursued a girl who worked sometimes at the Red Light and sometimes at Big Al's Old Chicago. I had worked my way into her consciousness by being funny and fast and, I suppose, contemptible. I finally got her to go out with me, and I took her to dinner—I don't remember where—and then back to my apartment. We were on the bed five minutes after I locked the front door, and we jammed for maybe another ten or fifteen minutes, and then it was all over. I lay back and looked at her. She had bad teeth and sharp bones and smelled as if she carried sesame oil around with her in an aerosol. "My God," I thought. "Who *is* this girl? And how am I going to get rid of her *now*?" After sex, all animals are sad; after *any* kind of pleasure, really. We're not built for pleasure. We're built for agony and for seeing things too clearly, which is often a terrible agony in itself. I loathed myself then, and I loathed myself now.

Dr. Yeniknani knocked lightly on my door and came in. He glanced briefly at the nurse's daily notes.

"Am I going home?" I asked.

He turned his bright, black eyes on me. "Hmm? Oh, yes. Your discharge orders have already been written. You have to arrange for someone to come and get you. Hospital policy. You can leave anytime."

"Thank God," I said, and I meant it. That surprised me.

"Praise Allah," said the doctor. He looked at the plastic box of daddies beside my bed. "Have you tried all of these?" he asked.

"Yes," I said. That was a lie. I had tried a few, under the supervision of a therapist; the data add-ons had been pretty much of a disappointment. I don't know what I'd expected. When I chipped in one of the daddies, its information was sitting there in my mind, as if I'd known all of it all my life. It was like staying up all night and cramming for an exam, without having to lose any sleep and without the possibility of forgetting any of the material. When I popped the chip out, it all vanished from my memory. No big deal. Actually, I was looking forward to trying some of the daddies that Lalla had in her shop. The daddies would come in very handy now and then.

It was the moddies I was afraid of. The full personality modules. The ones that crammed you away in some little tin box inside your head, and someone you didn't know took over your mind and body. They still spooked the hell out of me.

"Well, then," said Dr. Yeniknani. He didn't wish me luck, because everything was in the hands of Allah, Who knew what the outcome was going to be anyway, so luck hardly entered into it. I'd learned gradually that my doctor was an apprentice saint, a Turkish derwish. "May God provide a successful conclusion to your undertaking," he said. Very well spoken, I thought. I had come to like him a lot.

"*Inshallah*," I said. We shook hands, and he left. I went to the closet, took out my street clothes, threw them on the bed—there was a shirt and my boots and socks and underwear and a new pair of jeans that I didn't remember buying. I dressed quickly and spoke Yasmin's commcode into my phone. It rang and rang. I spoke my own, thinking she might be at my apartment; there was no answer there, either. Maybe she was at work, although it wasn't two o'clock. I called Frenchy's, but no one had seen her yet. I didn't bother leaving a message. I called a cab instead.

Hospital policy or not, nobody gave me a hard time about leaving unescorted. They wheeled me downstairs and I got into the cab, holding a bag of toilet articles in one hand and my rack of daddies in the other. I rode back to my apartment feeling a bewildering emptiness, no emotions at all.

I unlocked my front door and went in. I figured the place would be a mess. Yasmin had probably stayed here a few times while I was in the hospital, and she was never great at picking up after herself. I expected to see little mounds of her clothes all over the floor, monuments of dirty dishes in the sink, half-eaten meals and open jars and empty cans all around the stove and table; but the room was as clean as when I'd last seen it. *Cleaner,* even; I'd never done such a thorough job of sweeping, dusting, and washing the windows. That made me suspicious: some skillful lockpicker with a yen for neatness had broken into my home. I saw three envelopes beside the mattress on the floor, stuffed fat. I bent over and picked them up. My name was typed on the outside of the envelopes; on the inside of each was seven hundred kiam, all in tens, seventy new bills fastened together with a rubber band. Three envelopes, twenty-one hundred kiam; my wages for the weeks I spent in the hospital. I didn't think I was getting paid for that time. I would have done it for free—the Sonneine on top of the etorphin had been quite pleasant.

I lay down on the bed and tossed the money to the side, where Yasmin sometimes slept. I still felt a curious hollowness, as if I was waiting for something to come along and fill me up and give me a hint about what to do next. I waited, but I didn't get the word. I looked at my watch; it was now almost four o'clock. I decided not to put off the hard stuff. I might as well get it over with.

I got up again, stuck a wad of a few hundred kiam in my pocket, found my keys, and went back downstairs. I began to feel just the beginning of some kind of emotional reaction. I paid close attention: I was nervous, not pleasantly so; and I was sure that I was fighting my way up the thirteen steps of the gallows, intent on putting my head in some as-yet-unseen noose. I walked down the Street to the east gate of the Budayeen and looked for Bill. I didn't see him. I got into another cab. "Take me to Friedlander Bey's house," I said.

The driver turned around and looked at me. "No," he said flatly. I got out and found another driver who didn't mind going there. I made sure we agreed on the cabfare first, though.

When we got there I paid the driver and climbed out. I hadn't let anyone know I was coming; Papa probably didn't expect to see me for another day. Nevertheless, his servant was holding the polished mahogany door open before I reached the top of the white marble stairs. "Mr. Audran," he murmured.

"I'm surprised you remember," I said.

He shrugged—I couldn't say if he smiled or not—and said, "Peace be upon you." He turned away.

I said "And upon you be peace" to his back and followed. He led me to Papa's offices, to the same waiting room I had seen before. I went in, sat down, stood up again restlessly, and began to pace. I didn't know why I'd come here. After "Hello, how are you?" I was depressed to find I had nothing else to say to Papa at all. But Friedlander Bey was a good host when it served his purposes, and he wouldn't let a guest feel uncomfortable.

In a while the communicating door opened and one of the sandstone giants gestured. I passed by him and came again into Papa's presence. He looked very tired, as if he had been handling urgent financial, political, religious, judicial, and military matters without rest for many hours. His white shirt was stained with perspiration, his fine hair mussed, his eyes weary and bloodshot. His hand trembled as he gestured to the Stone That Speaks. "Coffee," he said, in a hoarse and peculiarly soft voice. He turned to me. "Come, my nephew, be seated. You must tell me if you are well. It pleases Allah that the surgery was successful. I have had several reports from Dr. Lisân. He was quite satisfied with the results. In that regard I am also satisfied, but of course the true proof of the value of the implants will be in how you use them."

I nodded, that's all.

The Stone arrived with the coffee, and it gave me a few minutes to settle my nerves while we sipped and chatted. I realized that Papa was looking at me rather closely, his brows drawn together, his expression mildly displeased. I closed my eyes in exasperation: I had come in my usual street clothes. The jeans and boots were fine in Chiri's club or for hanging out with Mahmoud, Jacques, and Saied, but Papa preferred to see me in the *gallebeya* and *keffiya*. Too late now, I told myself; I'd started off in the hole, and I was going to have to climb out of it and gain some more ground to get back in his good graces.

I shook my cup back and forth a little after the second refilling, indicating that I had had enough. The coffee things were cleared away, and Papa murmured something to the Stone. The huge man left the room also. This was the first time, I believe, that I'd been alone with Papa. I waited.

The old man pressed his lips together while he thought. "I am glad that you thought enough of my wishes to undergo the surgery," he said.

"O Shaykh," I said, "it is—"

He shut me up with a quick gesture. "However, merely having the surgery will not solve our problems. That is unfortunate. I have had other reports that told me you were reluctant to explore the full benefits of my gifts. You may be thinking that you can satisfy our arrangement by wearing the implants, but not using them. If you are thinking that, you are deluding yourself. Our mutual problem cannot be solved unless you agree to use the weapon I have given you, and use it to the utmost. I have not had such augmentation myself because I believe my religion forbids it; therefore, one might argue that I am not the proper person to advise you on this matter. Yet I think I know a thing or two about personality modules. Would you care to discuss a proper choice with me?"

The man was reading my mind, but that was his job. The odd thing was that the deeper in I got, the easier it seemed to be to talk to Friedlander Bey. I wasn't even properly terrified when I heard myself declining his offer. "O Shaykh," I said, "we do not even agree on the identity of our enemy. How then can we hope to choose a suitable personality as an instrument of our vengeance?"

There was a brief silence during which I heard my heart give one good bam! and start on another. Papa's eyebrows raised a little and fell back into place. "Once again, my nephew, you prove to me that I was not mistaken in my choice of you. You are correct. How then do you propose to begin?"

"O Shaykh, I will begin by making a closer ally of Lieutenant Okking, and getting all the information he has in the police files. I know certain things about some of the victims that I'm sure he does not. I see no reason to give him this information now, but he may require it later. I will then interview all our mutual friends; I think I will find further clues. A careful, scientific examination of all the available data should be the first step."

Friedlander Bey nodded thoughtfully. "Okking has information you do not have. You have information he does not have. Someone should assemble all that information in one place, and I would rather that person be you, and not the good lieutenant. Yes, I am pleased with your suggestion."

"All who see you, live, O Shaykh."

"May Allah grant that you go and come in safety."

I saw no reason to tell him that what I truly planned to do was make a closer scrutiny of Herr Lutz Seipolt. What I knew of Nikki and her death made the whole affair more sinister than either Papa or Lieutenant Okking were willing to admit. I still had the moddy I'd found in Nikki's purse. I'd never mentioned that moddy to anyone. I would have to find out what was recorded on it. I also hadn't mentioned the ring or the scarab.

It took me another few minutes to ease myself out of Friedlander Bey's villa, and then I couldn't find a taxi. I ended up walking, but I didn't mind because I was having a fierce argument with myself all the way. The argument went like this:

Self$_1$ (afraid of Papa): "Well, why not do what he wants? Just collect all the information and let him suggest the next step. Otherwise, you'll just be asking for a broken body. If not a dead one."

Self$_2$ (afraid of death and disaster): "Because every step I take is directly toward two—not one, but two—psychopathic murderers who don't care half a chickpea if I live or die. As a matter of fact, either or both of them would probably give considerably more than that just for the chance to put a bullet between my eyes or slit my throat. That's why."

Both selves had considerable stores of logical, reasonable things to say. It was like being at a mental tennis match: one would bash a statement across the net, and the other would bash a refutation right back. They were too evenly matched, the rally would go on forever. After a while I got bored and stopped watching. I had all the equipment, after all, to become El Cid or Khomeini or anybody else, and why was I still hesitating? Nobody else around here had any of my qualms. I didn't think of myself as a coward, either. What would it take to get me to chip in that first moddy?

I got the answer to that the very same night. I heard the sunset call to prayer as I passed through the gate and headed up the Street. Outside the Budayeen, the muezzin sounded almost ethereal; inside the gate, the same man's voice had somehow gained a reproachful note. Or was that my imagination? I wandered over to Chiriga's nightclub and sat down at the bar. She wasn't there. Behind the bar was Jamila, who had worked for Chiri a few weeks ago and then quit after my Russian was shot in the club. People come and go around the Budayeen; they'll work in one club and get fired or quit over some dumb-ass little thing, go work someplace else, eventually make the circuit and end up back where they started. Jamila was one of those people who can make the circuit faster than most. She was lucky to hang onto a job in one place for seven days running.

"Where's Chiri?" I asked.

"She's coming in at nine. You want something to drink?"

"Bingara and gin over ice, with a little Rose's." Jamila nodded and turned away to mix it. "Oh," she said, "you had a call. They left a message. Let me find it."

That surprised me. I couldn't imagine who would leave

a message for me, how they'd known I'd come in here tonight.

Jamila returned with my drink and a cocktail napkin with two words scrawled across it. I paid her and she left without another word. The message was *Call Okking*. What a fitting beginning to my new life as a superman: urgent police business. No rest for the wicked; it was becoming my motto. I unclipped my phone and growled Okking's commcode, then waited for him to answer. "Yeah?" he said at last.

"Marîd Audran," I said.

"Wonderful. I called the hospital, but they said you'd been discharged. I called your house, but there wasn't any answer. I called your girl friend's boss, but you weren't there. I called your usual hangout, the Café Solace, but they hadn't seen you. So I tried a few other places, and left messages. I want you here in half an hour."

"Sure, Lieutenant. Where are you?"

He gave me a room number and the address of a hotel run by a Flemish conglomerate, in the most affluent section of the city. I'd never been in the hotel, or within so much as ten blocks of it. That wasn't my part of town.

"What's the situation?" I asked.

"A homicide. Your name has come up."

"Ah. Anyone I know?"

"Yes. It's odd that as soon as you went into the hospital, these bizarre killings stopped. Nothing unusual for almost three weeks. And the day you're released, we're right back in the Reign of Terror."

"Okay, Lieutenant, you've got me and I'll have to confess. If I'd been smart, I would have arranged a murder or two while I was in the hospital, to throw off suspicion."

"You're a wise guy, Audran. That just makes your predicament worse, all the way around."

"Sorry. So you never told me: who's the victim?"

"Just get here fast," he said, and hung up.

I gulped my drink, left Jamila half a kiam tip, and hurried out into the warm night air. Bill was still missing from his usual place on the wide Boulevard il-Jameel outside the Budayeen. Another cab driver agreed to the fare I offered him, and we rumbled across town to the hotel. I went straight up to the room, and was stopped by a police officer standing inside the yellow tape "crime scene" barrier. I told him Lieutenant Okking was expecting me. He asked me my name, and then let me pass.

The room was like the inside of a slaughterhouse. There was blood everywhere—pools of blood, streaks of blood on the walls, blood spattered on the bed, on the chairs and bureau, all over the carpet. A murderer would have had to spend a lot of time and energy making certain his victim was sufficiently dead to splash all that blood so much, thoroughly soaking the room. He'd have to kill the wretch with stab after stab, like a ritual human sacrifice. It was inhuman, grotesque, and demented. Neither James Bond nor the nameless torturer had worked this way. This was either a third maniac, or one of the first two with a brand-new moddy. In both cases our scanty clues were now obsolete. That's all we needed at this point.

The police were completing the job of bundling the corpse into a body bag on a stretcher, and moving it out the door. I found the lieutenant. "So who the hell got the business tonight?" I asked.

He looked at me closely, as if he could gauge my guilt or innocence from my reaction. "Selima," he said.

My shoulders slumped. I felt immensely exhausted all of a sudden. "Allah be merciful," I murmured. "So why did you want me here? What does this have to do with me?"

"You're investigating all this for Friedlander Bey. And besides, I want you to look in the bathroom."

"Why?"

"You'll see. Be prepared, though; it's pretty sickening."

That just made me less eager to go into the bathroom. I did, though. I had to, there was no choice. The first thing I saw was a human heart, hacked from Selima's chest, sitting in the bathroom sink. That made me retch right there. The sink was fouled with her dark blood. Then I saw the blood smeared all over the mirror above the sink. There were uneven borders and geometric patterns and unintelligible symbolic marks drawn on the glass. The most unsettling part were the few words written in blood in a dripping handwriting, that said *Audran, you next.*

I felt a faint, unreal sensation. What did this insane butcher know about me? What connection did I have with the monstrous slaying of Selima, and of the other Black Widow Sisters as well? The only thought I had was that my motivation up until now had been a kind of gallant desire to help protect my friends, those who might be future victims of the unknown mad murderers. I had had no personal interest, except possibly a desire for revenge, for Nikki's killing and for the others. Now, though, with my name written in congealing blood on that mirror, it *had* been made personal. My own life was at stake.

If anything in the world could induce me to take the final step and chip in my first moddy, this was it. I knew absolutely that from now on, I'd need every bit of help I could get. Enlightened self-interest, I called it; and I cursed the vile executioners who had made it necessary.

14

First thing the next morning, I paid a call on Laila at her modshop on Fourth Street. The old woman was just as creepy as ever, but her costume had undergone some slight revision. She had her dirty, thin gray hair shoved up under a blond wig full of ringlets; it didn't look so much like a hairpiece as something your great-aunt would slip over a toaster to hide it from view. Laila couldn't do much with her yellowed eyes and wrinkled black skin, but she sure tried. She had so much pale powder on her face that she looked like she'd just busted out of a grain elevator. Over that she had smeared bright cerise streaks on every available surface; to me it appeared that her eye shadow, cheek blush, and lipstick had all come out of the same container. She wore a sparkly pair of plastic sunglasses on a grimy string around her neck—cat's-eye sunglasses, and she had chosen them with care. She hadn't bothered to find herself some false teeth, but she had swapped her filthy black shift for an indecently tight, low-cut slit-skirted gown in blazing dandelion yellow. It looked like she was trying to shove her head and shoulders free of the maw of the world's biggest budgie. On her feet she wore cheap blue fuzzy bedroom slippers. "Laila," I said.

"Marîd." Her eyes weren't quite focused. That meant that she was just her own inimitable self today; if she had been chipping in some moddy, her eyes would have been focused and the software would have sharpened up her responses. It would have been easier to deal with her if she *had* been someone else, but I let it go.

"Had my brain wired."

"I heard." She snickered, and I felt a ripple of disgust.

"I need some help choosing a moddy."

"What you want it for?"

I chewed my lip. How much was I going to tell her? On one hand, she might repeat everything I said to anyone who came into her shop; after all, she told me what everybody else said to her. On the other hand, nobody paid any attention to her in the first place. "I need to do a little work. I got wired because the job might be dangerous. I need something that will jack up my detective talent, and also keep me from getting hurt. What do you think?"

She muttered to herself for a while, wandering up and down the aisles, browsing through her bins. I couldn't make out what she was saying, so I just waited. Finally she turned around; she was surprised that I was still there. Maybe she'd already forgotten what I'd asked. "Is a made-up character good enough?" she said.

"If the character is smart enough," I said.

She shrugged and mumbled some more, snagged a plastic-wrapped moddy in her clawlike fingers, and held it out to me. "Here," she said.

I hesitated. I recalled thinking that again she reminded me of the witch from *Snow White;* now I looked at the moddy like it was a poisoned apple. "Who is it?"

"Nero Wolfe," she said. "Brilliant detective. Genius for figuring out murders. Didn't like to leave his own house. Someone else did all his legwork and took the beatings."

"Perfect," I said. I sort of remembered the character, although I don't think I ever read any of the books.

"You'll have to get somebody to go ask the questions," she said. She held out a second moddy.

"Saied'll do it. I'll just tell him he'll get to knock some heads together whenever he wants, and he'll jump at the chance. How much for both of them?"

Her lips moved for a long time while she tried to add two figures together. "Seventy-three," she whined. "Forget the tax."

I counted out eighty kiam and took my change and the two moddies. She looked up at me. "Want to buy my lucky beans?" I didn't even want to *hear* about them.

There was still one little item troubling me, and it may have been the key to the identity of Nikki's killer, the torturer and throat-slasher who still needed silencing. It was Nikki's underground moddy. She may have been wearing it when she died, or the killer may have been wearing it; as far as I knew, goddamn *nobody* may have been wearing it. It may just be a big nothing. But then why did it give me such a sick, desperate feeling whenever I looked at it? Was it only the way I recalled Nikki's body that night, stuffed into trash bags, dumped in that alley? I took two or three deep breaths. Come on, I told myself, you're a damn good stand-in for a hero. You've got all the right software ready to whisper and chuckle in your brain. I stretched my muscles.

My rational mind tried to tell me thirty or forty times that the moddy didn't mean anything, nothing more than a lipstick or a crumpled tissue I might have found in Nikki's purse. Okking wouldn't have been pleased to know that I'd withheld it and two other items from the police, but I was getting to the point where I was beyond caring about Okking. I was growing weary of this entire matter, but it was succeeding in pulling me along in its wake. I had lost the will even to bail out and save myself.

Laila was fiddling with a moddy. She reached up and chipped it in. She liked to visit with her ghosts and phantoms. "Marîd!" She whined this time in the thrilling voice of Vivien Leigh from *Gone With the Wind*.

"Laila, I've got a bootleg moddy here and I want to know what's on it."

"Sure, Marîd, nevah you mind. Just you give me that little ol'—"

"Laila," I cried. "I don't have time for any of that goddamn Southern belle! Either pop your own moddy or force yourself to pay attention."

The idea of popping out her moddy was too horrifying for her to consider. She stared at me, trying to distinguish me in the crowd. I was the one between Ashley, Rhett, and the doorway. "Why, Marîd! What's come ovah you? You seem so feverish an' all!"

I turned my head away and swore. For the love of

Allah, I really wanted to hit her. "I have this moddy," I said, and my teeth didn't move apart a fraction of an inch. "I have to know what's on it."

"Fiddle-dee-dee, Marîd, what's so important?" She took the moddy from me and examined it. "It's divided into three bands, honey."

"But how can you tell what's recorded on it?"

She smiled. "Why, that's just the easiest thing in the world." With one hand, she popped the Scarlett O'Hara moddy and tossed it carelessly somewhere beside her; it hit a rack of daddies and skittered into a corner. Laila might never find her Scarlett again. With the other hand she centered my suspect moddy and chipped it in. Her slack face tightened just a bit. Then she dropped to the floor.

"Laila?" I said.

She was twisting into grotesque positions, her tongue protruding, her eyes wide and staring and sightless. She was making a low, sobbing sound, as if she'd been beaten and maimed for hours and didn't even have the strength left to cry out. Her breathing was harsh and shallow, and I heard it rasp in her throat. Her hands were bundles of dry black sticks, scrabbling uselessly at her head, desperate to pop the moddy out, but she couldn't control her muscles. She was crying deep in her throat, and rocking back and forth on the floor. I wanted to help her, but I didn't know what to do. If I'd come any closer, she might have clawed me.

She wasn't human anymore, it was horribly easy to see that. Whoever had designed that moddy liked animals— liked to *do* things to animals. Laila was behaving like a large creature; not a housecat or small dog, but a caged, furious, tormented jungle animal. I could hear her hiss, I could see her snapping at the legs of the furniture and striking out at me with her nonexistent fangs. When I stooped near her, she swung on me quicker than I thought possible. I tried to grab at the moddy and came away with three long, bloody slashes down my arm. Then her eyes locked on mine. She crouched, pulling her knees forward.

Laila leaped, her thin, black body launched toward me.

She gave a shrieking, wailing cry and stretched out her hands for my neck. I was sickened by the sight, by the change that had come over the old woman. It wasn't just Laila attacking me: it was the old hag's body possessed by the corrupt influence of the moddy. Ordinarily, I could have held Laila away with one hand; today, however, I found myself in mortal danger. This beast-Laila would not be happy merely with cornering me or wounding me. It wanted me dead.

As she flew toward me, I sidestepped as neatly as I could, giving her a lot of movement with my arms the way a matador fools the eye of the bull. She crashed into a bin of used daddies, flipped on her back, and drew her legs up as if to disembowel me. I brought my right fist down hard on the side of her face. There was a muffled crack of bone, and she collapsed limply in the bin. I bent down and chipped out the bootleg moddy and tucked it away with my other software. Laila wasn't unconscious long, but she was stunned. Her eyes wouldn't focus, and she was muttering deliriously. When she felt better she was going to be very unhappy. I looked quickly around her shop for something to fit her vacant implant. I ripped open a new moddy package—it was an instructional unit, I think, because it came with three daddies. Something about giving dinner parties for Anatolian bureaucrats. I was sure Leila would find that one fascinating.

I unclipped my phone and called the hospital where I'd had my own amping done. I asked for Dr. Yeniknani; when he answered at last, I explained what had happened. He told me an ambulance would be on its way to Laila's shop in five minutes. He wanted me to give the moddy to one of the paramedics. I told him that whatever he learned about the moddy was confidential, that he shouldn't divulge the information to the police or even Friedlander Bey. There was a long pause, but finally Dr. Yeniknani agreed. He knew and trusted me more than he trusted Okking and Papa put together.

The ambulance arrived within twenty minutes. I watched the two male paramedics carefully lift Laila on a stretcher and put her into the wagon. I committed the moddy to one of them and reminded him to give it to no one but Dr. Yeniknani. He nodded hurriedly and climbed back behind the steering wheel. I watched the ambulance drive off, out of the Budayeen, toward whatever medical science might or might not be able to do for Laila. I clutched my own two purchases and locked and shut the door to the old woman's shop. Then I got the hell out of there. I shuddered on the sidewalk.

I'd be jammed if I knew what I'd learned. First—granting the huge condition that the bootleg moddy originally belonged to the throat-cutter—did *he* wear it or did he give it to his victims? Would a timber wolf or a Siberian tiger know how to burn a helpless person with cigarettes? No, it made better sense to picture the moddy chipped into a raging but well-secured victim. That accounted for the wrist bruises—and Tami, Abdoulaye, and Nikki had all had their skulls socketed. What did the assassin do if the victim wasn't a moddy? Probably just iced the sucker and sulked all afternoon.

All I could figure was that I was looking for a pervert who needed a savage, caged carnivore to get his juices flowing. The notion of resigning flashed through my mind, the often-played scene of quitting despite Friedlander Bey's soft-spoken threats. This time I went as far as to imagine myself beside the cracked roadway, waiting for the ancient electric bus with its crowd of peasants on top. My stomach was turning, and it had only just so much room to move.

It was too early to find the Half-Hajj and talk him into being my accomplice. Maybe about three or four o'clock he'd be at the Café Solace, along with Mahmoud and Jacques; I hadn't seen or spoken to any of them in weeks. I hadn't seen Saied at all since the night he'd sent Courvoisier Sonny on the Great Circle Route to paradise, or somewhere. I went back home. I thought I might take the Nero Wolfe moddy out and look at it and turn it over in my hand a couple of dozen times and maybe peel off the shrinkwrap and find out if I'd have to swallow a few pills or a bottle of tende to get the nerve to chip the damn thing in.

Yasmin was in my apartment when I got there. I was surprised; she, however, was upset and hurt. "You got out of the hospital yesterday, and you didn't even *call* me," she cried. She dropped down on the corner of the bed and scowled at me.

"Yasmin—"

"Okay, you said you didn't want me to visit you in the hospital, so I didn't. But I thought you'd see me as soon as you came home."

"I did want to, but—"

"Then why didn't you *call* me? I'll bet you were here with somebody else."

"I went to see Papa last night. Hassan told me that I was supposed to report in."

She gave me a dubious look. "And you were there all night long?"

"No," I admitted.

"So who else did you see?"

I took a deep breath and let it out. "I saw Selima."

Yasmin's scowl turned into a grimace of utter contempt. "Oh, is that what trigs you these days? And how was she? As good as her advertisements?"

"Selima's on the list now, Yasmin. With her sisters."

She blinked at me for a moment. "Tell me why I'm not surprised. We *told* her to be careful."

"You just can't be that careful," I said. "Not unless you go live in a cave a hundred miles from your nearest neighbor. And that wasn't Selima's style."

"No." There was silence for a while; I guess Yasmin was thinking that it wasn't her style, either, that I was suggesting that the same kind of thing might happen to her. Well, I hope she was thinking that, because it's true. It's always true.

I didn't tell her about the blood-o-gram Selima's killer left for me in the hotel suite's bathroom. Somebody had figured Marîd Audran for an easy mark, so it was time for Marîd Audran to play things close to the chest. Besides, mentioning it wouldn't improve Yasmin's mood, or mine, either. "I got a moddy I want to try," I said.

She raised an eyebrow. "Anybody I know?"

"No, I don't think so. It's a detective out of some old books. Thought he might help me stop these murders."

"Uh huh. Did Papa suggest it?"

"No. Papa doesn't know what I'm really going to do. I told him I was just going to follow along after the police and look at the clues through a magnifying glass and all that. He believed me."

"Sounds like a waste of time to me," said Yasmin.

"It *is* a waste of time, but Papa likes things orderly. He operates in a steady, efficient, but dreary and minimal-velocity way."

"But he gets things done."

"Yes, I have to admit that he gets things done. Still, I don't want him looking over my shoulder, vetoing every other step I take. If I'm going to do this job for him, I have to do it my way."

"You're not doing the job just for him, Marîd. You're doing it for us. All of us. And besides, remember the *I Ching*? It said no one would believe you. This is that time evil, patterned scars and filed teeth ... "I'll be right you think is right, and you'll be vindicated in the end."

"Sure," I said, smiling grimly, "I only hope my fame doesn't come posthumously."

" 'And covet not that which Allah hath made some of you excel others. Unto men a fortune from that which they have earned, and unto women a fortune from that which they have earned. Do not envy one another, but ask Allah of His bounty. Behold! Allah is the Knower of all things.' "

"Right, Yasmin, quote at me. Suddenly you're all religious."

"*You're* the one worrying about where your devotions lie. I *already* believe; I just don't practice."

"Fast without prayer is like a shepherd without a crook, Yasmin. And you don't even fast, either."

"Yeah, but—"

"But nothing."

"You're evading the subject again."

She was right about that, so I changed evasions. "To be or not to be, sweetheart, *that* is the question." I tossed the moddy a few inches into the air and caught it. "Whether 'tis nobler in the mind—"

"Will you plug the goddamn thing in already?"

So I took a deep breath, murmured "In the name of God," and plugged it in.

* * *

The first frightening sensation was of being suddenly engulfed by a grotesque glob of flesh. Nero Wolfe weighed a seventh of a ton, 285 pounds or more. All Audran's senses were deceived into believing he had gained a hundred and thirty pounds in an instant. He fell to the floor, stunned, gasping for breath. Audran had been warned that there would be a time lag while he adjusted to each moddy he used; whether it had been recorded from a living brain or programmed to resemble a fictional character, it had probably been intended for an ideal body unlike Audran's own in many ways. Audran's muscles and nerves needed a little while to learn to compensate. Nero Wolfe was grossly fatter than Audran, and taller as well. When Audran had the moddy chipped in he would walk with Wolfe's steps, take things with Wolfe's reach and grasp, settle his imaginary corpulence into chairs with Wolfe's care and delicacy. It hit Audran harder than he had even expected.

After a moment Wolfe heard a young woman's voice. She sounded worried. Audran was still writhing on the floor, trying to breathe, trying merely to stand up again. "Are you all right?" the young woman asked.

Wolfe's eyes narrowed to little slits in the fat pouches that surrounded them. He looked at her. "Quite all right, Miss Nablusi," he said. He sat up slowly, and she came toward him to help him stand. He waved at her impatiently, but he did lean on her a bit as he got to his feet.

Wolfe's recollections, artfully wired into the moddy, mixed with Audran's submerged thoughts, feelings, sensations, and memories. Wolfe was fluent in many languages: English, French, Spanish, Italian, Latin, Serbo-Croatian, and others. There wasn't room to pack so many language daddies into a single moddy. Audran asked himself what the French word for al-kalb was, and he knew it: le chien. Of course, Audran spoke perfect French himself. He asked for the English and Croatian words for al-kalb, but they eluded him, right on the tip of the tongue, a mental tickle, one of those frustrating little memory lapses. They—Audran and Wolfe— couldn't remember which people spoke Croatian, or where they lived; Audran had never heard of the language before. All this made him suspect the depth of this illusion. He hoped they wouldn't hit bottom at some crucial moment when Audran was depending on Wolfe to get them out of some life-threatening situation. "Pfui," said Wolfe.

Ah, but Nero Wolfe rarely got himself into life-threatening situations. He let Archie Goodwin take most of those risks. Wolfe would uncover the Budayeen's assassins by sitting behind his familiar old desk—figuratively, of course—and ratiocinating his way to the killers' identities. Then peace and prosperity would descend once more upon the city, and all Islam would resound with Marîd Audran's name.

Wolfe glanced again at Miss Nablusi. He often showed a distaste for women that bordered on open hostility. How did he feel toward a sex-change? After a moment's reflection, it seemed the detective had only the same mistrust he held for organically grown, nothing artificially added, lo-cal, high-fiber females in general. On the whole, he was a flexible and objective evaluator of people; he could hardly have been so brilliant a detective otherwise. Wolfe would have no difficulty interviewing the people of the Budayeen, or comprehending their outré attitudes and motivations.

As their body grew more comfortable with the moddy, Marîd Audran's personality retired even further into passivity, able to do little more than make suggestions, while Wolfe assumed more control. It became clear that wearing a moddy could lead to the expenditure of a lot of money. Just as the murderer who'd worn the James Bond moddy had reshaped his physical appearance and his wardrobe to match his adopted personality, so too did Audran and Wolfe suddenly want to invest in yellow shirts and yellow pajamas, hire one of the world's finest chefs, and collect thousands of rare and exotic orchid plants. All that would have to wait. "Pfui," grumbled Wolfe again.

They reached up and popped the moddy out.

There was another dizzy swirl of disorientation; and then I was standing in my own room, staring stupidly down at my hand and at the module it held. I was back in my own body and my own mind.

"How was it?" asked Yasmin.

I looked at her. "Satisfactory," I said, using Wolfe's most enthusiastic expression. "It might do," I admitted. "I have the feeling that Wolfe will be able to sort through the facts and find the explanation, after all. If there is one."

"I'm glad, Marîd. And remember, if this one isn't good

enough, there are thousands of other moddies you can try, too."

I put the moddy on the floor beside the bed and lay down.

Maybe I ought to have had my brain boosted a long time ago. I suspected that I'd been missing a bet, that I'd been wrong and everybody else had been right. Well, I was all grown-up and I could admit my mistakes. Not out loud, of course, and never to someone like Yasmin, who'd never let me forget about it: but deep down inside I knew, and that's what counted. It had only been my pride and fear, after all, that had kept me from getting wired sooner—my feeling that I could show up any moddy with my own native good sense and one cerebral hemisphere tied behind my back. I unclipped my phone and called the Half-Hajj at home; he hadn't gone out yet for lunch, and he promised to pass by my apartment in a few minutes. I told him I had a little gift for him.

Yasmin lay down beside me while we waited for Saied to arrive. She put a hand across my chest and rested her head on my shoulder. "Marîd," she said softly, "you know that I'm really proud of you."

"Yasmin," I said slowly, "you know that I'm really scared out of me wits."

"I know, honey; I'm scared, too. But what if you hadn't done your part in all this? What about Nikki and the others? What if more people are killed, people you could have saved? What could I think about you then? What would *you* think?"

"I'll make a deal with you, Yasmin: I'll go on and do what I can and take whatever chances I can't avoid. Just stop telling me all the time that I'm doing the right thing and that you're so glad I may be dead in the next half-hour. All the cheering in the reserved seats is great for your morale; but it doesn't help me in the least, after a while it gets kind of tiresome, and it won't make bullets or knives bounce off my hide. Okay?"

She was, of course, hurt, but I meant exactly what I'd said; I wanted to nip all this "Go out there and get 'em, boy!" choo in the bud. I was sorry that I'd been so hard on Yasmin, though. To cover it, I got up and went to the bathroom. I closed the door and ran a glass of water. The water is always warm in my apartment, summer or winter, and I rarely had ice in the little freezer. After a while you can drink the tepid water with its swirling, suspended particles in it. Not me, though. I'm still working on that. I like a glass of water that doesn't stare back at you.

I took my pill case from my jeans and scrabbled out a cluster of Sonneine. These were the first sunnies I'd taken since I got out of the hospital. Like some kind of addict I was celebrating my abstinence by breaking it. I dropped the sunnies into my mouth and took a gulp of warm water. There, I thought, *that's* what will keep me going. A couple of sunnies and a few tri-phets are worth a stadium full of well-wishers with their bedsheet banners. I closed the pill case quietly—was I trying to keep Yasmin from hearing? Why?—and flushed the toilet. Then I went back into the big room.

I was halfway across the floor when Saied knocked on the door. *"Bismillah,"* I called, and swung it open.

"Yeah, you right," said the Half-Hajj. He came into the room and dropped himself on the corner of the mattress. "What you got for me?"

"He's amped now, Saied," said Yasmin. He turned toward her slowly and gave her that rough-and-tough glare of his. He was in that hitter frame of mind again. A woman's place is in *certain areas* of the home, seen and not heard, maybe not even seen if she knows what's good for her.

The Half-Hajj looked back at me and nodded. *"I* was wired when I was thirteen years old," he said.

I wasn't going to arm-wrestle with him about anything. I reminded myself that I was asking him to help me, and that it would truly be dangerous for him. I flipped the Archie Goodwin moddy to him, and he caught it easily with one hand. "Who is it?" he asked.

"A detective from some old books. He works for the greatest detective in the world. The boss is big and fat and never leaves his home, so Goodwin does all the legwork for him. Goodwin is young and good-looking and smart."

"Uh huh. And I suppose this moddy is just an end-of-Ramadân gift, a little late, right?"

"No."

"You took Papa's money, and you took his wire-job, and so you're really going out after whoever's been disenfranchising our friends and neighbors. Now you want me to chip in sturdy, reliable Goodwin and ride along with you after adventure or something."

"I need someone, Saied," I said. "You were the first person I thought of."

He looked a little flattered by that, but he was still far from enthusiastic. "This just isn't my line," he said.

"Chip it in, and it will be."

He looked at that one from both sides and realized I was right. He took off his *keffiya*, which he'd shaped into a kind of turban, popped out the moddy he was wearing, and plugged in Archie Goodwin.

I walked by him, toward the sink. I watched as his expression lost focus and then reformed subtly into something else. He seemed more relaxed, more intelligent now. He gave me a wry, amused smile, but he was measuring me and the new contents of his mind. His eyes took in everything in the room, as if he'd have to make an item-by-item catalog of it all later. He waited, giving me a look that was part insolence and part devotion. He wasn't seeing me, I knew; he was seeing Nero Wolfe.

Goodwin's attitudes and personality would appeal to Saied. He'd love the chance to jazz me with Goodwin's sardonic remarks. He liked the idea of being devastatingly attractive; wearing that moddy, he'd even be able to overcome his own aversion to women. "We'd have to discuss the matter of salary," he said.

"Of course. You know that Friedlander Bey is underwriting my expenses."

He grinned. I could see visions of expensive suits and intimate dinners and dancing at the Flamingo whirl through his rectified mind.

Then, suddenly, the grin receded. He was riffling through Goodwin's artificial memories. "I've been punched around more than a little, working for you," he said, thoughtfully.

I wiggled a finger at him, in Wolfe's manner. "That is

part of your job, Archie, and you are well aware of it. I surmise it is the part you enjoy most."

The grin filled his face again. "And you enjoy surmising about me and *my* surmising. Well, go ahead, it's the only exercise you get. And you might be right about that. Anyway, it's been a long time since we had a case to work on."

Maybe I should have had my Wolfe moddy chipped in, too; without it, watching the Half-Hajj do his sidekick imitation solo was almost embarrassing. I gave a Wolfe grunt because it was expected, and paused. "Then you'll help me?" I asked.

"Just a minute." Saied popped the moddy out and chipped in his old one. It took less time for him to get used to going from a moddy to his own naked brain and into a second moddy. Of course, as he said, he'd been doing it since he'd been thirteen; I'd only done it once, a few minutes ago. He looked me over sourly, from my face down to the floor and back up again. When he started talking, I knew immediately that he wasn't in a good mood. Without Goodwin's moddy to make it all seem fun and romantic and excitingly risky, the Half-Hajj was having none of it. He stepped closer to me and spoke with his jaws clenched tightly together. "Look," he said, "I'm real sorry Nikki got killed. It bothers me that somebody's aced out the Black Widow Sisters, too, though they were never friends of mine; it's just a bad thing all the way around. As for Abdoulaye, he got what was coming to him and, if you ask me, he got it later than he deserved. So it comes down to a grudge match between you and some blazebrain on account of Nikki. I say *wonderful*, you got the whole Budayeen and the city and Papa himself on your side. But I don't see where you get the goddamn nerve"—and he poked me real hard in the chest with a forefinger that was like a heavy iron rod—"to ask me to screen you from everything bad that might happen. You'll take the reward, all right, but the bullet holes and the stab wounds you figure you can palm off onto me. Well, Saied can see what you're doing, Saied isn't as crazy as you think he is." He snorted, almost amazed at my audacity. "Even if you get out of all this alive, Maghrebi, even if everybody in the world thinks you're some kind of hero, we're going to have to settle this business between us." He looked at me, his face fierce and red, his jaw muscles working, trying to cool down enough to get his rage out coherently. At last he gave up; for a few seconds I thought he was going to slug me. I didn't move an inch. I waited. He raised his fist, hesitated, then grabbed the Archie Goodwin moddy from his other hand. He threw the moddy to the floor, chased it a few yards as it skidded across the room, then raised one foot and brought it down, crushing the plasty moddy beneath the heavy wooden stacked heel of his leather boot. Shattered pieces of the plastic case and bright, colored bits of the circuitry within flew in all directions. The Half-Hajj stared down at the ruined moddy for a moment, his eyes blinking stupidly. Then he slowly looked up at me again. "You know what that guy *drinks*?" he shouted. "He drinks *milk*, goddamn it!" Deeply offended, Saied headed toward the door.

"Where are you going?" asked Yasmin timidly.

He glanced at her. "I'm going to find the biggest porterhouse steak in the city and put it where it belongs. I'm going to have a hell of a good time in honor of how close I came to getting conned to death by your boyfriend here." Then he threw open the front door and stalked out, slamming the door shut behind him.

I laughed. It had been a great performance, and just the release I had been needing. I wasn't looking forward to the reckoning Saied had threatened; but if the two assassins didn't make the matter trivial, I was sure that the Half-Hajj would get over his anger soon enough. If I did end up a hero, unlikely as it seemed, he'd be in an unpopular minority, sounding spiteful and envious. I was sure that Saied would never stay in any unpopular group if he could do anything about it. I'd just have to keep breathing long enough, and the Half-Hajj would eventually be my friend again.

My good humor, I guessed, coincided with the rising of the sunnies. See, I told myself, how already they're helping you stay in control? What good would it have done to get into a fistfight with Saied?

"Now what?" asked Yasmin.

I wished she hadn't asked that. "I'll go find another moddy, as you suggested. In the meantime, I have to put all the information together the way Papa wants, and try to sort all this out and see if there's a definite pattern or line of investigation to follow."

"You weren't being a coward, were you, Marîd? About getting the brain implants?"

"Sure, I was afraid. You know that. I wasn't being a coward about it, though. It's more as if I was putting off the inevitable. I've felt like Hamlet a lot lately. Even when you admit that the thing you fear *is* inevitable, you're not sure it's still the correct thing to do. Maybe Hamlet could have solved things with less bloodshed another way, without forcing his uncle's hand. Maybe getting my brain amped only seems right. Maybe I'm overlooking something obvious."

"If you just diddle with yourself like this, more people will die, maybe even yourself. Don't forget, if half the Budayeen knows you're on the killers' trail, the killers know it, too."

That hadn't yet occurred to me. Even the sunnies couldn't buoy me up after that piece of news.

An hour later I was in Lieutenant Okking's office. As usual, he didn't show much enthusiasm when I looked in on him. "Audran," he said. "Collected another dead body for me? If all's right with the world, then you're dragging yourself in here mortally wounded, desperate for my forgiveness before you kick off."

"Sorry, Lieutenant," I said.

"Well, I can dream, can't I?"

Ya salaam, he was always so goddamn amusing. "I'm supposed to work more closely with you, and you're supposed to cooperate willingly with me. Papa thinks it best if we pool all our information."

He looked like he'd just sniffed something decomposing nearby. He muttered a few words unintelligibly under his breath. "I don't like his high-handed butting in, Audran, and you can tell him that for me. He's going to make it harder for me to close this case. Friedlander Bey's only endangering himself more by having you interfere with police business."

"He doesn't see it that way."

Okking nodded glumly. "All right, what do you want me to tell you?"

I sat back and tried to look casual. "Everything you know about Lutz Seipolt and the Russian who was killed in Chiri's club."

Okking was startled. It took him a moment to compose himself. "Audran, what possible connection could there be between the two?" he asked.

We'd been through this before; I knew he was just stalling. "There have to be overlapping motives or some broad conflict we don't understand, being played out in the Budayeen."

"Not necessarily," said the lieutenant. "The Russian wasn't part of the Budayeen. He was a political nobody who set foot in your quarter only because you asked him to meet you there."

"You're doing a good job of changing the subject, Okking. Answer the question: Where is Seipolt from and what does he do?"

"He came to the city three or four years ago, from someplace in the Fourth Reich, Frankfurt, I think. He set himself up as an import-export agent—you know how vague a description that is. His main business is food and spices, coffee, some cotton and fabrics, Oriental rugs, junk copper and brass pieces, cheap jewelry, Muski glass from Cairo, and other minor things. He's big in the European community, he seems to turn a nice profit, and he has never shown any signs of being involved in any high-level illicit international trade. That's about all I know."

"Can you imagine why he pulled a gun on me when I asked him a few questions about Nikki?"

Okking shrugged. "Maybe he just likes his privacy. Look, you aren't the most innocent-looking guy in the world, Audran. Maybe he thought you were there to put the arm on him and run off with his collection of ancient statuary and scarabs and mummified mice."

"Then you've been to his place?"

Okking shook his head. "I get reports," he said. "I'm an influential police administrator, remember?"

"That's right, I keep forgetting. So the Nikki-Seipolt angle is a dead end. What about the Russian, Bogatyrev?"

"He was a mouse working for the Byelorussians. First his kid went missing, and then he had the bad luck to stop this James Bond's slug. He has even less of a connection to the other murders than Seipolt does."

I smiled. "Thanks, Lieutenant. Friedlander Bey wanted me to make sure you hadn't turned up any new evidence lately. I really don't want to disrupt your investigation. Just tell me what I should do next."

He made a face. "I'd suggest that you go on a fact-finding mission to Tierra del Fuego or New Zealand or somewhere out of my hair, but you'd only laugh and not take me seriously. So check on anyone who had a grudge against Abdoulaye, or if anyone particularly wanted to kill the Black Widow Sisters. Find out if any of the Sisters had been seen with an unknown or suspicious person just before she was killed."

"All right," I said, standing up. I'd just been given a first-class runaround, but I wanted Okking to think he had me snowed. Maybe he had some definite leads that he didn't want to share with me, despite what Papa had said. That might explain his offhand lying. Whatever the reason, I planned to come back soon—when Okking wasn't around—and use the computer records to dig a little deeper into the backgrounds of Seipolt and Bogatyrev.

When I got home, Yasmin pointed to the table. "Somebody left a note for you."

"Oh yeah?"

"Just slipped it under the door and knocked. I went to the door, but there wasn't anybody there. I went downstairs, but there was nobody on the sidewalk, either."

I felt a chill. I tore open the envelope. There was a short message printed out on computer paper. It said:

AUDRAN:
YOU'RE NEXT!
JAMES BOND IS GONE.
I'M SOMEONE ELSE NOW. CAN YOU GUESS WHO?
THINK ABOUT SELIMA AND YOU'LL KNOW.

IT WON'T DO YOU ANY GOOD, BECAUSE
YOU'LL BE DEAD SOON!

"What does it say?" asked Yasmin.

"Oh, nothing," I said. I felt a little tremor in my hand. I turned away from Yasmin, crumpled the paper, and stuffed it in my pocket.

15

Since the night Bogatyrev had been killed in Chiriga's place, I had felt almost every strong emotion a person can. There had been disgust and terror and elation. I had known hate and love, hope and despair. I had been by turns timid and bold. Yet nothing had filled me so completely as the fury that surged in me now. The preliminary jostling was over, and ideas like honor, justice, and duty were submerged beneath the overpowering need to stay alive, to keep from being killed. The time for doubt had passed. I had been threatened—*me*, personally. That anonymous message had gotten my attention.

My rage was directed immediately at Okking. He was hiding information from me, maybe covering up something, and he was endangering my life. If he wanted to endanger Abdoulaye or Tami, well, I guess that's police business. But endangering me—that's *my* business. When I got to his office, Okking was going to learn that. I was going to teach it to him the hard way.

I was striding fiercely up the Street, seething and rehearsing what I was going to say to the lieutenant. It didn't take me long to get it all worked out. Okking would be surprised to see me again, only an hour after I'd left his office. I planned to storm in, slam his door so hard the glass would rattle, shove the death threat into his face, and demand a complete recitation of facts. Otherwise I would haul him down to one of the interrogation rooms and bounce him off his own walls for a while. I bet Sergeant Hajjar would give me all the help I wanted, too.

As I got to the gate at the eastern end of the Budayeen,

I faltered a bit between steps. A new thought had rammed its way into my mind. I had felt that little tickle of unfinished business this morning when I'd talked to Okking; I'd felt it after seeing Selima's corpse, too. I always let my unconscious mind work on those tickles, and sooner or later it puzzled them out. Now I had my answer, like an electric buzzer going off in my head.

Question: What is missing from this picture?

Answer: Let's take a close look. First, we've had several unsolved murders in the neighborhood in the last several weeks. How many? Bogatyrev, Tami, Devi, Abdoulaye, Nikki, Selima. Now, what do the police do when they hit a brick wall in a homicide investigation? Police work is repetitive, tedious, and methodical; they bring in all the witnesses again and make them go over their statements in case some vital clue has been neglected. The cops ask the same questions five, ten, twenty, a hundred times. You get dragged down to the station, or they wake you up in the middle of the night. More questions, more of the same dull answers.

With a scoreboard showing six unsolved, apparently related killings, why hadn't the police been doing more plodding and inspecting and badgering? I hadn't had to go through my stories a second time, and I doubt that Yasmin or anyone else had to, either.

Okking and the rest of the department had to be laying off. By the life of my honor and my eyes, why weren't they pursuing this thing? Six dead already, and I was sure that the count would go higher. I had been personally promised at least one more corpse—my own.

When I got to the copshop I went by the desk sergeant without a word. I wasn't thinking about procedures and protocol, I was thinking about blood. Maybe it was the look on my face or a midnight-black aura I was carrying with me, but no one stopped me. I went upstairs and cut through the maze of corridors until I came to Hajjar, sitting outside Okking's meager headquarters. Hajjar must have noticed my expression, too, because he just jerked a thumb over his shoulder. He wasn't going to stand in my way, and he wasn't going to take his chances with the boss, either. Hajjar wasn't smart, but he was tricky. He was going to let Okking and me beat on each other, but he wasn't going to be nearby himself. I don't remember if I said anything to Hajjar or not. The next thing I recall, I was leaning over Okking's desk with my right fist wrapped tightly in the bunched cotton cloth of his shirt. We were both screaming.

"What the hell does this mean?" I shouted, waving the computer paper in front of his eyes. That's all I could get out before I was spun around, dropped, and pinned to the floor by two policemen, while three more covered me with their needle guns. My heart was already racing, it couldn't beat any faster without exploding. I stared at one of the cops, looking into the tiny black mouth of his pistol. I wanted to kick his face in, but my mobility was restricted.

"Let him go," said Okking. He was breathing hard, too.

"Lieutenant," objected one of the men, "if—"

"Let him go. *Now.*"

They let me go. I got to my feet and watched the uniforms holster their weapons and leave the room. They were all muttering. Okking waited for the last one to cross the threshold, then he slowly closed the door, ran a hand through his hair, and returned to his desk. He was spending a lot of time and effort calming himself. I suppose he didn't want to talk to me until he got himself under control. Finally he sat down in his swivel chair and looked at me. "What is it?" he asked. No bantering, no sarcasm, no cop's veiled threats or wheedling. Just as my time for fear and uncertainty had passed, so had Okking's time for professional disdain and condescension.

I laid the note on his blotter and let him read it. I sat down in a hard, angular plastic chair beside Okking's desk and waited. I saw him finish reading. He closed his eyes and rubbed them wearily. "Jesus," he murmured.

"Whoever that James Bond was, he traded in that moddy for another one. He said I'd know which one if I thought about it. Nothing rings any bells with me."

Okking stared at the wall behind me, calling up the scene of Selima's murder in his mind. First his eyes got a little wider, then his mouth fell open a bit, and then he groaned. "Oh my God," he said.

"What?"

"How does Xarghis Moghadhîl Khan sound?"

I'd heard the name before, but I wasn't sure who Khan was. I knew that I wasn't going to like him, though. "Tell me about him," I said.

"It was about fifteen years ago. This psychopath proclaimed himself the new prophet of God in Assam or Sikkim or one of those places to the east. He said a gleaming blue angel presented him with revelations and divine proclamations, the most urgent being that Khan go out and jam every white woman he could find and murder anybody who got in his way. He bragged about settling two or three hundred men, women, and children before he was stopped. Killed four more in prison before they executed him. He liked to hack organs out of his victims as sacrifices to his blue metal angel. Different organs for different days of the week or phases of the moon or some goddamn thing."

There was anxious silence for a few seconds. "He's going to be a lot worse as Khan than he was as Bond," I said.

Okking nodded grimly. "Xarghis Moghadhîl Khan by himself makes the whole of the Budayeen's collection of thugs look like cartoon cats and mice."

I closed my eyes, feeling helpless. "We've got to find out if he's just some lunatic hatchet man or if he's working for somebody."

The lieutenant stared past me at the far wall for a moment, turning some idea over in his mind. His right hand toyed nervously with a cheap bronze figure of a mermaid on his desk. Finally he looked at me. "I can help you there," he said softly.

"I was sure you knew more than you were telling. You know who this Bond-Khan guy is working for. You know I was right about the murders being assassinations, don't you?"

"We don't have time for back-patting and medal-pinning. That can come later."

"You'd better come across with the whole story now. If Friedlander Bey hears that you're holding back this information, he'll have you out of your job before you have time to say you're sorry."

"I don't know that for sure, Audran," said Okking. "But I don't want to test it."

"So spell it out: Who was James Bond working for?"

The cop turned away again. When he glanced back at me, there was anguish in his expression. "He was working for me, Audran."

The plain truth is, that wasn't what I was expecting to hear. I didn't know how to react. *"Wallâhî il-'azîm,"* I murmured. I just let Okking take care of explaining it however he wanted.

"You're stumbling around in something bigger than a few serial murders," he said. "I guess you know that, but you don't have any idea how *much* bigger. All right. I was getting money from a European government to locate somebody who had fled to the city. This person was in line to rule another country. A political faction in the fugitive's homeland wanted to assassinate him. The government I work for wanted to find him and bring him back unharmed. You don't need to know all the details of the intrigue, but that's the basic idea. I hired 'James Bond' to find the man, and also to disrupt the other party's attempt to assassinate him."

I took a few seconds to take that all in. It was a pretty good sized chunk to swallow. "Bond killed Bogatyrev. And Devi. And Selima, after he became Xarghis Khan. So I was on the right track from the beginning—Bogatyrev was iced on purpose. It wasn't an unfortunate accident, as you and Papa and everybody else kept insisting. And that's why you haven't been digging deeper into these murders. You know exactly who killed them all."

"I wish I did, Audran." Okking looked tired, and a little sick. "I don't have the slightest idea who's working for the other side. I have enough clues—the same awful M.O., the bruises and handprints on the tortured bodies, a pretty good description of the killer's size and weight, a lot of little forensic details like that. But I don't know who it is, and it scares me."

"*You're* scared? You got a hell of a lot of nerve. Everybody in the Budayeen has been hiding under their covers for weeks, wondering if these two psychos would tap them next, and *you're* scared. What the hell are you scared of, Okking?"

"The other side won, the prince was assassinated; but the murders didn't stop. I don't know why. The assassination should have ended the matter. The killers are probably eliminating anyone who might identify them."

I chewed my lip and thought. "I need to back up a little," I said. "Bogatyrev worked for the legation of one of the Russian kingdoms. How does he tie up with Devi and Selima?"

"I told you I didn't want to give out all the details. This gets dirty, Audran. Can't you be satisfied with what I've already told you?"

I felt myself getting furious again. "Okking, your fucking hit man is coming after *me* next. I've got a goddamn *right* to know the whole story. Why can't you tell your killer to lay off now?"

"Because he's disappeared. After the prince was killed by the other side, Bond dropped out of sight. I don't know where he is or how to get in contact with him. He's working on his own, now."

"Or else someone else has given him a new set of instructions." I couldn't suppress a shudder when the first name that crossed my mind was not Seipolt's—the logical choice— but Friedlander Bey's. I knew then that I'd been kidding myself about Papa's motives: fear for his own life, and a laudable interest in protecting the other citizens of the city. No, Papa was never so straightforward. But could he somehow be behind these terrible events? It was a possibility I could neglect no longer.

Okking was lost in thought, too, a glint of fear in his eyes. He played with his little mermaid some more. "Bogatyrev wasn't just a minor clerk with that Russian legation. He was the Grand Duke Vasili Petrovich Bogatyrev, the younger brother of King Vyacheslav of Byelorussia and the Ukraine. His nephew, the crown prince, had gotten to be too much of an embarrassment at court and had to be sent away. Neofascist parties in Germany wanted to find the prince and bring him back to Byelorussia, thinking that they could use him to topple his father from the throne and replace the monarchy with a German-controlled 'protectorate.' Remnants of the Soviet Communists supported them; they wanted the monarchy destroyed, too, but they planned to replace it with their own sort of government."

"A temporary alliance of the far right wing and the far left," I said.

Okking smiled wanly. "It's happened before."

"And you were working for the Germans."

"That's right."

"Through Seipolt?"

Okking nodded. He wasn't enjoying any bit of this. "Bogatyrev wanted you to find the prince. When you did, the duke's man, whoever he is, would kill him."

I was astonished. "Bogatyrev was setting up the murder of his own nephew? His brother's son?"

"To preserve the monarchy at home, yes. They'd decided it was unfortunate but necessary. I told you it was dirty. When you wander into the highest level of international affairs, it's almost always dirty."

"Why did Bogatyrev need me to find his nephew?"

Okking shrugged. "In the past three years of the prince's exile, he'd managed to disguise himself and hide pretty well. Sooner or later, he must have realized his life was in danger."

"Bogatyrev's 'son' wasn't killed in a traffic accident, then. You lied to me; he was still alive when you told me the matter was closed. But you say the Byelorussians *did* kill him, after all."

"He was that sex-change friend of yours. Nikki. Nikki was really the Crown Prince Nikolai Konstantin."

"Nikki?" I said in a flat voice. I was unnerved by the accumulated weight of the truths I'd demanded to hear, and by the weight of regret. I remembered Nikki's terrified voice during that short, interrupted telephone call. Could I have saved her? Why hadn't she trusted me more? Why didn't she tell me the truth, tell me what she must have suspected? "Then Devi and the other two Sisters were killed—"

"Just because they were too close to her. It didn't make any difference whether or not they really knew anything dangerous. The German killer—Khan, now—and the Russian guy aren't taking any chances. That's why you're on the list, too. That's why . . . this." The lieutenant opened a drawer and took something out, flipped it across his desk toward me.

It was another note on computer paper, just like mine. Only it was addressed to Okking.

"I'm not leaving the police station until this is all over," he said. "I'm staying right here with a hundred fifty friendly cops watching my back."

"I hope none of them is Bogatyrev's knifeman," I said. Okking winced. The idea had already occurred to him, too.

I wished I knew how long the hit lists were, how many names followed mine and Okking's. It was a shock when I realized that Yasmin could very well be on them. She knew at least as much as Selima had; more, because I'd told her what I knew and what I guessed. And Chiriga, was her name there? What about Jacques, Saied, and Mahmoud? And how many other people that I knew? Thinking about Nikki, who'd gone from prince to princess to dead, thinking about what I had ahead of me, I felt crushed; I looked at Okking and realized that he was crushed, too. Far worse than I. His career in the city was over, now that he had admitted to being a foreign agent.

"I don't have any more to tell you," he said.

"If you learn something, or if I need to get in touch with you . . ."

"I'll be here," he said in a dead voice. "*Inshallah.*" I got up and left his office. It was like escaping from prison.

Outside the station house, I unclipped my phone and spoke into it as I walked. I called the hospital and asked for Dr. Yeniknani.

"Hello, Mr. Audran," came his deep voice.

"I wanted to find out about the old woman, Laila."

"It's too soon to tell, to be quite frank. She may recover with the passage of time, but it doesn't seem likely. She is old and frail. I have her sedated and she's under constant observation. I'm afraid she might fall into an irreversible coma. Even if that doesn't happen, there's an extremely high probability that she will never regain her intelligent faculties. She will never be able to care for herself or perform the simplest tasks."

I took a deep breath and let it out. I felt that I was to blame.

"All is as Allah ordains," I said numbly.

"Praise be to Allah."

"I will ask Friedlander Bey to take upon himself the cost of her medical expenses. What happened to her was a result of my investigations."

"I understand," said Dr. Yeniknani. "There is no need to speak to your sponsor. The woman is being treated as a charity case."

"I speak for Friedlander Bey as well as myself: we cannot adequately express our thanks."

"It is a sacred duty," he said simply. "Our technicians have determined what was recorded on that module. Do you wish to know?"

"Yes, of course," I said.

"There are three bands. The first, as you know, is a recording of the responses of a large, powerful, but starved, maltreated, and ruthlessly provoked cat, apparently a Bengal tiger. The second band is the brain impression of a human infant. The last band is the most repellent of all. It is the captured, fading consciousness of a very recently murdered woman."

"I knew I was looking for a monster, but I've never heard anything so depraved in all my life." I was thoroughly disgusted. This lunatic had no moral restraints on him at all.

"A piece of advice, Mr. Audran. Never use such a cheaply manufactured module. They are crudely recorded, with a great deal of harmful 'noise.' They lack the safeguards built into the industrially made modules. Too frequent use of underground moddies results in damage to your central nervous system, and through it, your whole body."

"I wonder where it will end?"

"Simple enough to predict: The killer will get a duplicate module made."

"Unless Okking or I or someone else gets to him first."

"Take heed, Mr. Audran. He is, as you say, a monster."

I thanked Dr. Yeniknani and returned the phone to my

belt. I couldn't stop thinking about how wretched and miserable a life Laila had remaining to her. I thought also about my nameless foe, who used a commission from the Byelorussian royalists as a license to indulge his repressed desire to commit atrocities. The news from the hospital changed my half-formed plans entirely. Now I knew precisely what I had to do, and I had some good ideas about how to get it done.

Going up the Street, I met Fuad the Terminally Witless. "*Marhaba,*" he said. He squinted up at me, one hand shading his weak eyes.

"How's it goin', Fuad?" I said. I wasn't in the mood to stand around and talk with him. I had some preparations to make.

"Hassan wants to see you. Something to do with Friedlander Bey. Said you'd know what he meant."

"Thanks, Fuad."

"Do you? Know what he means?" He blinked at me, hungry for gossip.

I sighed. "Yeah, right, I know. Got to run." I tried to tear myself away from him.

"Hassan said it was really important. What's it all about, Marîd? You can tell me. I can keep a secret."

I didn't answer; I doubted that Fuad could keep *anything*, least of all a secret. I just clapped him on the shoulder like a pal, and gave him my back. I stopped in Hassan's shop before I went home. The American kid was still sitting on his stool in the empty room. He gave me a chilling comehither smile. I was sure now: this boy liked me. I didn't say a word, but ducked into the back and found Hassan. He was doing what he was always doing, checking invoices and packing lists against his cartons and crates. He saw me and smiled. Apparently he and I were on good terms now; it was so hard keeping track of Hassan's moods that I had stopped trying. He set down his clipboard, put one hand on my shoulder, and kissed my cheek in the Arabic manner. "Welcome, O my darling nephew!"

"Fuad said you had something to tell me from Papa."

Hassan's face grew serious. "That is only what I told Fuad. I tell you this from *myself*. I am worried, O Maghrebi. I am *more* than worried—I am terrified. I have not slept soundly for four nights, and when I do nap, I have the most horrible dreams. I thought nothing could be worse than when I found Abdoulaye . . . when I found him. . . ." His voice faltered. "Abdoulaye was not a good man, we both know that; yet he and I were closely associated for a number of years. You know that I employed him, even as Friedlander Bey employs me. Now I have been warned by Friedlander Bey that—" Hassan's voice broke and he was unable to say anything for a moment. I was afraid that I would have to watch this bloated pig go to pieces right in front of me. The idea of patting his hand and saying "There, there," was absolutely loathsome. He got himself collected, though, and went on. "Friedlander Bey warned me that more of his friends may yet be in danger. That includes you, O clever one, and myself as well. I am sure you understood the risks weeks ago, but I am not a brave man. Friedlander Bey did not choose me to perform your task because he knows I have no courage, no inner resources, no honor. I must be harsh with myself, because now I can see the truth. *I have no honor.* I think only of myself, of the danger that may confront me, of the possibility that I may suffer and end up just as—" At that point Hassan did break down. He wept. I waited patiently for the shower to pass; slowly the clouds parted, but even then no sun glimmered through.

"I'm taking my own precautions, Hassan. We all should take precautions. Those who've been killed died because they were foolish or too trusting, which is the same thing."

"I trust no one," said Hassan.

"I know. That may keep you alive, if anything will."

"How reassuring," he said dubiously. I don't know what he wanted—a written promise that I would guarantee his scabrous, pitiful little life?

"You'll be all right, Hassan; but if you're so afraid, why not ask Papa for asylum until these killers are caught?"

"Then you think there *are* more than one?"

"I know it."

"That makes it all twice as bad." He struck his chest with his fist several times, appealing to Allah for justice: what had Hassan ever done to deserve this? "What will you do?" the plump, fat-faced merchant said.

"I don't know yet," I said.

Hassan nodded thoughtfully. "Then may Allah protect you," he said.

"Peace be upon you, Hassan," I said.

"And upon you be peace. Take with you this gift from Friedlander Bey." The "gift" was another envelope thick with crisp currency.

I went back out through the cloth hanging and the bare shop without giving Abdul-Hassan a glance. I decided to stop in to see Chiri, to give her a warning and some advice; I also wanted to hide out there for half an hour and forget that I was running for my life.

Chiriga greeted me with her characteristic enthusiasm. *"Habari gani?"* she cried, the Swahili equivalent of "What's up?" Then she narrowed her eyes when she saw my implants. "I heard, but I was waiting to see you before I believed. Two?"

"Two," I admitted.

She shrugged. "Possibilities," she murmured. I wondered what she was thinking. Chiri was always a couple of steps ahead of me when it came to figuring out ways to pervert and corrupt the best-intentioned of legal institutions.

"How've you been?" I asked.

"All right, I guess. No money, nothing happening, same old goddamn boring job." She showed me her sharpened teeth to let me know that while the club might not be making money and the girls and changes weren't making money, *Chiri* was making money. And she wasn't bored, either.

"Well," I said, "we're all going to have to work to keep it all right."

She frowned. "Because of the, uh . . ." She waved a hand in a little circle.

I waved a hand in a little circle, too. "Yeah, because of the 'uh.' Nobody but me wants to believe these killings aren't over and that just about everybody we know is a possible slabsitter."

"Yeah, you right, Marîd," said Chiri in a soft voice. "What the hell you think I should do?"

She had me there. As soon as I talked her into agreeing, she next wanted me to explain the logic the assassins were using. Hell, I'd wasted a lot of time running up and down looking for that, too. Anybody could get bumped, anytime, for any reason. Now when Chiriga asked for practical advice, all I could say was "Be careful." It looked like you had two choices: you went about things just the same but with more eyes open, or you could go live on another continent just to be on the safe side. The latter is assuming you didn't pick the wrong continent and walk right into the heart of the matter, or let it follow along with you.

So I shrugged and told her it looked like a gin and bingara kind of afternoon. She poured herself a big drink, poured me a double on the house, and we sat around and looked into each other's unhappy eyes for a while. No kidding, no flirting, no mentioning the Honey Pílar moddy. I didn't even look at her new girls, and Chiri and I were huddled together too closely for the others to barge in and say hello. When I killed my drink I took a glass of her tende—it was starting to taste better. The first time I'd tried it, it was like I'd bitten into the side of some animal that had died under a log a week ago. I stood up to go, but then some true tenderness that I wasn't quick enough to hide made me touch Chiri's scarred cheek and pat her hand. She flashed me a smile that was almost back to full strength. I got out of there before we both decided to retire to Free Kurdistan or somewhere.

Back at my apartment, Yasmin was working on being late to work. She had got up early that morning to drop her pain and suffering on me, so to get to Frenchy's late she just about had to go back to sleep and start all over again. She gave me a drowsy smile from the mattress. "Hi," she said in a small voice. I think she and the Half-Hajj were the only people in the city who weren't completely terrified. Saied had his moddy to simulate courage, but Yasmin just had me. She was absolutely confident that I was going to protect her. That made her even dumber than Saied.

"Yasmin, look, I got a million things to do, and you're going to have to stay at your own place for a few days, okay?"

She looked hurt again. "You don't want me around?" Meaning: you got somebody else now?

"I don't want you around because I'm a big, shiny target now. This apartment is going to be too dangerous for anybody. I don't want you getting into the line of fire, understand?"

She liked that better; it meant I still cared for her, the dizzy bitch. You have to keep telling them that every ten minutes or they think you're sneaking out the back. "Okay, Maríd. You want your keys back?"

I thought about that a second. "Yeah. That way I know where they are, I know somebody won't lift them from you to get into my place." She took them out of her purse and tossed them toward me. I scooped them up. She made going-to-work motions, and I told her twenty or thirty times that I loved her, that I'd be extra crafty and sly, and that I'd call her a couple times a day just to check in. She kissed me, took a quick glance at the time and gave a phony gasp, and hurried out the door. She'd have to pay Frenchy his big fifty again today.

As soon as Yasmin was gone, I started putting together what I had, and I soon saw how little that was. I didn't want either of the freezers to pop me in my own house, so I needed a place to stay until I felt safe again. For the same reason, I wanted to look different on the street. I still had a lot of Papa's money in my bank account, and the cash I'd just gotten from Hassan would let me move around with a little freedom and security. It never took me long to pack. I stuffed some things into a black nylon zipper bag, wrapped my case of special daddies in a T-shirt and put it on top, then zipped the bag and left my apartment. When I hit the sidewalk, I wondered if Allah would be pleased to let me come back to this place. I knew I was just worrying myself for no good reason, the way you keep pushing at a sore tooth. Jesus, what a nuisance it was, being desperate to stay alive.

I left the Budayeen and crossed the big avenue into a rather pricey collection of shops; these were more like boutiques than like the souks you'd expect. Tourists found just the souvenirs they were looking for here, despite the fact that most of the junk was made in other countries many thousands of miles away. There probably aren't any native arts and crafts in the city at all, so the tourists browsed happily through gaily colored straw parrots from Mexico and plastic folding fans from Kowloon. The tourists didn't care, so nobody had any kick coming. We were all very civilized out here on the edge of the desert.

I went into a men's clothing store that sold European business suits. Usually I didn't have the money to buy half a pair of socks, but Papa was staking me to a whole new look. It was so different, I didn't even know what I needed to get their sweat all over the Oxford suits. I told him I genuinely interested in helping customers. I let him know I was serious—sometimes *fellahîn* go into these shops just to get their sweat all over the Oxxford suits. I told him I wanted to be outfitted completely from the ground up, I told him how much I was willing to spend, and let him put the wardrobe together. I didn't know how to match shirts and ties—I didn't know how to *tie* a tie, I got a printed brochure about different knots—so I really needed the clerk's help. I figured he was getting a commission, so I let him oversell me by a couple of hundred kiam or so. He wasn't just putting on an act about being friendly, the way most shopkeepers do. He didn't even shrink away from touching me, and I was about as scruffy then as you could get. In the Budayeen alone, that takes in a wide range of shabbiness.

I paid for the clothes, thanked the clerk, and carried my packages a couple of blocks to the Hotel Palazzo di Marco Aurelio. It was part of a large international Swiss-owned chain: all of them looked alike, and none of them had any of the elegance that had made the original so charming. I didn't care. I wasn't looking for elegance or charm, I was looking for a place to sleep where no one would sizzle me in the night. I wasn't even curious enough to ask why the hotel in this Islamic stronghold was named after some Roman son of a bitch.

The guy at the desk didn't have the attitude of the salesman at the clothing store; I knew immediately that the room clerk was a snob, that he was paid to be a snob, that the hotel had trained him to raise his natural snobbery to ethereal heights. There was nothing I could say to crack his contempt; he was as set in his ways as a sidewalk. There was something I could do, though, and I did it. I took out all the money I had with me and spread it out on the pink marble counter. I told him I needed a good single room for a week or two, and I'd pay in cash in advance.

His expression didn't change—he still hated my guts—but he called over an assistant and instructed him to find me a room. It didn't take long. I carried my own packages up in an elevator and dumped them on the bed in my room. It was a nice room, I guess, with a good view of the back ends of some buildings in the business district. I had my own holo set, though, and a tub instead of just a shower. I emptied the zipper bag onto the bed, too, and changed into my Arab costume. It was time to pay another call on Herr Lutz Seipolt. This time I took a few daddies along with me. Seipolt was a shrewd man, and his boy Reinhardt might give me problems. I chipped in a German-language daddy and took along some of the body-and-mind controls. From now on I was only going to be a blur to normal people. I didn't plan to hang around anywhere long enough for someone to draw a bead on me. Marîd Audran, the superman of the sands.

Bill was sitting in his beat-up old taxi, and I got in beside him on the front seat. He didn't notice me. He was waiting for orders from the inside, as usual. I called his name and shoved his shoulder for almost a minute before he turned and blinked at me. "Yeah?" he said.

"Bill, will you take me out to Lutz Seipolt's place?"

"I know you?"

"Uh huh. We went out there a few weeks ago."

"That's easy for *you* to say. Seipolt, huh? The German guy with the thing for blondes with legs? I can tell you right now, you're not his type at all."

Seipolt had told me he didn't have a thing for *anybody* anymore. My God, Seipolt had lied to me, too; I tell you, I was shocked. I sat back and watched the city scream by the car as Bill forced his way through it. He always made the trip a little more difficult than it had to be. Of course, he was avoiding things in the road most people can't even *see*, and he did it well, too. I don't think he smacked a single *afrit* all the way out to Seipolt's.

I got out of the cab and walked slowly to Seipolt's

massive wooden door. I knocked and rang the bell and waited, but no one came. I started to go around the house, hoping to run into the old *fellah* caretaker I'd met the first time I'd come out here. The grass was lush and the plants and flowers ticked along on their botanical timetables. I heard the chirping of birds high in a tree, a rare enough sound in the city, but I didn't hear anything that might mean the presence of people in the estate. Maybe Seipolt had gone to the beach. Maybe Seipolt had gone shopping for brass storks in the *medînah*. Maybe Seipolt and blue-eyed Reinhardt had taken the afternoon and evening off to make the rounds of the city's hot spots, dining and dancing under the moon and stars.

Around the big house to the right, between two tall palmettos, was a side door set into the whitewashed wall. I didn't think Seipolt ever used it; it looked like a convenience for whoever had to carry the groceries in and the garbage out. This side of the house was landscaped with aloes and yucca and flowering cactus, different from the front of the villa and its tropical rain-forest blossoms. I grabbed the doorknob, and it turned in my hand. Somebody had probably just gone into town for the newspaper. I let myself in and found myself looking down a flight of stairs into an arid darkness, and up a shorter flight into a pantry. I went up, through the pantry, through a well-equipped and gleaming kitchen, and into an elaborate dining room. I didn't see anyone or hear anyone. I made a little noise to let Seipolt or Reinhardt know I was there; I wouldn't want them to shoot me down, thinking I was spying or something.

From the dining room I passed through a parlor and down a corridor to Seipolt's collection of ancient artifacts. I was on familiar ground now. Seipolt's office was just . . . over . . .

. . . there. The door was closed, so I crossed to it and rapped on it loudly. I waited and rapped again. Nothing. I opened the door and stepped into Seipolt's office. It was dim; the drapes were closed across the window. The air was stifling and stale, as if the air-conditioning wasn't working and the room had been shut up for a while. I wondered if I dared go through the stuff on Seipolt's desk. I went up to it and riffled quickly through some reports on the top of a stack of papers.

Seipolt lay in a kind of alcove formed by the bay window behind his desk and two file cabinets against the left-hand wall. He was wearing a dark suit, stained darker now with blood, and when I first glanced over the desktop I thought he was a charcoal-gray throw rug on the light brown carpet. Then I saw a bit of his pale blue shirt and one hand. I took a few steps toward him, not really interested in seeing just how badly cut to pieces he was. His chest was opened from his throat to his groin, and a couple of dark, bloody things were spilled out on the carpet. One of his own internal organs had been crammed into his other stiff hand.

Xarghis Moghadhîl Khan had done this. That is to say, James Bond, who worked for Seipolt. Until just recently. Another witness and lead obliterated.

I found Reinhardt in his own upstairs suite, in the same shape. The nameless old Arab had been murdered on the lawn in back of the house, as he worked among the lovely flowers he nurtured in defiance of nature and climate. All had been killed quickly, then dismembered. Khan had crept from one victim to the next, killing fast and quiet. He moved more silently than a ghost. Before I went back into the house, I chipped in a few daddies that suppressed fear, pain, anger, hunger, and thirst; the German daddy was already in place, but it looked as if it wouldn't be very useful this afternoon.

I headed toward Seipolt's office. I intended to go back in there and search through the desk. Before I got to the room, though, someone called out to me. *"Lutz?"*

I turned to look. It was the blonde with the legs.

"Lutz?" she asked. *"Bist du noch bereit?"*

"Ich heisse Marîd Audran, Fräulein. Wissen Sie wo Lutz ist?" At that point my brain swallowed the German add-on whole; it wasn't as if I could just translate the German into Arabic, but as if I was speaking a language I'd known since early childhood.

"Isn't he down here?" she asked.

"No, and I can't find Reinhardt either."

"They must have gone into the city. They were saying something about that over lunch."

"I'll bet they've gone to my hotel. We had a dinner engagement, and I understood that I was to meet him here. I hired a car all the way out here. What a damn stupid thing. I guess I'll just give the hotel a ring and leave a message for Lutz, and then call another taxi. Would you like to come along?"

She bit her thumbnail. "I don't know if I should," she said.

"Have you seen the city yet?"

She frowned. "I haven't seen *anything* but this house since I've *been* here," she said grumpily.

I nodded. "That's how he is, he drives himself too hard. He always says he'll take it easy and enjoy himself, but he works himself and he works everybody around him. I don't want to say anything against him—after all, he's one of my oldest business associates and dearest friends—but I think it's bad for him to keep going the way he does. Am I right?"

"That's just what I tell him," she said.

"Then why don't we go back to the hotel? Maybe once we're there together, the four of us, we'll get him to relax a little tonight. Dinner and a show, as my guests. I insist."

She smiled. "Just let me—"

"We must hurry," I said. "If we don't get back quickly, Lutz will turn around and come back here. He's an impatient man. Then I'll have to make still another trip out here. It's an awful ride you know. Come along, we don't have any time to spare."

"But if we're going out to dinner—"

I should have guessed. "I think that dress suits you perfectly, my dear; but if you prefer, why, I beg that you allow me to accommodate you with another outfit of your choice, and whatever accessories you feel are necessary. Lutz has given me many gifts over the years. It would give me great pleasure to acknowledge his generosity in this small way. We can go shopping before dinner. I know several very exclusive English, French, and Italian shops. I'm sure you'd enjoy that. Indeed, you might choose your garments for the evening while Lutz and I take care of our little business. It will all work out beautifully."

I had her by the arm and out the front door. We were walking up the gravel drive to Bill's taxi. I opened one of the car's rear doors and helped her in, then I walked around the back of the cab and got in the other side. "Bill," I said in Arabic, "back to the city. The Hotel Palazzo di Marco Aurelio."

Bill looked at me sourly. "Marcus Aurelius is dead, too, you know," he said as he started up the taxi. I got a frosty feeling wondering what he meant by "too."

I turned to the beautiful woman beside me. "Pay no attention to the driver," I said in German. "Like all Americans, he is mad. It is the will of Allah."

"You didn't phone the hotel," she said, giving me a sweet smile. She liked the idea of a new suit of clothes and jewelry just because we were going to dinner. I was just a crazy Arab with too much money. She liked crazy Arabs, I just knew it.

"No, I didn't. I'll have to call as soon as we get there."

She wrinkled up her nose in thought. "But if we're *there*—"

"You don't understand," I told her. "For the common run of guests, the desk clerk is capable of handling matters like this. But when the guests are, shall we say, special—like Herr Seipolt or myself—then one must speak directly with the manager.

Her eyes got bigger. "Oh," she said.

I looked back at the freshly watered garden that Seipolt's money had imposed on the very edge of the creeping dunes. In a couple of weeks, that place would look as dry and dead as the middle of the Empty Quarter. I turned to my companion and smiled easily. We chatted all the way back to the city.

16

At the hotel, I left the blonde in a comfortable chair in the lobby. Her name was Trudi. Trudi Nothing, she told me blithely, just Trudi. She was a close personal friend of Lutz Seipolt. She'd been at his house for more than a week. They'd been introduced by a mutual friend. Uh huh. That Trudi, she was just the nicest, most outgoing girl—and Seipolt, you couldn't *ask* for a sweeter man, down under all that murder and intrigue he wore just to fool people.

I went to make my phone call, but it wasn't to anyone in the hotel that I needed to talk—it was Okking. He told me to babysit Trudi until he could get his fat ass moving. I popped out the daddies I was wearing, then put back the German-language one; I wouldn't be able to say a word to Trudi without it. That's when I learned Vital Important Fact #154 about the special add-ons Papa had given me:

You Pay For Everything In This World.

See, I *knew* that. I learned it many years ago at my mama's knee. It's just that it's something you keep forgetting and have to relearn every once in a while. Don't Nobody Get Nothing For Free.

All the time I'd been out at Seipolt's, the daddies were holding my hormones in check. When I went back into the house to search Seipolt's desk, I would have been helpless with nausea, knowing that the hacked-up bodies hadn't been dead very long, knowing that bastard Khan might *still* be around the place somewhere. When Trudi called out "Lutz?" I would have split my skin jumping in twenty directions at once.

When I popped the daddies out, I found out that I hadn't avoided those terrible feelings, I'd only postponed them. Suddenly my brain and my nerves were tied in an agonizing jumble, like a tangled ball of yarn. I couldn't untwist the separate emotional currents: there was wide-eyed, gasping horror, stifled by the daddies for a few hours; there was sudden fury directed at Khan, for the satanic method he had chosen to remain unknown, and for making me witness the results of his heinous acts; there was physical pain and utter weariness, as the fatigue poisons in my muscles rendered me almost helpless (the daddy had told my brain and the meat part of me to ignore injury and fatigue, and I was suffering from both now); I realized that I was awfully thirsty and I was getting pretty damn hungry; and my bladder, which the daddies had ordered not to communicate with any other part of my body, was near bursting. ACTH was pouring into my bloodstream, making me even more upset. Epinephrine pumped out of my adrenals, making my heart beat faster still, getting me ready for fight or flight; it made no difference that the threat was long gone. I was getting the entire reaction I would normally have experienced over a period of three or four hours, condensed into a solid, crippling blow of emotion and deprivation.

I chipped those daddies back in as fast as I could, and the world stopped lurching. In a minute, I was smoothly back in control. My breathing became normal, my heartbeat slowed down, the thirst, hunger, hatred, tiredness, and the sensation of my full bladder all vanished. I was grateful, but I knew that I was only postponing the payback yet again; when it came due at the end of all this, it would make the worst drug hangover I'd ever known seem like a quick kiss in the dark. Paybacks, *ils sont un motherfucker, n'est-ce pas, monsieur?*

I would have to agree with that.

As I was going back to the lobby and Trudi, someone called my name. I was glad I had the daddies back in; I never liked having my name called in public places anyway, particularly when I was in disguise. "Monsieur Audran?"

I turned and gave one of the hotel clerks a cool look. "Yes?" I said.

"A message for you, monsieur. Left in your box." I could tell he was having trouble with my *gallebeya* and *keffiya*. He was under the impression that only Europeans stayed in his nice, clean hotel.

It was moderately impossible that anyone had left a message for me, on two counts: the first was that no one knew I was staying here, and the second was that I'd checked in under a made-up name. I wanted to see what kind of foolish mistake had been made, and then throw it in the faces of the hotel's stuffed shirts. I took the message. Computer paper, right?

AUDRAN:
SAW YOU AT SEIPOLT'S, BUT THE TIME WASN'T RIGHT.
SORRY.
I WANT YOU ALL TO MYSELF, ALONE AND QUIET.
I DIDN'T WANT ANYONE TO THINK YOU WERE JUST PART OF
A RANDOM GROUP OF VICTIMS.
WHEN THEY FIND YOUR BODY,
I WANT TO BE SURE THEY KNOW
YOU RECEIVED INDIVIDUAL ATTENTION.

                                                        KHAN

My knees were trying to buckle, brain implants or no. I folded the note and put it in my shoulder bag.

"Are you all right, monsieur?" asked the clerk.

"The altitude," I said. "It always takes me a while to adjust."

"But there is none," he said, bewildered.

"That's just what I mean." I went back to Trudi.

She smiled at me as if life had lost its savor while I was away. I wondered what she thought about all by herself. All "alone and quiet." I winced.

"I'm sorry to have been gone so long," I murmured. I gave her a little bow and took the chair beside her.

"I was just fine," she said. She took a long time uncrossing her legs and crossing them the other way. Everyone between here and Osaka must have watched her do it. "Did you speak to Lutz?"

"Yes. He *was* here, but he had some urgent matter to clear up. Something official, with Lieutenant Okking."

"Lieutenant?"

"He's in charge of making sure nothing awkward happens in the Budayeen. You've heard of that part of our city?"

She nodded. "But why would the lieutenant want to talk with Lutz? Lutz doesn't have anything to do with the Budayeen, does he?"

I smiled. "Forgive me, my dear, but you sound a trifle naive. Our friend is a very busy, very industrious man. I doubt if anything happens in the city without Lutz Seipolt knowing about it."

"I suppose so."

That was all bull; Seipolt was middle-management, at best. He was certainly no Friedlander Bey. "They are sending a car for us, so we'll all meet together just as we planned. Then we can decide what we'll do for the rest of the evening."

Her face lit up again. She wasn't going to miss out on her new outfit and the free night on the town, after all.

"Would you care for a drink while we wait?" I asked. That's how we passed the time until a couple of plainclothes gold shields shuffled tiredly across the thick blue carpet toward us. I stood up, made some introductions, and we all left the hotel lobby the best of friends. We continued our pleasant little conversation all the way to the precinct station. We went upstairs, but I was stopped by Sergeant Hajjar. The two plainclothesmen escorted Trudi in to see Okking.

"What happened?" asked Hajjar grimly. I think he was being all cop now. Just to show me he could still do it.

"What do you think happened? Xarghis Khan, who worked for Seipolt and your boss, covered a few more of his tracks. Very thorough, this guy is. If I were Okking, I'd be nervous as hell. I mean, the lieutenant is a stand-out uncovered track himself."

"He knows it; I've never seen him so shook. I made him a present of thirty or forty Paxium. He took a bunch of 'em for lunch." Hajjar grinned.

One of the uniformed cops came out of Okking's office. "Audran," he said, and jerked his head at me. I was just part of the team, they all had a lot of respect for me.

"In a minute." I turned back to Hajjar. "Listen," I said, "I'm going to want to look through what you pull out of Seipolt's desk and file cabinets."

"I figured," said Hajjar. "The lieutenant's too busy to worry about all that, so he'll tell me to take care of it. I'll make sure you get first crack at it."

"All right. It's important, I hope." I went into Okking's glass-walled enclosure just as the two soft-clothes guys led Trudi out. She smiled at me and said *"Marhaba."* That's when I guessed that she spoke Arabic, too.

"Sit down, Audran," said Okking. His voice was hoarse. I sat down. "Where's she going?"

"We're just going to question her in a little more depth. We're going to sift her brain thoroughly. Then we'll let her go home, wherever the hell that is."

It sounded like good police work to me; I just wondered if Trudi would be in any shape to go when they got done sifting her. They'd use hypnosis and drugs and electrical brain stimulation, and it all left you feeling kind of wrung out. That's what I've heard.

"Khan is getting closer," said Okking, "but the other one hasn't made a peep since Nikki."

"I don't know what that means. Say, Lieutenant, Trudi isn't Khan, is she? I mean, could she ever have been James Bond?"

He looked at me like I was crazy. "How the hell would *I* know? I never met Bond in person, we just dealt over the phone, by mail. As far as I know, *you're* the only living person who ever saw him face-to-face. That's why I can't get over this little, nagging suspicion I have, Audran. There's something not quite right about you."

About *me*, I thought; a lot of damn nerve again, coming from a foreign agent cashing checks from the National Socialists. I was unhappy to hear that Okking wouldn't be able to pick Khan out of a lineup, if we should get so lucky. I didn't know if the lieutenant was lying, but he was probably telling the truth. He knew he was high on the list, if not next, to be slashed. He'd been serious about not leaving that room, too: he'd set up a cot in the office, and there was a tray with an unfinished meal on it on his desk.

"The only thing we probably know for sure is that both of them use their moddies not only to kill but to spread a little terror. It's working fine, too," I said. "Your guy—" Okking shot me an ugly look, but hell, it was the truth. "Your guy's changed from Bond to Khan. The other guy is the same as he was, as far as we know. I just hope the Russians' bumper has gone home. I wish we could know for sure that we don't have to worry about him anymore."

"Yeah," said Okking.

"Did you get anything useful out of Trudi before you sent her downstairs?"

Okking shrugged and flipped over half a sandwich on the tray. "Just the polite information. Her name and all that."

"I'd like to know how she got involved with Seipolt in the first place."

Okking raised his eyebrows. "Easy, Audran. Seipolt was the highest bidder this week."

I let out an exasperated breath. "I figured that much, Lieutenant. She told me she'd been introduced to Seipolt by somebody."

"Mahmoud."

"Mahmoud? My friend, Mahmoud? The one who used to be a girl over by Jo-Mama's before his sex change?"

"You right."

"What's Mahmoud got to do with this?"

"While you were in the hospital, Mahmoud got promoted. He took over the position that was left vacant when Abdoulaye got creased."

Mahmoud. Gone from sweet young thing working in the Greek clubs to petty shakedown artist to big-time white slaver in a couple of easy steps. All I could think was "Where else but in the Budayeen?" You talk about equal opportunity for all. "I'll have to talk to Mahmoud," I muttered.

"Get in line. He's coming in here in a little while, as soon as my boys can roust him."

"Let me know what he tells you."

Okking sneered. "Of course, friend; didn't I promise you? Didn't I promise Papa? Anything else I can do for you?"

I got up and leaned over his desk. "Look, Okking, you're used to looking at pieces of bodies splashed around nice peoples' living rooms, but I can't do it without throwing up." I showed him my latest message from Khan. "I want to know if I can get myself a gun or something."

"What the hell do I care?" he said softly, almost hypnotized by Khan's note. I waited. He looked up at me, caught my eye, and sighed. Then he pulled open a lower drawer in his desk and took out some weapons. "What do you want?"

There were a couple of needle guns, a couple of static pistols, a big seizure gun, and even a large automatic projectile pistol. I chose a small Smith & Wesson needle gun and the General Electric seizure cannon. Okking put a box of formatted needle clips on his blotter for me, twelve needles to a magazine, a hundred magazines in the box. I scooped them all up and tucked them away. "Thanks," I said.

"Feel protected now? They give you a sense of invulnerability?"

"You feel invulnerable, Okking?"

His sneer tilted over and crashed. "The hell," he said. He waved me out of there; I went, as grateful as ever.

By the time I got out of the building, the sky was getting dusky in the east. I heard the recorded cries of muezzins from minarets all over the city. It had been a busy day. I wanted a drink, but I still had some things to do before I could let myself ease off a little. I walked into the hotel and went up to my room, stripped off my robe and headgear, and took a shower. I let the hot water pound against my body for a quarter of an hour; I just rotated under it like lamb on a spit. I washed my hair and soaped my face two or three times. It was regrettable but necessary: the beard had to come off. I had gotten clever, but Khan's reminder in my mailbox made it plain that I still wasn't clever enough. First, I cut my long reddish-brown hair short.

I hadn't seen my upper lip since I was a teenager, so the short, harsh swipes with the razor gave me some twinges of regret. They passed quickly; after a while I was actually curious about what I looked like under it all. In another fifteen minutes I had eliminated the beard completely, going back over every place on my neck and face until the skin stung and blood stood out along bright red slashes.

When I realized what I reminded myself of, I couldn't look at my reflection any longer. I threw cold water on my face and toweled off. I imagined thumbing my nose at Friedlander Bey and the rest of the sophisticated undesirables of the city. Then I could find my way back to Algeria and spend the rest of my life there, watching goats die.

I brushed my hair and went into the bedroom, where I opened the packages from the men's store. I dressed slowly, turning some thoughts over in my mind. One notion eclipsed everything else: whatever happened, I wasn't going to chip in a personality module again.

I would use every daddy that offered help, but they just extended my own personality. No human thinking machine of fact or fiction was any good to me—none of them had ever faced this situation, none of them had ever been in the Budayeen. I needed to keep my own wits about me, not those of some irrelevant construct.

It felt good to get that settled. It was the compromise I'd been searching for ever since Papa first told me I'd volunteered to get wired. I smiled. Some weight—negligible, a quarter-pound, maybe—lifted from my shoulders.

I won't say how long it took me to get my necktie on. There were clip-on ties, but the shop where I'd bought everything frowned on their existence.

I tucked my shirt into my trousers, fastened everything, put on my shoes, and threw on the suit jacket. Then I stepped back to look at my new self in the mirror. I cleaned some dried blood from my neck and chin. I looked good, faster than light with a little money in my pocket. You know what I mean. *I* was the same as always: the *clothes* looked first-rate. That was fine, because most people only look at the clothes, anyway. It was more important that for the first time, I believed the whole nightmare was close to resolution. I had gone most of the way through a dark tunnel, and only one or two obscure shapes hid the welcome light at the end of it.

I put the phone on my belt, invisible beneath the suit coat. As an afterthought, I slipped the little needle gun into a pocket; it barely made a bulge, and I was thinking "better safe than sorry." My malicious mind was telling me "safe *and* sorry"; but it was too late at night to listen to my mind, I'd been doing that all day. I was just going down to the hotel's bar for a little while, that's all.

Nevertheless, Xarghis Khan knew what I looked like, and I knew nothing about him except that he probably didn't look anything like James Bond. I remembered what Hassan had said only a few hours ago: "I trust nobody."

That was the plan, but was it practical? Was it even possible to go through a single day being totally suspicious? How many people did I trust without even thinking about it—people who, if they felt like getting rid of me, could have murdered me quickly and simply? Yasmin, for one. The Half-Hajj, I'd even invited him up to my apartment; all he needed to be the assassin was the wrong moddy. Even Bill, my favorite cabbie; even Chiri, who owned the hugest collection of moddies in the Budayeen. I'd go crazy if I kept thinking like that.

What if Okking himself was the very murderer he was pretending to track down? Or Hajjar?

Or Friedlander Bey?

Now I was thinking like the Maghrebi bean-eater they all thought I was. I shook it off, left the hotel room, and rode the elevator down to the mezzanine and the dimly lighted bar. There weren't many people there: the city had few enough tourists to begin with, and this was an expensive and quiet hotel. I looked along the bar and saw three men on the stools, all leaning together and talking quietly. To my right there were four more groups, mostly men, sitting at tables. Recorded European or American music played softly. The theme of the bar seemed to be expressed in potted ferns and stucco walls painted pastel pink and orange. When the bartender raised his eyebrows at me, I ordered a gin and bingara. He made it just the way I liked, down to the splash of Rose's. That was a point for the cosmopolitans.

The drink came and I paid for it. I sipped at it, asking myself why I'd thought sitting here would help me forget my problems. Then she drifted up to me, moving in an unhuman slow-motion as if she were half-asleep or drugged. It didn't show in her smile or her speech, though. "Do you mind if I sit with you?" Trudi asked.

"Of course not." I smiled graciously at her, but my mind was roiling with questions.

She told the barman she wanted peppermint schnapps. I would have put fifty kiam on that. I waited until she got her drink; I paid for it, and she thanked me with another languorous smile.

"How do you feel?" I asked.

She wrinkled her nose. "What do you mean?"

"After answering questions all day for the lieutenant's men."

"Oh, they were all as nice as they could be."

I didn't say anything for a few seconds. "How did you find me?"

"Well," she gestured vaguely, "I knew you were staying here. You brought me here this afternoon. And your name—"

"I never told you my name."

"—I heard it from the policemen."

"And you recognized me? Though I don't look anything like the way I did when you met me? Even though I've never worn clothes like these before or been without my beard?"

She gave me one of those smiles that tell you that men are such fools. "Aren't you glad to see me?" she asked, with that glaze of hurt feelings that the Trudies do so well.

I went back to my gin. "One of the reasons I came down to the bar. Just on the chance you'd come in."

"And here I am."

"I'll always remember that," I said. "Would you excuse me? I'm a couple drinks ahead of you."

"Sure, I'll be fine."

"Thanks." I went off to the men's room, got myself in a

stall, and unclipped my phone. I called Okking's number. A voice I didn't recognize told me he was in his office, asleep for the night, and he wasn't going to be awakened except for an emergency. Was this an emergency? I said I didn't think so, but that if it was I'd get back to him. I asked for Hajjar, but he was out on an investigation. I got Hajjar's number and punched it.

He let his phone ring a while. I wondered if he were really investigating anything or just soaking up ambience. "What is it?" he snarled.

"Hajjar? You sound out of breath. Lifting weights or something?"

"Who is this? How'd you get—"

"Audran. Okking's out for the night. Listen, what did you learn from Seipolt's blonde?"

The phone went mute for a moment, then Hajjar's voice came back on, a little more friendly. "Trudi? We knocked her out, dug around as deep as we could, and brought her back up. She didn't know anything. That worried us, so we put her out a second time. Nobody should know as much nothing as she does and still be alive. But she's clean, Audran. I've known tent stakes that had more going for them than she does, but all she knows about Seipolt is his first name."

"Then why is she still alive and Seipolt and the others aren't?"

"The killer didn't know she was there. Xarghis Khan would have jammed the living daylights out of her, then maybe killed her. As it happened, our Trudi was in her room taking a nap after lunch. She doesn't remember if she locked her door. She's alive because she'd only been there a few days and she wasn't part of the regular household."

"How'd she react to the news?"

"We fed her the facts while she was under, and took out all the horribleness for her. It's like she read about it in the papers."

"Praise Allah, you cops are nice. Did you put anybody on her when she left?"

"You *see* anybody?"

That stung me. "What makes you so sure I'm with her?"

"Why else would you be calling me about her this time of night? She's clean, sucker, as far as we could tell. As for anything else, well, we didn't give her a blood test, so you're on your own." The line went dead.

I grimaced, clipped the phone back on my belt, and went out to the bar. I spent the rest of that gin and tonic looking for Trudi's shadow, but I didn't see a likely candidate. We went out to have something to eat, to give me the chance to ease my mind. By the end of the supper, I was sure no one was following either Trudi or me. We went back to the bar and had a few more drinks and got to know each other. She decided we knew each other well enough just before midnight.

"It's kind of noisy in here, isn't it?" she said.

I nodded solemnly. There were only three other people in the bar now, and that included the block of wood who was making our drinks. It was just that time when either Trudi or I had to say something stupid, and she beat me to it. It was right then that I simultaneously misplaced my caution and decided to teach Yasmin a lesson. Listen, I was mildly drunk, I was depressed and lonely, Trudi was really a sweet girl and absolutely gorgeous—how many do you need?

When we went upstairs, Trudi smiled at me and kissed me a few times, slowly and deeply, as though morning wasn't coming until after lunch some time. Then she told me it was her turn to use the bathroom. I waited for her to close the door, then I called down to the desk and asked them to be sure I was awake by seven the next morning. I took out the small plastic needle gun, threw back the bedspread, and hid the weapon quickly. Trudi came out of the bathroom with her dress hanging loosely, its fastenings left undone. She smiled at me, a lazy, knowing smile. As she came toward me, my only thought was that this would be the first time I'd ever gone to sleep with a gun under my pillow.

"What are you thinking about?" she asked.

"Oh, just that you don't look bad, for a real girl."

"You don't like real girls?" she whispered in my ear.

"I just haven't been with one for a while. It's just worked out that way."

"You like toys better?" she murmured, but there was no more room for discussion.

17

When the phone rang, I was dreaming that my mother was shouting at me. She was screaming so loud that I couldn't recognize her, I just knew it was her. We started arguing about Yasmin, but that changed; we fought about living in the city, and we fought about how I could never be expected to understand anything because the only thing I ever thought about was myself. My part was limited to crying "I am not!" while my heart thudded in my sleep.

I thrashed awake, bleary and still tired. I squinted at the phone, then picked it up. A voice said, "Good morning. Seven o'clock." Then there was a click. I put the phone back and sat up in bed. I took a deep breath that hesitated and hitched two or three times on the way in. I wanted to go back to sleep, even if it meant nightmares. I didn't want to get up and face another day like yesterday.

Trudi wasn't in bed. I swung my feet to the floor and walked naked around the small hotel room. She wasn't in the bathroom, either, but she had written a note for me and left it on the bureau. It said:

Dear Marîd—

> *Thanks for everything. You're a dear, sweet man. I hope we meet again sometime.*

> *I have to go now, so I'm sure you won't mind if I borrow the fare from your wallet.*

> > *Love ya,*

> > *Trudi*

> *(My real name is Gunter
> Erich von S.
>   You mean you really didn't
> know, or were you just being
> nice?)*

There is very little I've missed in my life, as far as sex goes. My secret fantasies don't concern what, they concern who. I'd seen and heard everything, I thought. The only thing I'd never heard faked—until, evidently, last night—was that involuntary animal catch in a woman's breathing, the very first one, before the lovemaking has even had time to become rhythmical. I glanced down at Trudi's note again, remembering all the times Jacques, Mahmoud, Saied, and I had sat at a table at the Solace, watching people walk by. "Oh, her? She's a female-to-male sex-change in drag." I could read *everybody*. I was famous for it.

I swore I'd never tell anyone anything ever again. I wondered if the world ever got tired of its jokes; no, that was too much to hope for. The jokes would go on and on, getting worse and worse. Right now I was certain that if age and experience couldn't stop the jokes, there was nothing about death that would make them stop, either.

I folded my new clothing carefully and packed it in the zipper bag. I wore my white robe and *keffiya* again today, making yet another new look—Arab costume but clean-shaven. The man of a thousand faces. Today I wanted to take Hajjar up on his promise to let me use the police computer files. I wanted to fill in a little background, on the police themselves. I wanted to find out as much as I could about Okking's link to Bond/Khan.

Instead of walking, I took a cab to the police station. It wasn't that I was getting spoiled by the luxury Papa was paying for; I just felt the urgent pressing of events. I was killing time as fast as it was killing me. The daddies were buzzing in my head, and I didn't feel muscle-weary, hungry, or thirsty. I wasn't angry or afraid, either; some people might have warned me that not being afraid was dangerous. Maybe I should have been afraid, a little.

I watched Okking eat a late breakfast in his flimsy

fortress while I waited for Hajjar to get back to his desk. When the sergeant came in, he gave me a distracted look. "You're not the only bakebrain I have to worry about, Audran," he said in a surly voice. "We've got thirty other jerks giving us fantasy information and inside words they dig out of dreams and teacups."

"You'll be glad I don't have a goddamn piece of information for you, then. I came to get some from you. You said I could use your files."

"Oh, yeah, sure; but not here. If Okking saw you, he'd split my skull. I'll call downstairs. You can use one of the terminals on the second floor."

"I don't care where it is," I said. Hajjar made the phone call, typed out a pass for me, and signed it. I thanked him and found my way down to the data bank. A young woman with Southeast Asian features led me to an unused screen, showed me how to get from one menu to the next, and told me that if I had any questions, the machine itself would answer them. She wasn't a computer expert or a librarian; she just managed traffic flow in the big room.

First I checked the general files, which were much like a news agency's morgue. When I typed in a name, the computer gave me every fact available to it concerning the person. The first name I entered was Okking's. The cursor paused for a second or two, then lettered steadily across the display in Arabic, right to left. I learned Okking's first name, his middle name, his age, where he'd been born, what he'd done before coming to the city, all the stuff that gets put on a form above the important double line. Below that line comes the really vital information; depending on whose form it is, that can be the subject's medical record, arrest record, credit history, political involvement, sexual preference(s), or anything else that may one day be pertinent.

As for Okking, below that double line there was nothing. Absolutely nothing. *Al-Sifr*, zero.

At first I assumed there was some kind of computer problem. I started over again, returning to the first menu, choosing the sort of information I was looking for, and typing in Okking's name. And waited.

Mâ shî. Nothing.

Okking had done this, I was sure. He had covered his tracks, just as his boy Khan was now covering his own. If I wanted to travel to Europe, to Okking's birthplace, I might learn more about him, but only to the point when he left there to come to the city. Since then, he did not exist at all, not officially speaking.

I typed in Universal Export, the code name of James Bond's espionage group. I had seen it on an envelope on Okking's desk once. Again, there were no entries.

I tried James Bond without hope, and turned up nothing. Similarly with Xarghis Khan. The real Khan and the "real" Bond had never visited the city, so there was no file on either of them.

I thought about other people I might spy on—Yasmin, Friedlander Bey, even myself—but I decided to leave my curiosity unsatisfied until a less urgent occasion. I entered Hajjar's name and was not astonished by what I read. He was about two years younger than I was, Jordanian, with a moderately long arrest record before coming to the city. A psychological profile agreed point for point with my own estimation of him; you didn't dare trust him as far as he could run with a camel on his back. He was suspected of smuggling drugs and money to prisoners. He was once investigated in connection with the disappearance of a good deal of confiscated property, but nothing definite came of it. The official file put forth the possibility that Hajjar might be profiting from his position on the police force, that he might be selling his influence to private citizens or criminal organizations. The report suggested that he might not be above such abuses of authority as extortion, racketeering, and conspiracy, among other law-enforcement frailties.

Hajjar? Come now, what ever gave you that idea? Allah forfend.

I shook my head ruefully. Police departments all over the world were identical in two respects: they all have a fondness for breaking your head open for little or no provocation, and they can't see the simple truth if it's lying in front of them naked with its legs spread. The police don't enforce laws; they don't even get busy until after the laws are broken. They solve crimes at a pitifully low rate of success. What the police are, to be honest, is a kind of secretarial pool that records the names of the victims and the statements of the witnesses. After enough time passes, they can safely shove this information to the back of the filing system to make room for more.

Oh yeah, the police help little old ladies across the street. So I'm told.

One by one, I entered the names of everyone who'd been connected to Nikki, beginning with her uncle, Bogatyrev. The entries on the old Russian and on Nikki matched exactly what Okking had finally told me about them. I figured that if Okking could excise himself from this system, he could alter its remaining records in other ways, too. I wouldn't find anything useful here except by accident or Okking's oversight. I went on with a diminished hope of success.

I had none. At last I changed my mind and read the entries on Yasmin, Papa, and Chiri, on the Black Widow Sisters, on Seipolt and Abdoulaye. The files told me that Hassan was likely a hypocrite, because he would not use brain implants for his business, on religious grounds, yet he was a known pederast. That wasn't news to me. The only thing that I might suggest to Hassan someday was that the American boy, who already had his skull wired, might be more useful as an accounting tool than just sitting on a stool in Hassan's bare shop.

The only person I knew on whom I didn't peep was myself. I didn't want to know what they thought about me.

After I searched the files for my friends' histories, I looked at telephone company records for the phones in the police station. There was nothing enlightening there, either; Okking wouldn't have used his office phone to call Bond. It was like I was standing at the hub of a lot of radiating roads, all of them dead ends.

I walked out of there with food for thought but no new facts. I like knowing what the files had to say about Hajjar and the others; and the reticence it showed toward Okking—and, not so mysteriously, toward Friedlander Bey—was provocative if not informative. I thought about it all as I wandered into the Budayeen. In a few minutes I was back at my apartment building.

Why had I come here? Well, I didn't want to sleep in the hotel room another night. At least one assassin knew I was there. I needed another base of operations, one that would be safe for at least a day or two. As I got more accustomed to letting the daddies help me in my planning, my decision making got faster and less influenced by my emotions. I now felt completely in control, cool and assured. I wanted to get a message to Papa, and then I would find another temporary place to sleep.

My apartment was just the way I'd left it. Truthfully, I hadn't been away long, although it felt like weeks; my time sense was all distorted. Tossing the zipper bag onto the mattress, I sat down and murmured Hassan's commcode into my phone. It rang three times before he answered. *"Marhaba,"* he said. He sounded tired.

"Hello, Hassan, this is Audran. I need to have a meeting with Friedlander Bey, and I was hoping you could fix it for me."

"He will be glad that you are showing interest in doing things the proper way, my nephew. Certainly, he will want to see you and learn from you what progress you are making. Do you wish an appointment for this afternoon?"

"As soon as you can, Hassan."

"I will take care of it, O clever one, and I will call you back to tell you of the arrangements."

"Thanks. Before you go, I want to ask you a question. Do you know if there's any connection between Papa and Lutz Seipolt?"

There was a long silence while Hassan framed his reply. "Not any longer, my nephew. Seipolt is dead, is he not?"

"I know that," I said impatiently.

"Seipolt was involved only in the import-export trade. He dealt only in cheap trinkets, nothing that would be of interest to Papa."

"Then so far as you know, Papa never tried to cut himself a piece of Seipolt's business?"

"My nephew, Seipolt's business was barely worth mentioning. He was just a small businessman, like myself."

"But, also like yourself, he felt he needed a secondary

income to make ends meet. You work for Friedlander Bey, and Seipolt worked for the Germans."

"By the life of my eyes! Is that so? Seipolt, a spy?"

"I'd be willing to bet you already knew that. Never mind. Did *you* ever have any dealings with him?"

"What do you mean?" Hassan's voice became harsh.

"Business. Import-export. You have that in common."

"Oh, well, I bought items from him now and then, if he offered some particularly interesting European goods; but I don't think he ever bought anything from me."

That didn't get me anywhere. At Hassan's request, I gave him a quick rundown of the events since my discovery of Seipolt's body. By the time I finished, he was thoroughly frightened again. I told him about Okking and the doctored police records. "That's why I need to see Friedlander Bey," I said.

"You suspect something?" asked Hassan.

"It isn't only the missing information in the files, and the fact that Okking's a foreign agent. I just can't believe that he has the full resources of the department looking into these murders, and yet he hasn't come forward with a single useful piece of information for me. I'm sure he knows much more than he's telling me. Papa promised that he'd pressure Okking into sharing what he knows. I need to hear all that."

"Of course, my nephew, don't worry about that. It shall be done, *inshallah*. Then you have no true idea of how much the lieutenant actually knows?"

"That is the way of the *flic*. He might have the whole case wrapped up, or he may know even less than I do. He's a master at giving you the runaround."

"He cannot give Friedlander Bey the runaround."

"He'll try."

"He won't succeed. Do you need more money, O clever one?"

Hell, I could always use more money. "No, Hassan, I'm doing fine for now. Papa has been more than generous."

"If you need cash to further your investigation, you have only to contact me. You are doing an excellent job, my son."

"At least I'm not dead yet."

"You have the wit of a poet, my darling. I must go now. Business is business, you know."

"Right, Hassan. Call me back after you've spoken with Papa."

"Praise be to Allah for your safety."

"*Allah yisallimak,*" I said. I stood up and tucked the phone away again; then I began looking for the one other object that I'd found in Nikki's purse: the scarab she had taken from Seipolt's collection. That brass reproduction tied Nikki directly to Seipolt, as did her ring that I'd seen in the German's house. Of course, with Seipolt now among the dear departed, these items were of questionable value. True, Dr. Yeniknani still had the homemade moddy; that might be an important piece of evidence. I thought it was time to begin preparing a presentation of all I'd learned, so that I could eventually turn it all in to the authorities. Not Okking, of course, and not Hajjar. I wasn't sure who the proper authorities were, but I knew there had to be some somewhere. The three items were not enough to convict anyone in a European court of law, but according to Islamic justice, they were plenty.

I found the scarab under the edge of the mattress. I unzipped my bag and stuffed Seipolt's tourist's souvenir down under my clothing. I packed carefully, wanting to be sure that everything I owned was out of the apartment. Then I kicked a lot of scraps and rubbish into low piles here and there. I didn't feel like spending a lot of time cleaning. When I finished, there was nothing in the room that showed that I'd ever lived there. I felt a stinging sadness: I'd lived in that apartment longer than in any other single place in my life. If anywhere could truly be called my home, this little apartment should be it. Now, though, it was a big, abandoned room with dirty windows and a torn mattress on the floor. I went out, shutting the door behind me.

I returned my keys to Qasim, the landlord. He was surprised and upset that I was going. "I've liked living in your building," I told him, "but it pleases Allah that now I must move on."

He embraced me and called on Allah to lead each of us in righteousness unto Paradise.

I went to the bank and used the card to withdraw my entire account, closing it. I stuffed the bills into the envelope Friedlander Bey had sent me. When I got myself another place to stay, I'd take it out and see how much I had altogether; I was kind of teasing myself by not peeking now.

My third stop was the Hotel Palazzo di Marco Aurelio. I was dressed now in my *gallebeya* and *keffiya*, but with my short haircut and clean-shaven face. I don't think the desk clerk recognized me.

"I paid for a week in advance," I said, "but business matters force me to check out earlier than I planned."

The desk man murmured. "We're sorry to hear that, sir. We've enjoyed having you." I nodded and tossed my room's tag onto the counter. "Just let me look at . . ." He keyed the room number into his terminal, saw that the hotel did indeed owe me a little money, and began getting the voucher printed out.

"You've all been very kind," I said.

He smiled. "It is our pleasure," he said. He handed me the voucher and pointed to the cashier. I thanked him again. A few moments later I crammed the partial refund in my zipper bag with the rest of my money.

Carrying my cash, my moddies and daddies, and my clothing in the zipper bag, I walked south and west, away from the Budayeen and away from the expensive shopping district beside the Boulevard il-Jameel. I came to a *fellahîn* neighborhood of twisting streets and alleys, where the houses were small, flat-topped, needing whitewash, with windows covered by shutters or thin wooden lattices. Some were in better repair, with attempts at gardening in the dry earth at the base of the walls. Others looked derelict, their gap-toothed shutters hanging in the sun like tongues of panting dogs. I went up to a well-kept house and rapped on the door. I waited a few minutes until it opened. A large, heavily muscled man with a full black beard glared down at me. His eyes were narrowed suspiciously, and in the corner of his mouth his teeth were chewing away at a splinter of wood. He waited for me to speak.

With no confidence at all, I launched into my story. "I

have been stranded in this city by my companions. They stole all our merchandise and my money, too. I must beg in the name of Allah and the Apostle of God, may the blessings of Allah be upon him and peace, your hospitality for today and for this evening."

"I see," said the man in a surly voice. "The house is closed."

"I will give you no cause for offense. I will—"

"Why don't you try begging where the hospitality is more generous? People tell me there are families here and about with enough to eat for themselves and also for dogs and strangers, as well. Me, I'm lucky to earn a little money for beans and bread for my wife and my four children."

I understood. "I know you don't need trouble. When I was robbed, my companions didn't know that I always keep a little extra cash in my bag. They greedily took everything in plain sight, leaving me with enough to live on for one or two days, until I can make my way back and demand a lawful accounting of them."

The man just stared at me, waiting for something magical to appear.

I unslung my zipper bag and opened it. I let him watch me shove the clothing aside—my shirts, my trousers, socks— until I reached down and pulled out a paper bank note. "Twenty kiam," I said sadly, "that's all they left me with."

My new friend's face went through a rapid selection of emotions. In this neighborhood, twenty-kiam notes made their presence felt with noise and shouting. The man may not have been sure of me, but I knew what *he* was thinking.

"If you would give me the benefit of your hospitality and protection for the next two days," I said, "I will let you have all the money you see here." I thrust the twenty closer to his widening eyes.

The man wavered visibly; if he'd had big, flat leaves, he would have rustled. He didn't like strangers—hell, *no one* likes strangers. He didn't like the idea of inviting one into his house for a couple of days. Twenty kiam, though, was equal to several days' pay for him. When I looked closely at him again, I knew that he wasn't sizing me up anymore —he was spending the twenty kiam a hundred different ways. All I had to do was wait.

"We are not wealthy people, O sir."

"Then the twenty kiam will ease your life."

"It would, indeed, O sir, and I desire to have it; however, I am shamed to permit such an excellent one as you to witness the squalor of my house."

"I have seen squalor greater than any you can imagine, my friend, and I have risen above it even as you may. I was not always as I appear to you. It was only the will of Allah that I be flung down to the deepest pits of misery, in order that I might return to take back what has been torn from me. Will you help me? Allah will bring good fortune to all who are generous to me on my way."

The *fellah* looked at me in confusion for a long while. At first, I knew he thought I was just crazy, and the best thing was to run as far away from me as possible. My babbling sounded like some kidnapped prince's speech from the old tales. The stories were fine for late at night, for murmuring around the fire after a simple supper and before sleep and troubled dreams. In the light of day, however, a confrontation like this had nothing to make it seem plausible. Nothing except the money, waving like the frond of a date palm in my hand. My friend's eyes were fixed on the twenty kiam, and I doubt that he could have described my face to anyone.

In the end, I was admitted into the house of my host, Ishak Jarir. He maintained a strict discipline, and I saw no women. There was a second floor above, where the family members slept, and where there were a few small closets for storage. Jarir opened a plain wooden door to one of these and roughly shoved me inside. "You will be safe here," he said in a whisper. "If your treacherous friends come and inquire about you, no one in this house has seen you. But you may stay only until after morning prayers tomorrow."

"I thank Allah that in His wisdom He has guided me to so generous a man as you. I have yet an errand to run, and if everything occurs as I foresee, I will return with a bank note the twin of that you hold in your hand. The twin shall be yours, as well."

Jarir didn't want to hear any of the details. "May your undertaking be prosperous," he said. "Be warned, though:

if you come back after last prayers, you will not be admitted."

"It is as you say, honorable one." I looked over my shoulder at the pile of rags that would be my home that night, smiled innocently at Ishak Jarir, and got out of his house suppressing a shudder.

I turned down the narrow, stone-paved street that I thought would take me back to the Boulevard il-Jameel. As the street began a slow curve to the left, I knew that I'd made a mistake, but it was going in the right direction anyway, so I followed it. When I got around the turn, however, there was nothing but the blank brick rear walls of buildings hedging in a reeking, dead-end alley. I muttered a curse and turned around to retrace my steps.

There was a man blocking my way. He was thin, with a patchy, slovenly kept beard and a sheepish smile on his face. He was wearing an open-necked yellow knit shirt, a rumpled and creased brown business suit, a white *keffiya* with red checks, and scuffed brown oxford shoes. His foolish expression reminded me of Fuad, the idiot from the Budayeen. Evidently he had followed me up the dead-end street; I hadn't heard him come up behind me.

I don't like people catfooting up behind me; I unzipped my bag while I stared at him. He just stood there, shifting his weight from one foot to the other and grinning. I took out a couple of daddies and zipped the bag closed again. I started to walk by him, but he stopped me with a hand on my chest. I looked down at the hand and back up at his face. "I don't like being touched," I said.

He shrank back as if he had defiled the holy of holies. "A thousand pardons," he said weakly.

"You following me for some reason?"

"I thought you might be interested in what I have here." He indicated an imitation-leather briefcase he carried in one hand.

"You a salesman?"

"I sell moddies, sir, and a wide selection of the most useful and interesting add-ons in the business. I'd like to show them to you."

"No, thanks."

He raised his eyebrows, not so sheepish now, as if I'd

asked him to go right ahead. "It won't take a moment, and very possibly I have just the thing you're looking for."

"I'm not looking for anything in particular."

"Sure you are, sir, or you wouldn't have gotten wired, now, would you?"

I shrugged. He knelt down and opened his sample case. I was determined that he wasn't going to sell me anything. I don't do business with weasels.

He was taking moddies and daddies out of the case and lining them up in a neat row in front of his briefcase. When he was finished he looked up at me. I could tell how proud he was of his merchandise. "Well," he said. There was an anticipatory hush.

"Well what?" I asked.

"What do you think of them?"

"The moddies? They look like every other moddy I've ever seen. What are they?"

He grabbed the first moddy in the line. He flipped it to me and I caught it; a quick glimpse told me it was unlabeled, made of tougher plastic than the usual moddies I saw at Laila's and in the souks. Bootleg. "You know that one already," the man said, giving me that sorry smile again.

That earned him a sharp look.

He pulled off his *keffiya*. He had thinning brown hair hanging down and covering his ears. It looked like it hadn't been washed in a month. One hand popped out the moddy he'd been wearing. The timid salesman vanished. The man's jaws went slack and his eyes lost their focus, but with practiced speed he chipped in another of his homemade moddies. Suddenly his eyes narrowed and his mouth set in a hard, sadistic leer. He had transformed himself from one man to another; he didn't need the usual physical disguises: the entirely different set of postures, mannerisms, expressions, and speech patterns was more effective than any combination of wigs and makeup could be.

I was in trouble. I held James Bond in my hand, and I was staring into the cold eyes of Xarghis Moghadhîl Khan. I was staring into madness. I reached up and chipped in the two daddies. One would let me get unnatural, desperate strength from my muscles, without weariness or pain, until the tissue actually tore apart. The second cut out all sound; I needed to concentrate. Khan snarled at me. There was a long, vicious dagger in his hand now, its hilt of silver decorated with colored stones, its guard of gold. "Sit down," I read his lips. "On the ground."

I wasn't going to sit down for him. My hand moved about four inches, seeking the needle gun under my robes. My hand moved a little and stopped, because I remembered that the needle gun was still beneath the pillow in the hotel room. By now the chambermaid would have found it. And the seizure gun was zipped away safely in my bag. I backed away from Khan. "I've been following you for a long time, Mr. Audran. I watched you at the police station, at Friedlander Bey's, at Seipolt's house, at the hotel. I could have killed you that night when I pretended you were just a goddamn robber, but I didn't want to be interrupted. I waited for the right moment. *Now*, Mr. Audran, now you will die." It was wonderfully simple to read his lips: the whole world had relaxed and was moving only half as fast as normal. He and I had all the time we needed. . . .

Khan's mouth twisted. He enjoyed this part. He stalked me back deeper into the alley. My eyes were fixed on his gleaming knife, with which Khan intended not only to kill me but also to hack my body to pieces. He meant to drape my bowels over the filthy stones and the refuse like holiday garlands. Some people are terrified of death; others are even more terrified of the agony that might come first. To be honest, that's me. I knew that some day I'd have to die, but I hoped it would be quick and painless—in my sleep, if I was lucky. Tortured first by Khan: that was definitely not how I wanted to go out.

The daddies kept me from panicking. If I let myself get too scared, I'd be souvlaki in five minutes. I backed away further, scanning the alley for something that would give me a chance against this maniac and his dagger. I was running out of time.

Khan's lips pulled back from his teeth and he charged me, uttering wordless cries. He held the dagger overhand at shoulder height, coming at me like Lady Macbeth. I let him take three steps, then I moved to my left and rushed him. He expected me to flee backward, and when I went at him he flinched. My left hand reached for his right wrist, my right arm swung behind his forearm and held his hand steady. I bent his knife hand back with my left hand, against the fulcrum of my right arm. Usually you can disarm an attacker like that, but Khan was strong. He was stronger than that nearly emaciated body should have been; the insanity gave him a little extra power, and so did his moddy and daddies.

Khan's free hand had me by the throat, and he was forcing my head back. I got my right leg behind his and pulled his feet out from under him. We both went down, and as we fell I covered his face with my right hand. I made sure to slam the back of his head into the ground as hard as I could. I landed on his wrist with my knee, and his hand opened. I threw his dagger as far as I could, then used both hands to beat Khan's head on the slimy pavement a few more times. Khan was dazed, but it didn't last long. He rolled out of my grasp and flung himself back on me, tearing and biting at my flesh. We wrestled, each trying to get an advantage, but we were grappling so tightly that I couldn't swing my fists. I couldn't even work my arms free. Meanwhile, he was hurting me, raking me with his black nails, drawing blood with his teeth, bludgeoning me with his knees.

Khan shrieked and heaved me to the side; then he leaped, and before I could get away, he landed on top of me again. He held my arms pinned with one knee and one hand. He raised a fist, ready to smash it down on my throat. I cried out and tried to roll him off, but I couldn't move. I struggled, and I saw the lunatic light of victory in his eyes. He was crooning some inarticulate prayer. With a wild bellow, he slammed his fist down and caught the side of my face. I almost lost consciousness.

Khan ran for his knife. I forced myself to sit up and search wildly for my zipper bag. Khan found the dagger and was coming at me. I got my bag open and threw everything out on the ground. Just as Khan was three feet from me, I nailed him with one long burst from the seizure gun. Khan gave a gurgling cry and toppled beside me. He would be out for hours.

The daddies blocked most of my pain, but not all; the rest they held at a distance. Still, I couldn't move yet, and it would be a few minutes before I could do anything useful. I watched Khan's skin turn a cyanotic blue as he fought to draw air into his lungs. He went into convulsions and then suddenly relaxed completely, only a few inches from me. I sat and gasped until I was able to shake off the effects of the fight. Then the first thing I did was pop the Khan moddy out of his head. I called Lieutenant Okking to give him the good news.

18

I found my pill case in the zipper bag and took seven or eight sunnies. I was trying something new. My body was aching after the fight with Khan, but it wasn't the pain so much; purely in the interest of science, I wanted to see how the opiate would affect my augmented sensations. While I waited for Okking, I learned the truth empirically: the daddy that cleared alcohol from my system at a faster rate also kicked out the sunnies, too. Who needs that? I popped that moddy and took another hit of Sonneine.

When Okking arrived he was buoyant. That was the only word to describe him. I'd never seen him so pleased. He was attentive and gracious to me, concerned for my wounds and pain. He was so nice, I figured the holo news people were around taping, but I was wrong. "I guess you're one up on me now, Audran," he said.

I figured he owed me a lot more than that. "I've done your whole goddamn job for you, Okking."

Even that didn't puncture his elation. "Maybe, maybe. At least now I can get some sleep. I couldn't even eat without imagining Selima, Seipolt, and the others."

Khan roused; without a moddy in his socket, however, he began to scream. I recalled how awful I felt when I took the daddies out after just a few days. Who knows how long Khan—whatever his real name was—had gone, hiding beneath first one moddy and then another. Maybe without a false personality chipped in, he wasn't able to confront the inhuman acts he'd performed. He lay on the pavement, his hands cuffed behind him and his ankles

248

chained together, thrashing and thundering curses at us. Okking watched him for a few seconds. "Drag him out of here," he said to a couple of uniformed officers.

They were none too gentle about it, but Khan got no sympathy from me. "Now what?" I asked Okking.

He sobered up a little. "I think it's about time for me to offer my resignation," he said.

"When the news gets around that you've accepted money from a foreign government, you're not going to be very popular. You've dented your credibility."

He nodded. "The word has already gotten around, at least in the circles that count. I've been given the choice of finding employment out of the city or spending the rest of my life behind bars in one of your typical wog hellholes. I don't see how they can fling people into those prisons, they're right out of the Dark Ages."

"You've put the numbers on your share of the population, Okking. You'll have a big welcoming committee waiting for you."

He shivered. "I think as soon as I get my personal affairs tied up, I'll just pack my bags and slip away into the night. I wish they'd give me a character reference, though. I mean, foreign agent or no, I've done good work for the city. I never compromised my integrity, except a few times."

"How many other people can honestly say the same? You're one of a kind, Okking." He was just the kind of guy who would walk away from this and turn it into a recommendation on his resume. He'd find work somewhere.

"You like seeing me in trouble, don't you, Audran?"

As a matter of fact, I did. Rather than answer, though, I turned to my zipper bag and repacked it; I'd learned my lesson, so I tucked the seizure gun under my robe. From Okking's conversation, I gathered that the formal questioning was finished, that I could go now. "Are you going to stay in the city until Nikki's killer is caught?" I asked. "Are you at least going to do that much?" I turned to face him.

He was surprised. "Nikki? What are you talking about? We got the killer, he's on his way to the chopping block right now. You're obsessed, Audran. You don't have any proof of your second killer. Lay off or you'll learn how fast heroes can become ex-heroes. You're getting boring."

If *that* wasn't a cop's way of thinking! I caught Khan and turned him over to Okking; now Okking was going to tell everybody that Khan had bumped them all, from Bogatyrev to Seipolt. Of course, Khan *had* killed Bogatyrev and Seipolt; but I was sure that he hadn't killed Nikki, Abdoulaye, or Tami. Did I have any proof? No, nothing tangible; but none of it hung together any other way. This was an international rat's nest; one side tried to kidnap Nikki and bring her alive to her father's country, and the other side wanted to kill her to prevent the scandal. If Khan had murdered agents of both parties, it made sense only if he was merely a psychotic who cut up people senselessly, in no pattern. That just wasn't true. He was an assassin whose victims had been put away to further his employers' scheme and to protect his own anonymity. The man who cut Seipolt up was not a madman, he was not really Khan—he only wore a Khan moddy.

And that man had nothing to do with Nikki's death.

There was still another killer loose in the city, even if Okking found it convenient to forget him.

About ten minutes after Okking and his crew and I went our separate ways, the telephone rang. It was Hassan, calling back to tell me what Papa had said. "I've got some news, too, Hassan," I said.

"Friedlander Bey will see you shortly. He will send a car for you in fifteen minutes. I trust you are at home?"

"No, but I'll be waiting outside the building. I had some interesting company, but they've all gone away now."

"Good, my nephew. You deserved some pleasant relaxation with your friends."

I stared up at the cloud-covered sky, thinking about my confrontation with Khan, wondering if I should laugh at Hassan's words. "I didn't get much relaxing done," I said. I told him what had happened from the time I'd last talked to him until they carted Okking's hired killer away.

Hassan stammered at me in amazement. "Audran," he said when he finally regained control, "it pleases Allah that you are safe, that the maniac has been captured, and that Friedlander Bey's wisdom has triumphed."

"You right," I said. "Give all the credit to Papa. He was giving me the benefit of his wisdom, all right. Now that I think about it, I didn't get a hell of a lot more help from him than I got from Okking. Sure, he backed me into a corner and made me go along with having my head opened; but after that he just sat back and tossed money my way. Papa knows everything that goes on in the Budayeen, Hassan. You mean to tell me both he and Okking have been standing around with their thumbs in their ears, absolutely baffled? I don't buy that. I found out what Okking's part in all this was; I'd like even better to know what Papa's been doing behind the scenes."

"Silence, son of a diseased dog!" Hassan dropped his ingratiating manner and let his real self peek out, something he didn't do very often. "You still have much to learn about showing respect to your elders and betters." Then, just as suddenly, the old Hassan, Hassan the mendacious near-buffoon, returned. "You are still feeling the strain of the conflict. Forgive me for losing my patience with you, it is I who must be more understanding. All is as Allah wills, neither more nor less. So, my nephew, the car will call for you soon. Friedlander Bey will be well pleased."

"There isn't time to get him a little gift, Hassan."

He chuckled. "Your news will be gift enough. Go in peace, Audran."

I didn't say anything, but broke the connection. I resettled my zipper bag on my shoulder and walked toward my old apartment building. I would meet with Papa, and then I would hide in Ishak Jarir's closet. The bright side was that Khan was now out of the picture. Khan had been the only one of the two murderers who'd shown any desire to eliminate me. That meant the other one probably felt like letting me live. At least, I hoped so.

While I waited for Papa's limo to come, I thought about my battle with Khan. I hated the man violently—all I had to do was call to mind the horror of Selima's mutilated corpse, the revulsion I had felt while stumbling upon the dismembered bodies at Seipolt's house. First he had killed Bogatyrev, Nikki's own uncle who wanted her dead. Nikki was the key; all the other homicides were part of the frantic coverup that was supposed to keep the Russian scandal secret. I suppose it worked—oh, a lot of people here in the city knew about it, but without a live crown prince to embarrass the monarchy, there was no scandal back in White Russia. King Vyacheslav was safe on his throne, the royalists had won. In fact, with some clever and careful work on their part, they could use Nikki's murder to strengthen their grip on the unstable nation.

I didn't care about any of that. Following the brawl with Khan, I'd let him live—for a little while. He had a date now with the headsman in the courtyard of the Shimaal Mosque. Let him relive his brutalities in terror of Allah in the meantime.

The limo arrived and carried me to Friedlander Bey's estate. The butler escorted me to the same waiting room I'd seen twice before. I waited for Papa to complete his prayers. Friedlander Bey didn't make a great show of his devotion, which in a way made it all the more remarkable. Sometimes his belief shamed me; on those occasions I called up memories of the cruelties and crimes he was responsible for. I was only fooling myself; Allah knows none of us is perfect. I'm sure Friedlander Bey had no such illusions about himself. At least he asked his God to forgive him. Papa had explained it to me once before: he had to take care of a great number of relatives and associates, and sometimes the only way to protect them was to be unduly hard on outsiders. In that light, he was a great leader and a stern but loving father to his people. I, on the other hand, was a nobody who did a lot of illicit things myself, to no one's benefit; and I didn't even have the saving grace to beg Allah's pardon.

At last one of the two huge men who guarded Papa motioned to me. I entered the inner office; Friedlander Bey was waiting for me, seated on his antique lacquered divan. "Once again you do me great honor," he said. He indicated that I should be seated across the table from him, on the other divan.

"It is my honor to wish you good evening," I said.

"Will you take a morsel of bread with me?"

"You are most generous, O Shaykh," I said. I didn't feel wary or self-conscious, as I had on my previous meetings with Papa. After all, I had done the impossible for him. I had to keep reminding myself that the great man was now in my debt.

The servants brought the first course of the meal, and Friedlander Bey steered the conversation from one trivial subject to another. We sampled a little of many different dishes, everything succulently prepared and fragrant; I decided to chip out the hunger-override daddy, and when I did, I realized just how hungry I was. I was able to do justice to Papa's banquet. I wasn't, however, ready to pop the other daddies out. Not quite yet.

The servants brought platters of lamb, chicken, beef, and fish, served with delicately seasoned vegetables and savory rice. We ended with a selection of fresh fruit and cheeses; when all the dishes were cleared away, Papa and I relaxed with strong coffee flavored with spices.

"May your table last forever, O Shaykh," I said. "That was the finest meal I've ever enjoyed."

He was pleased. "I give thanks to God it was to your liking. Will you drink some more coffee?"

"Yes, thank you, O Shaykh."

The servants were gone and so, too, were the Stones Who Speak. Friedlander Bey poured my coffee himself, a gesture of sincere respect. "You must agree now that my plans for you were all in order," he said softly.

"Yes, O Shaykh. I am grateful."

He waved that aside. "It is we, the city and myself, who are grateful to you, my son. Now we must speak of the future."

"Forgive me, O Shaykh, but we cannot safely think of the future until we are secure in the present. One of the murderers who menaced us has been accounted for, but there is yet another at large. That evil one may have returned to his homeland, it is true; it is some time now since he struck down his victims. Yet it would be prudent for us to consider the possibility that he is still in the city. We would be well advised to learn his identity and his whereabouts."

The old man frowned and pulled at his gray cheek. "O my son, you alone believe in the existence of this other assassin. I do not see why the man who was James Bond, who was also Xarghis Khan, could not also be the torturer who slew Abdoulaye in so unspeakable a manner. You mentioned the many personality modules Khan had in his possession. Could not one of them make him the demon who also murdered the Crown Prince Nikolai Konstantin?"

What did I have to do to persuade these people? "O Shaykh," I said, "your theory requires that one man was working for both the fascist-communist alliance *and* the Byelorussian loyalists. He would, in effect, be neutralizing himself at every turn. It would postpone the outcome, which might be to his advantage although I don't understand how; and he would be able to report positive results to both sides for a time. Yet if all that were true, how would he resolve the situation? He would finally be rewarded by one side and punished by the other. It's foolish to think that one man might simultaneously be protecting Nikki *and* trying to murder her. In addition, the police examiner determined that the man who killed Tami, Abdoulaye, and Nikki was shorter and heavier than Khan, with thick, stubby fingers."

Friedlander Bey's face flickered with a weak smile. "Your vision, respected one, is acute but limited in scope. I myself have sometimes found it worthwhile to support both sides of a quarrel. What else can one do when one's beloved friends dispute a matter?"

"With your forgiveness, O Shaykh, I point out that we are speaking of many cold-blooded homicides, not quarrels or disputes. And neither the Germans nor the Russians are our beloved friends. Their internal bickerings are of no importance to us here in the city."

Papa shook his head. "Limited scope," he repeated softly. "When the infidel lands of the world break apart, we are revealed in our strength. When the great Shaitans, the United States and the Soviet Union, each fell into separate groups of states, it was a token from Allah."

"A token?" I asked, wondering what all this had to do with Nikki and the wires in my skull and the poor, forgotten people of the Budayeen.

Friedlander Bey's brows drew together, and he looked suddenly like a desert warrior, like the mighty chieftains who had come before him, all wielding the irresistible Sword of the Prophet. "Jihad," he murmured.

Jihad. Holy war.

I felt a prickle on my skin, and the blood roared in my ears. Now that the once-great nations were growing helpless in their poverty and dissension, it was time for Islam to complete the conquest that had begun so many centuries before. Papa's expression was very much like the look I had seen in the eyes of Xarghis Khan.

"It is what pleases Allah," I said. Friedlander Bey let out his breath and gave me a benevolent, approving smile. I was humoring the man. He was more dangerous now than I ever suspected. He had almost dictatorial power in the city; that, coupled with his great age and this delusion, made me walk carefully in his presence.

"You will do me a great favor if you will accept this," he said, leaning over the table with still another envelope. I suppose someone in his position thinks money is the perfect gift for the man who has everything. Anyone else might have found it offensive. I took the envelope.

"You overwhelm me," I said. "I cannot adequately express my thanks."

"The debt is mine, my son. You have done well, and I reward those who carry out my wishes."

I didn't look in the envelope—even I knew that would have been a breach of manners anywhere. "You are the father of generosity," I said.

We were getting along just fine. He liked me a lot better now than at our first meeting, so long ago. "I grow tired, my son, and so you must forgive me. My driver will return you to your home. Let us visit together again soon, and then we shall speak of your future."

"On the eyes and head, O lord of men. I am at your disposal."

"There is no might or power save in Allah the exalted and great." That sounds like a formula reply, but it's usually reserved for moments of danger or before some crucial action. I looked at the gray-haired man for some clue, but he had dismissed me. I made my farewells and left his office. I did a lot of thinking during the ride to the Budayeen.

It was a Monday evening, and Frenchy's was already getting crowded. There was a mix of naval and merchant marine types, who'd come fifty miles from the port; there were five or six male tourists, looking for one kind of action and about to find another; and there were a few tourist couples looking for racy, colorful stories they could take home with them. There was a sprinkling of business-men from the city, too, who probably knew the score but came in anyway to have a drink and look at naked bodies.

Yasmin was sitting between two sailors. They were laughing and winking at each other over her head—they must have thought they'd found what they were looking for. Yasmin was sipping a champagne cocktail. She had seven empty glasses in front of her. Very definitely, *she* had found what she was looking for. Frenchy charged eight kiam for a cocktail, which he split with the girl who ordered it. Yasmin had cleared thirty-two kiam already off those two jolly sea rovers, and from the look of it there was more to come, the night was still young. And that's not including tips, either. Yasmin was wonderful at pulling tips. She was a joy to watch; she could separate a mark from his money faster than anyone I knew, except maybe Chiriga.

There were several seats open at the bar, one near the door and a few in the back. I never liked to sit near the door, you looked like some kind of tourist or something. I headed for the shadowy interior of the club. Before I got to the stool, Indihar came up to me. "You'll be more comfortable in a booth, sir," she said.

I smiled. She didn't recognize me in my robes and without my beard. She suggested the booth because if I sat on the stool, she wouldn't be able to sit next to me and work on my wallet. Indihar was a nice enough person, I'd never gotten into any kind of hassle with her. "I'll sit at the bar," I said. "I want to talk to Frenchy."

She gave me a little shrug, then turned and sorted out the rest of the crowd. Like a hunting hawk she sighted three affluent-looking merchants sitting with one girl and one change. There was always room for one more. Indihar pounced.

Frenchy's barmaid, Dalia, came over to me, trailing her wet towel on the counter. She made a couple of passes at the spot just in front of me and plopped a cork coaster down. "Beer?" she asked.

"Gin and bingara with a hit of Rose's," I said.

She squinted her eyes at me. "Marîd?"

"My new look," I said.

She dropped her towel onto the bar and stared at me. She didn't say a word. That went on until I started to get self-conscious. "Dalia?" I said.

She opened her mouth, closed it, then opened it again. "Frenchy," she cried, "here he is!"

I didn't know what that meant. People all around turned to look at me. Frenchy got up from his seat near the cash register and lumbered over to me. "Marîd," he said, "heard about you taking on that guy that wiped the Sisters."

It dawned on me that I was a bigshot now. "Oh," I said, "it was more like *he* took *me* on. He was doing pretty well, too, until I decided to get serious."

Frenchy grinned. "You were the only one that had the balls to go after him. Even the city's finest were ten steps behind you. You saved a lot of lives, Marîd. You drink free in here and every other place on the Street from now on. No tips, either, I'll give the word to the girls."

It was the only meaningful gesture Frenchy could make, and I appreciated it. "Thanks, Frenchy," I said. I learned how quickly being a big shot can get embarrassing.

We talked for a while. I tried to get him to see that there was still another killer around, but he didn't want to know about it. He preferred to believe the danger was over. I had no proof that the second assassin was still in the city, after all. He hadn't used a cigarette on anybody since Nikki's death. "What are you looking for?" asked Frenchy.

I stared up at the stage, where Blanca was dancing. She was the one who had actually discovered Nikki's corpse in the alley. "I have one clue and an idea of what he likes to do to his victims." I told Frenchy about the moddy Nikki had in her purse, and about the bruises and cigarette burns on the bodies.

Frenchy looked thoughtful. "You know," he said, "I do remember somebody telling me about a trick they turned."

"What about it? Did the trick try to burn her or something?"

Frenchy shook his head. "No, not that. Whoever it was said that when she got the trick's clothes off, he was all covered with the same kind of burns and marks."

"Whose trick was it, Frenchy? I need to talk to her."

He gazed off toward the middle of next week, trying to remember. "Oh," he said, "it was Maribel."

"Maribel?" I said in disbelief. Maribel was the old woman who occupied a stool at the angle of the bar. She always took that stool. She was somewhere between sixty and eighty years old, and she'd been a dancer half a century ago, when she still had a face and a body. Then she stopped dancing and concentrated on the aspects of the industry that brought more immediate cash benefits. When she got even older, she had to lower her retail markup in order to compete with the newer models. Nowadays she wore a red nylon wig that had all the body and bounce of the artificial lawns in the European district. She had never had the money for physical or mental modifications. Surrounded by the most beautiful bodies money could buy, her face looked even older than it was. Maribel was at a distinct disadvantage. She overcame that, however, through shrewd marketing techniques that stressed personalized attention and customer satisfaction: for the price of one champagne cocktail, she would give the man next to her the benefit of her manual dexterity and her years of experience. Right at the bar, sitting and chatting as if they were all alone in a motel room somewhere. Maribel subscribed to the classical Arab proverb: the best kindness is done quickly. She had to carry most of the conversation, of course; but unless you watched closely—or the guy couldn't keep the glazed look off his face—you'd never know that an intimate encounter was taking place.

Most girls wanted you to buy them seven or eight cocktails before they'd even begin to negotiate. Maribel's clock was running out, she didn't have time for that. If Yasmin was the Neiman-Marcus—and she was, in my opinion—then Maribel was the Crazy Abdul's Discount Mart of hustlers.

That's why I found Frenchy's story hard to believe.

Maribel would never have the opportunity to see scars on her trick. Not sitting at the corner of the bar like that.

"She took this guy home," said Frenchy, grinning.

"Who'd go home with Maribel?" It was hard to believe.

"Someone who needed the money."

"Son of a bitch. *She* pays men to jam her?"

"Money cycles through this world like anything else."

I thanked Frenchy for the information and told him I needed to talk to Maribel. He laughed and went back to his stool. I moved over to the seat beside her. "Hi, Maribel," I said.

She had to look at me a while before she recognized me. "Marîd," she said happily. Between the first syllable and the second, her hand plopped in my lap. "Buy me a cocktail?"

"All right." I signaled to Dalia, who put a champagne cocktail in front of the old woman. Dalia gave me a crooked smile and I just shrugged helplessly. The girls and changes in Frenchy's club always got a tall stainless-steel cup of ice water with their drinks. They said it was because they didn't like the taste of liquor, and to get all that alcohol down they had to drink ice water with it. They sipped some champagne or some hard liquor, then went to the ice water. The marks thought it was tough on these poor girls, having to guzzle two or three dozen drinks every night if they didn't enjoy the stuff. The truth was that they never swallowed the drink; they spit it out into the metal cup. Every so often Dalia would take the cup away and empty it on the pretext of freshening up the ice water. Maribel didn't want the spit-back cup. She liked her booze.

I had to admit, Maribel's hand was as skilled as any silversmith's. Practice makes perfect, I guess. I was about to tell her to stop, but then I said to myself, what the hell. It was a learning experience. "Maribel," I said, "Frenchy told me you saw somebody with burn marks and bruises all over his body. Do you remember who?"

"I did?"

"Somebody you went home with."

"When?"

"I don't know. If I could find that person, he might be able to tell me something that would save some lives."

"Really? Would I get some kind of reward for that?"

"A hundred kiam, if you can remember."

That stopped her. She hadn't seen a hundred kiam in one lump since her glory days, and they belonged to another century. She hunted through her disordered memories, desperately trying to come up with a mental picture. "I'll tell you," she said, "there *was* somebody like that, I remember that much; but I can't for the life of me remember who. I'll get it, though. Will the reward still be good—"

"Whenever you remember, give me a call or tell Frenchy."

"I won't have to split the money with him, will I?"

"No," I said. Yasmin was on stage now. She saw me sitting with Maribel, she saw Maribel's arm moving up and down. Yasmin gave me a disgusted look and turned away. I laughed. "Thanks, but that's all right, Maribel."

"Going, Marîd?" asked Dalia. "That didn't take very long."

"Rotate, Dalia," I said. I left Frenchy's, worried that my friends, like Okking, Hassan, and Friedlander Bey, believed they were all safe now. I knew they weren't, but they didn't want to listen to me. I almost wished something terrible would happen, just so they'd know I was right; but I didn't want to bear the guilt for it.

In the midst of their relief and celebration, I was more alone than ever before.

19

"**Y**ou do not wish it."

Audran looked at him. Wolfe sat there like a self-satisfied statue, his eyes half-closed, his lips pushing out a little, pulling in, then pushing out again. He turned his head a fraction of an inch and gazed at me. "You do not wish it," he said again.

"But I do!" cried Audran. "I just want all of this to be over."

"Nevertheless." He raised a finger and wiggled it. "You continue to hope that there will be some simple solution, some way that doesn't threaten danger or, what is yet worse to your way of thinking, ugliness. If Nikki had been murdered cleanly, simply, then you might have tracked her killer down relentlessly. As it is, the situation becomes ever more repellent, and you desire only to hide from it. Consider where you are now: huddled in the linen closet of some impoverished, nameless fellah." He frowned disapprovingly.

Audran felt condemned. "You mean I didn't go about it the right way? But you're the detective, not me. I'm just Audran, the sand-nigger who sits on the curb with the plastic cups and the rest of the garbage. You always say yourself that any spoke will lead the ant to the hub."

His shoulders raised a quarter of an inch in a shrug, and then fell. He was being compassionate. "Yes, I say that. However, if the ant walks all the way around the rim three-quarters of the circumference before choosing a spoke, he may lose more than merely time."

Audran spread his hands helplessly. "I'm getting near the hub in my own clumsy way. So why don't you use your eccentric genius and tell me where I can find this other killer?"

Wolfe put his hands on the arms of his chair and levered

himself up. His expression was set and he barely noticed me as he walked by. It was time to go up to his orchids.

When I chipped out the moddy and replaced the special daddies, I was sitting on the floor of Jarir's closet, my head on my drawn-up knees. With the daddies back in, I was invincible—not hungry, not tired, not thirsty, not afraid, not even angry. I set my jaw, I ran my hand through my rumpled hair, I did all those valiant things. Step aside buddy, this is a job for . . .

For me, I guess.

I glanced at my watch and saw that it was early evening. That was all right, too; all the little throat-slashers and their victims would be out.

I wanted to show that bloated Nero Wolfe that real people have their own low cunning, too. I also wanted to live the rest of my life without feeling forever like I had to throw up in the next few seconds. That meant catching Nikki's killer. I took out the envelope of money and counted it. There was over fifty-seven thousand kiam. I had expected a little more than five. I stared at all that money for a long time. Then I put it away, took out my pill case, and swallowed twelve Paxium without water. I left the little room and passed Jarir. I didn't say a word to him going out.

The streets in that part of town were deserted already, but the nearer I got to the Budayeen, the more people I saw. I passed through the eastern gate and went up the Street. My mouth was dry despite the daddies that were supposed to keep the lid clamped down on my endocrines. It was a good thing I wasn't afraid, because I was scared stiff. I passed the Half-Hajj and he said a few words; I just nodded and went by as if he'd been a total stranger. There may have been a convention or a tour group in town, because I remember little knots of strangers standing in the Street, staring into the clubs and the cafes. I didn't bother walking around them. I just shoved my way through.

When I got to Hassan's shop, the front door was closed. I stood there and stared at it stupidly. I couldn't remember it ever being closed before. If it had just been me, I'd have reported it to Okking; but it wasn't just me. It was me and my daddies, so I kicked the door beside the lock, one, two, three, and it finally sprang open.

Naturally, Abdul-Hassan, the street-american kid, wasn't on his stool in the empty shop. I crossed the shop in two or three strides and ripped the cloth hanging aside. There was no one in the storeroom in the back, either. I hurried across the dark area between the stacks of wooden crates, and went out the heavy iron door into the alley. There was another iron door in the building across the way; behind it was the room in which I'd bargained for Nikki's short-lived freedom. I went up to it and pounded on it loudly. There was no response. I pounded again. Finally a small voice called out something in English.

"Hassan," I yelled.

The small voice said something, went away for a few seconds, then shouted something else. I promised myself that if I lived through this, I was going to buy that kid an Arabic-language daddy. I took out the envelope of money and waved it, yelling "Hassan! Hassan!"

After a few seconds, a small crack opened. I took out a thousand-kiam note, put it in the kid's hand, showed him all the rest of the cash, and said "Hassan! Hassan!" The door shut with a whuff and my thousand kiam disappeared.

A moment later the door opened again, and I was all ready for it. I grabbed the edge and pulled, wrenching the door out of the kid's grasp. He cried out and swung with it, but he let go. I flung the door open, then doubled over as the kid kicked me as hard as he could. He was too short to reach where he was aiming, but he still hurt me pretty bad. I grabbed a fistful of his shirt and slapped him a few times, then whacked the back of his head against the wall and let him fall into the refuse-strewn alley. I let my breathing catch up; the daddies were doing a fine job, my heart was pumping away as if I were just humming along with Fazluria, not running for my life. I paused only to bend down and snap back the thousand-K bill the *'ricain* kid was still holding. "Take care of the fîqs," my mother always taught me.

There was no one in the ground-floor room. I thought about slamming and locking the iron door behind me, so that the American kid or any other bogeyman couldn't sneak up without my knowing, but I decided instead that I might need a handy exit in a hurry. I made no noise as I walked carefully and slowly toward the stairway against the wall to my left. Without the daddies I would have been elsewhere, whispering into a stranger's ear in some romantic language. I took out my rack of daddies and considered them. The two corymbic implants I had were not fully loaded; I could still chip in another three, but I was already wearing everything I thought I might need in a crisis. All but one, to tell the truth: there was still the special black daddy that plugged directly into my punishment cells. I didn't think I'd ever use that one voluntarily; but, if I had to face somebody like Xarghis Moghadhîl Khan again with nothing but a butter knife, I'd rather go out a snarling, vicious beast than a rational, whimpering human being. I held the black daddy in my left hand and went on up the stairs.

In the room above there were two people. Hassan, smiling faintly and looking just a little distracted, was standing in a corner and rubbing his eyes. He looked sleepy. "Audran, my nephew," he said.

"Hassan," I said.

"Did the boy let you in?"

"I gave him a thousand and took the decision out of his hands. Then I took the thousand out of his hands, too."

Hassan gave me his little ingratiating laugh. "I am fond of the boy, as you know, but he's an American." I'm not sure what he meant by that, "He's an American, so he's a little stupid," or "He's an American, there are plenty more."

"He won't be bothering us," I said.

"Good, O excellent one," said Hassan. His eyes flicked down to Lieutenant Okking, who was spread-eagled on the floor, his wrists and ankles tied with nylon cords to rings set into the walls. It was obvious that Hassan had used this set-up before—often. Okking's back, legs, arms, and head were marked with cigarette burns and streaked with long, bright slashes of blood. If he was screaming I didn't notice, because the daddies had my senses concentrated on Hassan. Okking was still alive, though. I could see that much.

"You finally got around to the cop," I said. "Are you sorry his brain isn't wired? You like to use your bootleg moddy, don't you?"

Hassan raised an eyebrow. "It is a pity," he said. "But, of course, *your* implant will suffice. I am already looking forward to that with pleasure. I owe you thanks, my nephew, for suggesting the policeman. It was my belief that my guest here was as witless a fool as he acted. You insisted that he was withholding information. I couldn't take the chance that you were correct." I frowned and looked at Okking's writhing body. I promised myself that later, when I was in my own mind, I'd get sick.

"All along," I said, as if we were merely discussing the price of beauties, "I thought there were two killers wearing moddies. I've been so stupid: it turned out to be one moddy and one old-fashioned crackpot. Here I was trying to outthink some international high-tech hoodlum, and it turns out to be the neighborhood dirty old man. What a waste of time, Hassan! I should be ashamed to take Papa's money for this." As I was saying all this, of course, I was edging slowly closer to him, looking down at Okking and shaking my head, and generally acting like a kindly police sergeant in a movie, trying to soft-talk a frantic slob from jumping off a ledge. Take my word for it: it's harder than it looks.

"Friedlander Bey has paid you the last kiam you'll ever see." Hassan actually sounded sad.

"Maybe, maybe not," I said, still moving slowly. My eyes were on Hassan's thick, stubby fingers wrapped around a cheap, curved Arab knife. "I've been so blind. You were working for the Russians."

"Of course," Hassan snapped.

"And you kidnapped Nikki."

He looked up at me, surprised. "No, my nephew, it was Abdoulaye who took her, not me."

"But he was following your orders."

"Bogatyrev's."

"Abdoulaye took her from Seipolt's villa."

Hassan only nodded.

"So she was still alive the first time I questioned Seipolt. She was somewhere in his house. He wanted her alive.

Then when I went back to demand answers from him, he was dead."

Hassan stared at me, fingering the blade.

"After Bogatyrev died, you killed her and dumped her body. Then you killed Abdoulaye and Tami to protect yourself. Who made her write those notes?"

"Seipolt, O clever one."

"Okking's the last, then. The only one left who can link you to the murders."

"And yourself, of course."

"Of course," I said. "You're a hell of a good actor, Hassan. You had me fooled. If I hadn't found your underground moddy"—his teeth flashed in a startled snarl—"and some things that connected Nikki to Seipolt, I would never have had anything to go on. Both you and the Germans' assassin did first-rate work. I would never have guessed you until I realized that every goddamn important piece of information passed through you. From Papa to me, from me to Papa. It was right in front of me the whole time, all I had to do was see it. Finally, I just *had* to figure it out—it was you, you and your goddamn fat, short, stubby fingers." I was only about ten feet from Hassan, ready to take another cautious step, when he shot me.

He had a small, white plastic pistol and he stitched a row of needles in the air in a big, looping arc. The last two needles in the clip caught me in the side, just below my left arm. I felt them faintly, almost as if they'd happened to someone else. I knew they'd hurt bad in a little while, and part of my mind beneath the daddies wondered if the needles were juiced or if they were just sharp bits of metal to tear my body apart. If they were drugged or poisoned, I'd find out soon enough. It had become time for desperation. I completely forgot I had my seizure gun with me; I had no intention of having a sharp-shooting match with Hassan, anyway. I took the black daddy and slapped it into place even as I was collapsing from the wounds.

It was like . . . it was like being strapped to a table and having a dentist drilling up through the roof of my mouth. It was like being right on the edge of an epileptic fit and not quite making it, wishing that it would either go away or seize me and get it over with. It was like having the brightest lights in the world blazing in my eyes, the loudest noises exploding in my ears, demons sandpapering my flesh, unnameable vile odors clogging my nose, the foulest muck in my throat. I would gladly have died then just to have it all stop.

I would kill.

I grabbed Hassan by his wrists and fastened my teeth in his throat. I felt his hot blood spurting in my face; I remember thinking how wonderful it tasted. Hassan howled with pain. He beat on my head, but he couldn't free himself from the purely insane, purely animal hold I had on him. He thrashed, and we fell to the floor. He got loose and slammed another clip into his pistol and shot me again, and again I leaped on his throat. I tore at his windpipe with my teeth, and my stiff fingers dug into his eyes. I felt his blood running down my arms, too. Hassan's shrieks were horrible, maddened, but they were almost drowned out by my own. The black daddy was still torturing me, still burning like acid inside my head. All my screaming, all the infuriated, savage ferocity of my attack, did nothing to lessen my torment. I slashed and clawed and ripped at Hassan's bloody body.

Much later, I woke up, heavily tranquilized, in the hospital. Eleven days had passed. I learned that I had mangled Hassan until he was no longer alive, and even then I did not stop. I had avenged Nikki and all the others, but I had made every crime of Hassan's look like the gentlest of children's games. I had bitten and torn Hassan's body until there was barely enough left to identify.

And I had done the same to Okking.

20

It was Doc Yeniknani, the gentle Sufi Turk, who released me from the hospital at last. I had taken my share of hurts from Hassan, but I don't remember getting them, for which I thank Allah. The needle wounds, lesions, and lacerations were the easy part. The med staff just crammed me back together and covered me all over with gelstrips. My medication was taken care of by computer this time—no snippy nurses. The doctor programmed a list of drugs into the machine, along with the quantity and how often I was allowed to request them. Every time I wanted a jolt, I just punched a button. If I punched it too often, nothing happened. If I waited just the right amount of time, the computer slipped me intravenous Sonneine right through my feeding tube. I was in the hospital for almost three months; and when I got out, my ass felt as nice and smooth as the day I was born. I will have to get one of those mechanical drug-pushers for myself. It could revolutionize the street narcotics industry. Oh, they'll put a few people out of work, but that's always been the price of free enterprise and progress.

The physical beating I took while I was reducing the former Hassan the Shiite to soup bones wasn't bad enough to keep me in bed so long. Actually, those wounds could have been treated in the emergency room, and I could have been out dining and dancing a few hours later. The real problem was inside my head. I had seen and done too many terrible things, and Dr. Yeniknani and his colleagues considered the possibility that if they just disconnected the punishment daddy and the other override daddies, when all the facts and memories hit my poor, unbuffered brain, I'd end up as crazy as a spider on ice skates.

The American kid found me—found us, I mean, me and Hassan and Okking—and called the cops. They got me to the hospital, and apparently the highly paid, highly skilled specialists didn't want any part of me. No one wanted to risk his reputation by taking charge. "Do we leave the add-ons in? Do we take them out? If we take them out, he might go permanently insane. If we leave them in, they might burn their way right down into his belly." All those hours that black daddy was still juicing the punishment center in my brain. I passed out again and again, but I wasn't dreaming about Honey Pílar, you can bet on that.

They popped the punishment chip first, but left the others in to leave me in a kind of insensible limbo. They brought me back to full, unaugmented consciousness slowly, testing me every step of the way. I'm proud to say that I'm as sane today as I ever was; I have all the daddies in their plastic box in case I get nostalgic.

I didn't have any visitors in the hospital this time, either. I guessed that my friends had good memories. I took the opportunity to grow my beard back, and my hair was getting long again. It was a Tuesday morning when Dr. Yeniknani signed my releases. "I pray to Allah that I never see you here again," he said.

I shrugged. "From now on, I'm going to get myself a quiet little business selling counterfeit coins to tourists. I don't want any more trouble."

Dr. Yeniknani smiled. "No one wants trouble, but there is trouble enough in the world. You cannot hide from it. Do you remember the shortest sûrah in the noble Qur'ân? It is actually one of the earliest revealed by the Prophet, may blessings be upon his name and peace. 'Say: I seek refuge in the Lord of mankind, the King of mankind, the God of mankind, from the evil of the sly whisperer, who whispers in the hearts of mankind, of the *djinn* and of mankind.' "

"*Djinn* and mankind and guns and knives," I said.

Dr. Yeniknani shook his head slowly. "If you look for

guns, you will find guns. If you look for Allah, you will find Allah."

"Well, then," I said wearily, "I will just have to start my life fresh when I get out of here. I'll just change all my ways and how I think and forget all the years of experience I've had."

"You mock me," he said sadly, "but some day you will listen to your own words. I pray to Allah that when that day comes, you will yet have time to do as you say." Then he signed my papers, and I was free again, me again, with nowhere to go.

I didn't have an apartment anymore. All I had was a zipper bag with a lot of money in it. I called a cab from the hospital and rode over to Papa's. This was the second time I'd dropped by without an appointment, but this time I had the excuse that I couldn't phone Hassan to make an arrangement. The butler recognized me, even favoring me with a minute change in his expression. Evidently I had become a celebrity. Politicians and sex stars may cuddle up to you and it doesn't prove a thing, but when the butlers of the world notice you, you realize that some of what you believe about yourself is true.

I even got to give the waiting room a miss. One of the Stones That Speak appeared in front of me, did an about-face, and marched off. I followed. We went into Friedlander Bey's office, and I took a few steps toward Papa's desk. He stood up, his old face so shriveled up in smiles that I was afraid it would snap into a million pieces. He hurried toward me, took my face, and kissed me. "O my son!" he cried. Then he kissed me again. He couldn't find the words to express his joy.

For my part, I was a little uncomfortable. I didn't know whether I should play the brick-fronted hero or the aw-shucks kid who just happened to be in the right place at the right time. The truth was, I only wanted to get out of there as fast as I could with another thick envelope of reward money, and never have anything to do with the old son of a bitch again. He was making it difficult. He kept kissing me.

At last it got thick, even for an old-fashioned Arab potentate like Friedlander Bey. He let me go and re-

treated behind the formidable bastion of his desk. It seemed
that we weren't going to share a pleasant lunch or tea and
swap stories of mangled corpses while he told me how
terrific I was. He just stared at me for a long time. One of
the Stones crept up beside me, just behind my right shoulder. The other Stone planted himself behind my left shoulder. It felt eerily reminiscent of my first interview with
Friedlander Bey, in the motel. Now, in these grander
surroundings, I was somehow reduced from the conquer-
ing hero to some slimy miscreant who'd been caught with
his hand in someone else's pocket, and was now on the
carpet. I don't know how Papa did it, but it was part of his
magic. Uh oh, I thought, and my stomach started to grum-
ble. I still hadn't learned what his motives had been.

"You have done well, O excellent one," said Friedlander
Bey. His tone was thoughtful and not wholly approving.

"I was granted good fortune by Allah in His greatness,
and by you in your foresight," I said.

Papa nodded. He was used to being yoked together with
Allah that way. "Take, then, the token of our gratitude."
One of the Stones shoved an envelope against my ribs,
and I took it.

"Thank you, O Shaykh."

"Thank not me, but Allah in His beneficence."

"Yeah, you right." I pushed the envelope into a pocket.
I wondered if I could go now.

"Many of my friends were slain," mused Papa, "and
many of my valued associates. It would be well to guard
against such a thing ever happening again."

"Yes, O Shaykh."

"I have need of loyal friends in positions of authority,
on whom I can rely. I am shamed when I recall the trust I
put in Hassan."

"He was a Shiite, O Shaykh."

Friedlander Bey waved a hand. "Nevertheless. It is time
to repair the injuries that have been done to us. Your task
is not finished, not yet, my son. You must help build a
new structure of security."

"I will do what I can, O Shaykh." I didn't like the way
this was going at all, but once again I was helpless.

"Lieutenant Okking is dead and gone to his Paradise,

inshallah. His position will be filled by Sergeant Hajjar, a man whom I know well and whose words and deeds I need not fear. I am considering a new and essential department—a liaison between my friends of the Budayeen and the official authorities."

I never felt so small and so alone in my life.

Friedlander Bey went on. "I have chosen you to administer that new supervisory force."

"Me, O Shaykh?" I asked in a quavery voice. "You don't mean me."

He nodded. "Let it be done."

I felt a surge of rage and stepped toward his desk. "The hell with you and your plans!" I shouted. "You sit there and manipulate—you watch my friends die—you pay this guy and that guy and don't give a good goddamn what happens to them as long as your money rolls in. I wouldn't doubt that you were behind Okking and the Germans *and* Hassan and the Russians." Suddenly I shut up quick. I hadn't been thinking fast, I'd just been letting my anger out; but I could tell by the sudden tightness around Friedlander Bey's mouth that I'd touched something pretty goddamn sensitive. "You *were,* weren't you?" I said softly. "You didn't give a flying fuck *what* happened to anybody. You were playing *both* sides. Not against the middle—there *wasn't* any middle. Just *you,* you walking cadaver. You don't have a human atom in you. You don't love, you don't hate, you don't care. For all your kneeling and praying, you got nothing in you. I've seen handfuls of sand with more conscience than you."

The really strange thing was that during that whole speech, neither of the Stones That Speak came any nearer or shoved me around or broke my face for me. Papa must have given them a signal to let me have my little oration. I took another step toward him, and he lifted the corners of his mouth in a pitiful, ancient man's attempt at a smile. I stopped short, as if I'd walked into an invisible glass wall. *Baraka.* The charismatic spell that surrounds saints and tombs and mosques and holy men. I couldn't have harmed Friedlander Bey and he knew it. He reached into a desk drawer and brought out a gray plastic device that fitted nicely into the palm of his hand. "Do you know what this is, my son?" he asked.

"No," I said.

"It is a portion of you." He pressed a button, and the screaming nightmare that had made an animal of me, that had driven me to rend and tear Okking and Hassan, flooded my skull in its full, unstoppable fury.

I came to in a fetal position on Papa's rug.

"That was only fifteen seconds," he told me calmly.

I stared at him sullenly. "That's how you're going to make me do what you want?"

He gave me that piece of a smile again. "No, my son." He tossed the control device in a gentle arc, and I caught it. I looked at him. "Take it," he said. "It is your loving cooperation I desire, not your fear."

Baraka.

I pocketed the remote control unit and waited. Papa nodded. "Let it be done," he said again. And just like that, I was a cop. The Stones That Speak moved closer toward me. In order to breathe, I had to keep skipping a couple of feet in front of them. They squeezed me out of the room and down the hall and out of Friedlander Bey's house altogether. I didn't have another chance to say anything. I was standing in the street, a lot richer. I was also some kind of imitation law-enforcement agent with Hajjar as my immediate boss. Even in my worst drug-induced half-crazed nightmares, I'd never concocted anything as horrible as that.

As the word does, it got around fast. They probably knew about it before I did, while I was still recuperating and playing solitaire with the Sonneine. When I went into the Silver Palm, Heidi wouldn't serve me. At the Solace, Jacques, Mahmoud, and Saied stared about six inches above my shoulder into humid air and talked about how much garlic was enough; they never even acknowledged my presence. I noticed that Saied the Half-Hajj had inherited custody of Hassan's American kid. I hoped they'd be very happy together. I finally went into Frenchy's, and Dalia set a coaster in front of me. She looked very uncomfortable. "Where you at, Marîd?" she asked.

"I'm all right. You still talking to me?"

"Sure, Marîd, we been friends a long time." She gave a long, worried look down at the end of the bar, though.

I looked, too. Frenchy stood up from his stool and came slowly toward me. "I don't want your business, Audran," he said gruffly.

"Frenchy, after I caught Khan, you told me I could drink free in here for the rest of my life."

"That was before what you done to Hassan and Okking. I never had no use for either of them, but what you did . . ." He turned his head aside and spat.

"But Hassan was the one who—"

He cut me off. He turned to the barmaid. "Dalia, if you ever serve this bastard in here again, you're fired. You got that?"

"Yeah," she said, looking nervously from Frenchy to me.

The big man turned back to me. "Now get out," he said.

"Can I talk to Yasmin?" I asked.

"Talk to her and get out." Then Frenchy turned his back on me and walked away, the way he'd walk away from something he didn't want to have to see or smell or touch.

Yasmin was sitting in a booth with a mark. I went up to her, ignoring the guy. "Yasmin," I said, "I don't—"

"You best go away, Marîd," she said in an icy voice. "I heard what you did. I heard about your sleazy new job. You sold out to Papa. I'd have expected that from anybody else; but you, Marîd, I couldn't believe it at first. But you did it, didn't you? Everything they say?"

"It was the daddy, Yasmin, you don't know how it made me feel. Anyway, *you're* the one who wanted me to—"

"I suppose it was the daddy that made you a cop, too?"

"Yasmin . . ." Here I was, the man whose pride sufficeth, who needed nothing, who expected nothing, who wandered the lonely ways of the world unappalled because there were no more surprises. How long ago had I believed that, actually been conned by it, seen myself that way? And now I was pleading with her. . . .

"Go away, Marîd, or I'll have to call Frenchy. I'm working."

"Can I call you later?"

She made a small grimace. "No, Marîd. No."

So I went away. I'd been on my own before, but this was something new in my experience. I suppose I should have expected it, but it still hit me harder than all the terror and ugliness I'd gone through. My own friends, my former friends, found it simpler to draw a line through my name and cut me out of their lives than to deal with the truth. They didn't want to admit to themselves the danger they'd been in, the danger they might be in again some day. They wanted to pretend that the world was nice and healthy and worked according to a few simple rules that somebody had written down somewhere. They didn't need to know what the rules were, precisely; they just needed to know they were there just in case. I was now a constant reminder that there *were* no rules, that insanity was loose in the world, that their own safety, their own lives, were always in jeopardy. They didn't want to think about that, so they made a simple compromise: I was the villain, I was the scapegoat, I took all the honor and all the punishment. Let Audran do it, let Audran pay for it, fuck Audran.

Okay, if that's how it was going to be. I thundered into Chiri's place and threw a young black man off my usual stool. Maribel got off a stool down at the end of the bar and wobbled drunkenly toward me. "Been looking for you, Marîd," she said in a thick voice.

"Not now, Maribel. I'm not in the mood."

Chiriga looked from me to the young black man, who was thinking about starting something with me. "Gin and bingara?" she asked, raising her eyebrows. That's as much expression as she showed me. "Or tende?"

Maribel sat down next to me. "You got to listen, Marîd."

I looked at Chiri; it was a tough decision. I went with vodka gimlets.

"I remember who it was," Maribel said. "The one I went home with. With the scars, who you was looking for. It was Abdul-Hassan, the American kid. See? Hassan must have put them scars on him. I *told* you I'd remember. Now you owe me."

She was pleased with herself. She tried to sit up straight on the stool.

I looked at Chiri, and she gave me just the merest hint of a smile.

"What the hell," I said.

"What the hell," she said.

The young black man was still standing there. He gave us each a puzzled look and walked out of the club. I probably saved him a small fortune.

ABOUT THE AUTHOR

Over the past two decades, George Alec Effinger's stories and novels have won him a reputation as one of science fiction's most consistently imaginative and innovative authors. His works are regularly nominated for the field's highest awards, and he recently received the Hugo and Nebula awards for his acclaimed novelette. "Schrödinger's Kitten." Effinger's novel starring Marîd Audran, *The Exile Kiss*, will be published by Doubleday Foundation in May 1991. He lives with his cat in New Orleans, LA.

Bantam Spectra Horror
because every spectrum is shadowed by the colors of the night...

☐ **The Demon by Jeffrey Sackett**
(28596-3 * $4.50/$5.50 in Canada)
An ex-sideshow geek moves into a small New York town, and on his heels follows a string of hideous and inexplicable murders.

☐ **The Horror Club by Mark Morris**
(28933-0 * $4.95/$5.95 in Canada)
Three young horror fans learn the true meaning of fear when they invite a new boy into their club who unleashes upon their hometown a terrifying, consuming evil.

☐ **The Amulet by A.R. Morlan**
(28908-X * $4.95/$5.95 in Canada)
Set in a quiet Wisconsin town, this is the chilling story of a woman's desperate struggle against the terrible power of a talisman which controls and changes the people around her.

☐ **House Haunted by Al Sarrantonio**
(29148-7 * $4.50/$5.50 in Canada)
From the four corners of the earth, five people are seduced into a sinister web of madness, murder and supernatural confrontation by a powerful spirit who longs for a doorway into the physical world.

Look for these bloodcurdling new titles on sale now wherever Bantam Spectra Books are sold, or use this page for ordering:

— —

Bantam Books, Dept. **SF103**   414 East Golf Road, Des Plaines, IL 60016

Please send me the items I have checked above. I am enclosing $ _____
(please add $2.50 to cover postage and handling). Send check or money order,
no cash or C.O.D.s please.

Mr./Ms._____

Address_____

City/State_____ Zip_____

Please allow four to six weeks for delivery.
Prices and availability subject to change without notice.   SF103 -- 4/91

BANTAM SPECTRA
SPECIAL EDITIONS

*A program dedicated to masterful works of fantastic fiction
by many of today's most visionary writers.*

☐ **Synners by Pat Cadigan**
(28254-9 * $4.95/$5.95 in Canada)
Synners create computer generated realities for art and entertainment, but when they inadvertently create a deadly virus spreading through the computer network, its up to them to stop it.

☐ **Winterlong by Elizabeth Hand**
(28772-9 * $4.95/$5.95 in Canada)
In the ruins of a post-Apocalypse Washington D.C., twins who were separated in childhood approach a reunion that could reshape human history.

☐ **Points of Departure by Pat Murphy**
(28615-3 * $3.95/$4.95 in Canada)
An outstanding collection of the short fiction of Pat Murphy, including the Nebula Award-winning "Rachel In Love" and an introduction by Kate Wilhelm.

☐ **Phases of Gravity by Dan Simmons**
(27764-2 * $4.50/$5.50 in Canada)
An ex-astronaut searches for the meaning in his life, guided by a mysterious woman who leads him through his personal "places of power." "Earth , air, fire, water: Dan Simmons. Warily, in awe, we watch him and marvel."--Harlan Ellison